For my Momma, because you never scolded me for staying up reading till the wee hours of the morning, even on school nights.

For my love, because you went to bed alone so many times while I wrote this book, and never gave me the guilt trip I so richly deserved.
I love you both, forever.

THE LAWS OF FOUNDING

BOOK ONE OF THE FOUNDING TRILOGY

NICOLE MCKEON

NICOLE YORK

CHAPTER ONE

I rushed across the hallway with one hand pressed firmly over my mouth and shoved my way into the bathroom. The door bounced off the bathtub with a dull clang as I stumbled into a cloud of humid air, groped for the toothpaste, and began brushing madly. The comfortingly domestic scent of my roommate's tea-tree shampoo slowly dispelled the vision of flames and nausea that inevitably followed that particular nightmare.

Once my stomach ceased threatening me with violence and a few eyedrops brought the world swimming back into focus, I found myself confronted with a fuzzy pink bath mat and a shower curtain spotted with aggressively colorful daisies.

When I had brushed my teeth before falling into bed last night, our bath mat had been white and the shower curtain pale blue. If Rayne thought turning our bathroom into a pre-teen paradise was a good idea, she had another thing coming. I was not prepared to put up with such violent displays of femininity so early in the morning.

Since we had agreed that common spaces would be decorated in neutral tones, I figured that questioning her decorating choices was a much better option than climbing back into bed despite the early hour. The feeling of blood on my hands was still so strong in my memory that the idea of walking back into my bedroom—even to change clothes—brought back my nausea, so I headed toward the kitchen instead.

Rayne sat on a barstool wearing multi-colored toe socks, sipping tea. Her damp blonde hair was piled on top of her head in one of those purposefully casual ballerina buns that I never managed to get the hang of. A sheaf of notes sat on the counter next to her saucer, the neatly printed words silently shaming me for ignoring my own homework.

As I passed the kitchen island, the leftover smell of oatmeal and blueberries made me think that a bit of breakfast might be just what I needed to calm my stomach.

"Allie," Rayne said, looking up from her notes, "I didn't know you were home. What time did you get in last night?"

I grunted in response and began pulling things out of the fridge.

"Well," she said in mock offense, "good morning to you, too."

"Sorry, Ray. I think I must have drank too much last night," I admitted while examining the egg carton, "my stomach needs something that hasn't been fermented before I can be civil."

"You don't remember how much you had to drink?"

I ignored the disapproval in her tone and shrugged, hoping my voice sounded more indifferent than I felt.

"I only remember having a few beers with Mat before I came home," I said as I lifted the side drawer, only to find it bare, and asked, "didn't I just buy a block of cheddar?"

"How would I know? I don't eat that stuff."

I would have laughed at the disgust in her voice if I wasn't too frustrated for amusement. My vague desire for food to fill my unhappy tummy had bloomed into a full-on craving that had me whining, "How can I possibly have an omelet without cheese?"

"The real question," she said, "is how you can put fried chicken placenta in your mouth."

"With profound pleasure," I countered, and set the carton of eggs aside to do a more thorough search of the bottom drawer of our fridge.

When the phone rang a second later, the ringer sounded strange—a muted digital tone rather than the sharp chime I was used to—and I wondered if Rayne replaced the phone as well as redecorating our bathroom. She sighed and climbed off her perch to skip across the room and chirp, "Hello," into the receiver. "Hey! Oh, I think she left it in her room. Okay. Yeah, I'll let her know. See you in a few."

I was already whisking eggs by the time she climbed back onto the barstool and resumed sipping her tea.

"I still can't believe we don't have any cheese in this place," I complained, churning my arm for all I was worth and watching the eggs blend into a smooth, bubbly froth. "I'm going to have to make a French omelet now when what I really wanted was ham and cheese."

Rayne eyed my bowl, stuck her finger in her mouth, and made a gagging noise. I laughed and turned back to my eggs.

"Your preferences have been noted. By the way, Barbie called, and she wants her bathroom back."

"We aren't going to have this argument again, are we?" she groaned, "we agreed to get new stuff for the bathroom on payday. You can wait two more weeks."

"Why don't I remember this argument?"

"Maybe because you don't pay attention to me when I talk?"

"Oh, please. Now you make us sound like an old married couple."

"We might as well be. You're always gone, and I'm the only one who cleans."

I snorted and began pulling spices out of the cabinet. "I clean. I did laundry last week. Besides, you work more hours than I do, so you're clearly the workaholic husband who leaves me to my own, desperate devices."

"Well, I don't have much choice if we want to pay bills, Allie. Unless you'd like to pick up more hours somewhere?"

She was starting to sound annoyed, which surprised me because both of us enjoyed a good verbal sparring match. I wasn't sure what she meant about my always being gone, but I decided to change the subject and preserve the peace.

"I don't want to fight," I said, "I just want to eat. Who called?"

"The only person who would be calling this early in the morning."

I turned from my omelet, pointed my spatula at her, and ordered, "Spill, woman. I'm hungry, and I have no time for riddles."

She sighed, placed her empty cup on the counter, and slipped lightly onto the floor. "It was Seth, of course. He wanted to know why you didn't answer your phone, and then said he would be here to pick you up in a few minutes. You may want to brush your hair."

"Who?"

"Very funny," she called over her shoulder as she headed toward her bedroom, ostensibly to put on a bra.

I pulled the pan off the heat and stalked after her. "Rayne, I'm not kidding, who are you talking about?"

"Seth, obviously," she said as she pulled her tank top back into place over a white sports bra. "You might want to change into something that doesn't say 'homeless' before he gets here."

"Who are you talking about?"

Rayne looked down at her arm and said, her voice hard, "Allie, let go."

I followed her gaze. White finger marks marred the skin of her arm where I'd grabbed her. I gaped at my hand, as shocked as if the limb had acted on its own. I'd never put my hands on Rayne. My stomach did a weird little flip-flop.

"I'm sorry," I whispered.

"You said you weren't going to drink anymore, Allie. You promised."

"I did?"

Dark blonde brows lowered accusingly at me, and I shook my head, lost. Having been my best friend since we were both twelve, Rayne knew why I sometimes needed to quiet my thoughts with a few drinks. I had built up a rather high tolerance during my teenage bouts with self-destruction, so I rarely drank too much; certainly not often enough that I'd need to promise her I would stop. I might not be the most dedicated scholar, but I did take my classes seriously enough not to get blasted on a Thursday night, so why would I make such a promise?

Unrelated details began clicking together in my mind like Legos, building a picture that scared me; no cheese, when that was one thing I never ran out of, our blue shower curtain replaced by daisies—pink bath mats? We'd agreed to avoid pink while decorating. Then there was the strange ringer on our phone, an agreement I couldn't remember, and my supposed promise to stop drinking.

My hands started shaking.

The doorbell rang, and Rayne walked away from me, rubbing her arm. I followed her but struggled to force my legs to move as dread took hold in the pit of my stomach.

A man stood in the doorway, smiling. He was handsome in an all-American, football player kind of way; light haired and wide chested with a strong, square jaw.

"Hey," he said, walking towards me, his eyes appreciative, "your hair looks great, did you do something to it?"

I stood rooted to the spot while my heart fluttered against my ribs like a bird trapped in a cage. He stopped in front of me and looked me up and down.

"Is this what you're wearing to the game? It doesn't look too festive."

He was teasing me. I opened my mouth to respond, but my mind had gone blank. Who was he? What game? I'd never been interested enough in any sport to attend games.

He reached out, put both hands on my waist, said, "You want to go change? I'll wait for you. I want a kiss, though," and leaned forward.

It was then, when I felt the warmth of his breath on my lips, that shock gave way to instinct. I slapped him, hard. He jerked his head back, letting go of me so quickly that I almost fell and had to grab the edge of the couch to regain my balance.

"What the hell, Allie?" he demanded, fingertips against the handprint on his cheek.

"I don't know who you are, but if you touch me again without my permission, I'll do worse than slap you."

His eyes grew wide as he stepped toward me, this time with his hands raised in a placating gesture that did nothing to stem my rising panic. The urge to run surged through my muscles like a lightning strike, but he was between me and the doorway. Rayne was simply standing there slack-jawed and unmoving. He continued to walk toward me, and I jerked backward, pointing a shaking finger at him. I couldn't remember his face no matter how hard I stared at it.

"Allie, it's okay, honey."

"No, I'm not okay. Get the hell away from me! Rayne, who is this guy? Get out of here before I call the cops."

Panting and sweating,, I felt as if the floor were about to drop from beneath my feet. The man, Seth, looked from Rayne to me with wide, worried eyes.

"Allie," Rayne said stepping toward me, "Allie, you're scaring me, what's going on? Did you drink anything besides beer last night? You didn't take any pills, did you?"

"She didn't drink anything last night," Seth said, eyes darting between Rayne and me, "we went to her brother's audition, and had dinner with her parents afterward."

"I don't even know you!" I yelled, putting both hands on my head and trying desperately to remember what I'd done last night.

Seth approached me again, but I held my hands in front of me with my palms out to ward him off as my throat tightened. I couldn't get enough air. My hands started to go numb. Vertigo hit me like a bus, and I toppled to the side, landing hard on my hands and knees.

"Allie!" they both shouted, leaning down to take me by the arms.

Full-fledged hysteria sunk its claws into my chest and I screamed, struggling against their hands and kicking at anything my legs could reach. My fingernails raked down one of Seth's cheeks before he caught my wrists and wrapped our arms behind my back.

"Call 911!" Seth shouted at Rayne, but his voice was hollow and far away as if he were at the end of a long tunnel. The outside of my vision darkened, closing in until there was no light left but a tiny pinpoint at the center.

I felt myself falling.

CHAPTER TWO

O nce, when I was about ten years old, far before my fear of deep water began, we had the kind of sweltering summer that forces families to the public pool daily just to avoid being cooped up with sweaty, cranky adolescents. I spent the whole summer convinced that I was a mermaid. I would dive down to the blue bottom of the pool and stay there for as long as I could, trying to move my legs with a fishy swish that would send my hair floating in clouds around my head.

One of the things I had loved the most about being underwater was the way sound was muted and filtered. I knew there was a world beyond that was loud and colorful, but the place I inhabited was one of languid, silent peace. That is the best way I can think of to explain what I felt as I woke up. My body was heavy and peaceful, and sound only reached me as if through cotton stuffed in my ears. Though I was beginning to drift toward consciousness, I instinctively knew that I didn't want to face whatever was waiting for me there.

Noises began to sharpen from far away tones to hard consonants and, slowly, speech and other sounds became intelligible. A dull, monotonous beeping noise set the rhythm for all the other noises around me: the hard-edged squeak of rubber-soled shoes on waxed floors, the dry rustling of fabric, and the *shhh* of paper sliding and turning. It was the antiseptic tang in the air that brought my mind fully awake, though; that was a scent with which I was familiar. It reminded me of my mom, and of hospital rooms.

It was the second time in a row I'd woken in a place that didn't belong to me, and the knowledge made me jerk upright. At least, I tried to jerk upright but my wrists, which had been wrapped in fleece-lined cuffs and belted to the side of the bed, pulled me up short. I was trapped.

I screamed.

I screamed at the absolute top of my register, which I'd never considered impressive until then, but may have reached glass-shattering decibels. Two more nurses ran into the room, and there were suddenly six hands pressing me down into the bed. I continued to scream and jerk my arms and legs in helpless panic, but the restraints held fast.

"Calm down, sweetie, everything is okay, you're safe," one of the nurses said in the kind of voice reserved for unruly livestock.

It wasn't enough to break through my panic. The sharp sting in my shoulder was, though, and I whipped my head to the side to see one of the nurses pulling a syringe out of my arm.

"What did you give me?" I shouted at her, jerking at my arm and lifting my head up off the bed to see my shoulder.

"It's just a mild sedative, Allison. It's going to help you stay calm."

"I don't want to be calm, I want you to take this crap off me!"

"We don't want you to hurt yourself or one of the nurses that are here to help you. This will keep everyone safe, so you can get better."

"There's nothing wrong with me!"

She compressed her lips and regarded me with sad eyes.

I realized quite suddenly that my panic wasn't helping my case at all. Letting my head fall back onto the pillow, I closed my eyes and tried to slow the breath that was sawing in and out of my lungs. I needed to get a hold of myself.

Okay, I thought, *I'm clearly in the mental ward of the hospital.*

That thought should have had me screaming again, but the panic disappeared as quickly as it had arrived. Was the sedative already starting to work?

Just stay calm, and go over everything, I told myself.

I'd woken up that morning in my own bed, and my room was the same as it had always been, at least as far as I could remember since my eyes had been cemented shut when I'd rushed out of it. The shower curtain and bath mat had been wrong, but several different circumstances could account for changes like those. Rayne had looked and acted the same as always, but there was the strange ringer on our phone, my supposed promise to quit drinking, and that guy Seth.

I racked my memory but thoughts were coming more slowly, and I had to dig them up and drag them through a thick sludge just to look at them. No matter how hard I tried, I couldn't remember having ever seen his face before, or anything else about him, but he acted as if I had known him and, what's more, known him intimately. The fact that I'd had no clue who the man was had obviously surprised my roommate. What did that mean?

"Hello, Allison." An older man, somewhere in his mid to late fifties with gray hair at his temples, walked in to pull a rolling stool up next to my bed. His white hospital coat was glaringly bright in the fluorescent light.

"I'm Doctor Reikowsky. How are you feeling?"

"Scared," I admitted, even though I seemed incapable of feeling any of the physical effects of fear.

He gave me a sympathetic smile. "I can understand that. I would be scared too if I woke up in a place I didn't recognize. Do you know where you are?"

"In the mental ward," I whispered. I tried to sound confident, but my voice was thin.

"Yes, you are. Do you know why?"

"I think...I think I maybe had a nervous breakdown."

The doctor put his heel on the rail of the stool and leaned his elbow on his knee. "I'd say that's a pretty fair assessment."

"How long have I been here?"

"Just a few hours. Your friends brought you. They said you had become violent, which was out of character for you. They were very worried about you, you know."

"Does my family know that I'm here?"

"Not yet. We've called but only gotten their machine so far. Your roommate warned us to expect that. She said they had stayed at a hotel last night while they were in town. I expect they're probably out for breakfast or something like that. I'm sure we will be able to get in touch with them soon."

"In town? But my mom only lives a half-hour outside of Seattle."

The doctor raised his eyebrows at me and wrote something on his clipboard.

"Someone will tell them I'm here?".

"Of course, we will, Allison. We are here to help you, you know." His eyes seemed so kind and understanding.

"Okay. Can you take these things off me?"

"As soon as we are sure that you won't hurt yourself or someone else. Do you feel the need to hurt anyone?"

"No," I lied.

Despite how nice this man was, and regardless of the blunted edges of my emotions, the nurses who had held me down and jabbed me in the arm definitely deserved a good punch in the face. It wasn't the urge I'm sure it would have been without the drugs they stuck in my arm but I really, really didn't like being held down; my memories of hospital rooms were less than welcome.

"That's a good sign," he assured me, and then asked, "Have you ever had a panic attack before?"

I started to say yes, I had one once when I was sixteen, but I didn't think I wanted to get into that episode with the person who was going to decide whether I needed to be committed. Anyway, I still wasn't certain if that experience had been a dream or not, so I revised my philosophy about honesty being the best policy in favor of not making matters worse.

"No," I said tonelessly.

"Do you have any idea what caused this attack?"

"I think so. Some guy I don't know came into my apartment and tried to kiss me."

I wanted to feel outraged about that, but I couldn't. The fact that my emotions weren't responding the way I expected them to should have made me uncomfortable, but it didn't.

Pulling a second clipboard from my bedside table and looking down at the writing, Doctor Reikowsky said, "Your roommate told us that you've been dating Seth for almost six months. She says he's close with your family and even goes on fishing trips with your father."

A shaft of panic lanced through me that the drugs were unable to dampen, and the machine I was hooked to started beeping faster. The doctor's mouth popped open as he looked at the machine and then at me, with his graying brows meeting above his eyes like kissing caterpillars.

"Why does it upset you to hear that?"

I swallowed and felt two hot tears slip out of my eyes to run down the sides of my face. Despite whatever drug they had given me, grief wrenched in my chest like a turning knife. Now I knew for certain that something was very, very wrong. This was not just a panic attack or strange amnesia or having gotten so drunk the night before that I messed up my brain. Something was horribly, terrifyingly wrong. This was something I couldn't possibly forget or else I truly had lost it.

"Because," I whispered, almost choking on the words as my heart grew heavy in my chest, "my dad died in a car accident when I was sixteen."

CHAPTER THREE

They committed me. I fought back.

Now, huddled in the corner of a padded room, I tried to wrap my head around the fact that something like this was happening to me, a completely average college student with a completely average life. My family hadn't come to the hospital and I wasn't allowed to call them, though the staff assured me they'd been notified that I was here. I'd also been assured that my father, whom I knew to be dead, was very much alive.

Thinking of him made my chest hurt. If these people were trustworthy, then I had spent the last five years living in a fantasy world. But I couldn't believe them. I couldn't believe them because I had been there; I had seen it, lived through it when I should have died in the car with him. I had felt his blood on my hands. I'd seen the fire. No, my father was dead. If I knew anything for certain, it was that.

So, where does that leave me?

In a mental institution with a dead father.

I laughed but within a few breaths, it turned into sobs. Sounds didn't echo in this room the way they should. Noise only seemed to travel a few feet before it died. It was supremely unsettling to know that no one would hear you if you screamed because the screams would never make it out of the room.

Shivering, I wrapped my arms around my knees and pulled them tight against my chest.

Okay, Allie, get a grip, I told myself. *Think this through. There are two possibilities here: either you're delusional, or you're not. Are you delusional?*

No, I'm not.

If you're not, then people are lying to you about some pretty big things, or they're mistaken. What are the chances that they're mistaken?

Pretty f-ing slim. My father was dead, that I knew.

They're lying to you, then. Why?

I didn't have an answer. What reason could they have to lie to me about my father's death? Who could benefit from that kind of lie? Thriller movie plots started to flash through my mind. The idea that anyone in a position of power would have it in for me, a B-average student who had never left her home state and had no outstanding talents to brag of—aside from memorizing movie lines—was almost laughable.

"I'm a twenty-one-year-old history major, for crying out loud!" Wasn't paranoia a symptom of psychosis?

I dropped my forehead onto my knees and squeezed my eyes shut, listening to the silence fall around me. I had always thought that "deafening silence" was a terrible cliché, but now I understood how true it could be. This wasn't the peaceful, mirror-pond stillness that feels like a warm blanket—it was oppressive and agitating, like a desperate scream that reached the frayed ends of breath but kept going. The urge to pound on the door, to beg to be let out—or even to fight my way free and run for it as soon as someone opened the door—made my limbs tremble. Running away was a specialty of mine.

The click of the lock turning was loud in the silence, and I jerked in surprise. As if in answer to my desperation, the door opened and a woman stood silhouetted in a halo of blinding fluorescent light, her faded blue scrubs hanging off a slender frame. Her face was beautiful but oddly angular, with high, sharp cheekbones and eyelashes so pale they were almost non-existent. She had silvery blonde hair cut to her shoulders and pulled into two tiny braids that looked completely incongruous next to her patrician face.

"Allison Chapter?" she asked, annunciating every syllable so cleanly that it sounded like a foreign language.

I nodded.

"Follow me, please."

I stood up but hesitated. "No restraints?"

"Do you want them?"

I shook my head violently.

"I did not think so. Follow me."

Then she turned and began walking down the hallway. I only hesitated for a second before bolting from the room. Stepping through that door and into a world with sound was like breaking the surface of the water when you'd been under for too long. The antiseptic tang in the air reminded me vividly of the hospital scent that always hung about my mother when she would come home from work. And of other things I didn't like thinking about.

"Where are we going?" I asked, but the woman cut me off with a preemptive command to keep my head down.

"Do not speak," she warned in a low voice.

Would they put the restraints back on me if I did? I wanted to take off running and call my mom on the first phone I could find. The ringer on her cell phone was usually turned off, so I couldn't be sure she would answer, but if I could leave her a message, then I could at least be sure that she knew what had happened to me.

"Do not try to run, Allison. Walk quietly, or they will notice you."

"Who will?" I asked, unnerved. How did she know I had been thinking about running? Then I scoffed at myself. I bet a lot of the patients in this place thought about running. Paranoia began to squeeze my shoulder muscles together, but I did as she said. My relief at being free of that room was so strong that I didn't want to bite the proverbial hand that fed me. Keeping my head down and my eyes on the unlikely purple ponies that dotted her scrubs, I managed to follow her all the way to the elevator without paying attention to much of the hospital and, apparently, without anyone from the hospital paying much attention to me.

As the elevator door began to close, I looked up and saw the face of one of my nurses as she rounded a corner and spotted me. For a second she simply stared with wide, shocked eyes and an open mouth. Judging by her expression, I was not supposed to be in the elevator. The woman next to me sighed, lifted one long-fingered hand to her ear, and said, "Diversion," very quietly. At that point, I began to realize that I wasn't simply being moved from one room to another or going somewhere else for another interview; something entirely different was happening.

I was suddenly certain that she wasn't a nurse, pony scrubs notwithstanding, and I had no idea where she wanted me to go, but it was either let her help me get away from the hospital long enough to make my escape or put myself back into the hands of the people who had drugged me and stuck me in a cell. I decided that my chances of escape were better with the woman who pressed the first-floor button with her immaculately manicured fingernail.

No matter how much I wanted to trust the doctors and nurses at the hospital, I knew I was not sick. Beyond that, anyone who would lie to me about my father's death was not the kind of person I wanted to trust with my life.

We had been on the sixth floor when we entered the elevator, and just as we reached level three, an alarm sounded. The elevator jerked to a stop.

"We will exit here," the woman instructed and pressed the 'door open' button on the wall. I was surprised when the doors opened with a casual little 'ding.' We walked into a hallway, where several hospital employees were rushing toward a desk, and turned immediately toward the stairwell. Much to my surprise, we made it to the first floor and out into the lobby without being noticed. Perhaps they were looking for someone who was sneaking or running, not casually strolling along as if all this commotion was business as usual. My companion took one of the emergency room wheelchairs and looked at me with a clear command in her eyes. I sat. She wheeled me out of the front doors of the hospital and into the cool air of an early fall night just as red lights began to strobe in the waiting room.

I took a deep breath and felt much of my tension melt away from just knowing that I could run if I needed to. The breeze that snaked up my back reminded me that I was still in a hospital gown, and made it very clear that one of the rear ties had come undone. Lovely. Walking through town bare-assed wasn't the best way for an escapee from the mental ward to go unnoticed. She stopped pushing the wheelchair once we reached the back of the parking lot, and I stood up, pinching the gown together behind my back and peering into the darkness to adjust my eyes.

"Thank you," I said as I turned to consider her impassive face. "I've got to say, though, I don't understand what just happened."

"I helped you escape from the hospital."

"I got that part, and I appreciate it, but I don't understand why. Who are you?"

A black van turned into the hospital parking lot just then and drove directly toward us, headlights off. I tensed and braced my feet instinctively.

"Um..." I looked from the approaching van to the unlikely stranger who'd just taken me out of the hospital. She must have seen the fear growing in my eyes because she put her hand to her ear again and said calmly, "She is going to run."

She was right.

Unfortunately, I didn't get the chance to run far. If the pavement was cold and hard beneath my bare feet, it was positively painful beneath my cheek. I had made it no more than 25 yards before someone leaped from the moving van and tackled me. Though I'd darted between the parked cars with all the speed and agility of a panicked rabbit, whoever had tackled me was far faster than I and, judging by the weight on my back and the fact that all the air had been forced from my lungs, much bigger as well.

"Get off me," I growled after sucking in a deep breath. Though I tried to buck the offender off, heaving and twisting to either side, they were heavy and strong and not going anywhere. I felt warm breath on my neck before a deep, faintly accented voice whispered, "Unless you want the world to see every inch of your backside, you should stop that writhing. I'm not going to hurt you, but I cannot let you run. You understand me?"

"You are hurting me," I spat, trying to ease the pressure on my hip bones as his weight ground them against the pavement. I hadn't considered that every movement would expose more of my naked rear end, which was only shielded now by the stranger's body. That thought was disconcerting enough that I went completely still.

He said, "I'm sure it's a nice enough arse, my girl, but it's not going to tempt me to ravish you here on the concrete. If I let you up, will you fight me?"

I didn't respond. He sighed, and I felt the moist heat of it on my ear before his weight disappeared. Before I could take a deep breath, I was hauled off the ground and pinned against his chest with my arms at my sides. His arms were wrapped securely around my torso as he dragged me toward the waiting van.

I did struggle then, trying to slam my head backward in the hope of reaching his nose but he was too tall for that and only grunted at my efforts. His arms were steel bands that my desperate strength could do nothing to break, and his grip was driving the wind out of me. Furious,

I tried to kick him but before I could introduce my heel to his groin, we were in the dark interior of the van, and it was moving away from the hospital. I dove for the door handle as soon as he released me, but it was locked. My heart leaped up into my throat as I watched the street lights blur past.

I was trapped.

CHAPTER FOUR

There were no seats in the back of the delivery van, so I sat on the floor and pulled my legs up underneath the hospital gown, wrapping my arms around my knees and wondering, again, how in the hell all of this had happened.

The van turned, and I tried to put my hands out to steady myself, but I wasn't fast enough to stop the momentum from rolling me to the side like an egg on a countertop. Luckily, I righted myself before showing the world any more of my undercarriage. Only briefly did I consider attacking the driver. For a second, the vision played out in my mind of the struggle for the steering wheel: the van would swerve across the road as we fought for control, tires would scream as we lost traction, the horrible crunching sound of twisted metal would—I swallowed hard and clenched my teeth. I wasn't brave enough for that kind of risk.

Instead of fighting my way free, I tucked enough of the gown beneath myself to keep my rear end off the cold floor and shivered as I settled in for a long wait. My captor grunted once and turned to look out the window. Just because I ruled out causing an accident in the hopes to escape from this kidnapping, that didn't mean I was helpless. I had a clear vision in my mind of the woman's face, so I felt certain I could give an accurate description to the police if I ever got the chance to give them my story.

The dashboard light was too faint to reach far into the cave-like interior, though, so I couldn't see much of the jerk's face beneath the hood of his jacket other than a long straight nose, a full bottom lip, and stubborn-looking chin. I thought of how much I'd like to break that nose and regretted not listening to my father when he tried to teach me self-defense.

I had begun to look like a woman much too early for my dad's comfort. Since I'd always been tall, the combination of height and womanly curves made me look much older than twelve. I started getting cat-called when I was thirteen and came home in tears from school one day because a bunch of old men who were fishing at the river near my house started barking at me from the back of their beer-filled pickup trucks. My dad had taken me out in the backyard that evening and showed me how to throw a punch, to knee someone in the balls, and other assorted dirty tricks that I didn't remember.

My dad had been a big man, tall and barrel-chested; the kind who tended to inspire either awe or fear. A sudden stab of longing for my dad made me hug my knees tighter against my chest. My mom had been more pragmatic about the whole affair and handed me a can of mace the next morning as I headed out the door for school.

"You've got hair as brassy as a new penny, Allie," she had told me, "and you're tall like your father, so you'll never be inconspicuous. You have to teach yourself how to be strong enough to deal with the attention because, as much as I would like to say things will change and it will go away, it won't." I had said that I'd be more than happy to dye my hair if she would buy me a box color from the store, and she'd calmly asked if I would have other parts of me fixed, too, when they began inconveniencing me.

"You can do what you want," she had said, looking at me with her solemn brown eyes and placing her hand on my cheek, "but you have my mother's cheekbones. Your eyes might be the same hazel color as your fathers, even down to the gold ring at the center, but the shape is mine and so are your brows. All the parts of you are proof that your father and I loved each other. Hair color can always be changed, I know," she said before I could get the words out, "just think long and hard about the reasons you want to change it. Sometimes what we need to change isn't on the outside."

I'd listened to my mother, but her advice had a side effect I didn't think she had intended. I started to develop something of an attitude, and the kind of biting sarcasm that made members of the opposite sex tend to steer clear. That was probably the reason I'd never had a real boyfriend. Sure, I'd had random make-out sessions at parties, but I'd initiated those myself. Being chased had always made me feel hunted, which was probably why I had been so shocked when a stranger showed up in my apartment to kiss me that morning. Had it only been that morning?

My stomach started to roil, and I groaned, curling in on myself and pressing my fists into my abdomen. A large, warm hand settled on my back, and I jerked away reflexively.

"Calm down. Put your head between your knees and breathe through your teeth."

I was tempted to ignore the jerk's advice and puke all over his boots, but common sense prevailed, and my nausea slowly subsided. Once my breathing was easier, he moved away again, and I relaxed enough to glare at him. Who were these people? And why were they doing whatever they were doing with me?

Might as well ask, I thought. *They're already kidnapping me, what else can they do?*

"Who are you?"

He looked at me from the shadows beneath his hood, but he didn't respond. "Where are you taking me?"

"Someplace safe."

"That doesn't mean anything."

"Someplace safe, Allison. We'll be there shortly, and your questions will be answered. For now, relax."

"That could be what you say to people to keep them calm before you sell them to some pimp or something," I snapped.

"It could be," he agreed calmly, "but it's not. You wouldn't believe me if I told you now, anyway. You've seen too many movies."

I sat back and folded my arms but jerked forward with a gasp when my naked back touched the cold inside wall of the van. Gooseflesh spread down my arms, and I rubbed it impatiently away. The stranger sighed, leaned away from the wall to pull his jacket off, then stepped forward and tossed it lightly over my exposed back. His body had warmed the inside of his jacket, which was lined with fleece and smelled of sandalwood and whiskey.

My first inclination was to pull it off and glare at him, but I hadn't realized how truly cold I'd been until I felt the warmth of his jacket. I opened my mouth to give him a reflexive 'thanks' but remembered getting tackled before being forced into a strange van. My mouth snapped shut, and I stared mutinously at the floor instead. He didn't bother to say anything else but turned again to look out of the window, giving me a clear view of his profile. He didn't seem like a serial killer, but how would I be able to tell? I'd heard too many stories of unwary girls being kidnapped and sold by charming human traffickers to trust someone just because they had a nice profile.

Yet you walked out of a hospital with a strange lady who looks like the Ice Queen without a second thought, I thought wryly.

"Two minutes," said the Ice Queen over her shoulder from the passenger seat. She sounded like an airline captain, as calm and assured as if we were about to pull into a resort and she expected thanks for a smooth ride. I lunged up off the floor and grabbed the back of her seat.

"What is going on?" I demanded, staring hard at the side of her face.

"We are taking you to a safe house," she said, unperturbed as ever.

"Safe from what? Why?"

"I will explain that to you once we are inside." We took another corner that forced me to swallow my next question and clutch the driver's seat for support. The van pulled into an alley in a suburban area, but we had only been in the car for 20 minutes, so we couldn't be that far outside of Seattle. Damn, I should have been paying better attention. I castigated myself as we turned into the garage of a comfortable looking two-story home. The lights were off, and I hadn't been able to see the house number.

"Come on," said the jerk from the back of the van.

I turned to glare at him, still unable to make out much of his face, and grimaced. Anything could happen once we got into that house. I might never walk back out again. Cold sweat beaded on my forehead as the driver and passenger doors opened and closed while the jerk just stared at me. Finally, he shook his head and started to mess with the front of his pants. I backed up, almost tripping over the cup holders, but he only looked up and snorted, then held out his hand.

Moonlight glinted off the blade of a knife. I flinched and grabbed the seatbacks, not sure if I wanted to run or hide.

"I already told you, I'm not going to hurt you," he said, "I swear it. Here, take this. You won't need it, but it will make you feel safer."

With a smooth motion, he flipped the knife and caught it by the flat of the blade, holding the hilt toward me. I took the proffered weapon hesitantly. Like the coat, it was still warm from his body. I adjusted my grip and took a deep breath. He was right; I did feel safer. At least I had something to fight back with, should anyone try to hurt me. He watched me for another second, nodded, and walked out the back doors of the van. It did cross my mind that this could be another tactic to put victims at ease so they wouldn't struggle, but the jerk could have manhandled me without much effort, or even tied and gagged me if he'd wanted to. There were three of them after all, and only one of me.

I climbed out of the van and looked down the long, dark alley as the cold pavement leeched the warmth from the soles of my bare feet. I could run. The jerk was leaning against the door of the van, though, and cleared his throat meaningfully. He would catch me if I ran. I could scream...and maybe end up back in the mental ward. With a sigh, I took a firm grip on the knife handle, straightened my shoulders, and walked into the open doorway. The house was sparsely furnished, but it was warm inside, and my feet sunk into the deep carpet. Wiggling my toes gratefully, I quickly scanned the room, hoping to see a phone.

"Go on," the jerk urged me, gesturing at the stairs as if reading my mind yet again. I held the gown closed with one hand, the knife clutched in the other, and walked forward. There was just enough light coming from an open door at the top of the stairs that I didn't need to feel my way up. The Ice Queen and the driver, a short, round man with a bald head and dark brown skin, sat in comfortable chairs against the far wall of the lighted room. Blackout curtains covered the room's only window. A large metal cabinet that reminded me of gym lockers sat against one wall, while a desk and four black backpacks were lined up neatly against the other.

The woman gestured toward the corner of the dented metal desktop and said, "Take those clothes and go change."

I grabbed them and walked toward the bathroom I'd seen near the stairway, glad to have the chance to cover myself with real clothing and, even more, for a moment alone to collect my thoughts. The landing was empty. Where had the jerk gone? *Probably lurking around some corner waiting to tackle someone*, I thought sourly as I pulled the bathroom door shut behind me.

Once I'd set the knife down on the counter, I had to take a second to admire the beautiful, interlacing knotwork carved into the dark wood of the hilt. It looked very old, as if the hard edges of the carving had been worn smooth over years of use, but that didn't diminish the almost hypnotic effect of the carving. Who just randomly had an antique knife like this?

After pulling on the soft, black v-necked sweater and matching black jeans, I added *how did they know what size clothes I wear*, to the list of questions I wanted to have answered, then turned to look at myself in the mirror. My eyes were bloodshot, and a bruise was already beginning to form over the cheekbone that had struck the ground when I'd been tackled earlier. The black clothes made me look almost unsettlingly thin and pale. A night of apparent debauchery, followed by a stint in the psychiatric ward and kidnapping, was enough to make me look a bit strung out.

I dropped the hospital robe into the garbage next to the sink. With a few deft twists of my fingers, I braided my hair, then splashed some cold water onto my face, grabbed the knife off the counter, and pulled open the door to walk smack into the chest of the Jerk.

"Oof," I grunted, backing up as quickly as possible. I was glad I had held the knife with the blade pointed at the ground.

"You are a solid one, aren't you?" he said ruefully, rubbing his collarbone where my head had struck it.

I started to deliver a scathing reply about just who was heavy when I looked up at his face, and the words died in my throat. Under the light of the bathroom, which I hadn't bothered to turn off, I could finally see his features. I was fairly tall, at five-foot-eight, but my head hovered right around his collarbones, so I had to look up to see his eyes, which were a dark blue that instantly reminded me of moonlight on the Pacific Ocean; pale gray at the center but nearly blue-black at the edges.

His hair was dark brown, lightly curling over his forehead, just long enough to touch the tops of thick, straight brows. The bridge of his nose had looked straight from the side, but it was bent just slightly, as if it had been broken at some point in the past. His lips were sculpted, fuller on the bottom, and twisted into a sardonic smile as I watched. Which made me realize that I was staring. Blood rushed up into my cheeks. I shook my head slightly, trying to make an excuse for myself but nothing came out. He sighed and took a step back to open up the hallway, gesturing toward the room where my other captors were waiting.

"Go on," he said. His voice was cool and resigned, as if making women become idiots with his face was something he was used to but not very happy about. I started to do just that but realized I had forgotten something. I turned back into the bathroom and came out a second later with his coat.

"Here," I said, holding it out toward him. He took the coat and nodded once, slowly, without looking at me.

Instead of bothering to wait for a reply, I hurried off toward whatever answers my captors were willing to give me.

CHAPTER FIVE

"I want to know your names," I said as I sat across from the people who had kidnapped me, folding my arms and trying to look as confident as possible.

"My name is Cecily," said the Ice Queen, who had changed into a filmy black blouse tucked into a very fashionable-looking pair of trousers. She had also taken down her braids and now sported a chic bob that fit her aristocratic features much better.

She gestured to the man sitting next to her, "And this is Abasi."

Abasi, who had driven the van, had a triangular goatee that hung several inches below his chin. His cheeks were rounded and jovial, but his eyes were very serious, and he sat with his surprisingly muscular arms folded over a belly as round as St. Nick's.

"Hello," he said with a slight dip of the head.

Cecily inclined her head to me and said, "And you are Allison Erin Chapter."

"How do you know me?" I asked, "how did you know where I was? What is all this?"

Abasi answered me in a voice that was deep and melodious, and there was a cadence to his words that I couldn't place. His goatee wiggled distractingly when he spoke. "We know who and what you are because it is our job to know."

"What I am is a tired, confused woman who wants some answers."

Amusement pulled at one corner of Abasi's mouth. "That is not all you are. If it were, you would be of no interest to us. No, you are much more than that. You are what is called a Walker. Walkers are very rare, Miss Chapter. We are careful to find them because they have the capacity for great good but also," he held up one finger, "great harm."

My brows drew down. "I'm sorry, I'm a what?"

"A Walker," he said slowly.

"Would you care to define that, and how you know I am one? Because this whole thing," I said gesturing vaguely, "and everything that has happened today—none of it makes any sense to me."

Cecily looked at Abasi, who nodded.

"Ronan?" she called, "Will you come in here, please. We need a quick demonstration."

The Jerk, whose name was apparently Ronan, walked quietly into the room. He was a big man—had to be around 6' 4"—but he walked with an athletic grace so compelling that I needed to remind myself forcefully that not an hour ago he had chased and tackled me in a parking lot. I scowled at him.

"Before I have Ronan begin this demonstration, let me ask you a question," Cecily said, leaning forward to place her hands on the desktop and lock eyes with me, "have you ever woken up in a place you did not recognize? A place that was not your own, with no knowledge of how you came to be there?"

My palms went cold, and I felt the blood drain from my face. The first time I woke up in a place I didn't recognize, I'd thought I was still dreaming. I had been sixteen years old. While I'd had similar experiences in dreams before, where the dream took place in my home or my school or somewhere else that I was familiar with, I never noticed all the subtle differences between the real place and the dream place until I woke up. It all seemed perfectly natural to me while sleeping. The biggest difference between dreams like those and my experience was that I only noticed those dissimilarities when I woke up. That's how I knew something was wrong; I had noticed that things were different inside what I thought was still my dream.

The color of the walls in "my" room had been wrong even though the shape of my bedroom was the same, and so was the furniture. The room smelled like patchouli, a scent that always made me nauseous. Posters of bands I didn't recognize, and pictures of people I didn't know had hung on the walls. The bed was neatly made, something I have never had the motivation to do, and a radio I didn't own was playing songs I'd never heard. These were things I never noticed in dreams. I even pinched myself, just like people do in the movies. It was so surreal that I'd had a rush of vertigo and my legs had given out. I ended up on my knees with my arms curled around myself, rocking back and forth and whispering, "wake up," over and over again.

At some point, I had opened my eyes to familiar walls and photos I recognized. Because there was no other explanation that made sense, I had told myself it was a dream. Rayne had told me once that she was could recognize when she was having a nightmare and wake herself up. I figured that was what had happened to me. For a long time, I even believed it. But when I looked up at Cecily, somehow, I knew that when she said, "a place that was not your own," she wasn't asking me if I'd ever gotten drunk and ended up in a parking lot or at a friend's house after blacking out. She knew.

I nodded numbly.

"What you did," she said, "is called Walking. It usually happens for the first time at some point during puberty or, more rarely, after a strong emotional upheaval."

She saw my face blanch and nodded sagely. "Yes, the activation of the ability seems to be tied to the pituitary gland, though that is a complex issue we do not fully understand, and the biomechanics have proven to be...elusive. In any case, when the ability is activated, it gives one the power to walk between verses. That is, inter-dimensional travel."

I laughed once, a bark of surprised incredulity, and said, "Walking between verses? What, you mean like different worlds? Magic?"

"Magic is a word we use to describe things we do not yet understand. No, Miss Chapter. What I am talking about is explainable by science, if only in theory. The most succinct description of this ability is inter-dimensional travel."

"Inter-dimensional travel. Seriously? Come on, Cecily, I want real answers. I've had a lot of really weird crap happen to me today, and I've even questioned my sanity. Now you're making me wonder about yours."

She turned to Ronan and nodded once. He looked at me and compressed his lips into an apologetic smile before closing his eyes, taking a deep breath, and disappearing as if he'd never been standing there.

I screamed.

It took a while for them to calm me down because I nearly peed all over myself when Ronan appeared again, moments later, holding a cup of what smelled like hot cocoa. After a lot of cajoling and being forced to touch Ronan's arm to prove that he was real, not some projection or trick of smoke and mirrors, I sat on the floor with the cocoa keeping my fingers warm, staring up at Cecily and doing my best not to look at Ronan, who scared the ever-loving crap out of me.

Part of my brain was screaming that I needed to bolt; no one stood between me and the doorway. The other part of my brain, the part I tried hard to ignore, whispered, *don't be a coward*. I clenched my jaw and nodded at Cecily to continue.

"How much of the sciences have you learned?" She asked.

"I took physics, but I didn't pay too much attention."

She sighed and draped one elegant hand over the armrest. "Very well," she said, "try to follow along. Earth existed in its true, singular form until the first Human being, a creature with self-consciousness, appeared. That was when we believe the first split happened."

"Split?"

"Say I offer you two drinks: one a glass of water and the other a glass of vodka. I have introduced two choices to you, which means two possible futures, correct?"

"Okay," I said, willing to accept that.

"If you chose the water, you are refreshed, and we continue our conversation. If you chose the vodka, you quickly become drunk," she ignored me as I muttered under my breath that it would take significantly more than that to get me drunk, and continued, "you assault me, and I'm forced to kill you. But neither of those two possible realities exist until after you've made a choice, do they?"

"Geez, that was a bit violent, don't you think?"

"The example must be dramatic. Once you choose, you have set the course for your future, but what happens to that other possible future? Does it cease to exist?"

I shrugged.

"Every time a human makes a decision," she continued, "they alter the possible future. I assume you learned that atoms vibrate?"

I nodded.

"Good," she said, "therefore, everything has a frequency. All of existence vibrates with a distinct pitch, a cosmic harmony if you will. A chair has a very different frequency than a living thing. A rat is different than a human, and no two humans are the same. Of course, this is all dramatically simplified because each piece of a system has a distinct frequency and each system its own harmony, but for the sake of brevity, we will simply say that each person vibrates. A Walker's vibrations are as different from those of a normal human being as a baby is different from a stone. Since inanimate objects make no choices, they remain an unchanging part of the cosmic melody. As human beings choose and act, they alter the melody and subtly change the song."

She paused for a breath in a very practiced way that made me think she must have repeated this speech countless times; the pause was just long enough to let the information sink in, but not so long to allow me to formulate more questions. "Because Walkers can change their own frequencies substantially," she continued, "their decisions and actions alter the fabric of reality in much more dramatic ways than the decisions of normal humans. Sometimes, decisions that have very far-reaching consequences are enough to split reality so that an entirely new earth appears that now follows the direction of the choice not taken."

I shook my head and said blankly, "A different dimension."

"Exactly. So, in one reality or verse, you drank the water, and, in the other, the vodka. Each line of the future follows the consequences of that choice."

"Are you telling me that what color socks I choose to wear could change the future?"

"No," she said very slowly, in the kind of voice a kindergarten teacher uses to explain to Billy why he can't pee in the flower pots, "not every single decision is enough to alter the course of your present reality. The atomic bomb, however, was. The truth is that, even in the most scientifically advanced verses, our understanding of this phenomena is theoretical at best; we only know that it does work."

I stood up and started to pace the room, pulling at the end of my braid. I had done my best to suspend disbelief and retain the enormous amount of information she spewed at me, but it wasn't easy.

"There's a reality where the atomic bomb was never invented?" I asked.

"Yes."

"Where Hitler won?"

Very quietly, "Yes."

I shivered. My mind was spinning like a top and hundreds of half-remembered bits of information from history classes and science fiction novels began clinging together and growing as they picked up speed, like a snowball rolling downhill. Things people claimed to be true but had never been explained—the Loch Ness Monster, fairy circles, or people disappearing without a trace in the Bermuda Triangle—might have more basis in reality than anyone imagined.

"And what you're telling me is that somehow, these Walkers can move from one reality, I mean one verse into another?"

She nodded.

"So, things like...I don't know...rocket ships to Mars?"

"Do exist," she finished.

"Aliens?"

"Not quite," Abasi said, clearly amused, "but verses advanced enough to seem like aliens, yes."

"And this vibration everyone has, Walkers can alter theirs to make them able to do," I swallowed, fought down the urge to hurl, and gestured to Ronan with a jerk of my head, "to do...that?"

Abasi smiled slightly and said, "Very good, Miss Chapter, yes. Not everyone understands that so quickly."

"So, you're saying that all the conspiracy theorists through history aren't crazy?"

A smile creased his face. "Oh, they are crazy; but many of them are also correct."

I sat on a bed in one of the small upstairs bedrooms with my legs folded underneath me, leaning my head back against the wall, grateful that they were willing to give me a few minutes to myself. What I'd learned made me wonder if leaving the psychiatric ward had been a good idea, after all. Questioning one's sanity isn't a comfortable proposition, so maybe it was best not to dwell on that.

The others were talking quietly in the large room at the top of the stairs. Their muffled voices reminded me of waking up in the hospital, and I shuddered. I never wanted to find myself captive like that, ever again. Apparently, according to Cecily, Walkers often ended up in the psych ward or mental institutions after Walking for the first time. That made sense, I supposed, considering that someone might find themselves surrounded by people who claimed to know them but whom they'd never met; people who try to convince them things happened in their lives that they couldn't remember, as I had.

What I wanted more than anything was someone to talk to. Someone who wasn't uptight like Cecily or might pop out of existence, as Ronan had done. I needed someone to tell me I wasn't losing my mind.

"You are not losing your mind," came a deep voice from the doorway. I looked up from where I'd dropped my head into my hands to see Abasi leaning against the doorframe with his massive arms folded across his chest and the corners of his mouth turned up.

"And no, I cannot read your mind. But that is what most people think when they first learn what they are."

He walked into the room and the bed sunk down under his weight. He only sat on the corner, but he was more solidly muscled than his soft midsection suggested.

"All of this is kind of hard to swallow," I admitted.

"I know it is. I find that the trick is to start off acting as if you did believe it, and soon enough you have all the proof you need."

"I don't know how to do that."

"You should try. We need to get you home, after all."

I had forgotten about that. With everything else there was to think about, I had forgotten the whole reason I ended up in the psychiatric ward in the first place.

"This...this isn't my world, is it?"

"No, my dear. It is not."

"I don't understand how this happened. How can I do something I don't know I can do?"

Abasi ran his thumb and forefinger down the sides of his triangular beard and looked at me quizzically. "Can you paint?"

"What?" I asked, surprised.

"Can you paint?"

"Um...no. I mean, I've never tried."

He tilted his head sideways and raised an expectant eyebrow at me.

"Okay," I said, "fair enough."

He laughed and gestured expansively, "So you see? Your first efforts at painting would not end up quite as you might hope, but that does not mean the ability is not there."

I supposed that made sense. "Why here, then?"

"The first few times they travel, people tend to walk to worlds in the Ververse that are the most like their own. They do it like you did, without thinking or sometimes because of some powerful emotion. This verse is very like that of True Earth."

And it was. If Seth hadn't come walking into my apartment, I might not have put together all the little clues that made this place different, at least not until... "Holy cow, Abasi, am I—I mean," I swallowed, "*I'm* here, too, aren't I?"

He nodded slowly. "Yes, you are. That is one of the reasons we needed to take you quickly. If a Walker meets themselves, it usually does not end well."

My attempts to control my breathing weren't very successful. I was having a hard time reconciling myself to the fact that there was more than just one of me out there. I climbed off the bed and stood in the center of the room with my arms wrapped around myself.

"Does that mean that she—I mean the me that lives in this verse...is she a Walker, too?"

He looked at me for a long time, his eyes kind and thoughtful. "No, Allison," he said and stood up to walk over and put his large hands comfortingly on my shoulders, "she is not you, my dear. She is only who you might have been, if things were different and other choices had been made. She is a different person."

The me—or the she—who lived in this verse still had her father. My father. She had a boyfriend. Were my parents, or her parents, still married, still happy? How many differences were there between us that stopped her from being me?

"If I saw her family, if I saw her father...my father...would he think—"

"I will not pretend that it has never been done," Abasi admitted slowly, "but Allison, it always ends in sorrow. She is not you. He is not *your* father."

I hesitated, imagining myself taking her place, even if only for long enough to hug him and hear his voice again. To hear him say, "I love you." I closed my eyes and felt hot tears hit my cheeks. He wouldn't be saying it to me, though. He'd be saying it to her.

"Wait Abasi," I said as my eyes flew open, "what happened to the other me when I showed up?"

"Nothing happened to her."

"But aren't we connected somehow? You said bad things happen if a Walker meets themselves, so wouldn't there be some kind of—" I snapped my fingers in a staccato rhythm, flipping through science-fiction books in my head until I came up with the word, "paradox! Wouldn't that be a paradox?"

He smiled at me. "No, Allison. How many times must I tell you that she is not you? You may share some history, but whatever happened between the split and our present time has made you two different people."

"But her family will still get the call that she escaped from the hospital," I said with a sinking feeling.

"Yes. She will have to live with the consequences of what happened while you were in her place. This is another reason we took you so quickly."

Guilt sunk its claws into my stomach. Any remaining hope I had of stealing a few, precious moments with my father was gone. I couldn't run around causing innocent people harm. I rubbed my eyes with the heel of my hand, took a steadying breath, looked at Abasi and nodded.

"Good!" he said, placing his hand on the small of my back and urging me toward the door, "let's get you home."

Cecily watched me with a remotely interested expression as we walked into the room; she was a cat who had spent all its energy playing with a mouse but wasn't beyond being tempted by some new toy.

"There is still much for you to learn, Allison, but that will take more time than we have tonight. Abasi and I must go, but Ronan will see you home."

Ronan was beautiful to look at but was also abrupt and more than a little intimidating, so the thought of having to spend any time alone with him made me ask Cecily, "Couldn't I...I mean, could Abasi maybe—"

She cut me off with a curt gesture, "No, I am sorry. It cannot be avoided, and we do not have much time. You are not the most pressing matter we have to deal with tonight."

She stood up, pulled a jacket off the back of her chair, and joined Abasi at the door.

"Do not worry, my dear," he said comfortingly, "soon you will be back in your own bed, back to your own life. Be grateful, because not everyone gets to go home."

They walked out of the room and were gone, leaving me alone with Mr. Tall Dark and Intimidating. I bit my lip. He was sitting on the window frame with his long legs stretched out and crossed at the ankles, looking at me with his head tilted to the side. My stomach made a loud, squelching noise. Ronan nodded as if he'd just made up his mind, then stood up and strode toward me.

"Come on," he said, "let's get you something to eat."

CHAPTER SIX

A s we passed through a beam of light beneath the arched street lamps, Ronan pulled his hood up over his dark hair and rolled his shoulders beneath the leather jacket. I shivered, wondering what had become of my self-possession. Not one to be intimidated easily, it bothered me that my initial instinct when walking with Ronan down a darkened street was to hide under a rock somewhere. It didn't help that his face was all but invisible beneath his hood.

"Where is your accent from?" I asked, just to break the silence.

"Ireland."

"Oh? Well, I'll refrain from the Lucky Charms jokes."

"You'd be the first."

"You can't really blame people, you know. The temptation is almost unbearable."

He grunted but didn't look back, and I had to lengthen my stride to keep up with him.

"How long have you, ah," I made a vague gesture, "been, you know, trapped in a Sci-Fi novel?" In his dark jacket and jeans, he seemed to disappear into the night between street lamps, reminding me uncomfortably of his disappearing act in the house, but the rhythmic tread of his long stride against the pavement was comfortingly solid.

"Science fiction? No, mine's a bit more like a fairy tale."

"You make that sound like it's a bad thing. Don't most people want their lives to be like fairy tales?"

"Maybe if they only know the Disney version. True fairy tales are a bit more gruesome. Look, we've only got another block before we reach the diner. Can you hold your tongue till then?"

When he looked back over his shoulder at me, his eyes were lost in the inky blackness beneath his hood. I swallowed a retort and clenched my jaw.

❧──•◆•──☙

The carpet in the diner looked older than me and was still riddled with cigarette burns from the days before it became a no-no to smoke in public. I scrunched my nose and slid warily across the pocked leather of the booth seat opposite Ronan. I didn't bother to hide my disdain.

"You're hungry, are you not?"

I glanced up from the table where 'Jenny is a slut' was scratched into the plastic surface in rude block lettering. The grimace on my face must have given me away.

"Yes," I admitted grudgingly.

"This place has food," he said with a shrug.

"If that's what you want to call it."

"Would you rather walk another five blocks?"

"Yes."

He blew out a breath and pulled the hood back, which tousled the dark curls on his forehead. There was a mole or something above his left eyebrow. A birthmark, maybe? He must have seen my eyes stray to the blemish because he pushed the hair around until it covered his forehead, and asked, "Are you always so contrary?"

I couldn't help but smile at that. "Yes."

The corners of his eyes crinkled just enough that only a charitable person would have called it a smile. A waitress appeared with two glasses of ice water and plunked them down, unceremoniously, on the scarred surface of the table.

"Breakfast served all night," she breathed out in a bored monotone, "what can I get you?"

"Can I get a menu?"

She gave me a dirty look and waddled off toward the front.

"Wow, great choice here, Ronan. Service with a smile."

"Give her a break, it's late, and she's probably tired."

I shrugged and took the menu with no more complaint. It was hard to order while she stood over the top of us, breathing loudly through her broken nose. Every now and then a high-pitched little wheeze would escape, and I had to bite my lip to keep a straight face.

"I'll just have two eggs over medium, sausage, hash browns and wheat toast, please."

She snatched the menu out of my hand. "You needed a menu for that? What about you?"

Ronan looked up and said blandly, "Same."

She grunted and left us looking at each other, me with my eyebrow raised, and him looking chagrined.

"Alright," he conceded, "next time you can choose the place."

I smiled triumphantly only to stop short as the smile froze on my face. "Next time?"

Ronan leaned back, as far as his large frame would allow, and draped one elbow over the back of the seat. He looked at me appraisingly for a moment, and I had that same absurd instinct to hide.

"We're going to be seeing a lot of each other for a while, Allison. You have a good deal to learn before you're safe on your own."

I grabbed the paper napkin wrapped silverware to give my hands something to do, and started spinning it on the table. "Maybe you can explain that to me a little bit. I think I have the broader points, but I still don't understand how you found me. If there are so many verses, wouldn't it be kind of hard to find just one person? I mean...kind of impossible, really, if Walkers are as rare as all that?"

Ronan sighed and settled in for what was clearly going to be a long talk. "How would you like to do this, Allie?"

He used my nickname without seeming to think about it, and the sound of it in his lightly accented voice made my stomach jump. I cleared my throat and asked the obvious follow-up. "What do you mean?"

"I can either sit back and give you a proper history of Walkers through the ages, or you can just ask me what you want to know."

I jumped on that immediately. "Let's start with who you are. All of you."

"Cecily, Abasi and I are Venatore. It's part of our job to find Walkers."

"Venatore? That sounds Latin."

"It is. It means hunter."

"Isn't it kind of strange that your group has a Latin name? I mean, they must speak all kinds of other languages in different verses, languages we don't have here."

"They do. But the founder of the Concilium is from a part of True Earth that spoke both Latin and English. He knew that the relative safety of our kind wouldn't be possible without some kind of law, so he created the Venatore, and tasked us with finding new Walkers and teaching the law to them, enforcing it when the need arose."

"That seems like an impossible job."

He grunted. "It isn't easy."

I pulled the butter knife out of the silverware bundle and started turning it over and over in my fingers. The light from the dusty lamp overhead caught on the flat surface of the blade and skittered off the wall as I twirled it.

"If you have a job—I mean if the Venatore are employed—there must be a central government, right?"

"There is, but it's not like a proper government. The Concilium have a set of rules meant to keep everyone safe, and the Venatore make sure the rules get enforced. That's about all there is to it. It's hard to police a society like ours when someone can disappear to a thousand different verses."

"I bet. What are the rules?"

He leaned forward then and rested his forearms on the tabletop. His eyes were serious, and I found it difficult to look away.

"This is important, girl, so pay close attention. Once I tell you these rules, you're bound by them, you understand?"

I nodded hesitantly, but then held my hand up as he opened his mouth and shouted, "Wait!"

Both his eyebrows raised so high that they got lost in his hair. If I hadn't just felt my stomach hit the floor, I'd have laughed at the surprise on his face.

"What's the matter?"

"Nothing."

He didn't believe me, to judge by the wry twist of his lips.

"It's just that rules are a big deal," I explained lamely. It sounded so dumb. How could I possibly explain myself in a way that didn't make me sound like a guilty five-year-old? Ronan watched me patiently, an interested gleam in his eye. I pressed my lips together and tried to think coherently about why knowing the rules of this new part of my life should make me feel so anxious.

"I guess it's just that people are willing to make allowances for you when you don't know any better. If you get into trouble, at least you can say that you didn't realize you were doing anything wrong. But once you know the rules, there's an expectation to live up to. All of this still doesn't feel real. If it's not real, it's safer. But, if there are rules..."

I left the thought hanging there, but Ronan was nodding. "Don't worry. There aren't many rules and, generally speaking, they're easy enough to follow," he assured me. An amused note crept into his voice, and he added, "and only one or two are punishable by death. No pressure."

That last comment should have had the panic back in full force but, oddly enough, the deadpan humor calmed my nerves more than any assurances or coddling could have done.

"Alright then," I was able to say with some aplomb, "lay it on me."

"Pay attention, then, because I will ask you to repeat these back to me later." Then his voice lowered into a measured pitch, and he said, "The Laws of the Founding were set down by the leader and founder of the Concilium, and they are these: no Walker may transport artifacts, technology or magical weapons to another verse, this is the First Law of the Founding. You shall not endanger another Walker's existence by revealing your gifts to mortal men; this is the Second Law. Your actions shall not deprive another Walker of freedom, property, health or life; this is the Third Law. Justice shall be rendered by a vote of the Concilium and ratified by a body of peers. If any Walker should break these laws, the Venatore shall bring the transgressor to the justice of the Concilium. Did you understand all of that?"

I sighed in relief. He had been right. It wasn't that bad. "Yep. Do unto others and keep your mouth shut. What I don't understand is, if you're the police force, why did you find me? Did I do something wrong?"

"No, you didn't. Like I said, part of what we do is find Walkers and train them how to use their abilities. If we teach you, you're less likely to break the rules, right? Which means it's safer for the rest of us and for the

verses you visit. It's better to find you now than wait till you've damaged
a society or conquered a continent."

I swallowed hard at the implications of that casual statement. "How
do you find them?"

Ronan sat back and ran his hands through the hair at the nape of
his neck, clearly thinking about how to answer me. His hair was a dark
brown, almost black, but not as dark as his lashes. He caught me staring
and quirked an eyebrow. I blushed.

"That's privileged information and not something I can share with
you," he said finally.

I thought I heard regret in his voice but didn't get the chance to ask
him why because our intrepid waitress appeared just then with an armful
of poorly cooked food, and dropped the plates in front of us before
walking away without another word. Ronan forked a rubbery egg into
his mouth, but I struggled to take a single bite. As much as I wanted
to eat, and I was terribly hungry, the oily sausage and deep-fried hash
browns made me think that death by starvation might not be such a
terrible way to go. I poked at one egg with my fork and grimaced.

Ronan stopped shoveling food into his face and asked around a
mouthful of potato, "Can't handle it, eh?"

Lips flattened into a determined line, I scooped up the egg and
crammed it in, chewing furiously. Some water helped me get the rubbery
thing down quickly, and my stomach growled. Apparently, my guts
didn't care what my palette thought of the skill of our cook; tummy
wanted food. Ronan watched intently as I trashed the rest of my dinner
as quickly as I could swallow. The faster it went down, the less I had to
taste. When I finished, I dropped my fork victoriously onto the plate and
smiled.

"Done."

Ronan had finished before me and had been sitting back with his arms
crossed over his chest. The corner of his mouth raised into an amused
grin, displaying a dimple on that side. "Competitive, are you?"

I shrugged. "A bit."

We sat in silence, looking at each other over yolk smeared plates.
With a few toast crumbs caught in the stubble at the corner of his wide
mouth and the memory of a dimple in one cheek, he looked much less
intimidating than he had after he'd tackled me in the parking lot. My
hand went to my cheekbone reflexively, and Ronan flinched.

"I am sorry about that," he said with a nod toward my face, "most
people do run, and I couldn't take the chance of letting you escape. We
might never have found you."

I shrugged it off, only regretting that his face had gone hard again. He
had seemed almost human for a second.

"Getting back to the rules," I pointed at him with my fork, "you
brought a cup of cocoa back from wherever you disappeared to. Why is
that okay, but moving technology around isn't?"

"A cup of cocoa is a far cry from a computer," he pointed out in a tone that implied I was missing an obvious answer.

"Humor me."

"What kind of impact do you think it would have if I showed up in the equivalent of Britain in 1492 with a television or a rocket launcher?"

Duh. "I suppose this was one of those instances where I should have believed my sci-fi novels," I admitted sheepishly. That had been an obvious answer once I took the time to consider it. Cecily had said that some verses were very different from this one, so it would be like showing up with alien technology.

"Okay, one point for your side. My next question is, how can you do it? I understand that Walkers can affect their own atomic frequencies, though I don't have the faintest idea how, but how does that ability extend to something like a cup of cocoa?"

He answered my question with another question. "Have you ever dodged something thrown at you, like a rock or a ball?"

"I have an older brother," I told him, laughing, "I've dodged a lot worse than that."

"But have you ever dodged something you didn't see coming?"

I had to think about that. My first instinct was to say no, but then I remembered walking through the park in front of my apartment with my friend Mateo when a sparrow decided that we were too close to her nest. She'd dive bombed us from behind, and I'd flinched out of the way so that she missed my ear by barely an inch. That suicidal little bird had chased Matt and me straight from the park and into a bus. Ronan slid out of his booth and motioned me to move over. I did, but with some apprehension. These booths weren't that wide, and Ronan was a big man.

I pushed back toward the wall to give him room, but he slid closer, his hip and thigh less than a foot from mine.

"Uncomfortable?" he asked, leaning toward me. His voice was low and his eyes intent. I could feel the heat radiating off his big body. The urge to lean farther away from him was strong, but my back was already against the wall.

"Yes, it is."

He slid away, and I relaxed. "I was inside your electromagnetic field," he explained, "you could feel how close I was, and it triggered your fight or flight reflexes."

"I could see you, though," I disagreed, "and I hardly know you, so it makes sense that it would be uncomfortable to be that close to someone I don't know. Just from an evolutionary standpoint, it would be dangerous for me to allow an unknown quantity close enough to do me harm."

"A fair point," he conceded, "but there's more going on than that. Close your eyes, this time." I didn't hesitate. Now I was intrigued. We'd slipped into full-on nerd territory, and my natural curiosity was strong enough to quell any misgivings. I closed my eyes.

"Notice how the rest of your senses become sharper when you can't see?" I did. Without the need to process all the information my eyes would have been sending my brain, I had more attention to spare for the smells and sounds around me. Even the weight of the clothes on my skin was noticeable. With a sudden squeak, I jerked my head to the side and my eyes flew open. Ronan's hand hung in the air centimeters from where my cheek had just been. Goosebumps were already rippling down my arms.

"You see? Even with your eyes closed your body knew."

"I could feel your warmth," I objected.

"What is warmth?" he asked.

It was a rhetorical question, so I didn't answer but I understood. "So, somehow we're able to affect the atomic frequencies of things that are inside our electromagnetic field?"

Ronan was in the process of sliding out of my side of the booth when he answered that they didn't know yet how we were able to do it but, yes, Walkers were capable of affecting inanimate objects within their field enough to transport them when they walked.

"It requires a good deal of concentration," he warned, "and it's even harder to bring a living thing, more dangerous, but still possible. This is why we don't reveal ourselves to the Legless. To walk with one of them could damage them or kill both the Walker and the Legless, not to mention the fact that no one wants to be studied for the sake of science. You can see why the rules are in place."

Gruesome pictures filled my head, and I couldn't help but ask the obvious follow-up question. "Walkers have tried to bring other people?"

"Yes, unfortunately. It can be done, but it's something we only try in extreme circumstances and, even then, there are some Walkers who aren't strong enough or just never get the hang of it. Your field isn't that large, in any case. Imagine trying to fit another person into it. What happens to the parts that get left out?"

I shuddered, deciding to let that question drop. From what he said, I'd have a lot of time to learn about the more intricate details, and now that my less than stellar dinner was starting to congeal into an oily knot in my guts, I had more pressing things on my mind.

"So, now you've found me, and I know about the rules, what happens next?"

"Now we get you home. After that, I'll check in on you and teach you a bit more about Walking between the verses. It will take a while to teach you to do it purposefully so that you aren't Walking on accident, or during a nightmare or when you're angry."

I shuddered. If every possible world existed, then I was sure there were some places I did not want to find myself by accident. "If you're a cop—"

"Venator," Ronan interrupted.

"Okay, if you're a Venator, how will you have time to help me with all this? Won't you be needed to catch bad guys or something?"

"I told you," he said patiently, "hunting isn't the only thing Venatore do, and there aren't so many Walkers that we can't take our time."

I started to ask what else was part of his job description when he sat suddenly still with his head cocked ever so slightly to the side, like a hound listening to a rabbit in the bushes. Suddenly, he lunged at me. His body forced us both down onto the seat just as the window across the aisle from us exploded inward.

CHAPTER SEVEN

I had only seconds to register how big Ronan's body was before I was being jerked to my feet and forced toward the back of the restaurant. Ronan kept himself between me and the front of the store, where all three huge plate windows had been shattered. We rushed past patrons and employees alike, some hiding beneath tables or behind partitions and some running toward the exits in a confused rush.

"Come on, lass, move," he growled at me and gave me very forceful encouragement with one big hand at the small of my back.

A series of sharp cracks split the air in the front of the diner, and I ducked instinctively.

"Were those gunshots?" I yelled, trying to make sure he could hear me over the screaming and the sound of clattering cookware.

"Yeah," he said as he stepped to the side of the rear exit. He had a dark pistol in his right hand.

"Why do you have a gun?" I asked faintly.

He ignored me and eased open the door to peer into the darkness. Once he was satisfied that there was no one in the alley, we left the diner behind and slunk into the shadows of the building and toward the street. Ronan walked with a kind of animal grace that was both fluid and predatory. I tried to force myself to relax but my hands were shaking, and I could hear every sound, from the wind in the alley to the crunch of glass beneath the feet of diners fleeing through the front of the restaurant. The tinny rattle of a soda can rolling across the pavement made me flinch and tense to run. I grabbed a handful of Ronan's coat to steady myself.

Just relax, Allie, I told myself, fighting the urge to flee, *this guy is practically a superhero, he can handle whatever is going on.*

We had made it two streets down, keeping to the shadows and moving quietly, when I tripped over a random piece of rubbish and gasped in pain as my ankle gave out. I landed on my knees, crying out in surprise, only vaguely conscious of a snapping sound, like someone breaking a branch near my left ear. Ronan, who had been just behind me, grunted and staggered, cursing. He grabbed me by the back of my jacket and jerked me into the shadows toward a stairwell that led down to a basement door.

The sound of Ronan growling profanities beneath his breath made me more uneasy than trying to walk on my sore ankle. Once we were in the stairwell, he put his back against the wall and reached inside his jacket. When he pulled his hand out there was blood on his fingertips. He ignored my gasp and grabbed my arm, pulling me against his chest, hard. I tried to pull back but he held me fast with one arm locked around my shoulders. His body went completely still. I could feel the thudding of his heart beneath my cheek and hear the shush, shush of my blood surging through my ears. Within a couple of breaths, his heartbeat began to slow noticeably, and I felt him begin to vibrate. At first, I thought he was shivering, but it was more like he was purring since the vibration seemed to be centered in his chest and rolled in waves out toward his limbs.

"Hang on to me and think of home," he said between clenched teeth.

The intensity of his voice had me responding without thought. I wrapped both arms around his waist and pressed my cheek hard against his chest, trying to draw a picture in my mind. I saw my apartment building, the large industrial elevator, and the hand-tied ribbon carpet that Rayne had made to sit outside our door. Ronan was shaking so hard that the reverberation of it rattled my entire body, making my brain bounce inside my skull until my bones hurt. I wanted to pull away and tell him to stop, that my teeth felt like they were going to shake loose, that my bones were going to pull away from muscles that were now tense with strain and cramping painfully. Suddenly my stomach dropped, and my mind went black.

"Allison."

I heard him speak, but for a moment I didn't recognize the name as my own. My limbs felt like they'd grown roots and attached themselves firmly to the earth. I drew in a long, shaky breath.

"Allison," he said again, his voice more insistent. I tried to say something, but my lips weren't cooperating. At least the shaking had stopped. My mouth was dry, and my eyelids felt cemented shut, just as they had when I'd awoken in my apartment only to find that it wasn't mine.

"Allison!"

I dragged my hand to my face and scrubbed it across my eyes.

"Mmhmm," I groaned and rolled over onto my stomach, pulling my hands and knees underneath myself. Once I got my eyes open, I wished I had kept them closed. My intestines coiled around themselves like snakes. I was suddenly violently ill. After losing what was left of my poorly cooked dinner, I spat and wiped my mouth with the back of my forearm.

"I'm sorry you had to see that," I said weakly, spitting again to rid myself of the taste. It didn't work.

"I've seen worse. Are we close to your flat?"

I sat down and scooted backward, away from the awful smell of my sickness, and blinked hard, trying work up a bit of moisture. It was still night, and we were still in an alley. I felt a chill run down my spine.

"Did we just...ah...walk?" I asked, looking up at Ronan whose face seemed to be perpetually shadowed underneath his hood.

"We did."

I blinked at the alley, trying to see the details. There was Mr. Soko's bike, chained to the railing of the back exit from our building, the red basket on the front-end zip tied to the handlebars. My nausea began to subside, and I sighed in relief; this was my place, I could feel it.

"Yes, we're right behind my building."

"That's good," Ronan said, and promptly passed out.

I kicked our door with the toe of my boot and shouted again, willing Rayne to be home. Ronan was barely conscious and his big body was so heavy that my knees threatened to buckle. His head lolled to the side, and I staggered.

"Ronan? Hang in there, okay? Are you awake?"

He lifted his head and made a concerted effort to take more of his own weight.

"I'm good," he lied.

I raised my leg to kick the door again, but it opened, and Rayne stood there, in a white tank top and sweatpants and ridiculous, fuzzy green slippers. She was unmoving, wide-eyed with one hand pressed against her chest as I pushed past her, dragging Ronan with me.

"Allie, what? Is he okay? What's going on? Should I call 911?"

As soon as I got close to the couch, I let him slide onto the cushion with a groan and a curse as he bumped his wounded arm.

"No," I said, dragging in a deep lungful of air, "you don't need to call the cops, but I do need towels, rubbing alcohol and boiled water. Hurry up!"

She stared at me for a long second as I began helping Ronan pull his arm out of his jacket while he cursed enthusiastically in what I assumed was Irish Gaelic, her lips twisted unhappily to the side.

"Okay," she agreed with obvious reluctance, "but you're going to tell me what happened to this guy."

And she disappeared into the hallway.

"Damn girl, could ye hurt my shoulder any more than you have done?"

I had the crazy urge to laugh. Up until then, his accent had been so subtle that I could barely tell that he had one, but when he was upset, it was a clear brogue.

"Got your Irish up, eh? You're the one that told me not to call 911, remember? If I remember correctly, you ordered me not to. So, you're just going to have to deal with my help whether it hurts or not, aren't you?"

He looked at me sharply, then grunted and moved his shoulder while I pulled his jacket the rest of the way off. The pain seemed to be keeping him awake better than my shouting had. He sucked air in through his teeth as I peeled the leather from his arm.

"Oh God, Ronan," I said, feeling faint, "you've lost a lot of blood."

Red stained his t-shirt from shoulder to hem and across the chest. The edges had already started to turn brown as the blood dried.

"Thanks for pointin' that out."

I swallowed and hurried to the kitchen, grabbing a clean dishtowel and the kitchen shears. Blood from the inside of his coat had smeared across my hands, and the sight of it made me lightheaded. The urge to run, to find anyone to help but me, made my leg muscles cramp. Ronan shifted his weight and hissed in pain, and the sound of it brought me back to myself.

Ignore the blood, I thought sternly, *it's not the first time you've seen it. Help this man who saved your life. You can do this much.*

He didn't move as I cut up the sleeve of his shirt and down across the shoulder to the chest, carefully peeling back the material to reveal the small entrance wound. The bullet had gone cleanly through the shoulder muscle and exited out the back at an angle without hitting the joint or the bone of his upper arm, from what I could tell. Blood was still welling from the wound, but it was only a slow ooze, and there was no spurting.

"Just flesh," I told him, relieved. He nodded but noticed my eyes roaming over the blood-soaked shirt.

"Don't worry. It's not as much as it seems."

"It was enough to make you pass out," I countered.

"I did that, but part of it was the—traveling."

Rayne hurried out of the back with a bottle of rubbing alcohol, a roll of paper towels, and the first aid kit from underneath the bathroom sink. "Will this be okay?"

"I think so," I said, taking the first aid kit and sliding the zipper open. My mom had made sure we were equipped with the granddaddy of all first aid kits. I pulled out gauze, sterile bandages, and Tylenol, and I even found a triangle sling tucked into the side.

"Do we still need boiling water?" Rayne asked, eyeing Ronan's shoulder with dismay.

I surveyed our equipment and dug back into the kit, hoping to find sterile water. It was there, thankfully.

"I don't think so," I told her, "but you should check the jacket to make sure that the hole in the shoulder closes all the way. Tell me if it looks like there's a piece missing."

She was already picking up the jacket when she asked, "Why?"

I pulled on a pair of plastic gloves and peeled open an antiseptic wipe. "I need to make sure the bullet didn't drag a piece of the jacket into his arm," I said as I began gently wiping the blood away from the wound.

"Bullet?" Her voice was faint as she eyed the coat like it was a poisonous snake.

"If a piece did get stuck in his arm," I shuddered, thinking about digging into the smooth muscle with forceps to remove a tiny piece of leather, and shook my head, saying firmly "then we'll have to call 911."

I glared at Ronan, daring him to contradict me. I knew the basics of first aid and a bit more, thanks to having a nurse for a mother, but not enough to find a stray piece of leather in a man's shoulder. If the bullet had dragged something into the wound, he would get an infection for sure. His lips were drawn tight, and his pupils dilated in pain, but he didn't argue with me.

"It looks good," Rayne said, though her voice was thin, "it doesn't look like anything is missing. The little hole closes all the way."

She pulled her hands away from the jacket to look down at her fingers and all the color drained from her cheeks. Her face went so white that it scared me.

"Rayne, don't faint," I warned, taking a step toward her.

She shook her head and hurried toward the kitchen with shaking hands, fingers red with Ronan's blood. I turned back to my patient, who had his eyes closed and was breathing in long, measured breaths. Sweat beaded his cheekbones, and he'd drawn both brows together so tightly that a deep crease had formed between them.

"Are you okay?" I asked.

He took another slow breath and then opened his eyes, the corner of his mouth turning up but not far enough to tease a dimple out of his cheek. "I'm all right. I've had worse than this and still lived to fight another day."

I noticed that his brogue had all but disappeared, blurred back into lightly accented American English. I regretted that. I had to admit to myself that, even though he had been growling at me at the time, hearing that accent in his deep voice had been sexy.

Not the right time to be thinking about that, I told myself sternly, disconcerted by the thought. After laying out a few towels to staunch any bleeding and cleaning the wound with sterile water, I applied some antibacterial lotion and made the best pressure dressing I could manage. Rayne sat on a barstool behind the couch with her arms wrapped around herself. Ronan didn't make another noise, only winced when I pulled the dressing tight. I had to lean over and wrap my arms around him to pull the sling into place and tie it above his opposite shoulder. He smelled just like his jacket had, only tainted by the metallic scent of blood. I felt his breath on my bare neck and the tickle of his dark curls against my ear.

Shivering, I leaned back and tried to sound business-like. "Okay, now we just need to get your arm into the sling, and that's about as good as I can make it."

He did make a noise as he bent his arm to slide it into the sling, but that couldn't be helped.

"Are you okay?" I asked once more, feeling rather maternal. I'd never used anything my mother had taught me about first aid, and having taken care of someone that way made me feel a strangely proprietary concern.

"I'll do," he said, adjusting the fit of the sling with his free hand. He looked at me and rubbed at the tension in his forehead with the long fingers of his right hand. "Thank you, Allison."

"You're welcome."

He looked into my eyes for a second longer and then gingerly turned so that he could see Rayne sitting behind him. "And you, Rayne. Thank you."

Color rose in her cheeks, and she nodded, the bun on top of her head wobbling a bit. I stood up and rubbed my hands down the thighs of my jeans, suddenly feeling the weight of the last 48 hours drag me toward the floor.

"You need sleep," Ronan said.

I eyed him, amused despite the fatigue. "If anyone needs sleep, it's you."

"I'll sleep here if you two don't mind?"

I did laugh then. "Your huge body on that sofa? Your legs would hang off from the knees down. No, you can sleep in my bed, and I'll sleep out here."

"I'm not going to take your bed from you."

"You were shot, and you need sleep a lot more than I do. How is your arm going to feel if you roll off that couch in the middle of the night?"

"It's already the middle of the night," he pointed out reasonably, though his face did go green at the idea.

"It's the middle of the morning," Rayne said from the back of the room, yawning and holding up the small clock that usually sat on the end table. "See?"

I folded my arms across my chest and savored the victory when he got carefully to his feet and stood still for a second as dizziness passed.

"Lead the way," he said. Once we were in my room, I pulled the door closed and followed him toward the bed.

"Why don't you just walk back to...whatever verse the Venatore are in? Couldn't they have doctored you up there?"

He sat gingerly and used his toes to try and work his boots off. "They could have, but I needed to make sure you were home safe. And then, well, I just didn't have the energy. It takes a fair bit of strength and concentration. Hard to do, when you're in pain, and maybe dangerous. Right now, I'm just too tired. We had a long day before we found you."

I snorted and bent to push his fumbling foot out of the way, grabbing the leather boot firmly by toe and heel.

"You don't have to do that," he protested, but the around his lips had gone pale in mute witness to the pain in his arm.

"Point your foot," I ordered.

"I can sleep with my boots on."

"You are a stubborn man, aren't you? Ronan, you saved my life from a drive-by shooting tonight, not to mention getting me out of the psych ward in a world I don't belong to. I think I can help you take off your boots so you can sleep comfortably."

He stopped fighting me and pointed his toes obediently. A few solid tugs and the boot slid off so quickly that I overbalanced and landed on my butt hard enough to make me say "umph." Like a gentleman, he kept his laughter quiet. It was the first time I'd seen him smile fully, or heard him laugh, and my lips curled in response.

"Is life as a Venatore always this much fun?" I asked when he'd finished laughing.

"No," he grunted, levering himself onto my blue flannel pillow, "sometimes it's much more exciting, and sometimes it hurts more. But," he raised one dark brow, and his eyes flicked toward my recently bruised rear end, "it's not always so funny."

I closed the door behind myself and stood for a moment trying to decide whether it was worth the effort to shower but before I realized I'd even decided, I was trudging toward the couch. The cushions were still warm from Ronan's body, and I sank down into them gratefully.

"It's time to explain a few things, Allie."

I groaned and buried my head in the ruffled throw pillow as the end of the couch creaked under Rayne's weight.

"Get your butt off my feet," I complained into the pillowcase.

She didn't move. Instead, she smacked me hard on the butt and said, "I mean it, Allie. You didn't come home last night, didn't call your mom, and now you show up at three in the morning with some random guy who's been shot, and we're not supposed to call the cops or take him to the hospital? What is going on?"

I wanted to ignore her and sink into oblivion, but I couldn't bring myself to do it. "I'm sorry," I said, rolling onto my side and curling around the pillow.

"Apology accepted. Now spill."

For a split second, I considered telling her everything. Rayne and I had been friends since our sophomore year in high school. We'd told each other everything, spent holidays with each other's families, and shared all our dirty secrets. She had stayed with me for days after the car accident, not speaking or trying to make me feel better, but just being there. I knew that what I had experienced in the last 24 hours was unbelievable, but maybe it would seem more real to me if I could tell my best friend.

I could still see the face of the other Rayne in my head, though. I could still see the fear and disbelief in her eyes as I lost my cool and flipped out in that other apartment that looked uncannily like this one. The rules Ronan had laid out in the restaurant, and the danger they presented, effectively and regretfully sealed my lips.

"He's my new tutor," I said, without thinking. "He was teaching me—physics—at a diner downtown. There was a drive-by shooting, and the windows exploded, it was crazy. People were screaming and running everywhere. We made it out the back, but I think a stray bullet hit Ronan." I was talking fast as scenes from the evening tumbled across my mind, not stopping to think out a lie but simply making it up as I went along, trying to tell as much of the truth as I could.

"Ronan didn't want to call the cops because we ran. I mean, we ran from the scene of a crime. I don't know if anyone else was hurt or anything. Someone could have..." I swallowed, realizing just how true the lie was, "someone could have died and we wouldn't have known it. I didn't stay to help or see if anyone was hurt. Ronan covered me with his body, you know, when the windows exploded. He's the reason I got out of there safely."

Tears were running down my cheeks, unchecked. I had run. Again. I'd been just as much of a coward this night as I had been when my dad had died.

"I didn't go back to help," I whispered.

Rayne made an incoherent little noise and knelt on the floor near my head. She wrapped her arms around my shoulders and held on as I cried.

"It's okay," she said, rubbing my hair, "it's okay, Allie. You're all right. No one could blame you. Would it have done anyone any good if you had been hurt or killed, too?"

I took a long, shaky breath and tried not to think of the people in the diner or our crabby waitress. Had she made it out of there? Did she have a family?

"Allie," Rayne said, her voice serious, "Allie. You have to stop feeling guilty for being alive."

I looked up into her light blue eyes, filled with tears of compassion and understanding. She was the kind of friend I could never deserve.

"I love you, Rayne-bow," I said, laying my head down on the pillow. She smiled at me and kissed my forehead.

"I love you, too, Allie-gator."

CHAPTER EIGHT

I sat in the shower with my head bowed, letting the hot water pound on my scalp, stream down my back, and pull soaking locks of hair over my face. While I had slept well the night before, when I wasn't sneaking into my room to make sure that Ronan was still breathing and not bleeding all over my bed, I hadn't slept comfortably.

Our couch was a thrift store find, and it was still in decent condition, but years of use squished the stuffing so flat that I felt every plank beneath me. Muscles had cramped up along the column of my spine and in my neck and shoulders, but I liked my showers unreasonably hot, which was helping relax the tension. I'd climbed into the shower as soon as I realized my mind was too busy to fall back to sleep after checking on Ronan for the last time. My body wasn't happy about it, so I dragged myself into the bathroom and sat on the shower floor, doing my best to reconcile myself to the events of the past two days.

When I was a little girl, we had a clothes dryer with a window in the door. I used to love the hypnotic effect of watching the clothes tumble over and over each other. Sometimes I would open the dryer door suddenly to try and catch a garment as it hung in the air for an instant before joining its companions on the bottom of the roller. I mostly failed, but that never stopped me from trying.

My brain felt a lot like the dryer, with thoughts tumbling endlessly over one another and me, standing behind the glass desperate to catch one, but hypnotized by the constant motion and intimidated by the sheer number of them.

Where to start?

How about with the fact that my life had suddenly turned into a science fiction novel with a side of gangland violence?

Had I really experienced a drive-by shooting? I scrubbed my hands over my face and groaned, pulling my fingers down the sides of my neck, and feeling the lumps of taut muscle beneath my slippery skin. The truth was that the whole idea of multiple universes, branching off again and again into a web so complex that my mind recoiled, was just too much to take in. Maybe it was better to stick closer to home and just let the bigger picture fall into place as it would. I was just going to have to take everything on authority and move on to things I could deal with, like getting control of my newfound ability before I accidentally woke up in the wrong verse again. The thought made me shiver despite the hot water, and I pulled back the shower curtain to look at the bath mat. It was still white. I let go an explosive breath to release the panic and began to lather my hair, deciding not to think any more about any of it.

When I stepped out into the fall sunshine, I had to stop and turn my face up to the sky. Fall was my favorite season because of the contrast of the crisp air and the warm sun, how the wind could bite my cheeks and make me shiver with delight at the same time.

"Mmm," I sighed contentedly, smiling at the feeling of goosebumps rolling down my arms while my face warmed. Ronan didn't stop to wait for my sun worship, striding purposefully across the street and into the shade of the maple trees in the small park across from our apartment building. I hurried to catch up. In the sunlight, I could see the lighter browns in his hair before it went almost black again in the shade. He walked with a confident, athletic stride that covered an impressive amount of ground. I had long legs, but I had to jog to keep up with him. You'd never know he'd been shot just the night before.

"Geez, are you always in a hurry?" I asked as I came alongside.

"Just a bit," he admitted, glancing down at me. "I'd like to get this looked at, and I've already left it too long as it is."

He stopped next to a bench that was in the far corner of the park, deeply shaded and screened from view by rhododendron bushes that stood nearly ten feet high. Standing in the park in the bright November sunshine, the last two days seemed less forbidding and much less likely. Ronan shifted his shoulder and winced slightly, adjusting the fit of his jacket over the wound.

"Thank you for tending this," he said with a tilt of his head toward the arm wrapped in the sling.

"I'm the one who should be thanking you," I countered, "you saved me more than once already, and I've only known you for two days. It's the least I could do."

"No thanks necessary, Allison. It is my job, after all, isn't it?"

"I guess it is," I said, feeling slightly deflated. He narrowed his eyes at my curt response, but I pretended not to notice and looked up into the red and yellow canopy, where sunlight filtered through the leaves.

"As soon as this heals enough, we'll start training. It shouldn't take too long for you to get the hang of Walking and learn how to control it so that you only travel when you mean to."

"How long do you think it will take? For you to heal, I mean."

"No more than a couple of days. The Venatore have very...advanced medicine. We can talk about that later," he said, "until then I want you to go about your normal routine as well as you can. You're in school?"

I nodded, remembering that I had a paper due that afternoon.

"Good. Focus on that. Until I see you again, try not to do anything too out of the ordinary. If you lose control of yourself and end up somewhere else, I might not be able to find you."

I swallowed hard. "Is that...is that likely to happen?"

"Probably not. You've made it this long, right? It's only that very strong emotion can trigger your abilities."

He seemed to hesitate for a second while indecision flickered in his eyes. "Do you have a boyfriend?" he asked finally.

My cheeks heated. "What does that have to do with anything?" I knew that I sounded rather peevish, but I couldn't help myself.

"Because," he said slowly, reaching up to break a dead twig off the branch just above his head, "sex can trigger strong emotion. So, if you've got a bloke you fancy, now would not be the time to climb into bed with him."

I snorted. "I'm pretty sure that's none of your business."

His eyes locked on mine and a jolt of recognition hit me hard in the pit of the stomach. Any time we'd spoken, he had always seemed to look toward me but never really at me, as if he took my presence for granted. This time, our eyes met fully, and for a moment, I was breathless. I knew I'd never seen Ronan before the night he tackled me outside the hospital, but there was something deep, a kind of acknowledgment that connected the two of us, as if my spirit looked at his and said, "Ah. It's you."

I held my hand to my chest, stunned, and felt suddenly exposed.

He opened his mouth, shut it, and blinked. I swallowed.

"It is my business," he said and pulled his gaze away to look at the piece of wood in his hand. He clenched his fist, and the twig between thumb and forefinger broke with a sharp snap. "It's my business because I don't want to have to go searching for you with no idea where to look. I need to know where I can find you so I can keep you safe, at least until you can manage it yourself. Unless you'd like to walk somewhere unfamiliar on your own?"

Freed from the force of his eyes, I felt myself settle uneasily back into my skin and faked a smile.

"Don't worry," I said with casual cheeriness, "I don't have a boyfriend and I don't make a habit of one-night stands, so I won't be orgasming my way into another dimension."

He barked a sharp, surprised laugh that brought out the dimples beneath the dark stubble on his cheeks. "I'll have to remember that line," he said, and just like that, the tension between us vanished.

"If I meet another Walker, will I know it? I mean, is there any way to tell?" I asked suddenly.

He didn't seem surprised that I asked, but his expression was guarded as he looked down at his hands and answered, "It's not likely. A very few of us can feel one another, a kind of reckoning, I'm told. The Venatore call the people who can feel magic Augurs, and they're damn rare. I can't feel it, though I've heard it described."

I nodded and wrapped my arms around my shoulders, feeling an unexpected and inexplicable sense of loss. *That must have been all that feeling was*, I thought.

"I doubt you'll see any in the next couple of days, though," he continued, not noticing that I'd stopped paying attention, "we are rather rare, too."

"When will I see you, then?"

"Within the next few days."

"Here at the apartment?"

He nodded.

"Okay," I said, pulling up the hood of my sweater against the wind that set the dry leaves rattling overhead.

Ronan looked over his shoulder to be sure that no one could see us and then his eyes took on a distant air, as if he were looking inward and not at the tall girl with the red hair standing just in front of him, hood up and arms wrapped protectively around herself. With a nod at me, he faded from my sight like a shadow when the sun appears. I stood for a few more moments looking intently at the empty space where a man once stood. The ground still held the evidence of his presence; a broken twig left forgotten atop leaves disturbed by his feet.

Despite having seen him disappear before, and even having walked between verses with him, the experience of watching someone disappear still made my stomach twist and my mind go blank with shock. No noise accompanied the action, but there was a feeling to it that defied description. The closest comparison I could think of was the way you could tell when someone has turned the TV on in a distant room, only magnified a hundred times. Soon, I would be doing the same thing, disappearing with little trace that I had ever been there in the first place.

How many unexplained missing persons were Walkers that had never come back? Rather than think about the implications of that, I headed numbly back up to my apartment and tried to turn my mind toward more mundane things, like the fact that I had a paper due in four hours. It was going to be hard to focus on a comparative study of mythologies now that I knew I might be much more intimately connected with mythological worlds than I could ever have believed.

That, in truth, those mythological worlds might not be make-believe, after all.

CHAPTER NINE

"Will you be here in time for dinner?"

The hopeful note in my mom's voice made my lips turn down unhappily. I didn't visit her nearly as often as I should, and now that I desperately wanted to see her, to feel safe with her arms around me and smell the faint scent of chemical cleaners that always seemed to hover beneath the smell of her lavender shampoo, I couldn't make the trip.

It had been two very long days since Ronan left and I was half expecting to see him at any moment. Every small noise made me jump and look toward the door. Rayne had retreated to her room, saying that I was stressing her out. Two days of expecting Ronan to appear, coupled with my own fear of disappearing in my sleep, had spun my anxiety into a whetstone that sharpened my natural sarcasm until it was razor-fine. I'd been cutting everyone in sight just to take the edge off. In fact, my tongue had gotten so dangerous that my manager sent me home early from my shift at the Co-op, and I'd been pacing the apartment like a caged animal ever since.

I couldn't even blame Rayne for hiding from me. Calling my mom had been an act of desperation, but one that I had clearly needed.

"I'd really like to see you, honey, it's been two weeks."

"I can't, mom," I said, feeling the full weight of regret settle on my shoulders, "I'm waiting on my physics tutor, and I can't miss him."

"But...you hate math."

"Hence the need for a tutor."

The line was silent for a moment, and I held my breath, hoping that she would believe me. "Okay," she said after the pause, "will we still see you for Thanksgiving, then? Ben's girl-fiend will be over, and I want you to meet her."

"Girl*friend*?"

"Nope, girl-fiend. That's why I want you to meet her. Maybe you can convince Ben that she's not good for him. "

"Uh oh," I said, laughing as a little bit of the tension eased, "Starting to feel like an evil mother-in-law already, are you?"

"Please don't say that. I honestly don't know what I will do if Ben decides to marry this one. I hope it hasn't gone that far."

My mom had a hard time reconciling herself to any of the girls my brother brought home after his rough breakup with Holly, who had been my mom's favorite since Ben's senior year in High School. They'd dated all through college, and my mom loved to refer to Holly as her future daughter-in-law. Things had gone south for them when my brother joined the acapella quartet The Rogues, and had started touring internationally. Four handsome guys singing Gaelic love songs was enough to build a solid fan base of rabid groupies who were sure to make any girlfriend jealous. Ben had never said what caused the breakup, though. In the aftermath, he had brought home one short-term fling after another, and it was starting to wear on my mom.

"He's only twenty-six, mom. He's got time. I don't think he's looking for Mrs. Right."

"Keep your fingers crossed," she said with a sigh, "Will you be here? Please? I need a buffer."

I chuckled, switched the phone to my other ear, and said, "I promise."

By the time I hung up, I had a sweaty ear and a kink in my neck, but at least my temper had been dulled. I didn't love talking on the phone, but I did miss my mom, and talking to her had helped keep my mind occupied.

The last couple of years had been rough for us. I'd been a less than stellar daughter for a while, but we'd started growing closer once I moved away for school. I think it made me realize how lucky I was to have a family that loved me. It was hard to maintain my teenage angst when I stopped being a teenager. With a sigh, I dropped my phone into my pocket and looked around the room for something to do. I'd already finished my homework, and Rayne was meditating to combat her irritation with my anxiety, so I was at loose ends. I'd already read every book in our apartment at least twice, so nothing sounded worth reading and, after spending an hour talking with my mom, I didn't much fancy messing with my phone.

I would have gone outside to clear my head, but a fall storm was in full swing, and the wind was gleefully tearing the remaining leaves off the trees while rain plastered them to the pavement. I walked around for a bit, picking things up and putting them down randomly, lost in thought. When a knock finally did break the silence, I was so zoned-out that I jumped and dropped the candle I'd been holding. It made a dull thud against the rug, missing my toes by millimeters, and rolled under the side table.

Heart thundering in my ears, I hurried to pull the door open. I had to move my gaze down about a foot from where I'd expected, to meet a pair of wide, soft brown eyes, instead of intense blue ones. These eyes were framed by thick, straight, black lashes below a pair of perfectly manicured brows that rose in surprise.

"Allie Cat! I thought you'd be at work, come here."

I couldn't help but smile as Mateo grabbed my neck with both soft hands and kissed my cheek. His cheek was as smooth as mine. Smoother, probably, since he visited the spa more than any normal human had a right to. Between school, his job as a barista in a chic little gourmet coffee shop during the day, and tending bar 3 nights a week, I had no idea where he got the time to look so put together. He held me at arm's length, gripping my shoulders, and narrowed his eyes at me. "Kitty, you're wearing makeup."

I brushed his hands off, ignoring the flush that climbed up my neck. "What, I'm not allowed to wear makeup?"

Mateo made a little clicking sound in the back of his mouth and shook his head. "Not makeup like that you're not. Why would you cover up those freckles, chica?" He fluttered a hand at my face and said, "No black eyeliner, either, your skin is too pale for it. You need something to play up your hazel eyes, not distract from them. It's brown for you."

I scowled. "Are we done critiquing my appearance, yet?"

He folded his arms across his chest, holding his elbow with one hand and putting the other on his jaw, considering me thoughtfully. "The tank top and jeans are a bit simple, but your curves look killer so you're okay there. Besides, you know I love it when you let all that fiery hair down. You look like a volcano goddess or something. Somebody should sacrifice a virgin to you. If you'd just let me get my hands on you, every man for 10 miles would follow you home."

I couldn't help but laugh at that. "Mat, how many times do I have to let you use me as a makeup dummy for school before I start getting paid for my pain and suffering?"

He snorted, and I said, "Besides, I don't want any man to follow me home. I've got enough on my plate as it is." Then I smiled roguishly at him and batted my eyelashes. "You're the only man in my life right now."

He smiled and rolled his eyes. "Pshhh, whatever. By the looks of your makeup, I'd say you wish there was a man." His tenor voice lowered to a growly bass, and he stepped toward me while affecting his father's thick Spanish accent. "You want someone to sweep you off your feet, kitty? Oh mi querida, come to me."

He reached out suddenly and wrapped both arms around me. I squealed as he dipped me with a flourish and kissed my neck madly with a bunch of "muah" sounds and squishy noises that made goosebumps run down my arms. I was laughing so hard I almost fell over as I pushed at his chest. He swung me back to my feet and gave me his best comic leer while I wiped my neck with the back of my hand, still shaking with amusement.

"I hope I'm not interrupting something."

I gasped and straightened, turning to see Ronan standing just inside the door to the stairwell. He was leaning against the doorframe with his arms crossed over his chest, dark hair plastered to his forehead, raindrops making runnels down his cheeks. He wore a black leather jacket, tee-shirt, and dark jeans that were also wet from the storm. He looked distinctly dangerous, and my stomach clenched in reflex.

"Ronan, ah, no, it's fine." I brushed hair out of my face then gestured to Mateo who stood with his weight balanced evenly between the balls of his feet, eyeing Ronan with a stare that was both assessing and calculating, his expression turned serious.

"This is my friend, Mateo."

One dark brow rose, and Ronan gave Mateo a sardonic bow.

"Um, Mat, this is Ronan. He's...my tutor," I finished lamely.

Mateo lifted his chin a fraction of an inch and said, "Hey."

The air between them seemed to crackle. Ronan outweighed Mateo by at least 40 pounds and was a good foot taller, but Mateo was a boxer and currently in protective mode; he wasn't intimidated. I couldn't even blame him for the protective impulse because Ronan looked like he could take someone apart with his bare hands and his expression wasn't friendly.

Mateo turned to look at me, brows drawn together and up in the middle in an expression that said, *are you sure this guy is cool?* I tried not to hold my breath and instead forced a smile and told him, "Rayne's in her room, meditating," and rolled my eyes.

"Not for long," Mateo said, relieved and grinning impishly. He squeezed my arm as he passed into the house and whispered, "I'll just be in the other room, okay?"

I took a second to calm myself before I turned toward Ronan, who hadn't moved. "So...you just going to stand there and try to intimidate everyone in the hallway, or what?"

"Are you sure you're not busy? You looked a bit distracted when I opened the door."

"Mat likes to tease me. Not that it's any business of yours."

"I see."

"Are we going to, uh, you know," I made a vague wiggly gesture with my fingertips, "practice?"

Ronan watched me for a second, his face blank, then uncrossed his arms and strode toward me to stop just inches away. I could feel the heat radiating off his body and refused the impulse to take a step backward. His nostrils flared, and he narrowed his eyes. Was he angry? Tension radiated from him, making his proximity disconcerting. He leaned closer.

"We're going to need somewhere private," he said in a low voice.

I swallowed but refused to be intimidated. "Could we just use the apartment? I mean, we aren't...Walking anywhere yet, are we?"

"No. Not yet. But your roommate has already seen me in less than favorable circumstances. I don't want to make her any more suspicious by talking about things where she might overhear." "I've told her you're tutoring me in theoretical physics," I said, letting a bit of smugness enter my tone, "so I think we're pretty free to talk about things, at least from a mechanical standpoint."

"Clever. All right. I'd rather not walk around in the rain anyway. Lead on."

I led him into the apartment, forcefully dispelling my unease. "We've got a car, so we wouldn't have to walk. But this is easier. Plus, I think if I left anywhere with you right now, Mateo might blow up my phone."

Ronan stiffened. "He'd blow your phone up? How?"

"No," I said, unable to restrain a laugh at the idea of Mat planting some little device on my phone, "no, no, it's just slang. I mean he'd constantly be calling or texting me to make sure I'm safe."

"Ah. He's protective of you."

"Yeah, he's one of my very best friends. Besides," I added, eyeing him up and down, "you don't exactly look...safe."

The corners of his eyes wrinkled but he didn't say anything. I cleared my throat. "Coffee or tea? Mateo gets us a gourmet coffee from Red Bean, downtown. Rayne has Earl Grey, but green tea is her favorite, so we have both."

"Tea, please. Earl gray, if you don't mind. You have cream?"

"I live with a habitual tea drinker. Yeah, we have cream. Fake stuff for Rayne and good old-fashioned heavy cream for me. It's even fresh from the farmer's market. I have to bribe her with foot rubs to pick it up for me."

Thinking that last bit had probably been too much information, I set the teapot on the burner and then pulled a stool up to the bar. Ronan sat across from me, completely silent, looking down at his long-fingered hands. The silence became suffocating. Whatever sense of ease I'd begun to feel with him before he'd left had disappeared. I had no idea what to say as all that had happened began to feel completely ridiculous and surreal. How could I start a conversation about interdimensional travel, for crying out-loud? It was so quiet that I could hear the muffled sound of laughter from Rayne's room at the end of the hall and the pat-pat-pat of water dripping from Ronan's hair and onto the counter.

"Oh geez," I said, hopping off the stool and hurrying toward the bathroom, calling over my shoulder, "hang on a sec."

I snagged a blue towel off the bathroom counter and glanced at myself in the mirror as I passed, then stopped. Mateo was right. The black eyeliner on my pale face made me look like a raccoon. I snagged a makeup remover wipe from Rayne's stash and quickly scrubbed my face with it as I hurried back down the hall.

"Here," I said, holding the towel out as I dropped the wipe into the garbage. Ronan took the towel with a muttered "thank you" and peeled his jacket off as I turned to the cupboard to take out a mismatched set of teacups that Rayne and I had found at an estate sale, and pulled the cream out of the fridge.

"Real stuff or fake stuff?"

He eyed the cartons suspiciously. "Is that even a question? Why eat fake food?"

"Why indeed." I put the imitation cream back in the fridge.

"Do you mind if I ask how a couple of college students manage to afford a flat like this?" The towel muffled his voice as he wiped the rain from his face. I shrugged.

"Rayne's uncle owns the building. He's nice."

Ronan made a noncommittal noise as I poured cream into the bottom of the cups. "If we keep our grades up, we get to live here rent-free—or, at least, cheap enough that I only need a part-time job. That's why all the furniture is such a hodge-podge. We find most of it at garage sales. Sugar?" I asked with the spoon hovering over the cup.

"No, thanks."

The cup and saucer looked almost like toys in his hands as he held them just under his nose and took a deep breath.

"Mmmm," he closed his eyes in pleasure. The rumble sounded like the purr of a big cat and made me smile.

"Should we talk in my room or? I mean, no one would believe us even if they did hear anything, so we could always sit on the couch."

Ronan looked over his shoulder, stretching the cotton shirt across his back and outlining the muscles as they bunched between his shoulder blades. "Maybe we should. Remember, not everyone who might overhear us is legless."

"Legless?"

"Non-Walkers."

"Ah. Would that be a problem? It's not like they wouldn't already know, after all."

Ronan set his cup down and looked at me seriously. "It's best to keep your hand close, Allison. Just because someone is a Walker, that doesn't make them your friend. Choose who and when to tell. It's safer that way."

My bed sank low beneath Ronan's weight. I had elected to sit on the chair next to my desk and pull my legs up underneath me. The bed would have been more comfortable, but being that close to him made me feel edgy, and this was not a conversation I wanted to miss because I was distracted by nerves.

"Where do we start?" I asked.

"Cecily gave you the basics, did she?"

"She did, yeah. The very basics, I think. She talked about how atoms vibrate and how each person has a unique frequency."

He set the teacup down on my bedside table right on top of my copy of Return of the King. I resisted the urge to jump up and save my paperback from potential water rings in favor of paying attention.

"Not only every person but everything. The same is true for every verse. Each has its own set of vibrations that form a unique harmony.

When you bring your frequency into harmony with it, you become a part of the song. It draws you, a bit like a magnet."

"The way you talk about Walking makes it sound more like singing with your whole body than actually walking."

Ronan blinked at me. "That's as good an analogy as any I've heard," he said.

"How do you know what the harmony is, though? And how could a person possibly change the frequency of their atoms? That seems like changing a pretty fundamental aspect of what they are. I mean, if a fish gives itself the ability to breathe air, is it still even a fish?"

Ronan leaned forward and put his elbows on his knees. "Walkers aren't human, strictly speaking. In keeping with your animal analogy, I suppose it would be similar to the difference between a wolf and a lap dog."

I was surprised to find myself less affected than I might have expected by the news that I wasn't human, 'strictly speaking.'

"As far as how a person could do it," he continued, "well that's the mystery, isn't it? We just know that we can do it. To be honest, the science of why is elusive because there are several working theories, and none of them completely falsifiable. The how is easier, though, and makes more sense in practice. Here's a good example." He began to hum deep in his chest, and I recognized the song immediately. It was a pop song I'd heard one too many times this summer.

"That's Miss Mary Jane, by Deaf Needle," I said.

He nodded and then changed the tune. The melody was the same, but the timing was different, and there were other subtle changes as well that altered the song just enough so that I could hear its roots.

"Mozart," I said, understanding.

Ronan spread his hands, and said, "That is True Earth. A piece of classical music that spawned a million covers and remakes. While each realm has a different twist on the original, they can all be traced carefully back to True Earth. Thousands and thousands of songs, too many to count. That's why we call it the Eververse."

"Do you know them all?" I asked, slightly awed.

He chuckled ruefully, making his face look open and friendly, and the sound was so infectious that I smiled as well. "No, never me. But I do know a fair few."

"You said before that it was hard—to Walk, I mean. So how was I able to do it in my sleep?"

"Ah, that has to do with your subconscious. Your mind is a lot more creative when you sleep, and less restricted by inhibitions or the boundaries of what you think is possible. In a dream, you might fly out your window, yeah?"

"Sure," I said, thinking about how often I'd done exactly that in a dream.

"But if I told you right now to jump out that window and fly into the city, you'd think I was mad, wouldn't you?"

"That or homicidal."

"Why?"

"Because humans can't fly."

Ronan raised both eyebrows. "Can't they?"

I paused and looked at him warily, unsure if this was a trick question. "Are you saying there are verses where people fly?"

"None I've been to, but there's a fair chance of it. After some of the things I've seen, I wouldn't count it out. The physics that govern this place don't apply to every verse. The farther you get from the original song, the more different the music. You see," he gestured toward his forehead, "as soon as you wake, your brain immediately starts telling you what's possible and what isn't. You're affecting your frequency with every thought, chaining yourself firmly to True Earth by unconsciously repeating the laws you know: gravity, and all that. You're singing the song over and over in your head. But," he raised a finger, "your unconscious mind isn't chained that way. It can sing any song. So, in sleep, you can change your frequency much easier. You bring yourself into harmony with the Realm most closely associated with your dream. For most people, it's a verse that's very like True Earth and similar to the life they live."

I supposed that made sense. My recurring nightmare had visited me the night before I'd woken up in that other place, only it was much more vivid than usual. The verse I'd ended up in had been very like my life on True Earth, down to the apartment, my bedding, Rayne's stupid socks, and even a lot of what was in our fridge. Of course, there were glaring differences as well. A thought struck me so hard that I felt it in my chest and all the air seemed to catch behind the lump in my throat.

"Ronan," I said, already knowing the answer to the question but needing to ask, "we know there are verses where my Dad didn't die in the car accident, right?"

His lips thinned, and he nodded.

The room started to spin a bit, and I latched onto the armrests of my chair to keep myself steady. "So... there are verses where he lived and I...died?"

"Allison," he said in a low voice, looking at me with grave blue eyes, "there are verses for almost every possibility. In some of them—in most of them—you were never even born."

Before that answer had a chance to sink in, my bedroom door swung open and Mateo walked in with Rayne's hand grasped firmly in his. "I am stealing Rayne, and she's going to be my wingman," he began as Rayne interrupted with, "wing woman," though she smiled as she said it.

Mateo shrugged and continued as if she'd never spoken, "We figured we'd head to the Atrium since Maggie is tending bar tonight. Do you two want to join?"

He looked at me pointedly, and I opened my mouth but hesitated. My first instinct was to look at Rayne for help. She had changed into a pair of high-waisted teal jeans with a cropped top that showed a two-inch strip of yoga-toned abdomen beneath a vintage jacket, her long blonde hair down and swirling in soft waves, delicate ankles showing above a pair of brown high-heeled booties. She looked like she'd just walked off the page of some fashion catalog. To top it off she was sweet and kind, and thoughtful. She managed to look effortlessly beautiful no matter what she wore. I looked down at my faded blue jeans and felt the familiar surge of jealousy. I was so used to feeling like a crow next to my swan of a best friend that the jealousy had almost become background noise, but at that moment it stabbed, hot and sharp.

"Come on you two," Rayne said, "how much studying can you do on a Friday night?"

Mateo looked meaningfully at the distance between Ronan and myself, a good six feet of floor space, and then looked at me with a question in his eyes. The glow of their concern warmed me from the inside and reminded me starkly of why I loved these two friends. The pangs of jealousy faded at once.

"I don't think so, Mat," I said, with a sidelong glance at Ronan who, I noticed, was watching Rayne thoughtfully, "if I take that one to the Atrium we might never get him out of there."

Mateo eyed Ronan, taking in the long line of leg and thigh, the breadth of shoulder, sensual lips, and blue eyes lit with humor. "You're probably right," he admitted, "we'd need a baseball bat to rescue him."

Ronan did laugh then, and everyone in the room watched him with a smile on their faces. "Thank you for the invitation, but we do have a lot of ground to cover before we begin our experiments. Can't have Allie taking any unnecessary risks, now can we? Safety first and all that." Mateo laughed, and his shoulders relaxed visibly at the unspoken promise. I knew Mateo well, but I hadn't noticed how tense he'd been until that moment. For whatever reason, he now trusted that I'd be safe alone with Ronan. Of course, I already knew that. Rayne missed this subliminal by play and looked directly at me, her smile only half faded.

"Are you sure you won't come? I can stay."

"No, it's okay. I think I had enough fun the last time I drank with Mat to tide me over for a while. Go find hot dates."

She hugged me briefly, and they were gone, leaving me in the apartment with Ronan, alone.

CHAPTER TEN

I was nursing my second beer when I realized it was midnight.
Grappling with the mechanics of my new reality for almost two hours made me think I was beginning to grasp the bones of it, but coming to terms with the true substance proved harder. It felt a lot like the difference between having someone hand you the blueprints to a building, and walking the halls in person. I was constructing ideas based on everything Ronan was telling me, but I knew it would be much different experiencing it for myself. To hear about a building was one thing, but to feel the brick and smell the air and stand on the threshold was another.

"When can I try this for myself?"

Ronan leaned back against my headboard and stretched his long legs with a stifled groan, folding his arms across his chest but giving no indication whether the bullet wound still pained him. I had to guess not, since he hadn't so much as flinched the entire time he'd been here.

"You shouldn't try it by yourself, at least not yet. It's customary for your guide to take you to a few places first so that you get used to Walking without putting yourself in any danger."

"Why is it dangerous? Could I end up in lava world or something?" My tone was light and half-joking, but it didn't hide my unease at the thought.

Ronan rolled to his feet and stretched his legs before leaning back against the wall near my window, taking a deep breath, and looking upward thoughtfully. "I began learning to walk the Ververse when I was 14," he said. "I was a smart lad, but stubborn and...well, I didn't always have the best judgment. We didn't know as much about Walking then, so it all felt more like magic. Anyway," he shrugged, "my teacher, he had a bit more faith in my patience than he should have. We'd Walked less than half a dozen times, but I learned quickly and was confident I could do it on my own. Angus warned me not to Walk without him, so I snuck away one night after he'd fallen asleep and Walked out of my own verse and right into a bloody battle."

He shook his head with amused dismay, "I was so shocked I nearly pissed myself. It's one thing to fight when you're prepared to do it. It's another when you intend to Walk yourself to someplace peaceful and end up with some bloke trying to take your head off with a broadsword."

I let out a long breath through pursed lips and shook my own head, trying to imagine Ronan as a gangly 14-year-old who wound up in a... "Wait," I said, incredulous, "did you say it was a sword fight?"

His eyes focused on me with steady blue intensity, but amusement still tugged at the corner of his mouth. "I did."

I wanted to ask him more but had no idea where to start.

"I managed to dodge the blow by falling backward onto my arse in the mud," he continued, "the bugger must have thought he'd gotten me—seeing me fall in the dark—because he spun around screaming and began hacking at some other poor bloke. I crawled out of there on my hands and knees. By the time I got control of myself enough to Walk back home, I was covered in mud and blood, shaking and cold and reeking something awful."

"Ronan," I asked "are you from here? True-Earth, I mean."

To my dismay, his face lost all traces of self-deprecating humor and his features stiffened into impassivity. "No," he said in clipped tones that didn't invite further questions, but studied my face like my thoughts were written in my bones in some strange language he couldn't read.

"When we found you," he asked, "was that the first time you Walked?"

I shook my head, hesitant to answer, but he was having none of that. "How old were you? Was it in your sleep?"

I swallowed and nodded, surprised to find that the terror from that time was still startlingly near the surface. "I was sixteen."

"That sounds about right. How did you get back?"

How could I answer that question when I didn't know the answer? He understood the bewildered look on my face, his intent expression softening a bit as he told me, "Not everyone does, you know." It was far too easy to imagine how someone might never come back. An accident, a nervous breakdown, maybe ending up in the middle of a battle like Ronan had. Or worse, not realizing what they had done and not being able to replicate it. The irony of spending the rest of your life stuck in the wrong place with the ability to go home, but never realizing you were capable of it, made me sick.

"If that's what happens to people, how were you able to find me in the hospital?"

"There are a few areas where Walkers tend to end up. The psychiatric ward is one of them."

"What are some others?"

"Places of power, usually. Places where people know there is some kind of force, but they don't always know what it is. Humans seem inclined to mark places of power with things: pyramids, henges, great monoliths, things like that. It also tends to happen more often when the verses pass close to each other, and the barriers are thin. That makes travel easier. We always find more Walkers near the equinoxes and the changes of the seasons than any other time."

I latched onto that piece of information and turned it over in my mind. "So that means the seasons are the same for each realm, then?" I asked.

"In many of them, yes, and those are the ones that tend to create the most inter-verse traffic. Remember, all the verses are still tied to True Earth and share the same history up to the point of the split. It's only after the split that things begin to change. The farther back the split, the more different the present."

"But even within those time frames, certain decisions could make a bigger difference than just the regular course of time, right? Even if other parts of the verse were a lot alike? Say Hitler had won. That could make a bigger difference than just a split of 50 years or so, couldn't it?"

"It could. Sometimes it does, and sometimes it doesn't. Say Hitler won but was assassinated shortly afterward; things might have continued much like they had in True-Earth history. There's no way to know. That's why I warned you against trying to Walk on your own for a while. You have no idea what the other verse will be like or how close it will be to your own."

The thought of a world in which Hitler had won made my skin go cold. If I Walked to a place like that unaware, I could stumble into the middle of a swordfight and end up in the mud without a head.

"Alright, you've convinced me. No Walking by myself."

"Smart girl."

Not smart, I thought to myself, *scared*.

"Don't patronize me, boyo," I said to cover my unease, mimicking a phrase my father was fond of saying to my older brother any time he got too big for his britches.

Ronan looked at me quizzically, his head cocked to one side, and both brows pulled together over the bridge of his nose. Then he went very still, narrowing his eyes as if he was trying to see through me to the wall on the other side. A trickle of unease slid cold down my spine and reminded me that I'd found Ronan incredibly intimidating the first night we met.

My butt started to vibrate. I gasped and practically leaped out of my chair, pressing my hand to my right hip and spinning like a dog chasing its tail. The metal case was warm from my body heat as I jerked the phone out of my back pocket with a good deal more force than necessary.

"Hello."

"Allie?" Rayne's voice crackled across the line. Something was wrong. "Can you come get me? I don't feel very good, but I don't want to make Mat leave. Can you, please?"

"Yeah," I said, spinning and groping for my jacket where I'd flung it over the back of the chair. The car keys jangled as I sunk my hand into the pocket. "Yeah, I'll be there in a minute. Are you okay, you don't sound good, how much have you had to drink?"

The line was silent for a second. "I don't feel very good, but I don't like these guys, either."

"You're still at the Atrium, right?"

"...yeah," she said, and her voice sounded far away.

"I'm on my way."

I walked into the hallway before I remembered that I'd left Ronan sitting on my bed. I stopped suddenly, intending to turn and let him know where I was going, but instead felt the weight of him hit me from behind. I grunted in surprise as his momentum catapulted me forward. Ronan jerked me backward by my shoulders, saving me from hitting my head on the opposite wall. Unfortunately, he wasn't so lucky. He'd pulled me at the same time I pushed myself backward, and I slammed into his chest hard enough to elicit an "oof."

I regained my balance and turned to face him just as he released my arms, which stung from the force of his grip.

"I'm sorry," I said, rubbing the back of my head with my free hand. There was a red welt just above the collar of his v-necked tee shirt, "this appears to be habit-forming."

"You've got a solid skull on you, Allie," he said ruefully, "we've got to stop running into each other this way."

"Maybe if you'd quit sneaking around."

"You sure you're not just a bit hard of hearing?"

I wanted to laugh but noticed that we were standing very close to each other; close enough that I could tell his dark blue irises were splintered in the middle with a lighter blue that spread from his pupil like ice forming on the surface of deep water. Against the thicket of his black lashes, the effect was striking enough I could have easily just stood there and stared at him like I used to stare at my Tiger Beat posters as a thirteen-year-old with raging hormones and a deep desire for sad love songs on the radio.

Rayne needed me, though, and I didn't have any time to admire my erstwhile tutor.

"I need to go pick up Rayne," I told him, "She didn't sound good."

"I'll come with you."

I glanced down at my phone, surprised again by the time. It was well past midnight. "Are you sure? You don't have to. I know it's late, you can head home if you want."

He locked the door as I spoke and then turned and motioned toward the stairs, saying, "after you."

We rode in silence through a tunnel of green lights. I was too distracted to hold a conversation. Rayne hadn't sounded at all like herself. She didn't usually drink enough to make herself sick, but if she was that far gone, she might not be making the best choices. Ronan hadn't said anything beyond giving me an amused, "Station wagon, eh?" when I unlocked the car door.

The Atrium was still crowded, and there was no parking for a block in any direction. I settled for a spot around the corner and was out of the car almost before I'd turned off the engine. I couldn't shake the feeling of unease that had settled in my gut since hearing Rayne's voice.

HERE, I typed in a quick text message with one thumb and hit send before stuffing the phone back into my pocket.

The interior of the club was dark. I began to sweat almost immediately in air heavy with the moisture of so many tightly packed bodies. I pushed through a crush of humanity toward the tables in the back where we usually sat and blinked into the darkness. There was no blonde head back there.

I turned to Ronan, who had been following closely, and shouted, "Keep looking, I'm going to check the bathrooms."

He nodded and walked toward the bar while I slid between two groups of men and into the hallway. The bathroom was empty. I held open the door of the men's room and shouted, "Rayne?" By the time I had circled the dance floor again, with no sight of her, I was in a full-fledged panic. My eyes darted around the room, and I spotted Ronan. Two men were standing next to him, smiling, and one was touching his forearm. I stepped close just in time to hear one of them say, "with Mateo out the back."

Ronan nodded and grabbed my hand, pulling me toward the back of the club.

Calm down, I told myself, even as I pulled my phone out of my pocket and started to text her, then gave up and dialed her number instead. We pushed through the back exit, and the cold air hit my sweaty skin like a slap. I shivered and pressed the phone hard to my ear.

"Hi, this is Rayne. Sorry, but I can't—" I thumbed the end button and started dialing again as Ronan pulled me deeper into the alley, my mind racing with dire possibilities even as I tried to calm myself. They probably caught a bus already. Mateo wouldn't just leave Rayne alone if she didn't feel good. Maybe he called her a cab or something?

Those were perfectly plausible explanations but didn't stop my stomach from twisting itself into tight knots. Ronan's hand was the only thing stopping me from running down the alley and screaming her name at the top of my lungs. When he stopped it almost jerked me off my feet, but he steadied me absently and then stood perfectly still, like a cat listening to the scratching of a mouse. It took me a second to realize that he was listening. I stopped, too, and let my arm relax so that my hand hung down to my side and pressed the ringing speaker of my phone against my jeans, muffling it. A car passed in the street and then Ronan jerked on my arm and we were running. The sound of a phone ringing in the distance was faint but clear, and I followed him toward it without thinking as my chest tightened in foreboding.

Halfway down the alley was an opening between two tall buildings on the left and a three-story parking garage on the right. There were three men, faintly lit from the right side by the fluorescent lights on the ceiling of the first floor of the parking garage. One was crouched, the other two arguing, but I couldn't make out what they were saying.

One of the men, taller than the others, gave the man he was fighting a two-handed shove. The shorter man stumbled backward and hit the brick wall with an audible *crack* and gasp of pain, leaving him dazed. The crouching man didn't seem to notice, but he was in the shadow of the lower wall with his back to us, and I couldn't see what he was doing. Had he stolen Rayne's phone? Was that why we heard the ringing?

The man who had struck the wall stumbled to the side before regaining his balance, bringing his face into a beam of light from the parking garage.

"Mateo," I whispered in shock just before the taller man growled something and swung at Mat's face. Mat's boxing training kicked in and he ducked to the outside as the fist flashed by his head. In the instant it took the taller man to recover, Mateo was on him.

The crouching man growled something and twisted to pull on whatever he was holding. As his body shifted to the side, I realized with a sudden, sinking feeling that the object in the shadow was Rayne. He held her by the forearm and pulled at her top as she wilted toward the pavement.

Mateo must have noticed what was happening because he shouted and charged, ignoring the wild swing of his former opponent. He grabbed Rayne's attacker by the back of the neck and knocked him to the ground with a sharp jab, but before Mateo could turn back toward the taller man, he was caught by a kick to his midsection, followed by a vicious punch that sent him gasping to his knees.

A rush of furious adrenaline flipped a switch in my brain, and everything slowed down so that I began noticing the smallest of details, like the red stain on the taller man's white button-up shirt, and one of Rayne's shoes left forgotten in a puddle. My heart thundered and my leg muscles bunched to lunge forward an instant before Ronan grabbed me by both shoulders. His face was hard, mouth drawn into a tight line that compressed his normally full bottom lip. The muscle in his jaw clenched above the sharp angle of the bone.

His hands were humming with tension, but his voice was completely steady when he said, "Call the police, Allison."

Then he turned and stalked down the alley with long, graceful strides that made no noise on the wet pavement.

"Cops," I said breathlessly and began fumbling with the buttons.

One of the men cried out in alarm, and my eyes snapped up before I pushed the second 1. They'd seen Ronan. Blood began to pound in my ears as the short man pushed himself to his feet. The taller man said something challenging and raised his chin toward Ronan, who had closed the distance in seconds. Suddenly, fists were flying, and I started running toward the fight, spitting out all the information I could remember to the woman who had asked, "What's your emergency" in a nasal voice.

Ronan slid to the right of one punch and grabbed the taller man's wrist with his left hand as it passed, using the forward momentum to pull the man toward him while leaning back to kick him in the stomach. The tall man doubled at the waist with his arm wrapped protectively around his midsection, and Ronan followed up with a knee to the man's head that dropped him, limp, to the ground.

The shorter man snarled something I couldn't hear over the voice of the 911 operator. Ronan was clearly a skilled fighter, but the shorter man was as broad across the shoulders as Ronan with forearms that belonged on Popeye. He moved like a wrestler, with his hands up and knees bent, and my stomach dropped when I saw him bend and shoot toward Ronan's legs with surprising speed. An instant later the shorter man was on his knees on the ground, whimpering, with Ronan bent over the top of him, their legs pointing in opposite directions. One of the man's wrists was gripped securely in Ronan's big left hand, and his neck was bent, obviously very painfully, down toward his chest by Ronan's right forearm and the weight of his shoulder.

"Ma'am...ma'am, are you still there? Is everything okay?"

I tried to answer but my tongue stuck to the roof of my mouth. Somehow I managed to croak, "Yes."

Ronan clearly had the thugs under control, so I stepped around the unconscious man on the pavement and hurried toward my fallen friends. Mateo pushed himself to a sitting position against the wall and groaned. The sharp bone of his cheek had disappeared beneath swelling that had already closed his left eye behind blooming purple lids, and his brows were drawn tightly together in pain. But he was at least conscious and moving, so I knelt over Rayne and began to shake her shoulder. She was almost completely limp, but her eyes were open and blinking lazily.

"Rayne?" I asked, turning her face toward me and peering into her eyes.

She didn't seem to see me, and my breath caught painfully. The pavement smelled of urine and alcohol so strongly that my stomach turned, but seeing Rayne lying in a puddle with splayed limbs, her clothes wet and torn, made everything else disappear. I pulled her torso up onto my thighs, cradling her head against my ribs. Her bare arms felt like ice.

"Rayne," I said again, shaking her shoulder, and willing her to look at me, "are you okay? Did they hurt you? Rayne, look at me."

Her eyes slid in my direction, unfocused, then rolled up behind closed lids.

"Rayne!" I shouted, slapping her cheek, but she didn't answer.

CHAPTER ELEVEN

I leaned over, setting my cheek against her lips and pressing my fingertips just beneath her jaw on the cool skin of her neck. Her heartbeat was strong and rhythmic but slow, and so was her breathing. At least she was breathing.

"How is she?" Ronan's steady voice helped to settle my nerves a bit.

"Um...she's breathing and her heartbeat seems fine, but I can't get her to wake up."

There was a sudden gasp, and I looked up to see Ronan lean harder on the neck of Rayne's attacker, who was now crying in pain.

"What did you do to the lass?" Ronan's voice was flat, and the sound of it sent a shiver down my arms that had nothing to do with the cold. He pressed a bit harder, and the man screamed, his legs stretching out behind him to try and relieve the pressure that must have been close to breaking his neck.

"Just a roofie!" he said in a high, choked voice, waving his free arm frantically, "that's it, I swear!"

Ronan looked at me with raised brows, but it took me a second to answer because relief made my head swim.

"It's a drug," I told him as moisture filled my eyes, "but people are usually ok after taking it."

Ronan looked down at the man and said icily, "If the lass is hurt, I'll see that you pay for it. Personally."

Tears ran unchecked down Mateo's cheeks as the EMT's pushed the gurney into the back of the ambulance and the doors closed, hiding Rayne's limp body from view. A wool blanket was wrapped around his shoulders as he stood by the open door of one of the police cars, but he still shivered. My heart went out to him. He wouldn't get over the agony of guilt until he saw Rayne awake and knew she'd be okay...maybe not even then. He barely looked me in the eye before giving me a half-hearted hug and climbing into the back of an ambulance. The guilt in his eyes was mirrored in my chest; neither of us had been able to protect someone we loved, and it didn't matter that it hadn't been our fault.

"Seems to be these guys' M.O.," the police officer was saying to Ronan, "This is the third time this month we've been called out for date rape. If your friend hadn't followed them outside and fought back long enough for you to get here, things might have ended very differently."

"Will Rayne be okay?" I asked.

"Probably," the officer said, making a notation on the metal clipboard he held, "most people recover from the symptoms of the drug by the next morning. She might not remember much of what happened, though," he gestured toward the ambulance with his pen, "they'll probably keep her overnight, just to be sure."

I nodded and wrapped my arms around my shoulders, wishing that I had a wool blanket but grateful for the presence of the police none the less. They'd arrived just minutes after Ronan had incapacitated the shorter attacker, followed closely by the ambulance. Both men had been handcuffed and stuffed in the back of police cars, bruised and sullen.

"Do you need anything else from us, officer?" Ronan asked as he settled his jacket onto my shoulders. Officer O'Goll lifted the papers on his clipboard and flipped through them with a professional eye.

"Nope. I've got your statements and your contact information." Then he looked up at Ronan, measuring his size and asked, "Are you sure you don't want the medics to take a look at you?"

Ronan shrugged and shook his head. Neither of the men had touched him. "Nah, I'm all right. Nothing worth bothering about."

"And Miss...Chapter, was it?" the officer asked, looking closely at my face. I nodded. "How are you feeling?"

He had a warm, friendly smile, despite his stern countenance and the bulge of muscle beneath his bulletproof vest, and he seemed to be genuinely concerned.

"I'm okay," I lied.

"You live close by, are you in school here?"

"Yeah, at UW."

He nodded and examined my face. His eyes were a soft gray, like an overcast sky. "This kind of thing isn't uncommon Miss Chapter. If you're going to be hanging out in places like the Atrium, it's safer to go in groups."

He reached out and gripped my shoulder, earnest and serious. "Concentrate on your studies and keep yourself out of trouble, all right?"

I pulled Ronan's coat a little bit tighter across my shoulders and said, "I will."

When we climbed into the station wagon, I pulled my keys from my pocket and reached for the steering column but couldn't get the key to slide in. My hands were shaking too badly. Ronan held out his steady hand, but I pushed it away impatiently, gritted my teeth, and stabbed the key at the hole. It slid home after the second try, and I turned the engine over with a growl, pulling out onto the road. The wet pavement reflected the city lights like an upside-down impressionistic painting, passing by with hypnotizing rhythm.

"Do you want to go to the hospital?" We had been silent long enough that Ronan's deep voice startled me, and I hit the brakes by reflex, giving him a dirty look before easing the gas pedal back down. Luckily the roads were practically empty this early in the morning, and there was no one behind me.

"I don't know," I admitted. "I called her parents, and they'll be there. I want to be there for her, though. I just feel..." I shook my head and shrugged, trying to get a grip on my elusive emotions. "I don't know how I feel."

"Tired?" he suggested.

"Exhausted."

"You should probably go home and get some sleep."

"I probably should," I agreed and turned right at the next light.

"Hospital?" he asked.

"Hospital."

⊷⊱ ⋅✦⋅ ⊰⊶

The hum of fluorescent lights reminded me of my brief internment in the psychiatric ward. It made the hair on the back of my neck stand up, even once we were back in my apartment. I'd stayed by Rayne's bed long enough to see her wake up, to hear that she would be okay, and to be forcibly removed by Sunny, Rayne's mom.

"I'm so sorry I wasn't with her," I'd said, taking Sunny's hand in my own shaking ones, "I'm sorry I let this happen."

"Allie, you're the only reason something worse didn't happen to Rayne. I can't begin to tell you how much it means to Cliff and me, what you did," she had said, wrapping me in a hug. But then she held me at arms-length, and her mellow voice had shifted into 'mom mode' before she said firmly, "but we love you, too, and you need to rest. You look dead on your feet. Ray is going to be okay, but she'll never forgive herself if you pass out from exhaustion and end up in bed next to her. Go sleep, and we will call you, okay? You hear me?"

I locked the apartment door and turned the deadbolt before pulling the chain into place and letting my head drop with a thud against the door.

"I'm sorry for all the excitement," I muttered, turning my head in place to look over at Ronan, who had started rifling through the cupboard. "It would be nice to go a few weeks without some new catastrophe."

He grunted something dismissive and pulled out a sachet of tea leaves before reaching for the teapot and filling it with water. I dragged myself away from the support of the door and stopped by the end of the counter, holding the countertop with both hands. The aftereffects of adrenaline left me shaky and off-balance.

"Hey."

Ronan stilled and turned to look at me. His expression was soft, despite the hard line of his lips. I hesitated. It was so easy to simply look into his eyes and forget about thinking.

"Thank you," I said.

Ronan nodded gravely and then took a step forward, leaned down, and lifted me effortlessly. The sudden change made my stomach lurch the way it did at the top of a roller coaster when you start to drop. He smelled like leather and sweet, sharp sweat. He laid me on the couch, grabbed the throw blanket from the back, and covered me in one smooth motion as the cushions sank welcomingly beneath me and I closed my eyes.

I hadn't yet fallen asleep when I smelled the warm, soothing fragrance of chamomile and lavender. It wasn't easy to pry my lids open, but the tea smelled like a slice of sanctuary, and I took the cup gratefully. Seeing Ronan with the mug in his hands brought back the image of him walking into Rayne's hospital room with two paper cups of steaming coffee for Ray's mom and dad, and a blanket for Mat, who had fallen asleep in a chair in the corner of her room. The warmth that blossomed in my stomach wasn't owed only to the tea.

"Thanks."

"Welcome." The couch sunk at my feet as Ronan leaned into the cushion and let his head fall back against the faded corduroy. The hair slid off his forehead and showed his profile, sharp against the light of the dawn through the far window. The line of his jaw, though covered in dark stubble, was still strongly carved and stark against the long column of his neck. Every bit of him radiated strength and certainty, and I found myself feeling not only grateful that he had been there to help Mateo and Rayne but also comfortable and safe in his presence.

My mind began to slip away from the events of the day, pulling out random impressions to examine with detached interest, like an old lady at a yard sale who wants to look at everything but buy nothing. I thought briefly of the time I'd had food poisoning when I was little, while my mom had been working graveyard at the hospital. My dad had wrapped me in blankets and sat by my side through endless replays of The Little Mermaid, holding the bucket every time I got sick. Most memories of sickness made me uneasy, but I trusted that nothing bad could happen to me so long as my Daddy was there.

That same feeling of peace stole over me as my mind went blank. My body had warmed the couch cushions and the blanket, the tea warmed my insides, and I had just enough time to think of how comfortable I was before all thought dissolved into sleep.

When the sudden, sharp sound of knuckles cracking against wood sliced through my dream, I catapulted off the couch, hair in my face, heart racing, and arms flailing.

"Wha?" I said, turning my head from side to side as if whoever woke me would be standing there to explain such rude behavior. The knock came a second time, and I spun toward the door, disoriented but stumbling toward the front of the room anyway.

"Okay," I called, trying to untangle my feet from the throw blanket that had slipped to the floor while I'd thrashed around in my sleep, "hang on."

"Miss Chapter? It's officer O'Goll."

After defeating the devil blanket, I weaved toward the door, still blinking and pushing hair out of my face. Officer O'Goll stood just outside the doorway in civilian clothes. "Miss Chapter?"

I shook my head and rubbed my eyes. "I'm sorry, I just woke up, and I'm not altogether here yet. What did you say?"

He smiled slightly and made a flipping gesture with his leather-gloved hand. Had he ridden a motorcycle here? "Don't worry about it. I just got off my shift, and I wanted to make sure you were okay. That must have been a traumatic experience last night."

"I'm okay."

"Good. Do you mind if I come inside? I'd like to ask you a few more questions about what happened last night. We've been looking for these creeps for a while, and I want to make sure the charges stick, so if you can remember anything else about what happened, I'd like to hear about it."

His grey eyes were earnest and intent on my face as I tried to make sense of what he wanted. More information about Rayne and Matt's attackers. Yes. I opened the door and stepped aside to allow him in. "I don't know how much I can help you, officer," I said slowly as I followed him into the living room, gathering the loose ends of my memories from the night before, "was there anything specific you needed to know?"

He turned around when he reached the couch, and the look on his face froze me. His eyes were intent, puzzled, and surprisingly angry. "I'd like to know why you're still alive."

I swallowed as ice condensed in the pit of my stomach. "What?"

"You had no pulse, I checked you myself." His voice was calm and almost bland, but his gaze held me pinned. As if I could have moved after a statement like that. My hand strayed unconsciously to the scar that ran across three inches of my scalp on the back of my head. He took a step forward, and I backed away, my throat closing tight with fear. He followed me step for step.

"You lost enough blood; I'm sure of that. We are not in the habit of leaving loose ends. You weren't breathing when we started the fire, so how are you still alive, Allison?"

I opened my mouth, but only a breathy squeak came out. Images of that day flashed before my eyes like the previews on a movie screen. The road had been red and gold with fallen leaves, and my father was smiling as he turned up the radio when my favorite song came on. I remembered my stomach dropping as our tires lost traction and fishtailed sideways near the corner, the lurch when the tires found purchase again but too late, the instant of weightlessness as we rolled off the embankment, and the violent slam of thousands of pounds of metal crashing onto the wet hillside. I saw my father's blood covering one side of his head, my hands, and the roof of the car beneath us.

"I suppose that's not important, as long as I finish it."

My head was shaking back and forth in disbelief, and I opened my mouth again but his arm shot out like a striking snake, and his gloved hand closed around my throat.

Ah, the thought hit me, *not a motorcycle. He's wearing gloves to hide his DNA when they find my body.*

The edges of my vision went black as his thumb and fingers closed on my arteries. I pounded on his arm, but his muscles were tight as steel bands. Before the world disappeared, I dropped to the floor, letting my weight land hard on my knees. His grip loosened just enough that I could fling myself to the side as his knee shot toward my face. The rough material of the jeans scraped my ear, and I fell to my stomach, coughing as air-rich blood rushed to my head, making me dizzy.

Before I could roll or crawl away, I was hauled off the ground by the backs of my arms. I kicked desperately as he pulled me toward the window, trying to get my legs underneath me. One heel connected with the coffee table, sending teacups crashing to the floor. I drew another deep breath preparing to scream but, before I could, I found myself on the floor yet again, crushed beneath a weight that forced all the air from my lungs. Then I was free, and I coughed as air scratched down my raw throat.

Officer O'Goll and Ronan grappled in a tangled knot of writhing arms and legs, grunting and swearing as they rolled over each other. A second later there was a strangled gasp followed by a meaty cracking noise, and then the mass went still. My heart froze for a split second, then beat hard as Ronan stood and pulled his leg out from beneath the officer's limp body.

"Is he..." I began, but couldn't finish.

"He is," Ronan growled, glaring at the body, "the wretched bastard."

Then he raised his eyes to look at me. They were a blazing, clear blue, like autumn skies on a cloudless day. "Are ye alright, lass?"

I nodded, unable to speak and unwilling to comprehend what had just happened. I hadn't noticed that Ronan was naked until that instant. His dark hair was plastered to his head, leaving water to run in shining rivulets down his bronzed skin. I could hear the faint sound of the shower, still running, in the bathroom behind me.

"Change your clothes," Ronan said and walked brusquely past me toward the hallway, seemingly oblivious to the fact that his body was on display.

"But the officer," I began, but my voice died out as I turned to look at the limp body of the dead man on the floor of my apartment. He was utterly still. I kept expecting to see his chest rise or an arm twitch, like the villains in movies who are never really dead.

"Allison, do you trust me?" Ronan was now standing only a few feet away; Ronan, who had saved my life and probably Rayne's and Mateo's, as well. Ronan, who had just killed a man before my eyes.

"Yes."

He reached toward my face with one big hand and held my chin between his thumb and forefinger. His skin was warm.

"I need to get you out of here," he said slowly, gently, "I need to take you somewhere safe. Change your clothes and get ready to leave, okay? I'll do the same."

I nodded dumbly, and he returned my nod before walking back down the hallway toward the bathroom, leaving me standing in the living room with the body of the man who had just tried to kill me...apparently for the second time.

CHAPTER TWELVE

The vibration began in my chest and radiated out to every part of me until my entire body was trembling. Since this would be my first time Walking as part of my training, Ronan had taken both of my hands in his and begun the process of bringing his atomic frequency into harmony with another verse, telling me to match him.

The strange full-body humming filled the air between us, like the tone of a bell. I felt the vibration even more strongly through his skin where our palms met. I could match Ronan's frequency with the same ease with which you'd match the pitch of a song on the radio or a note played on a well-tuned piano; only, I wasn't doing it with my voice. The vibration grew stronger and more intense until I thought my muscles would peel off my bones like palm fronds in a hurricane, but the world dropped away, and my vision went white.

Panting on my hands and knees, I tried to regain my balance as the ground spun around me. I closed my eyes tight and breathed through my teeth, willing myself not to throw up. The sensation of vertigo abated much more quickly than it had the last time, though nausea remained, in part because of the awful taste in my mouth. After a few minutes, I pushed myself to my feet and held both hands out to steady myself as my vision adjusted. It took several seconds to generate enough moisture to swallow, even longer to blink tears into my sandpapery eyes.

The reassuring weight of Ronan's hand settled on my shoulder as my surroundings came into focus. We were standing in a meadow in the center of a deciduous forest that was ablaze with fall colors. A stand of aspen trees to my right looked like a group of struck matches; their tops flamed shaped and yellow as the sun. The meadow seemed impossibly green, with knee-high grass and a couple of huge stones, more than twelve feet high, standing upright and moss-covered in the center. Above us, the cloudless sky was achingly blue and the air was sharp enough to sting my cheeks, causing goosebumps to ripple down my arms. I took a deep breath and exhaled dreamily.

I knew, on a very deep level, that this was not my verse. It was almost the same way you can tell when some band covers a song you know; it might sound like the original song, but there's always something that gives the game away. Whether it's the timing or the inflection of the singer's voice, subtle hints tell you that it's not the original. At the same time, I did feel welcome in this new place. I was smiling when I turned to look at Ronan, but the smile faded when I saw his face. His eyes were hard and serious, his mouth flat. When he held out his hand, I took it without thinking, following him to the edge of the clearing where fallen trees had left convenient seating.

He gestured to the log, and I sat, wary of his mood. The feeling of satisfaction at having Walked to this beautiful place deserted me as a vision of Officer O'Goll's grey eyes replaced the foliage.

"What happened?" His voice wasn't unkind, but it rang with command.

"What do you mean?"

"With the police officer," he said impatiently, "tell me what happened, all of it."

"Why?" Ronan's brows lowered, and I felt, suddenly, the impertinence of my question. I had no reason not to tell Ronan what had happened; I owed him that at least for saving my life. But my natural inclination to do the exact opposite of anything anyone ordered me to do had trumped my better judgment. I didn't like autocratic Ronan. It reminded me too much of the sullen Jerk who had tackled me in the parking lot of the hospital.

"Why?" he asked, incredulous. "Because an officer of the law was doing his best to toss you from a window, Allie, and I killed him for it. You'll be telling me what happened and you'll be telling me now."

I swallowed, hard, and told him what had happened exactly as I remembered it, word for word. I stumbled over the memories of the accident and realized exactly why I hadn't wanted to tell him.

"And then you must have heard something because, the next thing I knew, the two of you were on the floor," I finished.

"Think hard, because every little detail may mean something; is that everything that happened?"

I shook my head and rubbed my palms hard against the fabric of my jeans, feeling again in memory the wet warmth of blood on my hands. Ronan stood very still for a moment and then began to pace with his lips pinched together between his teeth so that his mouth disappeared into a flat line. I tried to look at the colors of the wood, breathe in the refreshing chill of the fall air, but the wonder of it left me. Ronan stopped and sat across from me on the flat edge of a broken stump, leaning forward to brace his elbows on his knees.

"Look," he began, and then sighed, his shoulders slumping, "something is going on that I don't understand, and I don't know what it is beyond the fact that someone is trying to kill you."

The skin on the back of my neck tightened. "Yes, well, you took care of that problem."

"No, Allie, I don't think I did. Someone tried to kill you the first night we met, as well, and I don't think it was that officer."

"What? You mean that drive-by shooting? That could have happened to anyone."

"Maybe," he agreed, "but random shootings don't usually include someone who follows victims into the alley and takes shots at them with silenced guns."

"But," I started to say, then shut my mouth, mind racing over the events of that night, "when I tripped, that's when you got shot, wasn't it? Not when the windows broke."

He nodded. "That's why I stayed with you that night. I suspected something was wrong, so I didn't want to leave you alone. But nothing had happened by that next morning, and I needed to have the wound healed, so—"

"Wait a minute. You were so tired and weak you barely made it to my bed."

The corner of his mouth turned up in a wry smirk. "Allison, I've been injured worse than that and continued to fight for hours. Don't get me wrong, it bloody hurt," he said, shrugging the shoulder in question, "but that's not why I stayed."

I huffed and crossed my arms, doing my best to pin him to the spot with my eyes. He looked back, unblinking. "Did you have to let me struggle to take off your boots if you were so tough?" I asked icily.

"I rather enjoyed it, actually. It would have been painful to do it on my own. Besides, you were so bossy about it."

I narrowed my eyes at him and wished I had something to throw at his smirking face. "If I had known you were faking it, I would have made you do it yourself, you jerk. You scared the crap out of me, Ronan, and I had to lie to my best friend. There was a lot of blood."

His face sobered. "Even a little bit of blood looks like a lot, Allison. It would have scared you worse if I had told you my suspicions on top of everything. I didn't want to worry you like that if it was nothing but a random act of violence, and the wound gave me enough reason to stay close to you for the night. After all, I only had unfounded suspicions then. That's why I felt safe enough leaving you the next day when nothing else happened. But after this afternoon, I'm sure of it; especially after what you've told me."

"But how can we know that it wasn't a coincidence? Maybe you looked like someone else or—I mean, don't we need more proof before making that assumption?"

"Hard proof would be nice, but difficult to come by in a situation like this. And look," he held his hand out to measure the height of his shoulder against my head, "the shot happened when you tripped. People who shoot with silenced guns in dark allies don't choose random targets. If you hadn't stumbled..."

A cold chill ran down my spine. "There's no chance it was a coincidence?"

"A chance, sure," he shrugged, "but do I think it's likely that someone would experience this many attempts on their life with no connection, one of those attempts by someone who can Walk between verses? I doubt it. It's safer for you if we assume they're connected."

"Officer O'Goll was a Walker? How do you know that?"

"He tried to Walk while we were fighting. That's why I had to kill him. He was strong enough to leave while fighting, and I couldn't risk him coming back with reinforcements."

"That's...three times," I said in a small voice, feeling shaken.

His eyes grew softer as he looked at me and his voice was gentle when he asked, "It happened when you were sixteen?"

I nodded. I hadn't spoken about the car accident since it had happened, not to anyone. My mom thought I didn't remember the details of the accident since I'd had a concussion and had never talked about it—but I did remember. I remembered every exquisitely painful instant. I hadn't realized that I'd started talking until Ronan reached out and took my cold hands off my knees, wrapping them in his large, warm ones.

"It was so fast," I was saying, "one instant we were singing and laughing, and the next...everything hurt, Ronan. When I woke up, I was on the roof of the car and my dad was hanging upside down from his seatbelt. It took me a second to realize that the car was upside down, everything looked so strange. His blood was dripping from the top of his head onto the ceiling, and I was laying in it. Both of his hands were hanging down and..."

I shuddered and closed my eyes. "I was able to get his seatbelt to unlatch. When his body landed next to me, I got sick. I couldn't help it. He was still warm, but he wasn't breathing. I was woozy, and it was hard to stay awake, but I tried everything my mom taught my brother and me. I did the rescue breathing, but there was no space for CPR. His lips were wet though, I think it was my blood, and I couldn't get the air to go through. It kept leaking out the sides and making these little squishing noises. I didn't think about trying to dry his face; I just kept trying to force air into his lungs and pounding on his chest until I couldn't feel my hands. I...think I started screaming at him."

I had. I'd screamed his name and pounded on his chest until the blood loss and pain overwhelmed the adrenaline, and I passed out on top of his body. I didn't fully wake up until two blood transfusions, 30 stitches in my head, a cast for the compound fracture in my left leg, and several days later. They said they'd found me 50 feet from the car. My father's body had been destroyed in the fire that would have killed me, too.

"I don't remember climbing away from the car," I admitted dully. I didn't speak for weeks after that. Then I had been on the outs with my Mom. I drank and partied and barely made it through my junior year. Somehow I got the best of my self-destructive period and threw myself into school, studying history because of my father's passion for it, but I still missed him terribly, and I still had nightmares filled with blood and fire. Every now and then, it took a few drinks to convince me that it would be safe to fall asleep.

Ronan's hands were warm and calloused, his knuckles scarred with small white lines, but his fingers were long and graceful as the rest of his body, dusted across the third joint with short, rough black hairs that caught the light as he turned my hands over so that they lay palm up in his. "I'm sorry, lass."

The sympathy in his deep voice made tears sting the backs of my eyelids. I blinked furiously and wiped my cheek on my shoulder, which was still sore from my fight with Officer O'Goll.

"He said I had no pulse," I said, feeling that familiar 'click' of information fitting together, "and he also said 'we.' That means there was someone else. So, I'm not safe even though he's dead—am I?"

Ronan shook his head.

"Why would someone want to kill me? I was a 16-year-old nobody living in a small town in Washington."

"I don't know," Ronan said as he stood and pulled me to my feet, "but I mean to find out."

He turned and began to walk away, still holding my hand, but I planted my feet and pulled on his arm, forcing him around to face me.

"My father is dead because someone wanted me dead."

Ronan hesitated and then nodded, unwilling to lie even to make me feel better, and said, "It seems that way."

I took a deep breath and let it out slowly, feeling heaviness settle firmly in my chest and begin to glow with the smoldering heat of a banked fire. "They're still out there somewhere then. And I can't—I mean I don't know..." I growled and ran my hands through my hair in frustration. "I wouldn't know how to find them or what to do to stop them. If they could find me in two separate verses, where would I be safe? Damn it!"

Frustration crept up my neck and into my cheeks in a hot wave. Had I not been through enough in the last week? And now I knew that my father was dead because some shadowy stranger wanted to kill me. As far as I could tell, there wasn't a damn thing I could do about it because the only person who might have been able to tell me anything was also dead.

"Gah, I just want to hit someone!" I growled between my teeth, balling my fists with impotent fury.

Ronan's answering smile was decidedly wolfish. "No worries, lass. I'm going to make sure you do it properly."

CHAPTER THIRTEEN

Its As Ronan led me out of the clearing and toward the forest, my mind raced over what the officer had said and the implications of what he'd done. We had lived in a small town just east of the Cascade Mountains when the accident—no, I had to stop thinking of it that way; when the murder happened. I'd been life-flighted to a hospital, and as soon I was released, we'd moved to the western side of the state. My mom hadn't been able to stay anywhere near where she'd built a life with my father. Too many memories, she said.

So, if O'Goll had been unaware of my recovery, he must not have been a police officer at the time or, at least, not on the eastern side of the state, or else he'd have known that I'd been sent to the hospital rather than the morgue. Was he in Seattle by accident? That would be an awfully big coincidence.

By the time we reached the edge of the forest, I was no closer to understanding why any of it had happened. At least Ronan had disposed of the body. I shivered, seeing the suddenly empty space on my living room rug as Ronan and the limp body of Officer O'Goll vanished.

Raucous cawing derailed my train of thought, and I jerked to a stop, spinning toward the noise. There, on a low hanging branch, sat a bird the color of blood and fire. It was as large as a peacock, and shaped much the same, with a long tail and feathers that came to a delicate point, like the head of a spade. There was a faint shimmer to the feathers, like the oil-on-water sheen of duck feathers, only it was a golden color rather than the blue-green of the fat little birds from my world. It's long neck stretched and the bird made an awful noise that was surprising coming from such a striking creature.

I let go of Ronan's hand and covered both my ears. "What is that?"

He looked back over his shoulder at the bird, who was now industriously grooming it's wing feathers. "Ah," he said, smiling, "that's a phoenix."

"Seriously? You're not teasing me?"

"No, that's a real phoenix."

I didn't bother to close my mouth. As I took an involuntary step forward, the bird lifted its head to turn a bead-black eye on me. Not finding me worth its time, it went back to methodically cleaning its feathers with a delicate yellow beak.

"It's so pretty."

"It is, that."

"Does it really die in fire and come back from its ashes?"

"It does, but not the way you'd think. It's hard to explain. Come on."

I left only reluctantly and because Ronan promised that I'd soon be seeing something that would take my mind off the mythical bird. He was right. I had never been out of the United States, so I'd never had the privilege of seeing castles in real life but, like every little girl, I dreamed of being a princess with the accompanying visions of castles and princes on white horses. The real thing was infinitely cooler.

I was sure that no castle from my world could match the splendor that sat high at the head of the wide valley opening below us. The white stone castle had blue and grey slate-roofed turrets complete with pinnacles, flags, towers, arching bridges, and stained glass windows as large as those in any gothic church. The entire thing glowed with reflected light, like the moon at dusk.

"It's as big as a city," I breathed.

"It is a city."

"It's amazing."

Ronan shifted his weight and peered past our shoes down the edge of the cliff we stood atop. It was at least 500 feet to the valley floor where a river curled lazily like a silver and blue snake that hugged the castle city's outer wall and disappeared around its flank.

"How do we get down?" I asked, trying not to look over the edge for too long.

"There's a path off that way," Ronan gestured with his chin but didn't take his eyes off the river below.

I looked back down at the water, imagined stepping into the fast-moving current, and asked, "Do we have to cross the river?"

"We do."

I gulped. "We don't have to swim, do we?"

He turned to look at me, brows raised. "Why would we do that? There's a bridge."

"Oh, okay," I said, shoulders dropping in relief, "will it take long to get there?"

Ronan's eyes had drifted back toward the river, gone almost opaque as he saw something far beyond the castle at the head of the valley or even the mountains that flanked it like sentinels. I recognized the look of insistent memory.

"Ronan?"

He jerked when I touched his shoulder and turned toward me so quickly that I flinched. He shrugged one shoulder and rubbed the back of his neck, looking embarrassed. "Let's go," he said, "the path is just that way, on the other side of the Rhododendron bushes."

I took one last, longing look at the castle before the foliage enclosed us in a private world of moist air that was thick with the musty scent of decaying leaves. Sunlight came through the red-gold canopy in long, luminous pillars that made the pathway look almost like the colonnade of a temple. The wood was quiet in the way that a church is quiet when the congregation is praying, filled with worshipful expectation punctuated by the small ecstatic noises of birds and scurrying rodents. The dirt path was a gradual downhill that skirted the edge of the cliff as it leveled off into the valley floor.

Long grasses took hold as the trees thinned and finally opened out into a verdant carpet. The grasses were still rich with purple and yellow blooms playing host to bees who were gorging themselves on the harvest. With the castle city blazing in the last light of the day like an expertly cut jewel, and the ripe valley laid out in a king's feast at its feet, it was the kind of scene that made the ten-year-old girl inside of me go dreamy-eyed with desire.

Ronan slid out of his jacket and slung it over one arm while pulling at the neck of his tee-shirt with the other, forcing air down and through the cotton. The fabric clung to the line of his shoulders and showed the shadow of muscle across his upper back where a damp spot clung to the skin between his shoulder blades. I could feel the sweat bead between my breasts and glanced down hurriedly to make sure there were no tell-tale sweat spots on my own shirt.

"This is kind of miserable," I said, taking a discreet sniff of my armpit. He glanced back over his shoulder at me, the sunlight making him draw his dark brows down.

"Seasons are a bit funny, here."

"It looks like it. Why?"

"Altitude, I think. The capital city is among the higher elevations of this continent."

I watched a black-capped bird snatch a butterfly out of the air in mid-flight. "It felt a lot cooler in the meadow. It's kind of strange."

Ronan grunted and gestured me forward with a jerk of his chin. "That's not the strangest thing you'll see, Allie. Remember, some of the verses are very different from True Earth. Plant and animal life evolved in interesting ways."

"Well, things here seem more or less familiar."

"So far."

I smiled, thinking of the phoenix and wondering what else I might see, but not daring to hope for anything too outrageous.

We began to encounter other people as the path broadened into a proper road and soon merged with a cobbled thoroughfare. The robes, hoods, tunics, hose, and boots worn by our fellow travelers had a distinctly medieval flair, but the pattern and cut of the clothing were very modern, almost futuristic. Even the weave of the cloth was nothing like the kind of roughly spun fabric I would have imagined and more like something out of a high-end boutique or maybe even the runway in Paris.

A large wagon rumbled past on my right side, pulled by two animals I could only compare to oxen. They were as large as buffalo with horns as thick as my thighs, driven by a man in a leather jacket so unexpectedly cool that I would have given my right arm to get my hands on it. Tightly packed sacks filled the back of the wagon, being presided over by a little girl with shiny brown curls that bounced as the wagon moved. She had a cloth doll pressed tightly to her chest and a small, dreamy smile on her chubby face. I wondered what she was daydreaming about. She caught sight of me and her eyes widened in surprise. She leaned back and pulled on the driver's sleeve. He glanced over his shoulder, and his eyes widened as well, but he said something short to the little girl, who cast her eyes down.

I reached up and tucked a flyaway strand of hair behind my ear. Now that I wasn't staring at everyone's clothing, I noticed that my hair had, once again, made me conspicuous. There was more than one sidelong glance from other people headed toward the castle and not a few whispers. My shoulders slumped beneath the weight of 'otherness' that always swamped me when I became the topic of stranger's conversations.

"Watch it," Ronan said, grabbing my left arm and jerking me to the side just in time to avoid planting my foot in a steam- ing pile of oxen poo. The smell hit me a second later, and I looked over my shoulder as the crowd parted around the mess like the red sea.

"This is worse than rush hour in Seattle," I said, watching a line of men on horseback in the grass beside the road, riding past all the pedestrians at a quick trot. A few stragglers, who had wandered out into the grass, leaped out of the way of the oncoming riders. Ronan made a sound in his throat that I couldn't definitively say was a laugh, but I had my suspicions. I looked at him narrowly and noticed that the wary expression was back. His eyes never stopped moving. His hands were relaxed, but the watchful tension I'd first noticed about him had tightened his shoulder muscles. He raised one dark brow at me, and I dropped my eyes. How many times was he going to catch me staring? I was not going to blush, though, I told myself fiercely. I reached back and braided my hair to mask my embarrassment.

"So..." I began, trying to recover, "are you going to explain what we're doing here? I mean, this place is beautiful and all but..."

I let the question hang and judged our distance to the castle gate. The thing was enormous, and maybe 200 yards off.

"No," he said easily.

That seemed unreasonable, so I glared at him. "Care to explain your reason for not sharing?"

"Can't you just trust that your teacher knows best?"

I pursed my lips. The tone of his voice told me that he was being contrary on purpose, but the last thing I wanted to do was fight with him in the middle of rush-hour traffic, so I sighed. "Whatever you say, Obi-Wan."

He stopped so suddenly that I crashed into his back with a breathless "oof" and grabbed his sides to steady myself.

"Sorry," I murmured as he bent down and scooped something up off the cobblestones.

I hadn't noticed before how smoothly the stones fit together. They'd have to be cut to perfection to fit that flawlessly. The crush of people increased at the gate, and as we tried to thread our way through the crowd, Ronan took my hand and began to pull me along behind him, his big body cleaving through the mass of people like the prow of a ship.

"You'd be handy on the football field," I shouted over the noise.

"American football? Never say so. I'll take rugby any day."

I remembered my brother's face after a particularly gruesome match and winced. "Rugby, eh? You'd have to say goodbye to that pretty face."

I could tell that he smiled because I saw his cheek bunch up beneath his eye.

The crowd dispersed after we passed beneath the portcullis, people moving off in every direction like cockroaches under a light. Ronan hesitated, scanning the crowd. He seemed to find what he was looking for because he pulled on my hand and said, "c'mon." It was the cart that had passed us before the castle gates. The leather jacket-clad man was holding the little girl on his knee, saying something into her ear while her cherubic face pinched into a heartbreaking little pout.

We stopped a couple of feet away and the man, I assumed him to be her father, looked down at Ronan from the driver's seat. His face cleared and he smiled, turning toward the girl and whispering in her ear. She gaped at her father, then her eyes flashed toward Ronan's free hand and her feathery little eyebrows raised.

"That's mine," she said, pointing.

Ronan lifted the doll. It was wearing a blue dress and had dark hair made of yarn tied into two braids. "Is it now?" he said, considering the figure with a serious expression. "I found her on the stones. Saved her just before a great bird could snatch her up and carry her off."

The little girl's mouth popped open. "You did?"

"Mmhmm. The bird said that he wanted her to come up to the mountain and be the queen of the birds."

"But he can't have her; she's mine! My mummy gave me to her," she insisted, her little body quivering with the desire to hop out of the wagon and retrieve her doll.

"Well, that's what I told the bird, but he said he loved her and that he would care for her. I said that somebody else loved her more, and would be heartbroken without her."

She nodded her head violently, brown curls bouncing, "I do!"

Ronan looked at her gravely. "He didn't believe me at first. He said that he would only let me have her if I could promise that she would be well taken care of. I gave my word of honor that she would be, and I never lie."

I hid my smile behind my hand.

"I will take care of her! I will, I promise! Della's my bestest friend."

"Alright then, Della?" he asked the doll. Then he lifted the little figure to his ear and cocked his head. "Mmm," he murmured, "I see. Della says she would never want to go home with anyone but you."

He lifted the doll, and the little girl whisked it into her arms and kissed the yarn hair wildly, tears flowing down her cheeks. Her father was grinning and nodded his thanks at Ronan while gathering his daughter up in his arms.

CHAPTER FOURTEEN

"**Y**ou look like a tourist in New York City," Ronan observed in a gently mocking tone as we walked down the wide streets of the city toward the castle.

"I feel like a tourist in New York City."

The castle city had broad, open streets lined with neat shops, potted trees, beautifully carved wooden signs, flower beds, random statues that reminded me of the pictures I'd seen of Michelangelo's David, and people who hurried off about their business with the content intensity of honey bees. It was picturesque in the extreme, almost surreal. What kept me staring like a goon, though, was the high, arching bridges and walkways that connected the second and third stories of some of the buildings. The skyways arced gracefully over our heads, as broad as three or four sidewalks, and had brightly colored silk buntings hanging from the curved buttresses that supported them from beneath.

With the sloping roof and towers of the main castle building looming just beyond, the whole city felt like a real-life Disneyland; magical in a sanitized, closely planned way. I couldn't help but stare, whether it made me look like a tourist or not. At least it kept me from noticing every passerby who gawked at me like a freak show exhibit.

"They're not staring at your hair," Ronan said.

I flinched and dropped my braid, unnerved at how well he could read my expression. "Oh yeah? Well, this has happened to me my whole life, it's nothing new."

"Why don't you dye it, if it bothers you?"

"Because it's the only noticeable trait I got from my dad other than height. Besides, I like my hair," I added, stubbornly.

"Good. I like it, too. It's not a color one sees often. Be a shame to dye it."

"Then why did you ask?" Ronan appraised me.

Heat rose in my cheeks, but I didn't look away. After a second he shook his head and turned his eyes toward the castle and the fifteen-foot-high inner wall that separated it from the rest of the city. "Why do they keep looking at me then, if it's not this beacon?"

I grabbed a handful of my braid and shook at him in illustration.

"You're a Walker, and people always notice a new Walker here."

I hesitated, then hurried my stride to catch him up as we crossed the open space between the buildings of the city and inner wall of the castle proper.

"People here know? I mean, they know what we are?"

"They know. It's part of their lives."

"How can they tell? I thought," I paused, trying to remember our conversations about the rules that were part-and-parcel to this new life, "isn't this kind of a secret? I thought you said there were only a few Walkers who could tell when there was another of us nearby."

Two blue and white liveried guards stood beneath the narrow gate that led through the wall to the castle. When they saw us, they stepped back and uncrossed their spears, nodding at Ronan.

"We aren't supposed to reveal what we are to people who would endanger Walkers, so it is a secret in a way," he said, nodding back to the guards, "but not here. This is the one place you don't have to hide what you are. Besides," he stopped walking and then turned to face me. His dark hair caught the reflected light from the white stone of the castle, and I could see the deep brown in the slightly curling locks that covered his forehead. He folded his arms and gave me a once over from head to toe, clearly amused. "Have you noticed what you're wearing? Blue jeans, a cotton Aerosmith tee shirt, and a pair of...are those Converse?"

"Vans," I said from the corner of my mouth.

"You are very clearly not from around here."

He had a point, and one that made me feel more than slightly stupid for missing something so obvious, but I wasn't about to let go of the answers he hadn't given me.

"Why isn't it a secret here, then? If someone showed up in Seattle wearing something crazy people wouldn't assume—" I cut myself off, realizing that you could wear just about anything and still pass yourself off as a local in Seattle. "My point is, strange clothing doesn't automatically make people think you're some kind of, I don't know, time-traveling Jedi from another world, Ronan. Why do people here know about us when no one else does?"

"Jedi don't exist in any verse that I know of."

"For real? Gah, that's a bummer. I was kind of hoping to get my hands on a lightsaber."

"Not going to happen, I'm afraid."

"You could have broken it to me a bit easier than that."

One corner of his mouth crooked up. "There's no easy way to tell someone that they'll never get to have an epic duel with the dark side."

"True," I admitted, as a smile crept across my face, "but there is an easy way to distract apprentices from completely valid questions by using Star Wars references, isn't there?"

He shrugged and admitted, "It has worked in the past."

"You were this close," I raised my thumb and forefinger to illustrate just how easily I could be distracted by tapping into my rampant inner geek.

"Not close enough, though, eh?"

"Spill the beans, Obi-Wan," I said, crossing my arms.

He turned and gestured across the courtyard with a tilt of his dark head, putting one hand on the small of my back. The skin there tensed immediately, and I could feel the heat of his palm through the thin fabric of my shirt.

"C'mon," he said, "I'll tell you about it as we walk."

The gentle pressure of his hand urged me forward with greater ease than any promise of information could have done. I'd never been so confused by another human being in my life.

"For the people of this verse," he said, "Walkers are a bit like celebrities; people you grow up knowing about, but who live in the background. In the rest of this world, people know about Walkers in a vague sort of way, like you might be aware of the celebrities in another country. But here in the capital," he made a gesture that encompassed the castle, the city, and the surrounding woodland, "Walkers are more an everyday fact of life."

"Why?"

We were just about across the circular courtyard, and the huge, elaborately carved wooden double doors of the entrance stood directly before us, flanked by two statues of dragons standing with outstretched wings and tails that curled sinuously around their back feet. When he didn't answer, I dug my heels into the cobblestones before we could walk between the dragons, forcing Ronan to stop or push me over. He did stop and looked down at me, exasperated.

"You know," he observed, "you may be the most irritating young Walker I've ever taught."

"Kudos to me. I'm not going into that building until you answer my question, Ronan. Why do people here know?"

He sighed but could tell that I was serious, and shook his head as if in surrender, but then his eyes gleamed speculatively. "I could just pick you up and carry you in, you know."

"You probably could," I agreed, then said quietly but with all the menace I could muster, "but you wouldn't walk away without regretting doing it."

He laughed then. Loudly. He threw his dark head back and laughed so hard that the guards at the main gate turned to look in our direction. "Lord, but you are a feisty baggage, aren't you? You know, your eyes turn the color of spring grass when you're angry."

He was smiling openly, as honest a smile as I'd seen from him, and my insides turned warm at the sight of it. The stubble of two days' beard growth made dimples stand out starkly in his cheeks. His eyes sparkled with mirth, framed by coal-dark lashes and slashing brows turned up at the center in amusement. The sight of him was enough to make me feel like a middle school girl staring at her first crush which, oddly enough, irritated me more.

"Allison," he began and then shook his head, changing his mind, and his eyes sobered. "Maybe someday we will turn that into a true threat." Not bothering to explain what he meant by that cryptic remark, he continued, "Look, people here know about us because this is the center of what you'd call our government. You remember when I told you about the Concilium?"

I nodded. It would be hard to forget since that was the first time I'd ever been shot at, but I didn't bother to say it; the knowledge was already in his eyes.

"This is where the Concilium is located. The headquarters of the Venatore is here, as well. Whatever there is of a central government for our people, it's here in Avalon."

CHAPTER FIFTEEN

I n my head, I choked and sputtered and let my jaw drop till it hit the floor, but in reality, I simply stood there looking stupid and wondering if he had implied what I thought he had, or if it was a coincidence of name. The question in my eyes must have been clear because a flicker of amusement crossed his features.

"Yes, it's that Avalon. Why do you think I didn't just tell you straight out? You'd have scoffed at me and not taken any of this seriously."

I shook my head dumbly. "No, I...okay maybe I would. I mean," I put my hands on my hips and eyed him suspiciously. I didn't know Ronan well enough to know how much he might know about mythology in my verse, if he was teasing me, or if teasing was even something Ronan did, which I doubted. But I didn't like being made to look a fool. "How would you know whether I would believe you or not? For that matter, how would you have guessed I would know what Avalon was?"

Ronan sighed in the long-suffering way my mother used to when I was trying to explain how I had lost yet another pair of shoes. "Do you think I'd be teaching you and not know anything about you? That I'd tell you I was Venatore and not look into your life at all? I'd not be teaching an unstable person, nor yet someone I thought would use their ability to hurt or dominate others. Yes," he said, completely unapologetic as storm clouds began to gather in my eyes, "I spied on you. Of course, I did. Or do you want me to be teaching people of questionable character how to disappear at will?"

I opened my mouth, righteous with the fury of my violated privacy, and then shut it again. It wasn't exactly as if I had "rights" per se, as a Walker. And, when I came to consider the breadth of this ability, did I want people who might use it badly to be taught by the same man who had ostensibly promised to uphold whatever laws or rules his government created?

"Okay, maybe not," I admitted, albeit grudgingly, "but I didn't expect you be spying on me, Ronan. I don't like it."

"I don't blame you."

"But you don't regret it."

"Not a bit of it."

I ground my teeth and, on impulse, pushed past him and grabbed the metal ring of the right-hand door, pulling with all my might. To my surprise, the huge door moved so easily that I over-balanced and stumbled backward, bumping my rear into the tail of the grey stone dragon. Trying to salvage whatever dignity I had left, I motioned magnanimously at the open door and said, "After you."

Ronan took a deep breath, held it for a minute, sighed forcefully through his nose, and strode through the door. I followed him, not bothering to close the door behind me. Okay, so he knew that I was studying History and had a particular interest in mythology. It wasn't like I tried to hide that from anyone. He could have seen it just by looking at the kinds of books I had in my bedroom.

Besides, I said to myself, *the man has seen your naked butt, so what's worse? It's not like knowing your college schedule somehow makes him privy to all your darkest secrets.*

We walked down a flight of stairs and into a vast chamber with a ceiling so high that the light of the huge, stained glass windows on either side didn't reach it. Stone pillars, embellished with curling vines lined the length of the chamber in pairs from one end to the other. Some of the people moving through the room wore clothing I had no references for, and in materials I couldn't have begun to name. People from other verses?

A woman passed us, and I had to look down to stop myself from gaping at her. She was the tallest and thinnest woman I'd ever seen, with skin so light that it was almost white. She moved with an unearthly grace that gave the impression that she was floating. Long, moon-pale hair trailed behind her as if a breeze lifted it. There were even a few animals in the room. A bear was ambling between the pillars and the outside wall, moving in and out of the light of the windows. No one seemed in the least concerned.

We turned right and walked out of the huge chamber and into a window-lined hallway flanked by small courtyards with freshly cut lawns. Ronan opened the double doors at the end of the hall and led me down several corridors until finally stopping at an unremarkable wooden door, and pulling out a key. The room was simply furnished with a bed, a table and chair, a large armoire, and a dresser with a ceramic pitcher and bowl on it. The single window at the end of the room opened on the courtyard I'd seen from the hallway.

"I'm feeling a bit overwhelmed," I said without preamble, and promptly curled into a ball on the bed without caring to whom it belonged.

"I'm not sorry I spied on you," Ronan said. I noticed the slight emphasis he placed on the word spied. Clearly, that wasn't how he saw what he'd done. "But," he continued, "I am sorry that it bothers you that I did it. It wasn't my intention to make you feel vulnerable."

I took a breath so deep that my lungs creaked, then let it out slowly, and tried to release my tension with it. "I don't think that's what bothered me," I admitted, sitting up and trying to gather my thoughts. "I think it's that I am vulnerable, and now I know it. I mean, last week my world was pretty mundane. My biggest worries were finals and making it home to visit with my mom. This kind of stuff," I gestured to encompass everything that had happened, "was only in books and movies. And really, accidents aside, I was safe. Now I'm effectively on the run from some supernatural stranger who wants me dead, and you're telling me that I'm in a place right out of legend that isn't just a figment of the imagination but a whole universe of its own. That is what you're telling me, right? This is the Avalon where King Arthur is supposed to be buried?"

"It is."

I groaned. "Yeah. So here I am, and none of this seems real except the fact that the way I see my life, the way I see other people, has completely changed. I'm questioning everything, and I haven't even had the time to think any of it through. When you said that you had sp— researched me," I amended when I saw his brows draw together, "well, it just reminded me that I don't know you, and that there's a whole reality beyond the one that I thought I knew, and that I can't trust anything—or anyone—to be what I think they are."

My voice trailed off as the truth of it settled on me with crushing weight. I didn't want to cry, or hide, or even be alone to think because I had no idea how to begin to process the fact that everything I thought I knew was only an illusion on the surface of reality; if there was a reality. Ronan scooted the chair toward the bed, looking at me with an intent blue gaze that was both direct and compassionate.

"Allie," he said slowly, "let me ask you a question. Do you know who you are? Not your name or where you come from, but do you know who you are?" He didn't wait for me to answer but continued, "You're still you, aren't you? So, nothing has actually changed, only the way you see things has changed."

"It doesn't feel that way."

"I know, but it's the truth. It happens to you all the time, only in smaller ways, so you don't think about it. See," he adjusted his weight, settling in for a serious talk. It reminded me so strongly of what my father used to do when he was getting ready to lecture me that I felt a random stab of grief, "your ideas about things always get changed when you encounter them for the first time. Take New York city; I bet you have an idea in your head of what it's like."

I nodded, noting with vague interest that I'd begun to picture the crowded streets and high-rise apartment buildings almost as soon as he mentioned the city.

"If you go there, some things will be the way you imagined, and some things will be so different that your ideas about New York will alter to fit the reality. New York didn't change, only the way you perceived it did. The reality of a thing is always different than our notions of it are, it's just that not everyone gets confronted with the reality of so many things, all at once. And those things haven't changed, just like New York didn't change."

"I don't think knowing that makes this any easier to handle, Ronan."

He gave me a small, empathetic smile. "Maybe not right now, but it will."

"I don't even know where to start," I admitted, a bit helplessly. I hated, hated feeling like I needed help and was even worse at asking for it, but Ronan had a way of helping without making me feel helpless; I appreciated that.

He stood up and whisked the chair back underneath the edge of the table in a single, fluid motion. His voice was matter-of-fact when he said, "Quit trying to figure everything out. Just do what you need to do, and tackle things as they come at you. Don't think about it so much, just do it."

"Well aren't you just a walking Nike advertisement."

He ignored my jibe, but I couldn't deny that his advice did make me feel a bit better.

"Alright," I said, scooting to the edge of the bed and sitting up straight, "I will be just like Scarlett O'Hara and worry about it tomorrow."

"Well done."

"So why are we here and when can we eat?"

CHAPTER SIXTEEN

T he Castle had a huge dining hall, as large as the pillared room I'd first seen, lined with wooden tables and bench seats. The wood was dark and smooth, polished to a high gloss, and laden with all the bounty of a fall harvest. I plunked a piece of cheese, a handful of grapes, ham, potatoes, and a still steaming roll onto the plate, staring at the almost opaque quality of the spoon before using it to spread a bit of butter onto my roll.

"What are these made of?"

Ronan glanced away from his plate, which was piled twice as high as my own, and looked at the spoon I held up for his inspection.

"Horn," he said around a mouthful of turkey.

I didn't speak anymore after that because my mouth was too full. After a long day I was starving, and the freshly harvested food, made in the castle kitchens and cooked that afternoon, was easily the best meal I'd ever tasted. Besides that, eating kept my mind busy and I didn't have time to worry about our reason for Walking to Avalon.

Think about it tomorrow, I reminded myself, imitating Vivian Leigh's southern accent in my head. "Ronan! When were you getting back?" A bear of a man had just approached the table and was clapping Ronan forcefully on the back, a face-splitting grin beneath his beard. His skin appeared to be permanently sunburned and was covered in the same curly brown hair sprouting profusely from his head.

"Just today, Molfus. I'm not staying, though."

Molfus' face fell, then he caught sight of me and his eyes widened. I stood up and reached for his hand, which completely swallowed my own.

"This is Allison," Ronan said, "a new Walker from True Earth."

The man's dark eyes widened, making his exceptionally hairy eyebrows disappear into his hairline.

"Really? It is being quite a while since we are having a new female from True Earth. Welcoming to Avalon, Allison," he said, and then leaned toward me with a stage whisper, "If Ronan starts to boring you with his moody silences, come finding me, and I will be taking over your training."

His conspiratorial grin made me smile by pure reflex. "Thanks, but I've made it my mission to irritate him as much as possible until my training is over. Maybe by the time I'm done with him, he won't be so boring."

Molfus snorted in amusement, and I shot a sidelong glance at Ronan, who was glaring at both of us.

"I am liking this one," he said to Ronan as he gestured to me with his thumb, "be bringing her by the armory sometimes."

Ronan turned back to his food and lifted a hand dismissively as Molfus stalked out of the room, clapping other diners on the back on his way out.

"He's a fun guy," I said, "when I can make it through his accent."

"That's what everyone thinks until they get in the ring with him. He might sound slow, but his mind is as quick as a bear trap, and his hands are faster. You done?"

I looked down at my plate, contemplating the food that was left. I had yet to try the fruit that looked like a boiled starfish.

"I may be able to stuff a few more mouthfuls in, but then we'd be getting into dangerous gastronomic territory."

"Leave it, then. The servants will clean it and feed the leftovers to the stray animals."

I followed Ronan from the room, wondering whether teasing him in front of another Walker, at least I assumed Molfus to be a Walker since his skin tone and accent were wildly different from any Avalonian I'd seen, was a good idea.

Would he be mad at me? He'd been mostly silent, and I was too chicken to ask if he was angry, so I said instead, "What did he mean, we haven't had any females from True Earth in a while?"

Ronan pulled the door open and motioned me through. "Female Walkers are statistically rare. Maybe only one in twenty, but we get less from True Earth for some reason."

"Really? Why?"

He shrugged, "We don't know for sure, though the scientists think it has something to do with genetics. It seems harder to pass on the gene, or whatever it is that gives us this ability, to female children."

I filed that piece of information away and asked the question that had been burning in my mind since Ronan suggested his plan to keep me safe. "So, um...are we going to see him?"

"Don't worry," Ronan said, eyeing my hands as I played with the end of my braid.

I dropped it guiltily and insisted, "I'm not worried, just...anxious."

"I think this is a good idea, Allie. It's the best way I can think of to protect you while we try to figure out who's trying to kill you. If he says yes, you can start training."

"Couldn't you just teach me what I need to know?"

"I could, but I don't have the time, and I'm still responsible for my job, remember? I thought about hiding you in some rarely visited verse, but they've already found you in two places."

I did understand, but that didn't stop the nerves from making my stomach muscles clench. We turned into a long corridor with high ceilings and tapestries hung between arching windows. A pair of stately white doors stood at the end, carved with dragons in flight who curled around each other, almost like yin and yang.

"But, I don't know if this is what I want to do, Ronan," I whispered frantically, "I didn't think I was going to have to make this kind of decision right now!"

He stopped and turned toward me, taking me by the shoulders. "Breathe, Allie. No oaths are required to train. You only swear when you graduate to the second strata, and we will have this mess sorted by then. When you're training here, you'll be as safe as anywhere in the Eververse, and when you're not training, I'll be with you. Okay?"

Ronan had laid out his plan for my safety before we made our way into the dining hall, and he'd sounded so certain that this was the best way to protect me that I'd hesitantly agreed. He'd saved my life more than once, and he was my mentor, so if I could trust anyone, it should be him. Besides, it wasn't as if I had a better plan. I swallowed hard and steeled myself to walk through the dragon doors.

Inside, the space was similar in size to a large living room but imbued with an atmosphere of quiet dignity. The room itself was circular, with a staircase along the wall that disappeared into the ceiling, and thin windows that let in slivers of moonlight. An iron chandelier hung from the exposed beams of the ceiling and cast a flickering shadow on a huge circular table beneath.

Made from many triangular-shaped pieces of wood, the table looked like a multicolored starburst. Copper trim had been hammered thin and shaped along the edges of the table like gilt on book pages, and dragons were worked into the copper in exquisite detail, down to the tiny scales and forked tongues. The wood was smooth and warm beneath my fingertips.

"Do you like the table?" I spun toward the sound of the voice and saw a man walking down the stair, one hand resting lightly on the banister. He was tall and straight with hair the color of iron and a close-cropped beard. Black eyebrows made the grey eyes beneath seem even lighter by comparison.

"Yes, sir, I do," I said, doing my best to keep any hesitation out of my voice. This was him, and I knew it.

"I have seen it for so long that sometimes I fail to remember how extraordinary it is. It is good to see it with fresh eyes."

He had crossed the room and stopped just in front of me, hands folded together at the belt on his waist.

"Sir," Ronan said from just over my shoulder, "may I present Allison Erin Chapter of True Earth. She would like your permission to begin training in the first strata as a Venatore."

For an insane moment, I felt the urge to do something ridiculous, like bow or curtsey, but he only smiled and held out one calloused hand to me. His hand was broad and strong—not elegant, but competent and powerful. I felt the warmth of it all the way up to my elbow.

"Allison, I am pleased to meet you," he said, covering our joined hands with his free hand and inclining his head only the slightest degree, never taking his eyes off mine. "I am Arthur Pendragon."

CHAPTER SEVENTEEN

I sat on the edge of my cot, looking down at the metal cuff that was now curled snugly around my left wrist just above the joint.

"This identifies you as an apprentice," Ronan had said as he attached the cuff with a small tool that looked like a soldering iron. There was no latch or clasp, no way to get the silver bracelet off my wrist. It had to be removed by someone who knew how. The wolf carved into the silver was so lifelike that I could imagine it moving through the night with predatory grace, hunting its prey with relentless intensity. That was what Venatore meant, after all: hunter.

I flopped back on the cot with an explosive sigh and flung one arm over my head wondering how I had just managed to become the Venatore's newest recruit.

"This can't be real life," I muttered, looking at my wrist for the hundredth time. Before agreeing to the training, Ronan had shot down my first suggestion, that I start taking some self-defense classes.

"No, that won't do. You can't learn fast enough, and they can only teach you martial techniques known in True Earth."

"A taser then, or mace or—?"

"No, no, no," he'd said, folding his arms across his chest. To be fair, he had logical and convincing reasons why each of those things wouldn't be enough to keep me safe, but enrolling in the sci-fi equivalent of the police academy hadn't been my first choice. Ronan held a trump card, though. "If you decide to complete your training, you'll have the best tools and knowledge chase down whoever was responsible for your father's death."

"I thought we would have it all figured out before then," I had said, eyeing him suspiciously.

"We will," he had assured me, "but no one can accurately predict the future. At least, not that I know of, yet, without consequences. Besides, we have ways to help you learn faster than you would by training in your verse."

I now had to figure out how to fit training in with my classes at the University of Washington and my part-time job at the Co-op. I also had to think of a convincing lie to tell Rayne and Mateo that would justify my soon-to-be weekly disappearances was another hurdle I'd have to leap. Maybe I could convince them that I'd gotten a job out of town? A sharp knock on the door made me sit up in a rush.

"Yes?" Ronan walked in wearing a clean pair of jeans, black boots, and a soft grey tee shirt that looked well worn, his ever-present leather jacket held in one hand.

"You look like you just walked out of Grease," I said, smiling at him, "all you need is some pomade for your hair and a T-birds logo for your jacket."

"I—what?"

"Judging by your expression I'm going to guess that you've never seen Grease."

"You'd guess right."

"Well then, you've never really lived."

He shrugged. "I think I'll be all right."

I bit my lower lip and plucked at the edges of the bracelet, wondering why it was so hard to talk about everything I was experiencing without feeling like a fool. In some ways, I had stumbled into a fairy tale the way kids always did in my favorite books when I was little, but talking about it as if the fantasy world were just as real as school and work and home only made it seem more surreal. It would be like Rayne telling me about her day only to slip in that she had tea with Buddha after her shift at the Co-op. The juxtaposition made my new reality seem even more unlikely, particularly in the face of what I had just done.

"Ronan?" I asked, looking up from the silver cuff.

"Hmm?"

"Did I really just meet King Arthur? The King Arthur?"

"Mmmhmm."

"Yeah, that's what I thought." I lay back on the cot again and covered my face with my hands. When I spoke, the words came out muffled between my palms. "I still can't believe I just met a real-life myth. Well, I guess he's not really a myth after all, is he?"

"I suppose not."

"I wish I could have talked to him longer; I wanted to ask him so many questions."

Ronan grunted. "You and everyone else who knows who he is."

"Is he always so intense?"

He thought about that for a moment before answering, "I don't know if intense is the right word, but every time I speak to him I get the feeling that, if he still needed knights for the roundtable, I'd drop to one knee and do something stupid."

"I felt the same way. It's probably a good thing he only looked me over and gave permission before you hurried me out of there. I would have been asking for a quest or something if we'd spent any more time with him."

"He is certainly a man who lives up to his myth," Ronan said, his tone melancholy. It struck me again that I'd just met King Arthur, the

Pendragon, the man who spawned a hundred myths and remained a part of my cultural psyche centuries after his supposed death. I shook my head in wonder.

"Holy crap, does this ever get easier?"

"Nope. You just learn new ways to deal with it."

I leaned on my elbow and tilted my head, giving serious thought to throwing my pillow at him. "You are a supremely frustrating human being, did you know that?"

"Yep. You ready to go?" I hesitated, pursing my lips and pulling them hard to the side, trying to decide whether to follow the impulse. Before I could think too much about it, I grabbed a handful of feather pillow and hurled it at him as hard as I could, picturing it hitting him solidly in the face with a satisfying '*fwap*' and a cloud of goose down. Instead, his hand shot out with a motion faster than my eye could track and caught the pillow with a much less satisfying, and rather wimpy sounding, 'poof.'

His eyebrows were pulled up in the middle, and he asked blandly, "What did you do that for?" I stood up and snatched the pillow out of his hand.

"Because you make me crazy," I snapped and slung the pillow at the bed before walking past him and out into the hallway.

"Allison," he said from behind me, his voice neutral.

"What?"

"We need to go this way to get out of the Castle."

I was half tempted to march off in the opposite direction just to spite him, but bit the inside of my cheek and spun on my heel.

"Lead the way then, James Dean." He gave me a pensive look, then shrugged one shoulder and walked down the hallway, his boots making a soft thudding sound on the stone floor. He was at least a head taller than most of the people we passed, which was a surprising number for this late hour. Walking behind him, it was hard not to look at the shape of him and the way his muscles slid beneath the grey fabric of his shirt. If I was honest with myself, it was difficult not to be completely aware of him anytime he was within my vision. That wasn't precisely true because if I even knew he was there, whether I could see him or not, it was like an electric current in the air that I could feel even if I wasn't thinking about it.

We walked down several corridors, but my body was on autopilot while my brain was somewhere else, so it took me a moment to catch up when I was suddenly shaking hands with a dark-skinned man whose bald head and triangle-shaped goatee were familiar.

"Hello again, my dear," he said with a voice that was deep and rich and had a musical quality that was almost hypnotic.

"Abasi!" I jerked suddenly to full consciousness as my mind ground into gear, let go of his hand, and hugged him instead, feeling inconceivably grateful for his presence. He patted my back and then took me by the upper arms and held me away from himself, looking pleased but a bit embarrassed. Despite only having met and spoken with him for a short time, he felt like a safe place to me. Maybe it was the kindness that was so evident in his eyes.

"Welcome to Avalon," he said, smiling, "you are looking much better than the last time I saw you. You remember Cecily," it wasn't a question, so I nodded and turned to the tall blonde, whose aristocratic face was as impassive as when I'd first met her in the hospital. Her skin was cold and her handshake abrupt and businesslike.

"Miss Chapter. I have been told that you are going to begin training for admittance to the Venatore."

"Looks like it," I said, and raised my wrist so that the silver bracelet caught the light of the candelabra.

"Let me be the first to welcome you to our ranks, assuming you are accepted into the second strata."

I smiled weakly, not sure whether I wanted the congratulations or not but still feeling that I ought to be polite even though there was something about her that made me itch to irritate an emotional reaction out of that stone face.

"Um, thanks."

"Will she be staying at the Bastion?" Abasi asked Ronan, who was standing quite casually but I could see the taught strain across his shoulders.

"No," he said shortly, "at least not for now. We'll be moving about a lot as she gets the hang of Walking, so she could come in out of anywhere."

Abasi's smile widened as he turned back to me, raising both brows. "And how is your progress? What do you think of your newly discovered ability?"

"It's a bit of a trip, honestly. Half the time it doesn't feel real, and the other half of the time just thinking about it makes me nauseous."

"Yes, yes, the nausea is common. Your body is doing something quite extraordinary, after all. But it passes with time. Tell me, how would you describe the first step?"

I opened my mouth but hesitated and looked at Ronan, helpless. "First step?"

Before Ronan could answer, Cecily said, "The first step is what we call the beginning of the process, when one brings their body into harmony with the verse to which they intend to Walk. While the action is physically the same for each of us, it seems that not every Walker activates their ability in quite the same way. Abasi has a pronounced interest in the mechanics of the process."

Abasi's round face was practically glowing with curiosity; his cheeks squeezed up so close to his eyes that they almost disappeared behind the corners of his smile. "Indeed, I do. It is a fascinating phenomenon, after all. Can you tell me—"

Ronan took a step forward then and put a hand on the small of my back, interrupting Abasi with an apologetic throat clearing. "Maybe Allison can explain it to you another time, Abasi? We're behind schedule."

Cecily let out a long breath through her nose and folded her arms, but Abasi seemed abashed.

"Oh of course, please don't let me keep you, my dear. I look forward to our next talk! Take care of yourself, now, and keep some candy or chewing gum on you, if you can." He laughed at my confused expression and leaned forward to say, "It helps with the nausea," and gave me a conspiratorial wink.

Cecily bent toward me in a slight motion that couldn't be called a bow so much as a simple acknowledgment of my presence, and said in her airline pilot voice, "Good luck, Miss Chapter. Until next we meet."

And just like that Ronan and I were walking down another corridor with strides so long that I started to lose my breath. Before I could say anything, we were outside in a courtyard and heading toward the outer wall of the castle.

"Ronan," I said, jogging a bit to stay abreast, "do you mind? Where are we going in such a hurry?"

He didn't answer, but he didn't slow down until we entered the deep shadow beneath the trees that lined the wall of the inner courtyard. With only a sliver of moon peeking through the clouds, we were all but invisible.

"What was that all about?" I huffed, surprised that walking could tire me out so quickly.

"Let me ask you a question, Allison. Who knew where you were, the night we took you from the hospital?"

My mind made an almost audible click, and I gasped. "You don't think...but they're Venatore! Don't you trust them?"

"Under most circumstances, I would say yes. Right now, I think it's safer for you if I'm suspicious of the only other people who knew where you were the first time you were attacked."

"Mmm," I said, biting my lip and thinking of Abasi's round cheeks and kind eyes. I couldn't imagine him trying to hurt someone. Cecily, on the other hand, was much harder to read and I couldn't say what she might be capable of.

"What would we do if it was them?"

Ronan's face went dark and hard. "You remember the rules I taught you?"

"Um...mostly?"

"Your actions shall not deprive another Walker of freedom, property, health, or life; this is the Third Law," he said with a voice like iron, "repeat it to me."

I did.

"Breaking one of the Laws of Founding means they'd be brought up on charges before the Concilium and sentenced."

"Sentenced to what?" I asked, unsure if I wanted to hear the answer.

"That depends on the circumstances. For self-defense, maybe nothing. For cold-blooded murder? Death."

I whistled, then a thought struck me like a kick in the guts, and I felt the blood drain from my face as I grabbed his sleeve. "Ronan, what about Officer O'Goll? You said he was a Walker..."

"He was trying to kill you. I reported to Arthur after you went back to your room. I've already been cleared of any charges."

Relief loosened my knees, and I had to brace my feet until I got myself under control.

"I'm not making any accusations yet, Allie," he said comfortingly, holding both my hands, "we don't know nearly enough. For now, I want you to keep a healthy suspicion in the front of your mind. Until we nail down whoever is behind this, you can't fully trust anyone. You're probably safer here in Avalon than anywhere else, so I'm not saying you need to live in fear, just be aware. I'm not jumping to any conclusions," he assured me, glancing back at the building, "but I'd rather not take any chances with your life."

CHAPTER EIGHTEEN

"It's dinner with your mom," Rayne said, leaning back on the toilet seat and tugging at the licorice that was pinched between her back teeth, "why all this?"

She gestured with the same licorice at the bathroom counter strewn with all the impedimenta of twentieth-century female beautification rituals. I was sitting on a kitchen chair with my feet tucked up on the bottom rung and staring hard at Mateo, who was descending on me with an eyelash curler and a smirk.

"I'm meeting my brother's girlfriend," I said through tense lips, trying not to move at all lest Mateo squeeze my eyeball with his beauty torture device. "And," I continued once my eye was a safe distance from any metal implements, "Thanksgiving is the only holiday my family dresses up for, you know that. Plus, Ronan is coming so I don't want to embarrass anyone with my haggard face."

That was nothing but the truth. I'd barely slept since my trip to Avalon as I tried to catch up on homework, write a four-page paper, do a bit of research into the mythology of Avalon, and still find time to spend with Rayne and Mateo, who were miffed that I'd skipped out on our last few get-togethers. The constant feeling of being hunted wasn't helping me sleep well, even though being home and back in my normal routine made the other half of my life seem much less likely.

The only blessing had been fewer hours at the Co-op since they'd brought on temporary workers to help during the holidays. Rayne snorted, and I heard the snapping noise of her licorice as she pulled the loose end free.

"I don't see why you're bringing your tutor to dinner with your family. Unless he's more than just a tutor?"

Mateo guffawed as he twisted the mascara wand inside the bottle. "Ray please, have you seen Alli when that guy is around?" he asked while brandishing the spiky little brush at my face, "she's like a cat in heat."

I punched at him blindly and connected with something satisfyingly solid. Mateo grunted, then started pumping the brush in and out of the bottle while giving me a lascivious sneer. I ground my teeth to cover a laugh.

"Ronan is a friend, okay? And he doesn't have anywhere to go for Thanksgiving."

"You realize you're celebrating the genocide of indigenous people, right?" I pushed Mat's hands away from my face and looked at my best friend, who had been distinctly prickly since Ronan had dropped me off at home. She'd been walking out the front door of the apartment building as we were walking in, and a gust of fall wind had wrapped my hair around my face. I'd fought my way free of the strands in time to see Rayne standing there dumbstruck, her eyes wide and soft, mouth hanging open.

"Ray, are you okay?" My first thought had been that she was still suffering from some side effects of the drug she'd been given. She was staring at Ronan as if she'd never seen him before, not bothering to close her mouth. I had taken her by the shoulders and tried to get her to focus on my face. "Rayne? Do you feel all right?"

Her eyes had refocused as she leaned to the side to see around me, giving Ronan a soft smile that made her cheeks flush. "I wanted to say thank you for what you did for Mat and me," she'd said, tucking a stray lock of blonde hair behind her ear. Ronan had only made a noncommittal noise while pulling up the hood of his jacket against the wind that was blowing his hair around. I didn't think he'd even looked at her while he said it. Was he embarrassed by her gratitude? Maybe she'd felt insulted by his manners and was irritated with me for not saying something to him about it.

"I'm not celebrating anything but the chance to stuff as much turkey into my face as humanly possible with no blonde guilt fairies bemoaning the cruelty of my delicious animal flesh dinner," I said flippantly, hoping to break the tension with our favorite argument. She made a retching noise and threw a piece of licorice at my head, which I barely managed to dodge by jerking to the side and away from Mateo's makeup brush.

"I can't work like this," Mat said and emphasized his complaint by throwing the damp washcloth I'd used to dry my face in Rayne's direction. She squealed around her mouthful of licorice and tried to dodge, but she was sitting too close to the wall and ended up hitting her head trying to evade the germy cloth. She slipped off the toilet seat and onto the floor between the wall and tank with a panicked squeak.

I tried not to laugh, I really did, but the sound escaped through my nose in an explosive snort, and Mateo lost it for a good five minutes, holding his sides and leaning against the countertop for support. Rayne laughed grudgingly at first, feeling the side of her head gingerly, but no one could resist Mateo's hilarity for long without at least smiling.

I watched my two friends laughing over stupid things and felt a surge of gratefulness. After the trauma of what happened at the Atrium, the fact that the three of us were sitting in the bathroom having a good old-fashioned makeover and teasing each other, was a blessing. Life didn't get much better. At least, that was how I felt until Mateo started getting serious about painting my face. Rayne even started taking handfuls of hair and twisting them up with the curling iron.

I comforted myself with the fact that at least this was the twenty-first century, and no one would be cinching me into a corset. After a while, I even began to enjoy the process. There was something nice about having people touch your face and play with your hair. Rayne and Mat were chatting happily, and I felt myself start to drift away, my mind slipping into that blank state of floating peace where all the noise in the room fades into a lullaby hum, and I didn't think of anything in particular. That is, until Mateo crop dusted me with hairspray.

"Ack!" I coughed and surged out of the chair, waving my hands in front of my face to get a gulp of air that wasn't contaminated with Aqua Net. I pulled the window open and stuck my face against the screen. "Gah, Mat, it's in my eyes!"

He made a disgusted noise and popped the lid back onto the bottle. "No, it's not. Your eyes were closed when I sprayed your hair. Besides, you'll need it. Your hair is so heavy those big curls will never stay in this rain."

Once the air seemed safe, I turned around and held out my arms. "Okay. How did you do? Am I fixed?"

Mat wrapped his arms around himself. "I'm just going to go ahead and pat myself on the back," he said, "because you, Allie Cat, are my little red-haired masterpiece."

I grinned at him and turned to check myself out in the mirror. He wasn't lying. "Ooooh," I breathed, genuinely impressed, "you do deserve a pat on the back. You better be acing your cosmetology classes. Good job, guys. You made me beautiful."

Rayne walked up beside me and looked at me in the mirror, her head tilted to one side. Her eyes were hard though, and I almost flinched at the expression. Rayne had never looked at me that way: like I'd just insulted her and she'd like to take me down a peg.

"You," she said flatly, "need to cut it out. You're beautiful, and you know it."

"You're my best friend, Ray; you're biased. Plus, Mat appears to be the god of makeup. It took almost two hours to make me look this good."

Mateo bowed.

"You don't need the makeup, Allie; you're just as pretty when you aren't trying so hard."

"Says the girl who gets proposed to by every guy she passes," I scoffed.

"That was only twice."

Mateo and I exchanged raised brows. "Yeah, because everybody gets marriage proposals from total strangers," Mateo said, dropping a baby wipe he'd been using to clean the counter into the garbage basket.

"The second guy was homeless," she said, exasperated.

"Still counts," I insisted, "Mat and I have never been proposed to."

"Not that kind of proposal, anyway," he said with a grin.

"I'd settle for either."

"You've really trained yourself not to see it, haven't you?"

Apparently, our levity wasn't working because Rayne was looking at me with irritated incredulity, her blue eyes narrowed to slits. My own ire began to rise.

"You mean, did I somehow miss that guys would like to find out if I've got red hair between my legs? No. I've known that since I was about thirteen years old and the first old guy asked me if the carpet matched the drapes. That's not the same thing, Rayne. It doesn't make you feel beautiful; it makes you feel gross."

She looked taken aback but hadn't given up. "That's not what I meant."

"Yeah? Enlighten me."

"Allison, how can you possibly miss the way that people's eyes follow you when you walk by? Don't you ever look at yourself?"

I turned to the mirror again, feeling off-balance and uneasy. I didn't like where this conversation was going.

"You're a striking person, Allie. Okay, maybe not conventionally beautiful, but there's something about you that draws people, and It's not just your hair, either. But you don't want to see it, do you? It's easier to blame it on your hair because you were born with it, and you won't change something you got from your father. You've been trying to make the real you invisible for so long, hiding in books and laughing off every guy that's interested in you, that you've finally convinced yourself that your looks aren't part of who you are. Well, I've got news for you; the only person you're fooling is yourself."

She stared at me for another second, then shook her head when I didn't answer and walked out of the bathroom. I looked at my reflection and tried to be objective. Sure, I was pretty enough in an objective sort of way, with regular features and clear skin, but there was nothing striking like she'd mentioned, aside from my coloring. I had none of the elegance physical beauty required.

More than that, being beautiful meant something else to me, it was a way of confidently being yourself, of being warm and generous. Rayne had that quality, though I was too irritated with her right now to admit it aloud. I wasn't honest enough or nice enough for true beauty.

"Is it just me, or has she been particularly crabby?"

"It's been a rough few weeks," Mat said with a sigh.

I had a sudden flashback to the dark alley, seeing Mat viciously struck as Rayne lay on the wet pavement, and immediately regretted having opened my mouth.

"I'm sorry, Mat. That was a stupid thing to say."

"Don't worry, Allie Cat," Mateo said, draping his arms across my shoulders and kissing my cheek, "blurting out your thoughts isn't stupid, just inconsiderate. It's part of your charm. Now come on," he was suddenly businesslike, pushing me down the hallway toward my bedroom, "let's get you into your outfit."

CHAPTER NINETEEN

R onan was uncomfortable. He kept rubbing his hand on the back of his neck and sighing, and shrugging his left shoulder. Generally so steady that he could almost be considered impassive, it was strange to see his big body fidget like a horse twitching off flies.

"You didn't have to come, you know," I reminded him with a mixture of amusement and irritation.

"I can't leave you unprotected."

"I was pretty unprotected while you were gone this last week."

He didn't answer and the car slowly filled with a guilty silence. I cleared my throat meaningfully. "I had one of the trainees watching you," he finally admitted.

I chewed my bottom lip and pulled into the passing lane with a little bit too much enthusiasm. *Chill out,* I told myself as I consciously eased my foot off the gas pedal, *it's better to have someone there. At least no creeper could have hurt you or Rayne. Just be grateful.*

Within a few breaths, I had myself back under control.

"Thank you," I said, trying to feel grateful.

He let go of his breath and made a noise in the back of his throat that I assumed was meant to be a 'you're welcome,' in crabby Irish.

"You could have just followed me or had your trainee keep an eye out tonight, you didn't have to come," I pointed out, not willing to give up my argument so easily.

"If you don't want me to be there, you could have just said so."

"No," I said, glancing at him, surprised, "I'm glad you'll be there. I just," I shrugged and made my own growly-throat sound. Why did being around this man confound me so much? When I had told him that I needed to spend Thanksgiving with my Mom and brother, his response had been, "No." I'd been incredulous but didn't intend to have my entire life controlled by the possibility that someone might try to harm me.

His answer to my stubbornness had been to come to dinner.

"It's just that you seem like you aren't very happy to be spending Thanksgiving with me."

My voice sounded pathetically plaintive, even to my own ears, and I gave myself a mental forehead smack.

Yeah, you really just said that, I thought savagely, *way to sound like a whiny brat. You're the one that practically forced him to go. Is it any wonder he's not happy about it?* I had to restrain myself from mashing down on the gas pedal. Not even my memory of the unguarded expression I'd surprised out of Ronan when I walked out into the hallway in the blue dress Mateo picked out was enough to ease my irritation with myself, and that was a look of surprised pleasure I'd immediately stowed away to enjoy later. I was still castigating myself, and breathing rather forcefully through my nose when I felt his hand settle on my knee. The heat of his touch was unexpected, and a tingle ran down my leg to my foot.

"Allison, it's not that I don't want to spend Thanksgiving with you," he said softly, "it's only... it's been a long while since I've spent any time with normal people doing normal things. And I've not spent a holiday with anyone I've cared for in—" he hesitated, and the sound of his indrawn breath was almost painful. "Well," his deep voice was soft and low, letting me hear the gravel at the bottom of it, "long enough that I don't properly remember the last time. I might not be the best company for regular people."

He said, 'regular people' the same way someone else might say 'celebrities' or 'the queen.' Without thinking, I took my right hand off the steering wheel and laid it carefully on his.

"I'm going to be very proud to introduce you to my mother, Ronan." His expression had softened, and his eyes were as vulnerable as I'd ever seen them. "I don't know how I'm going to introduce you," I continued breezily, trying to cover the sudden rush of emotion that made my heart beat faster, "I mean, people don't normally bring their physics tutor to a family dinner, do they?"

He chuckled and said easily, "I don't suppose they do," then added in an amused tone, "unless they're shagging each other."

Heat raced from the back of my neck and down my spine, making my joints feel weak. He hadn't removed his hand from my leg, and I was hesitant to take my hand off his, but the connection suddenly felt electric, so I let go to grab the steering wheel in both hands. We might have superpowers, but I was sure neither of us would survive a crash at 70 miles per hour, and touching Ronan made my hands shake.

"I suppose I could always tell them that you're a member of a secret interdimensional police force and you're mentoring me in the use of my newly discovered supernatural powers," I said, trying to keep my voice light. I wasn't very successful, but Ronan didn't seem to notice.

"Why not just tell them that I'm teaching you the ways of the force?"

"I guess it kind of amounts to the same thing, doesn't it?"

"No cool force-pushes or mind control, though."

"Or lightsabers."

"Or lightsabers," he agreed. Then suggested, "I'm your bodyguard?"

"True, but not likely. Why would a random college student need a bodyguard? I could just say that you're my friend and you didn't have anywhere to go for Thanksgiving," I supposed, "that's as close to the truth as anything."

"Sympathy case, eh?" he said, sounding disgruntled.

"Poor little interdimensional super cop," I patted his arm, "nowhere to go on a holiday he probably doesn't even celebrate."

He snorted, and a thought struck me.

"Do you?" I asked, "celebrate any holidays, I mean?"

He hesitated long enough to make me nervous. I wanted to see the expression on his face so I could get an idea of what he was thinking, but I could only slip a couple of sidelong glances his way between passing slowpokes in the fast lane and double checking my rearview mirror; I wasn't exactly going the speed limit.

"I used to, as a boy, but I got out of the habit after I started Walking. There is one holiday that I connected with after the first time I experienced it. If I'm not busy with badass interdimensional cop stuff," he cast an amused glance in my direction, "I like to observe it."

I grinned. "What holiday?"

"It's hard to explain. I'm not sure it translates well."

"We've still got time," I assured him, "and I'd like to know if you don't mind sharing."

He shifted in his seat and rubbed the side of his jaw with the palm of his hand. The sound of the short brown hair rasping against his skin could be heard even above the hum of my car tires on the road. When he finally spoke, his voice was subdued. The bass rumble at the bottom of his register made me want to arch my back like a cat being stroked.

"I left my world because I was forced to. An injury, you see. My mentor Walked me to another verse and left me to recover with the monks while he tied up loose ends. Well," he made a sound of vague frustration, "monk isn't exactly right, but that's the best word I can think of to compare it to; the word doesn't translate. The monks, the Ushdni, don't spend all their time praying or studying, they just help people. All people. Anyway, it took me quite a while to heal, so I was there long enough to learn the language. In that verse, the continents never separated, so there's a unity among the people that isn't common in verses where oceans divide the continents. They only have one language. There's a sense in that place that you're part of something bigger than yourself, but it's not mindless like an ant colony or a bird flock; I don't think I can describe it in a way that makes any sense.

But there was a holiday there, in Endre I mean—that's the name of their verse—that I got to experience shortly before my mentor came back for me. They call it Mish'da. It means, as roughly as I can translate, 'remember' but even that isn't exactly right because it also means 'wash away.' Kind of like the way a trace of your footprint is left in the sand, even after the wave washes most of the footprint away."

I made an encouraging noise in my throat and waited while he thought his way through how to explain.

"From the time they wake up until the time they fall asleep, they don't speak, don't work, or do any chores. They're supposed to spend the entire day in silence thinking about the people who have made an impact on their lives. Parents and lovers take up a lot of thought, but you're encouraged to remember other people like teachers or friends, even strangers who have been kind."

Ronan's voice had taken on a kind of far-away quality, and I realized that he wasn't talking to me, anymore. He'd gotten caught in the memory, like an ocean wave, and it had carried him out to sea. "You think of people, and the things they did that moved you, and you let the gratitude fill you up. As you remember, you take a little glass bead, one for each person you think of, and put them on a bracelet or necklace. When you think you're full to bursting with gratitude and you can't remember anyone else, you start to think of all the people who ever hurt you. People who insulted you, people who tricked you, people you loved who betrayed you. You take that gratitude, and you use it to help you forgive them. You let them go." He took a deep, ragged breath and I let out a breath I wasn't aware of holding.

"The next day," he continued, "you wake up, and you're supposed to be free, clean. You're free from hatred and from guilt because anyone you wronged was supposed to be forgiving you, too. Then you do your best to be the kind of person who becomes a bead, and if you happen to come across anyone who you'd thought of during Mish'da, you take the bead off your bracelet, and you give it to them. You tell them, 'pi aren di'icta dala mish'da narushni-ecte.'"

"What does that mean?"

"Love for you has made me clean."

I took the next exit ramp and pulled off onto the shoulder, pushing the shifter into park, and leaning back far into my seat as I thought of Ronan's words, and the beauty of a holiday dedicated both to grateful remembrance, and honest forgiveness. Ronan's face was carefully blank, but his eyes had hung onto the ocean and still looked far away.

"What about the ones you forgave?" I asked quietly, "what do you say to them?"

He turned and locked eyes with me, his pupils were wide in the twilight and pushed the blue of his iris' to a small ring around the black hole in the center: haunted eyes.

"You don't say anything to them. They're forgiven."

CHAPTER TWENTY

"Hey baby girl, happy Thanksgiving!"

It didn't seem to matter how old I got, my mother's hugs always made me feel like I was a little girl. I could lay my cheek on the top of her head, I was a Walker, a college student who lived on her own, but when my mom hugged me, I was just a daughter. It felt good. I smelled the faint bite of cleaning solution beneath her shampoo. Even though she didn't work at the hospital anymore, opting to work in a private practice where the hours were more reasonable, she still smelled the same as she had when I was little.

"Happy Thanksgiving, Momma." She leaned back and held me at arm's length with a huge smile on her generous mouth.

"You look great, sweetie! That blue makes your skin look like ivory. And this bracelet is gorgeous, wow! It looks like an antique. And who's this?"

She dropped my arm, which I tucked behind my back to hide the cuff around my wrist, and turned to look at Ronan with friendly curiosity in her brown eyes.

"This is my friend, Ronan. He lives away from family," I added by way of explanation.

"Happy Thanksgiving Ronan," she said as she stepped forward and wrapped her arms around him. I bit my lips at the expression on his face. She seemed to hug him for an awfully long time, and the look of panic in his eyes increased as the seconds dragged. Even I was starting to get embarrassed.

'Sorry' I mouthed over her shoulder.

"It's great to have you for dinner," she said, finally stepping back and turning to me and whispering, "the more people between me and the girl-fiend, the better. Come on in."

We walked through the entry and toward the living room, following the silky swish of my mom's slacks. She had been a dancer when she was young, and she still had a regal grace that was captivating to watch. People seemed to naturally defer to her, which made her a remarkably effective nurse. When you added her natural grace and self-possession to thick dark hair, a willowy frame, and doe eyes, it was no wonder my dad had fallen head over heels for her. I noticed that she was wearing a pair of socks with boggle-eyed turkeys stitched all over them, and grinned. Most people would probably think of my mom as a classy lady. Most people didn't know about her affinity for ridiculous holiday socks. She had a Christmas pair with actual lights on them that played Rudolph the Red-Nosed Reindeer. We passed the staircase and moved into the grey carpeted living room.

"Most everything is ready," my mom explained, "except the mashed potatoes and putting the pumpkin pie in the oven." She reached up and tucked in a stray lock of brown hair that had escaped her sleek bun.

"Mom," I began, intending to tell her that she had a smear of flower across her brow, but stopped before I could ruin this vision of her all mussed from cooking. There was something about it that warmed me up from the inside. I said instead, "I love you."

Her eyes went soft. "I love you, too, sweetie. I'm so glad you're here."

"Where's Ben?"

She rolled her eyes and then blew a sharp breath out through her nose. "He stepped outside with the fiend. Apparently, the little idiot uses one of those e-cigarettes."

I looked over my shoulder to be sure the happy couple was nowhere close enough to hear the derision in her voice. "Mom, you can't call her that," I scolded. I knew she was talking about the girlfriend because no one could call Ben 'little.'

Mom looked indignant. "Oh yes, I can. Those things are dangerous. Besides, you'd be proud of me; I haven't said one sarcastic thing to her or your brother yet."

"You want a pat on the back for that?"

"Yes," She laughed, "I do! Keeping my temper is hard around that woman. You'll see." Then her eyes turned to Ronan, and she said, "So, Ronan, are you in school with Allie? You look old enough to have graduated already."

"Al!" I spun at the sound of my brother's voice and hurtled toward him without stopping to think. Tall and well built like my dad, my older brother was one of the few people who could swallow me up in a hug. I didn't get to see him nearly as much as I liked.

"I missed you, B."

"I missed you, too." He let go of me, smiling, and said, "God, you look even more like mom than the last time I saw you."

"I'll take that as a compliment," I said. He reached out and tugged on a red curl that escaped from whatever braided mess Rayne had created on the back of my head. "Still just as red as dads. Did Rayne get her hands on you?"

"You could tell, huh?"

"Yeah, it looks like the kind of thing she'd do. I think she wore her hair the same way for your prom, like a bird's nest on the top of her head."

"She used a recycled hairstyle on me? What a punk. How do you remember that, anyway?"

"Mom made me take about six thousand pictures, remember?"

"Yeah, I do actually. You made my date really nervous."

Ben laughed and rocked back on his heels, "I almost forgot right! That poor nerdy dude. He looked like a scared mouse. I s believe you let that guy take you to your senior prom."

I smacked his chest and said in Jeff's defense, "He was a nice smart, too. No one gave him enough credit."

Ben smiled down at me, his straight, thick brown brows the center and an indulgent smile making lines appear at t   ıer his hazel eyes above a carefully cultivated 5 o'clock shadow. "Baby s always trying to rescue the lost birds."

"Ugh, please don't bring up those birds."

He laughed. "It's not my fault they died, Mother Theresa."

I remembered the little, naked bodies, so still with their oversized beaks hanging open. "Gah, Ben, why do you have to be so mean?"

"Benny isn't mean," said a sugary sweet voice that went perfectly with a sugary sweet face, "he's the sweetest guy around."

"Al, this is Trisha. Trish, this is my sister Allison."

Trisha was tucking herself neatly under my brother's arm and looking up at him with a proprietary smile as she rested a perfectly manicured hand on his stomach. Trisha was too stereotypical to be a real person. Her hair was bottle blonde and perfectly curled in precise waves, she had a not-so-subtle tan that the Pacific Northwest can't provide in November and a pair of shoes that could have paid for a month's rent in my building. She held out her hand to me, and I took it. It was like holding a jellyfish.

"It's so nice to finally meet you, Allison! Benny talks about you all the time. I love your hair color! I wish I could pull off something like that."

"It's not all it's cracked up to be," I assured her.

Ben looked over my shoulder and lifted his chin. "Who's this?"

"Oh, I'm sorry!" I turned to look in Ronan's direction feeling like a terrible host. He'd taken off his coat to reveal a dark blue v-neck sweater with a white collared shirt beneath; sleeves pulled up to the elbows. The fabric fitted him like a glove, catching a bit behind the belt around his low-slung jeans. My mouth hung open for a second before I got control of myself and snagged his sleeve to pull him forward.

"Benny didn't tell me you had a boyfriend," Trisha pouted up at Ben.

I clenched my jaw. "Ronan's not—" I began, but he was already leaning forward and taking Ben's hand in one of those manly handshakes intended to establish the natural male pecking order.

"I'm Ronan," he said over the top of my voice. He wasn't smiling, exactly, but his voice was pleasant and amused.

"Good to meet you, Ronan. You'll be joining us for dinner, then?"

"Nah, I'm her bodyguard," he said with a jerk of his head in my direction.

Ben barked out a laugh and raised a brow at me. "In that dress, she needs one. You want a drink?"

"I'd love one." Ronan had neatly sidestepped any questions about who he was and, just like that, I was alone with the walking stereotype who stepped forward and grabbed both my hands.

"I'm so glad you're here, I just couldn't wait to meet you. I love your dress; it goes so good with your hair. Where'd you get it?"

"Erm...I don't actually know. My friend picked it out for me. You can look at the tag if you want."

I'd said the last flippantly, but she promptly spun me around and pulled at the back of my dress.

"Nicole Miller, I knew it."

I looked down at my dress, feeling self-conscious, "Is it as bad as Ben says?"

She scoffed. "No. It's a classic sheath dress. You could wear it to an office party. It's fine. Trust me. He's your big brother though, that's the kind of thing they say. You look chic, don't stress."

Just when I was beginning to think that I might have misjudged my brother's girlfriend, she leaned in and said, "Your boyfriend is totally hot. Those lips, oh my god. How long have you been dating!?"

"We aren't. Ronan is just a friend. He didn't have anyone to spend Thanksgiving with."

"Aww, aren't you sweet for inviting him! Benny," she called over her shoulder, "can you get me a glass of wine? Make sure it's chilled, though. Does your mom have any frozen blueberries to put in the glass?" and then whispered to me, "men never do anything right without exact instructions. I'm glad I brought that Pinot Noir, it's going to be so much better with dinner than that white zinfandel your mom drinks."

I bit my lips and made a noncommittal noise. The way she emphasized every few words made my back teeth grind. I didn't think people talked that way outside of TV shows.

"So, tell me about school! What are you majoring in? Wait, let me guess..." she pressed her palms together, index fingers against her bubblegum pink lips, and rolled her eyes upward; thinking was obviously a physical effort for Trisha. "I got it! I bet you're majoring in History."

"How...did Ben tell you that?" Trisha's laugh was like little chiming bells—at least, little chiming bells if someone attacked them with one of those plastic xylophone sticks that toddlers play with. "Of course he did, silly. What, do you think I'm psychic?" More laughter. "I mean, I am a little bit," she added conspiratorially, "but I don't usually tell people because I don't want them asking me things, you know? Like, lottery numbers or something."

I forced an approximation of an interested sound from my throat and mentally congratulated my mom for having held onto her tongue for so long around this woman. Like a miraculous intervention, my mom called from the kitchen, "Allie, can you come peel potatoes?" I exited the room on a wave of grateful relief.

◆》──◆◆◆──《◆

"This looks incredible, Mrs. Chapter," Ronan said from his seat next to me. My mom's smile was deeply gratified. Apparently, Ronan could be quite charming when he put his mind to it, as evidenced by the flush on my mom's cheeks and my brother's now easy manner.

The turkey looked like it had come straight off the pages of a magazine. Trisha's sweet potato pie, though, looked like the Stay Puffed Marshmallow Man had barfed on top of a pan of doggy kibble. I kept that thought to myself and piled my plate as high as I could with stuffing, deviled eggs, green bean casserole, mashed potatoes and gravy, and my mom's famous turkey. Ronan was already halfway through with seconds by the time I took my last bite of green bean. He was humming as he ate.

"Now can you see why I had a hard time settling for microwaved sausage and rubber eggs?" I asked, but I couldn't help smiling at his obvious enjoyment of my mom's cooking.

"I do. It's hard to settle for second-rate food if this is the kind of thing you ate growing up," he conceded, before stuffing a piece of dinner roll into his mouth.

My mom laughed. "Don't let her fool you. She was such a picky eater as a little girl. I had to make two separate dinners just to get her eat."

"Mmhmm, I'd believe it. I had to double-dog-dare her to get her to eat sausage and eggs when I could hear her stomach growling from across the table."

"That sounds like Allie," Ben said, smiling a big brother kind of smile at me, half indulgent and half exasperated.

I pointed my butter knife at him across the table. "Don't start with me, Benjamin," I warned. My threat was made ridiculous when the butter I had been using on my roll just seconds before slid off the tip of the knife and landed with a plop on top of Trisha's untouched pan of half-melted yams.

"Oops." I shot her a sideways glance, but she was too busy texting on her crystal-encrusted cell phone to notice that I'd defiled her dish. Was she Instagramming the deviled eggs?

"So, Ben," I said quickly, trying to divert attention away from discussing my personal shortcomings, "how did you and Trisha meet?"

"On tour," he said, wiping his mouth with a napkin and giving Trisha a roguish wink. She blushed and leaned into his shoulder with a happy little sigh. I barely restrained an eye roll.

"We had just gotten back from South Carolina and checked into the hotel the booking agent got us in Seattle. Trisha was the club rep who came to meet with us. The rest is kinda history."

"It's been two months of nothing but bliss," she said.

Ronan coughed loudly and covered it by swallowing the rest of his wine.

Trisha perked up like a puppy and asked, "Oh, is that the last of the wine? I'll go break out the Pinot. Would everyone like some?"

My mom looked at Trisha with a polite but resigned smile and said, "Sure."

Trisha grabbed the four glasses and flounced into the kitchen. I grabbed my glass of sparkling cider and raised it at Ben in a mocking salute.

"Shut up," he breathed across the table at me.

"What? I didn't say anything."

"Don't play innocent, brat. She's sweet, leave her alone."

"I have been the soul of courtesy," I insisted over the rim of my glass.

"You two had better stop," my mom warned from the front of the table.

"Uh oh, she broke out the 'mom' voice. Watch it, Al. You're not too old to be spanked."

"Benjamin."

He looked at my mom with wide, innocent hazel eyes. "What? I'm on your side, here."

She grinned unwillingly and pointed the end of her fork at him, "You control yourself."

Just then, Trisha entered the room with 4 wine glasses balanced delicately on a serving tray and an extra glass with what could only be a refill of my designated driver, non-alcoholic beverage.

How nice.

She practically preened as she handed everyone their glasses and told them exactly why this wine paired so well with turkey. My mom thanked her and then gave me an exasperated widening of the eyes. I returned a sympathetic smile and then shook my head in wonder as Ronan fill his plate for the third time.

"Slow down, speed racer, nobody's going to steal the bird," I laughed as Ronan forked an entire leg onto his plate. Trisha sat down, settling her dress neatly, and then looked at me.

"Speaking of birds, I'd like to hear the rest of this bird story you two were talking about earlier."

I groaned, and Ben smiled. "Oh, it's no big deal. Allison is just a murderer, that's all."

"Ben," my mom warned, "don't torture your sister."

Ronan started choking on a bite of something and grabbed his water glass, slogging back deep gulps to wash whatever it was down the hatch.

"A murderess, eh?" he wheezed, mischief in his blue eyes.

I gave Ben a hard look and didn't spare his girl-fiend, either. "Yeah, I'm a cold-blooded killer, Trisha," I said, deadpan.

She opened her mouth and then looked at Ben, confused.

"Don't ever go swimming with her," Ben said to Ronan, grinning at me the whole time, "you never know if you'll make it out of the water alive."

"First of all, Dad had to pull your ass out of the water, too, if I remember correctly."

"He pulled you out first because you couldn't handle yourself."

"No, he pulled me out first because he loved me more."

"Ha! It's because you can't be trusted near water."

"You two," my mom interjected, a pained look on her face, as she held a napkin to her mouth "can we not talk about that at the dinner table, please? I've never been so scared in my life. I thought I'd lost all three of you."

The break in her voice made me glare at Ben. "See what you did?"

"What? You just don't want to admit that it was your fault because you have water issues."

"Water issues?" Ronan asked.

"Our rubber boat sank when we were fishing with my dad," I told him, "Ben likes to bring it up because I couldn't swim very well."

"No," Ben said, "I bring it up because you practically drowned me to save yourself!"

"How does that relate to baby birds?" Ronan looked lost by the labyrinthine twists of our argument.

"Because Allie drowns anything that goes into the water with her," Ben answered Ronan with a malicious smile.

"Oh please, how was I supposed to know that baby birds weren't supposed to take a bath? I was five years old!"

"Maybe because they were robins and not penguins?" Ben asked as he took a drink of the wine Trisha had so graciously brought in. At least it was having a better reception than her yams.

"You washed baby birds?" Trisha asked.

Clearly, I was going to have to give some backstory here, and I wasn't happy about it. The sinking boat wasn't my favorite memory. I'd never had a problem with deep water until then, but when I remembered being filled with the visceral fear that I was going to be dragged to the bottom of the lake by slimy hands, a fear which followed me into adulthood, it made my skin crawl. At least the baby bird story had the advantage of having become family legend that got trotted out at nearly every holiday or family gathering, which meant that it was less painful by dint of sheer repetition.

"Allie was always in trees," Ben said to Ronan, but I cut him off quickly.

"I'll tell the story if you don't mind."

Ben smiled and sat back, gesturing magnanimously with his wine. "Be my guest."

"I found a bird's nest on the bottom branch of a maple tree in our backyard when I was about five," I began. "The birds were still really small, they didn't have any feathers or anything, and I was completely fascinated by them. I sat on the branch and watched them all afternoon. Their little naked heads were so cute, with their buggy eyes and their big open mouths. But I never saw the momma bird come back, so I started to think that they had been abandoned. You always hear about how the momma bird won't come back if there's a human smell on the nest. Anyway, it didn't occur to me that the parents wouldn't come in while I was so close to the nest. I figured that they'd probably been eaten by our neighbor's cat or something, so I was going to have to take care of the babies."

"I found her in the garage with a nest of dead baby birds and a bucket of suds," my mom said, her eyes and voice soft, "you know those blue buckets people use to wash cars?"

"So, you can imagine why I panicked when our boat sank," I interjected, "I was already traumatized."

"She cried for two days," Ben said after polishing off the rest of his wine, ignoring my attempt to end the conversation, "and then she had a funeral for them in the backyard. She browbeat everyone into standing there while she sang amazing grace and buried them in a shoebox."

"You weren't very nice about it," I accused him.

"I was ten!"

"That's no excuse."

"It's a perfect excuse."

Trisha asked plaintively, "You teased her about it, didn't you?"

"Naturally," I said, "teasing me is his favorite pastime."

He grinned impishly. "She got me back, though. I think she hit me with about 200 rocks that summer. I still have a lump on one side of my head."

"You threw rocks at him?"

"Every chance I got," I confirmed.

Ben leaned across the table toward Ronan and said in a stage whisper, "she's got a really good arm."

Ronan smiled at me, revealing both dimples, and my heart stopped beating for a second. "I've experienced that myself."

"I've never—"

"You have so," he cut in, "you hit me in the face with a pillow."

"You caught it before it hit your face, that doesn't count."

"It would have hit me in the face, though," he said reasonably.

"You know," Ben gestured toward us with the empty wine glass, "if she throws stuff atcha, it means she likes ya."

"I'll take that on your authority, mate."

"I know 'cause she threw me all the time."

"I'd like to throw something at you right now," I muttered, fingering my butter knife.

"You won ledder do that, wull you ma?"

"Wow, how much have you had, Ben? Cut that one off," I said, looking at my Mom.

She was staring at her half-empty wine glass with her brows pinched together in the middle. "Allie, you should tell us the truth about thisss guy," Ben slurred and blinked hard, trying to get his eyes to focus on Ronan. My heart jumped up into my throat. I thought he'd misspoken earlier, but he was stumbling over his words.

"What do you mean?"

Ben leaned to one side alarmingly. "I think he's gunna be more that jus yer friend. You lookit im, I saw you. And he looksit you like a sunrise. I kin feel it. Isnee?"

"Allison, call 911."

I turned to look at my mom. Her lips had gone white, and she gripped the edge of the table with both hands. Her eyes were wide and locked onto me, but I could tell that she couldn't see me clearly. Ben slid off his chair and landed on the floor with a thud.

"Ben!" I leaped to my feet but went abruptly still when I heard the snick of a gun hammer being locked into place.

CHAPTER TWENTY-ONE

"Sit down."

Trisha's voice was cool and controlled. I lowered myself into my seat.

"It's too bad that you didn't drink the wine," she said, "this would have been so much easier."

Ronan started to move but froze as the barrel of the gun in Trisha's perfectly manicured fingers trained itself on me.

"If you move, Venatore, I'll shoot her in the head." Ronan's jaw muscle clenched and I could hear the air whistle in as his nostrils flared.

"Trisha," I said, trying to sound calm but raging inside, "I need to get to Ben, I need to see if he's okay."

She tilted her head to the side and gave me an amused lift of one blonde brow. All traces of vapidity were gone from her face, replaced by cold competence. "That idiot drank too much, too fast. If he wasn't such a lush, you'd all be caught up to him by now and sleeping soundly on the floor." She must have seen the resolve on my face, because she said, "If you get up, I'll shoot you."

My mom was breathing heavily; her forehead rested on the table between her hands which were trembling wildly despite being pressed hard against the wood.

"Momma," I breathed as terror sunk sharp claws into my chest.

"No," she whispered against the wood, "no, no, no, no."

I had to stop this somehow. I had to get to my mom, to Ben, and make sure they were going to be all right.

"Just sit still and wait. I'll only hurt you if you force me to, Venatore," Trisha warned, her eyes calculating and locked distrustfully on Ronan.

"How do you know me?" Ronan demanded. His voice was flat, controlled, and completely emotionless. The sound of it pulled my eyes away from my mom who was mumbling something over and over in a whisper. Ronan's face had gone completely blank. The air around him crackled with the energy of coiled muscles and the barely restrained lust for violence.

"Don't try it," she warned, "we have no vendetta against you, Venatore, but you will not Walk from this place. If either of you disappears, I'll shoot these two," she gestured at my family with a quick tilt of the head, "and I'll start with Ben. Now, pick up your glasses and drink."

I looked down at the amber liquid, sparkling with bubbles of carbonation, and my heart gave a terrified little flutter. My favorite holiday drink looked so innocent, but it was waiting to pull me into unconsciousness that could be the last time I ever closed my eyes.

The pink cell phone vibrated against the table and Trisha glanced down at it quickly, color draining from her cheeks as she looked at Ronan and me with renewed intensity.

"Drink!" she shouted.

"No." My voice sounded like a stranger's voice, calm and firm.

Trisha's lips thinned, and she reached down with one hand to pull a steak knife from the folded napkin by her plate. "Maybe your brother wouldn't mind a few new scars, then. What do they say? Chicks dig scars?"

The phone on the table vibrated again, and Trisha's eyes dropped to the screen. My mom lunged up out of her seat with the same explosive, liquid grace that had carried her across the stage. Trisha let out a little squeak of surprise as everything erupted at once.

Ronan moved with violent speed, but a crack like thunder filled the dining room, and the acrid, sour smell of sulfur stung my nose. Ears ringing, I didn't move for half a second out of sheer surprise that I didn't have a burning hole in my chest. Ronan had already vaulted across the table before Trisha could fire a second shot. She clearly hadn't counted on the speed he was capable of. I watched his shoulders tense hard enough to make the muscles on his back stand out stark against his blue sweater and then I heard a muffled, fleshy popping noise and he relaxed. I didn't bother to try to see what had become of my brother's erstwhile girlfriend.

"Momma!" A staggering wave of grief crashed over me with enough force to drive all the air from my lungs. She was completely still, lying on her side with a red flower blooming across her pale satin blouse and beginning to puddle on the tabletop. Her eyes were closed, long eyelashes lying against her cheeks. The valley of her eye socket was filled with a pool of tears. Lips that had so often kissed my forehead were parted slightly. The streak of flower still dusted the edge of her brow, and her face was strangely peaceful. If I had caught her napping, she would have looked just like this; cheeks still faintly pink and the delicate blue veins beneath the thin veil of her eyelids like the pattern on dragonfly wings. I don't know how long I stood there before I started to move.

Was I moving? No, someone was moving me.

"Allison, we have to go!"

I looked at Ronan, but I didn't comprehend the noises he was making.

"Bloody hell," he growled and lifted me into his arms to walk up the stairs with me.

"Wait," I said, as I realized I was being pulled from my family, "wait no. Ben. Ben! Momma!" Fighting did me no good. Ronan wouldn't give beneath my blows, my screaming, or my nails digging into his flesh. He took the stairs two at a time despite my struggles. My old bedroom door slammed open under his boot, and he stepped into the room with me held against his chest, his long arms keeping mine locked against my sides as I fought madly to get loose.

"Let me go! Ronan, my mom, my brother!"

"Think of Avalon, Allie," he said, tightening his arms around my shoulders even as I tried to kick him.

"No! My family!"

His arms locked like a vice, pushing the air out of me as he dropped his head next to mine. I gave him as vicious a head-butt as I could manage. He ignored my blow.

"Allison," he said softly into my ear, "your mother is dead. Ben will be okay. I've called 911. If I don't get you out of here right now, whoever Trisha was texting will be here, and then we'll both be dead. You hear me?"

I bit his chest muscle hard enough to feel the skin give beneath his sweater and he swore, letting go just long enough to shake me hard. "You can't help them! Damn it, Allie, d'you hear me? If you want to protect your brother you need to get the bloody hell out of here. They'll leave him be if you're not here."

All the strength left my muscles as I was crushed under the realization that my existence had caused the death of my entire family. The sound of splintering wood echoed up the stairwell. Ronan stiffened. Someone was kicking in the front door. He pulled me hard against his chest again and wrapped both arms around my waist, lifting me off my feet and pressing his cheek against mine.

"Think of Avalon," he said through his teeth.

I tried. I couldn't stop seeing the smear of flour across my mother's brow. Ronan had begun to hum, and I felt the vibration of it, but I couldn't match him. I knew what to do, but my body wasn't responding to me anymore, and I couldn't force my mind into any semblance of order because there was nothing there to grab onto.

Thudding footsteps vibrated in the floorboards as muffled voices moved about in the dining room. I held my breath, terrified that I would hear another gunshot. Ronan was shaking in earnest now, hard enough to make my teeth rattle. I closed my eyes and repeated, Avalon, Avalon, Avalon, but all I could see was the blood that stained my mom's shirt.

Ronan was close to Walking; as his frequency began to shift from harmony with my own plane to harmony with Avalon, I knew that he would Walk without me and tear my body apart as he left. My skin felt as if it was being pulled inside out. I had the incredible sensation that I was suddenly moving in every direction at once; backward, forward, up and down, inside and outside, my cells screaming at me as they tried to fly apart. The pain was amazing.

Focus, I screamed inside my head as sirens began to wail in the distance. I tried to see the castle, the countryside, the field of butterfly flowers, but nothing was happening. Terror, pain, and grief wrenched through my gut.

There were footsteps on the stairs.

Stars started to pop at the outside of my vision, and my hands went numb.

I heard and then felt both of my shoulders dislocate.

Ronan would leave, and my entire family would die in this house. The killers would find my body ripped to pieces on the floor of my old bedroom...if there was anything left to find.

Heat began to roll off Ronan in wave after wave, coming faster and washing over me in a frantic rhythm as the energy of Walking infused his cells and began to pull him out of my verse and into another.

He was leaving, and it was killing me.

"Ronan," I whimpered.

Ronan growled, bent his head, and kissed me as the world went dark.

Chapter Twenty-Two

W hen I first began to take notice of things again, there was only grief. It was heavy and cold, and it killed every other feeling, including curiosity. I didn't ask how I had managed to make the journey, or how someone had found Ronan and me, both unconscious, in the field above the valley.

I didn't care.

When they'd set my shoulders and secured my arms in slings, I didn't make a sound because, while I felt the pain, it didn't seem to matter to me that it hurt. I didn't care that Ronan had left almost as soon as they'd found us and revived him, and I didn't care that he'd been gone three days.

The entire world consisted of four grey stone walls and a window into the courtyard. Sunlight and shadow moved across the frozen grass as if timed to music that I couldn't hear. The sun crossed the lawn and crawled up the opposite wall, picking out every stone as if they were drawn in ink.

Someone came in to feed me since I couldn't yet lift my arms, but I rarely ate.

I slept.

I woke.

I slept.

I was lying in bed with the blankets cocooned around me when Abasi walked in. He stopped in the doorway and looked at the room with his full lips pinched into a thin line above his goatee.

"When did you last bathe, my dear?" He didn't seem to expect an answer, just turned and closed the door behind himself before pulling out the desk chair by my window. It squeaked beneath his weight.

"It's been five days. You cannot stay in here forever, child. Would you honor the memory of your family by wasting away?"

I flinched and closed my eyes against the disarming kindness in his dark eyes.

"I don't want to be alive," I whispered. My voice was dry and raspy with disuse.

"But you are. You are alive. You are alive and starving yourself will not do. Who is there to right this wrong if not you? Who will survive your family name if not you? Would you grieve the spirit of your mother by killing her child?"

Mention of my mother sent a cold shaft of aching across my chest, and my vision began to swim. *I don't deserve to be alive,* I wanted to say. My dad. My mom...it was all my fault. And Ben—my thoughts died when I pictured him sliding off his chair with vacant eyes rolling back into his head. I squeezed my eyes shut and let the tears roll down my cheeks. I hadn't been strong enough to save any of the people I loved. Instead, I had run—the only one left alive. Again.

Abasi said other things, but finally retreated with a heavy sigh and bowed shoulders when I refused to respond. I pushed my face into my pillow and pulled the blankets up over my head, letting sleep pull me under.

"Ben is all right, Allison."

I jerked upright with a thundering heart. Blankets were tangled around me, and I fought for a few panicked moments to free myself and turn toward the voice I knew so well. The hope that had sprung up in my chest at his half-heard words was almost as sharp as the grief had been.

Ronan stood next to the desk with his arms folded over his chest, dark hair curling over his forehead. His face was blank, and his eyes were distant above a few days-worth of beard growth. He looked more like a stranger now than he had on the night we'd met.

"What?" I asked breathlessly with both hands clenched in the blankets to control their shaking.

"Ben is in the hospital, but he's going to be okay. The paramedics pumped his stomach. He'll recover."

I closed my eyes and let the relief pour through me. I couldn't stop a strangled cry from escaping so I covered my face with both hands and shook with wracking sobs until it felt like the force of it would crush my lungs. When the sobbing began to die out, I was weak and as tired as if I had run a marathon.

Ronan was gone.

I retreated again to the meager comfort of my bed.

The next morning brought Ronan back to my room.

"You're going to start training today," he said with no preamble.

I looked at him dumbly.

"You need to learn how to protect yourself."

"But Ben," I began, but Ronan cut me off with a sharp gesture.

"You're not going home until you can protect yourself."

The tone of his voice was flat and authoritative, which made my hackles rise immediately. His jaw clenched and both hands curled into fists when he saw the defiance in my face, but he closed his eyes and took a deep breath. When he opened them, the stranger was gone and the Ronan I'd come to know was standing before me. There was something else, something I couldn't place, in his expression.

"Look, Allie," he began, but this time I cut him off. I had a feeling I didn't want to know whatever he was trying to tell me.

"Where did you go?" I asked.

He opened his mouth, closed it, and looked at me hard. Finally, seeming to come to some decision, he said, "I went back to your mom's house. I went to Ben's apartment. I tried to find Trisha's place. I went to the hospital."

"Why?" I was dumbfounded. I knew that Ronan was a cop or, at least, what amounted to one, but I hadn't stopped to think about what he did outside of tackling college students in hospital parking lots and some vague idea about hunting down smugglers who tried to take magic swords into other worlds. He pulled out my chair and sank into it, rubbing the back of his neck. There were dark olive smudges beneath his eyes and lines etched into the corners of his mouth that hadn't been there before.

"I needed to check Trisha's cell phone. That's why I left you so quickly. I took a glance at it before we Walked, but it was locked, and I didn't have a lot of time to get you out of there. I couldn't chance Walking with it, because sometimes the shift short-circuits delicate technology. I didn't find anything that would help me figure out who she had been working for. When I got back, her body was already gone," he looked at me with wary eyes, "so was your mom's."

I bit my lips. "I can't leave him alone, Ronan. What if they find him? What if..." my throat constricted at the thought of what might happen to my brother if whoever wanted me dead found out that my brother was still alive. Would they find him and torture him to find out where I was? Would they use him to get to me or kill him, outright? I shied away from that mental image and asked instead, "Does he know?"

"He most likely knows only what the cops have told him."

"Which is?"

"That your mother is missing, that her blood was on the table, and that foul play is suspected, but they can't confirm anything because they can't find the body. Or Trisha. Or us."

"He must feel so alone. Ronan, I can't just leave him like that, not knowing. I can't."

Ronan stood and walked to the bed, grabbing my upper arms in both hands and bringing his face inches from mine. There was no tenderness in his eyes, only firm resolve and hard practicality.

"Allison, if you try to Walk right now, while you're grieving, there's a good chance you'll hurt yourself, if not worse. You don't have the experience to master yourself. I almost killed you bringing you here."

I remembered the agonizing feeling that my cells were trying to fly in a dozen different directions at once, the sudden wrench of my shoulders dislocating, and me trying desperately to bring myself into harmony with Avalon but not being able to make my body obey. I'd been sure I would die.

"Is that why you were so weak, after getting shot? I thought it was the bullet wound, but you said—"

"Yes. Walking is dangerous when you don't do it with a clear head. Being wounded like that made it harder, so the trip affected me more than usual. But to Walk with the grief and shock, you were experiencing; well that made the trip almost impossible."

He said almost, and I had a sudden, startling memory of his kiss. I didn't realize I'd touched my lips with my fingertips until I looked up and saw his blue eyes fixed on my mouth, inches away, the dark indigo of his iris shattered with fragments of icy blue that splintered out from the middle like a starburst.

"It was the only way I could think of to bring your body into harmony with mine," he said, his voice remote.

I nodded, mutely, and tried to swallow to bring moisture back to my suddenly dry mouth. "But, Ben. I can't—"

He cut me off again, with a shake of my shoulders, "Damn it, Allie! Can you not listen to a bleedin' word I say!? I'll make sure that he's somewhere safe, all right, if you promise me that you won't walk until I tell you it's safe."

I hesitated, and his grip tightened, his eyes boring into mine. "How will Ben feel if you die, too? Promise me," he demanded.

"I promise." He looked at me for a long moment and then nodded once, let go of my shoulders, and walked out of the room.

CHAPTER TWENTY-THREE

Molfus stood with sunshine gleaming on his dark head, and his meaty forearms crossed over an impressive expanse of hairy chest, a smile wide beneath his beard. There were ten or so groups of partners sparring in the practice field, some with weapons like swords and knives, others with weapons whose use I couldn't even guess at, and still others engaged in hand to hand combat. They were tossing each other around, grappling, and performing acrobatics that made Olympic gymnasts look lazy.

I took in the scene, which looked more like something out of a D-rated action flick than real life, and gave the dark-haired man an incredulous raise of my brows. His amused chuckle sounded like someone had hit an empty whiskey barrel with a rubber sledgehammer.

"Don't be worrying, kishma, you will be learning."

"Kishma?"

"Yes, it is Molradiam. It is meaning little fox."

"I suppose I'll take that as a compliment. Molradiam, where is that?"

"In True Earth, it would being all of Eastern Europe."

"Wow. That's a lot of ground. So, what is the name of your... realm?" I made an inarticulate gesture, "or your verse?"

"Yurth."

He pronounced it like, 'your-the.' I chuckled. "Yurth, eh? That's...unique."

Apparently, Yurthlings had a strong grasp of sarcasm because he caught mine easily and lowered his caterpillar brows at me. "Not all realms are being so different, you know. Most are even calling their verse Earth."

I shrugged, abashed. I hadn't wanted to be here. I wanted to be with Ben. I wanted to be spending my time trying to figure out why someone would want me dead, not learning how to fight. It didn't seem to matter how many times I searched through my past; I couldn't figure out what I'd done to make myself a target. Knowing that I was a danger to my friends and family made me want to snatch them up and hide them away somewhere.

The logical part of my mind knew that Ronan was right, though. After all, they tell you in airplane safety briefings that you should put on your own oxygen mask before trying to help someone else, but the emotional side of my brain didn't care what the logical side had to say. I wasn't happy about my promise to Ronan. In fact, the temptation to break my word and go home was so strong that keeping my sarcasm from turning into a weapon was making me so tense that I wanted to bite people. There was no reason to take that out on Molfus, though.

"I'm sorry."

He waved it off and turned, motioning for me to follow.

"This life, it is taking some getting used to. Come, we will getting you ready for your first day. This way."

As we walked toward the edge of the practice field and presumably toward the armory, I asked him something that had been niggling me. "How is it you speak English? I mean, with so many different worlds how is it that everyone I've met so far speaks English?"

Granted, some of it was with strange accents, peppered with words I didn't recognize or intonations that were completely foreign, but it was still discernable.

"You can thanking Arthur for that. There are other—what is the word—bases?" he looked at me for confirmation, and I nodded. "Other Bases of Walkers in other verses and they are speaking many other languages. But here, it is English. This is why Ronan is bringing you here and not to another place."

"King Arthur," I clarified.

Molfus laughed, "Don't let him hearing you call him that. He hasn't being a King since he is leaving True Earth."

"But that's who he was, right?"

"Yes, he is being the man from your legends. And it is not just True Earth that is telling stories of him."

We passed out of the sunlight of the training grounds and into the Bastion itself. The building was a fortress-like structure at the rear of the main castle of Avalon, with high walls, turrets, and other impedimenta of defense. A paper that had been delivered along with my lunch gave instructions on where to meet Molfus, and I hadn't had any trouble finding the place. The air inside was cool and dry and, while the construction was much the same as the main castle building, the Bastion was obviously militant. The furnishings were bare and utilitarian, though well-made and still pleasing to the eye. Molfus gave instructions to a teenage girl, who began strapping me into a kind of padded cotton vest when I tried to pick up our conversation.

"So, Arthur—why did he leave Earth? Was he killed like the story says or what? And how did he come to be the leader of the Concilium?"

Molfus had pulled a slightly bruised apple out of heaven knew where followed by a long-bladed knife from a sheath on his thigh, and was leaning against the wall peeling slices from the fruit and watching the progress of my outfitting with mischief in his eyes. "The stories are not being so far off, the ones that I am hearing. The Merlin is bringing him here, and the Lady is healing him."

"Merlin?" My voice was a couple of octaves too high, but I didn't bother to try and hide my incredulity, "are you kidding me?"

"Merlin was being from Avalon, and a wise man. There was being a prophecy, you see."

"Ahh, yes. A prophecy. Naturally."

Molfus ignored me and continued, "And the Merlin must be following it. He is training Arthur to be using his powers."

"What about this lady? Who is she?"

The teenage girl, who had to be maybe fourteen, stopped strapping a protective guard to my shin and looked up at me with surprised brown eyes. "The Blue Lady," she said it slowly and raised her voice at the end like a question, as if she couldn't quite believe anyone could be so ignorant. I gave her a quelling look out of the corner of my eyes, and she fastened another strap around my calf.

"It is she who is giving Arthur the sword," the big man explained, "but too many men...shehlany. Bah, what is being the name for the word when a man is wanting something that is not his own?"

"Jealous?"

He shook his head. "No, this is not being the word."

"Coveting?"

"Yes! Yes, too many men were coveting the power of the sword. It could conquering entire continents, maybe even worlds."

The girl was thumping and jerking on the shin guard, making sure it would stay in place, and my stomach started to knot up as I wondered what I was about to do that would require so much padding. I replayed our conversation to distract myself, and it hit me.

"You're talking about the Lady of the Lake! Wait a minute, are you saying that Excalibur is a real sword? Magical, I mean?"

"I do not know if magical is being the right word. It was forging by the Old Ones, who were having great knowledge and skill that is lost to the worlds for many ages. The sword is bonding with its bearer. It is giving the skill and knowledge of every bearer that is holding it, and it will never be breaking or needing sharpening. Armor cannot standing before it. Arthur was seeing the danger such a weapon could being in the hands of men who hungers for power. So, that is being the first law when Arthur is making the Concilium; that no weapon should be being brought from one realm into another. It was for the sword that Mordred was trying to kill his father."

I ran my mind back over all the stories I'd ever heard or read of King Arthur and what I'd studied for my classes as I tried to adjust to my new reality when another thought struck me like a bolt of lightning. "Molfus...the earliest stories I've heard of about King Arthur are from the fifth century. That would make him over 1500 years old."

Molfus scratched at his beard and rolled his eyes upward in thought. "I suppose he is being that."

I choked. He said it as if a person living 1500 years was no big deal and only a matter of calculation.

"But, that can't be," I sputtered, "I mean how can that happen? People don't live that long."

The Master at Arms held up one sausage-shaped finger and said calmly, "Most people are not living that long. Some people are."

"Walkers?"

"Some of them."

All the blood rushed from my head as a wave of dizzy relief swept over me. For a few terrifying moments, eternity had stretched out into a dark, unknowable abyss that threatened to swallow up everyone and everything I loved while I watched. If only some Walkers suffered that fate, then I was probably safe.

"You scared me for a second there," I admitted with my hand on my chest as if I could calm my racing heart just by holding it down.

"Why should it be scaring you that Walkers are living long?"

My heart skipped a beat and then redoubled. "What do you mean living long? Are all Walkers long livers?"

Molfus threw his meaty hands into the air. "Is Ronan teaching you nothing? What has he been doing these last weeks?"

"Mostly keeping me alive," I admitted.

Molfus stopped pacing and eyed me from underneath his bushy black brows with obvious frustration, folding his arms over his chest. "You are being told how you are Walking between this verse and another?"

I'd begun to think of Molfus as a kind of big, jolly teddy bear but seeing him now, only very slightly irritated, reminded me that this was the Master at Arms of Avalon, the man who oversaw training of the Venatore. I was suitably intimidated, even though I could tell his frustration wasn't aimed at me. I simply nodded.

"Alright then, you are knowing that a Walker is having the power to change how their own atoms vibrate. If you are being able to make this kind of changes inside your body, what other changes are being possible?"

One of my dad's good friends had back surgery when I was younger, and my mother had cooked him several days' worth of dinners for reheating when he got home from the hospital. I remembered the day we brought the dinners to his house and Frank had asked my dad to help him put on a strange belt. The belt was wide at the back and narrow in front, with cords coming out of one side that hooked into a little machine. He'd said that it was called "vibration therapy" and that there were elements in the belt that would vibrate at a frequency that sped up the healing process. Supposedly, it was going to help his bones heal faster. I hadn't thought about that in ages, but it came back to me forcefully now.

"Are you saying that some Walkers can train their minds to make their atoms vibrate in ways that can heal their bodies? Is that how they live so long?"

"This may be, though not all are being able to learn such a thing. For some, it is being part of their race to be long-lived. On True Earth, you are calling them demigods, but this is not so. As a man is living longer than a fly, so some races are living longer than others."

He shrugged his massive shoulders as he said it, and I was glad to see that the frustration had left his face. Both my parents were regular old humans, and I had no interest in eternity, so my mind was settled on that count; I wouldn't be living forever, thank goodness. But if I could train my mind to assist in healing my body, then maybe I could at least protect myself a bit better while I hunted for whoever was trying to kill me.

If I survived, then it would be nice never to have to suffer through a sprained ankle or broken arm. My mind immediately started to speculate on just how much I could control if I could train my mind well enough. Never another runny nose! That would be fantastic. I hated having mucus stream out of my face. My speculations were short-lived because the girl had just tightened the final strap on my padded armor and held up two padded gloves with a smug little smile.

"You'll want these," she said.

Training at the Bastion proved rather more specialized than I had guessed. Molfus led me down a corridor and into a circular room with nothing but a horn cup sitting in the center of a low table. The liquid inside was the color of whiskey or apple cider but more viscous, almost like honey.

"Ambrosia plant nectar. You will be drinking it every morning during your training. It is being very difficult to harvest, so do not be wasting any."

A faintly sweet smell rose from the cup, and I took a cautious sip. It was sweet, but only slightly, and had a bite that reminded me of dry wine. It was also thick and rather like trying to drink syrup. Molfus gave me a pointed look. *Bottoms up*, I thought resignedly, and sucked as much as poured the rest of the liquid from the cup.

Warmth began to spread through my body, and my muscles started to tingle in the way they do when your foot falls asleep, only without the little stabs of almost-pain. I opened my mouth, but Molfus cut me off before I could speak.

"Yes, this is being normal. Come."

As we headed back toward the training grounds, I felt as if I was moving through water, pushing myself forward, having to expend more than normal effort to move, but my mind was racing as if I'd just downed caffeine pills. I could feel every sensation that I normally ignored as background noise; the slide of my joints in their sockets, the pull and stretch of my leg muscles, the subtle shift of my hips as I transferred the weight from one leg to the other, and even the smooth way my ribs expanded as I breathed. I wasn't doing anything more than walking, but my mind was able to pick out and analyze every motion of my body without shifting focus away from following Molfus or taking note of what was around me.

"What is this stuff doing to me?"

"Heightening your connection to your body. It is increasing your muscle memories so training will be taking you less time to perfect."

I whistled, impressed. "So I could be a black belt in a couple of weeks? Because that would be amazing."

Molfus looked over his shoulder at me and said, "I am not knowing this word."

"Um, it's like an expert or a master."

"Ha!" Molfus stopped walking to laugh at me. Partners who had been sparring in the training field stilled and stared in our direction. My face went up in flames. "Miss Chapter, no one is mastering anything in so short a time. If you can be walking without limping in two weeks, I will be shaving my beard."

That sounded ominous.

CHAPTER TWENTY-FOUR

D anet reached down and hauled me to my feet for what felt like the hundredth time.

"Didn't I tell you not to cross your feet when you move?"

I grunted and lurched upward. Danet was taller than me by about two inches, but she outweighed me by a good twenty pounds of pure muscle. She wasn't bulky necessarily, but corded and hard, with broad shoulders and long legs. She was one of the few instructors without a current pupil, and she had the bonus of knowing what it was like to be a woman fighting against men. It had taken me a while to ignore the fact that her skin had a distinct blue tint.

"When your base is a-wrong, you have no roots," she said with a sideways kick to the outside of my right foot, "you see? But when your base is a-strong," she illustrated by slapping her thighs, "not even a great wind can push you down. Come, again."

We fought until my muscles began to give out, then she made me run two miles. It was the worst two miles of my life. I fell into bed without eating and was asleep instantly. That set the tone for the next week.

I woke up early, drank my Ambrosia nectar, ate, ran, fought in the training grounds, ran, ate and slept. Danet was a patient teacher but almost entirely without pity. I was only learning the beginning stages of unarmed combat, but I was covered in bruises and sporting a fantastic black eye. Despite the discomfort, I threw myself into the training with the wild abandon I had previously reserved only for good food and drunk karaoke. When I trained, I had no time to think about anything other than the split second I had to act within; no time to think about mom, about Ben, or that I was so far behind in my classes now there would be no hope to rescue the semester. It was also likely I'd already been fired from my job, so there was that to worry about as well, not to mention how concerned Rayne and Mateo must be.

I only had a brief time to worry while I was stuffing food into my mouth and, even then, I was so exhausted that I could only give my real life a cursory glance before sleep claimed me. I discovered that Ambrosia nectar did exactly what Molfus claimed it would and, after only two weeks, the motions of basic hand to hand combat had become very natural to me. I was no more beginning to think my way through a move than my body was in smooth motion, as if I'd been practicing for years. Of course, being able to throw a beautiful right hook didn't mean that I had good timing or even a solid grasp of when to use my newly found skill. I was still hesitant to get hit and wary of actively trying to hurt anyone, so I was constantly getting scolded.

"Toollah, you could have struck me three times if you didn't hesitate! My blows will not kill you. Look at you. You are a-young and strong; you will heal."

One time, when I'd pulled a punch and thrown myself completely off balance, Danet had gone off on a cursing fit in her own language, cheeks flushed an intriguing purple, her capable hands waving wildly. I'd had the urge to drop my head and dig the toe of my shoe into the ground. At that point, I'd only been training for a week. I'd never been in a fight, apart from Officer O'Goll, and that experience was the last thing I wanted to think about. The urge to rescue my pride, to prove that I could be good at this, had warred with my desire to get my training over with so I could get home and, as a result, I'd said nothing, and my training had continued with me suitably chastised.

Now, I was standing before her fury again, having hesitated with a kick that would have knocked her backward, and she was railing at me in two or three languages. Once she had let off enough steam, she looked at me with her head bowed in exasperation and demanded, "What will I have to do to see you motivated?"

"I am motivated!" I huffed, "I've been training from the time I wake up until the time I fall asleep, Danet. I don't know what else you want me to do."

"I want you to care!" she pushed my chest with both hands, "For someone gifted so greatly by nature, you have no fire. All the fire is in your hair, but there is none in your fighting."

I fingered my yellowing black eye and said, "Yeah, well there's enough in yours for both of us." She didn't detect my sarcasm. I couldn't explain the real reason I wasn't gung-ho to attack her because I knew telling her, 'I'm only here long enough to learn how to protect myself, so I can go home' would not go over well.

Danet turned suddenly and began walking off the training field and ordered, "Come," over her shoulder.

I rolled my eyes and followed.

The sounds of combat faded into the distance as we left the high walls of the Bastion behind us and climbed the grassy foothills between the castle and the mountains. Despite the clear sky, the air was crisp with the promise of snow, stinging my cheeks and bare arms, but the sun was warm on my back, and the smell of grass made me realize how much I'd grown accustomed to the scent of body odor and leather.

I drew deeply of the smell, held it until my lungs began to tingle, and let it out slowly. Danet turned and sat on the grass, then motioned for me to do the same. Her dark blonde hair, so striking against the pale blue of her skin, hung in a plat over her shoulder and she began to pull the braid apart with deft motions. "My family was killed by a raiding warlord when I was a-fifteen," she said. Her voice was low and melodious, unconcerned as if she was repeating a memory so well worn by use that its edges were too dull to cut. "My father was a farmer with large fields and many servants, wealthy by the standards of our village. I was-a very happy. There was no warning. One morning, before the sun rose, we heard the thunder of an army. They set fire to the house with us inside. My mother took my baby brother and ran out the front door, and they shot her when she got clear from the smoke. She was pregnant, and they had no use for her.

They were going to try to take my father, to force him to fight for them, but he was so enraged by my mother's death that he attacked them, and they cut him down. I did not have enough strength to fight, and I was young enough to be trained as a slave, so they took me away as my home burned."

I tried to swallow past the lump in my throat, wondering if I should say something to her or put my hand on her shoulder for comfort, but her eyes looked so far away that I was half afraid a touch would break the spell. Instead, I hugged my knees tight to my chest and tried not to picture Danet as she must have been that evening, dragged away crying while her former life disappeared in a cloud of smoke.

"I was in camp for three weeks. I was still untouched, and the warlord wanted to take my woman's flower before he turned me over to the trainers. I attacked him there, in his a-tent. He was not expecting such rage from a young girl, I think. I scared him so badly that he Walked, right before my eyes. I had my hands around his throat when he did it, and I felt it happen. That's when I knew I could follow him."

She was silent for so long that I began to wonder if I should say something, but what could I say? There were no words that could make up for a loss like that. 'I'm sorry,' sounded trite even in my own mind. Danet cleared her throat and looked at me with unflinching eyes.

"When the Venatore found me, I swore I would become able to stop men like the warlord; that I would find him, and give him a-justice for my family. There are other men and women like the warlord, ones that use this great gift in ways that shame the Shining One. I will find those who abuse this gift, and I will stop them. I know why I fight, Toollah. You must discover why you fight."

I thought of my father, of Ben, and my mom. Of course, I thought of Rayne and Mateo and what they must be going through, hearing of my mother's murder and my disappearance with no idea where I was or what happened to me. Was Ben out of the hospital yet? My mind started racing with all the pain and turmoil caused by this mystery person, whoever wanted me dead. The same fury I had felt in the clearing after Officer O'Goll had attacked me came roaring back to life, burning away the last of my grief and replacing it with a fierce determination that solidified into iron resolve still red-hot from the forge and burning in my chest.

"Did you give him justice?" I asked.

Danet's smile was as sharp as the blade of a knife.

Training was easier after that. I'm sure some of that was due to my muscles beginning to harden and my endurance building up, but Danet said that the Ambrosia nectar also increased the body's ability to repair itself. I gathered that it was rather like steroids and vaguely hoped that I wouldn't start growing chest hair.

She still scolded me for not attacking with as much fervor as I should and warned me that I would get myself hurt for holding back when I should be driving forward, but attacking her with all my might remained difficult for me. I couldn't compartmentalize the Danet who was my teacher from the Danet I must try to beat to a bloody pulp. Knowing why she had become Venatore didn't make the thought of hurting her any more palatable.

After another week, I was landing some solid blows, even surprising her sometimes, and doing a much better job defending myself. The black eye had faded, and though I landed on the ground more often than not, I was starting to feel more capable. I had just been congratulating myself for smoothly taking Danet down and extricating myself before she could catch me in a painful joint lock when a familiar voice froze me.

"How's she doing, then?"

Danet grunted as she stood to brush the grass and dirt off her hip, and said, "Well enough. She has a-promise as a technician, but no killer instincts."

Ronan made a noise in the back of his throat that was a kind of vocal shrug and said, "That's about what I expected. Can she protect herself well enough to be on her own for a few days?"

Up until this point, Ronan had been speaking from behind me, and I had stood with my back to him, stiff as a board, fists clenched at my sides. I turned to face him and let my eyes roam slowly and purposefully over his body. Despite looking drawn and tired, with his hair unkempt and the line of his mouth drawn down, the muscles of his torso were easily visible beneath a black t-shirt, and far too distracting. His eyes were unreadable, but a subtle flush crept up his neck at my blatant scrutiny, and the scornful little sneer that I knew was on my lips. I was too angry to care, and I didn't bother to hide it from my eyes, either.

"Would you care to find out how well I can protect myself?" I asked through my teeth.

Danet laughed at the startled expression on Ronan's face but stopped when she saw my eyes.

"Ronan is not the right person to test your new skills on, Toollah. You are no match for him."

Ronan had the mask on, his face completely unreadable, and that made me even more furious.

"I understand if you'd rather not. We wouldn't want to hurt your pride, would we? Though, it is part of your duty to help train new Walkers, and you always do your duty, don't you?"

The flush was now up to his high cheekbones and irritation began to gleam in his eyes. "Indeed, lass," he said quietly, "I do."

Danet had said nothing during this exchange, but now she stepped forward and put her hand on Ronan's forearm. "I have-a never seen her this angry. We have not trained for fighting during strong emotion yet, Brooagah. She may not have control."

Ronan shrugged and said confidently, "Don't worry, Danet. I won't let her hurt herself."

"I am-a more worried that she will try to hurt you."

"Ronan's a big strong man," I said with a cold little smile, "he can take care of himself, can't you boyo?"

His jaw muscle clenched, and he dropped his jacket, stepping forward toward the edge of the practice green Danet and I had been using to spar. I'd seen Ronan fight before, even if only briefly, and I recognized the change in the way he moved; from casual athletic grace to predatory stalking. I bared my teeth.

"If this is what ye're after, little girl," he said in a tone of blatant condescension, "I'm more'n happy to see that you get it."

I attacked.

The combination of strikes to the body and face that I had been practicing with Danet came quickly and smoothly, but Ronan was fast and either parried or dodged each blow, stepping just enough in either direction that my fists were always an inch short. He almost looked bored, which only stoked the fire in my chest.

I threw a jab with my left, and when his head slid just outside my reach, I leaned back and struck out with my right foot, landing a solid kick to the stomach that forced a surprised grunt from Ronan and a quick reply of strikes that I was only barely able to dodge. The look of boredom was gone from his face, replaced by an expression that I had seen from cats that waited hungrily for their prey to make that singe, fatal misstep.

This time Ronan came in, faster than I was prepared for, with a fluid string of motions that was completely unfamiliar and left me sitting on the ground gasping for air.

"What was that?" I panted, pushing myself to my feet, then crouching again as I brought my hands up.

"Experience," he said, then smiled at me and struck again. This time I was prepared, but the stinging on my backside hadn't made me wary, as it would have done if I was sparring with Danet; it made me angry.

Ronan had left me here for weeks with no word about my brother, no word about who Trisha might have been working for, no idea where he had gone or when he'd be back, and only a promise wrung from me in the grip of grief to keep me from finding out everything my heart was so desperate to know. I came in with a furious combination, landing a solid cross and grunting as he countered with a sharp, short punch to my ribs on my unguarded side. I dropped low and surged upward with my entire body, sinking my fist into his diaphragm and barely avoiding a downward elbow by blocking it with my forearm.

I opened the space between us and tried not to wince as a charlie horse cramped the muscle of my forearm. He wheezed, and I smiled to myself; my blow had been hard enough to affect him. He flung out a kick that I barely blocked with the outside of my leg and then shot in, wrapping his arms around my straight leg and driving me to the ground with this shoulder in my hips.

I bucked and squirmed, trying to push myself backward and away but he was too big, too heavy, and too strong. He was quickly in my guard, with his stomach pressed between my legs and the weight of his upper body driving the air from my lungs. I attacked his kidneys with my heels, lifting my foot and then driving my heel down into his back with all the force I could muster from the ground, but he surged forward, crushing me into the grass again with a huff of forcefully expelled air as he pushed himself farther up, leaving my legs locked around his hips while he smothered me with his wide chest.

I tried short punches to his ribs, but I had no leverage and couldn't hurt him. I knew I couldn't hurt him. Frustration welled up and poured out of my eyes in a hot, angry tide.

"Damn you!" I growled, as he passed my guard and pinned both my legs beneath his own, shifting until he was sitting on my hips. I planted my feet against the ground and tried to rotate my hips, but that only gave him the opportunity to slide his legs underneath my body and lock around my middle, making it harder for me to breathe.

With his chest still pressing me flat, he slid his arms up and fought for my wrists. It was a short fight, no more than fifteen seconds, total. His hands were big enough that he could pin both wrists in one hand. I bucked desperately and garnered enough furious force to spin us both. Ronan let go of my hands to brace himself as we rolled and I swung at his face. Pain exploded up my arm as my fist connected with his cheekbone, and within seconds he had my hands pinned again.

"Arrrrrgh!" I shouted furiously, crying between panting breaths, "damn you, Ronan. You left me," I growled and struggled to free my hands, glaring into his surprised face, "you left me!"

Then all the strength went out of my body, and I collapsed on top of him, limp and crying pathetically, too bewildered by my sudden transformation from fury to despair to care that a circle of onlookers surrounded us. The last few weeks exploded inside my head and leaked out my eyes as pain, and loss, and loneliness forced its way up my throat and tore out in sobbing breaths. Ronan lay stiff beneath me for a moment, then I felt his body relax, and his arms came up to wrap themselves around me.

I heard, as if far away, Danet's voice urging people to get back to whatever they were doing. Ronan shifted and surged to his feet, taking me with him. I buried my face in his shirt and let the pain, frustration, and weeks of worry roll over me like ocean breakers.

CHAPTER TWENTY-FIVE

Ronan hadn't carried me back to my room. For the last fifteen minutes, I'd had no attention to spare for anything other than my own self-pity. Shame seemed more than happy to take its place, though, and the voice inside my head said, *well done, coward. You've attacked the only person who's tried to keep you safe, and now he sees how ungrateful and selfish you really are.*

I was curled on Ronan's lap with his arms around me, one hand cradling my cheek against the warmth of his chest.

He's even trying to comfort you after you did your best to throttle him, my inner voice sneered at me, independent woman, eh? How many times have you broken down in front of him, now?

"Is this your room?" I asked quickly, trying to silence my thoughts.

His voice was low and gravely, vibrating in his chest beneath my cheek. "It is, that."

The room was surprisingly bright, with large windows on two walls looking out over the grassy lawns between the castle and the outer walls. I had been half sure Ronan would live in some dim dungeon room that was as austere as he could often be. Instead, the room was bright and warm in a masculine way, with heavy-looking, angular furniture, and fabrics in shades of beige and grey. It managed to seem almost luxurious despite relatively few furnishings and felt comfortable without being ostentatious. "

It's nice," I allowed, still feeling drained and subdued. My forearm hurt, and that made my eyes begin to mist again.

That's your own fault for picking a fight with him, I reminded myself, you're the one who forced him to spar with you.

My emotions didn't seem to care. It was a reminder of my own piss poor self- control, and the stereotypically feminine side of my personality, a part that I had always half detested as weak, was saying in a pathetic little voice, *he hurt you.*

"Allie," Ronan began and then shifted to pull my legs around so that I was half astride his lap and looking him full in the face. The mask he'd worn during our sparring match was gone, and his eyes were clouded. "I'm sorry I left you."

I shook my head as guilt stabbed at me. "You don't have anything to be sorry for. You still have work to do, and I know teaching me to Walk is only part of your job. I don't have any kind of claim on your time, and you've been generous enough to help me as much as you have."

I took a deep breath and continued, "I'm the one who should be sorry, I didn't have any call to goad you that way. I just feel... half the time I'm angry and the other half I want to break down and cry. I don't know what's wrong with me."

"You're grieving, lass. It's natural. And I do have call to apologize. I did need to leave, but I could have talked to you, told you where I was going and why so that you'd not be left wondering, but I was... well, let's just say I've had my own issues to work though."

He reached down and lifted my chin so that he could see my eyes; so close, the light blue splinters at the center of his irises glittered like stars. "It was selfish and thoughtless, and I've no excuses. Will ye forgive me?"

I nodded, feeling the guilt subside a bit and the knots in my stomach loosen. "Do you forgive me?"

"There's nothing to forgive, lass." I reached up and gently touched the swelling high on his right cheekbone that was just beginning to bruise and raised my brows at him.

The sound of his laughter vibrated through his body to mine. "Alright, maybe a little bit to forgive. That's what happens when you tangle with a vixen; you get bitten. I'll have a good few bruises by tomorrow. Your skill has developed faster than I anticipated."

I smiled. "That's what Danet said."

"She's a bonny fighter. She's handed me my arse more than once, and she's only been at it a quarter of the time. If she compliments you, you can believe it."

"Do you think I've come far enough to go home? I don't know how much more I can take without seeing my brother, without letting Ray know that I'm okay. I'm so far behind in school, and my mom's—"

He put his thumb over my lips, and I stilled, grateful; I didn't want to talk about my mom and funerals in the same sentence. "Hush. I know. And I'm sorry that you've been worried for so long. That's something else I need to apologize for. I meant to tell you straight out as soon as I saw you but watching you spar with Danet—distracted me. Then when you got your hackles up..." He hesitated and went silent.

I assumed he'd finish his thought, but his lips remained pursed. I pulled his hand away by the wrist and shook him, "You're going to make me crazy, what is it?"

"First," he said, letting our hands drop into my lap, "your brother is fully recovered. He's fine and staying with his bandmates in a rented flat north of Seattle. As far as I can tell, there's nothing that ties that place to you."

I closed my eyes and fought back a relieved sob. "Thank you," I whispered.

"The other thing, though. The police still haven't found your mum's body, Allison. According to all the sources, I could check, they've not found any trace of where her body could've been taken...or Trisha's."

"Oh, God."

The room went out of focus, and I held on to Ronan until I felt stable. "But her blood was everywhere," I said, "and Ben was unconscious before anything happened. Trisha is the only one who could have shot Mom but with no body and no gun...holy crap, Ronan," my mind made fast and furious connections, "is it even safe for me to go home? They've got to consider me as a suspect since no one else was there. I mean, my fingerprints would be on my plate and glass, maybe ballistics could show that the bullet came from the opposite direction if they had mom's...mom's body. Damn it, how can I go see Ben and Rayne?"

"I'm not sure. I checked every avenue that I could, but I can't find any trace of who Trisha could have been working with. What has me worried is that she got close to Ben before we found you. That means someone must have known about you before the time you Walked. How? And if they did, why did they wait to attack you until after you'd Walked, when you would be harder to kill?"

I shrugged, at a loss. "Ben said that Trisha worked for the club that he was going to perform at in Seattle, right? Maybe we can find out more about her from them if we can talk to Ben and his room- mates. The company she worked for must know something about her. All we have to do is get to their apartment without drawing any notice so Ben can tell us who she worked for."

Ronan nodded thoughtfully and bit his lips together until they flattened out, looking at my hair. I grabbed a lock and felt again the frustration of being so noticeable.

"I could dye it," I suggested.

His eyes flashed to my face, "Don't you dare!"

My insides warmed. Ronan liked my hair.

"What about a hat?" he suggested.

"I could braid it and tuck it up into a beanie, I guess, but what about you? You aren't exactly non-descript."

"Yeah, but I'm better at sneaking than you are. We'll just have to come from different directions and space it out a bit, so we don't arrive together."

Our hands were still joined in my lap, and Ronan had begun making absent-minded circles in my palm with his thumb.

I swallowed and said quickly, "Yeah, if we show up together, it would be a dead giveaway to anyone who was watching. I mean, we could always Walk if we were caught, but I don't think we're allowed to do that in front of normal people."

He hummed in agreement, eyes far away as he considered our next steps. I felt like the entire room was constricting down to our hands and the motion of Ronan's thumb. I tried to pull my mind away and got distracted by the fact that I was still sitting on his lap, my legs across his at an angle, the broad expanse of his chest mere inches from my own. I took a furtive breath to steady myself and let it out slowly, but it didn't help. My hand had started to tingle, and I couldn't keep my mind off it.

Then I noticed that I could actually feel the rush of his blood beneath his skin where he touched me. Confused, I closed my eyes and concentrated on the sensation; the rhythm was steady, pulsing with the ebb and flow of all life, as if his heartbeat was the metronome, and the entire universe a cosmic symphony timed to the steady beating of it. Everything slowed, and a familiar sensation blossomed inside me as I noticed the throb of my own pulse, matching his, and a sense of recognition that drew me toward him like gravity. *I know you,* I thought with a sense of wonder.

Ronan's sudden, short inhale surprised me out of my reverie, and I found him looking at me, wide-eyed with shock. The high, sharp planes of his cheekbones were slightly flushed, and I could see his pulse visibly at the base of his neck. Awareness crackled in the air between us like static electricity. Ronan's eyes dropped to my lips, and his pupils dilated. My lips began to tingle. He let go of my hand and fitted both of his own to my cheeks to cup my face tenderly. The force of his gaze held me riveted.

"Allie," he breathed, shaking his head, "I—"

I kissed him. Without bothering to think, I leaned in and fitted my lips to his slowly and deliberately, letting the smooth skin of his lower lip slide between my own. I wouldn't let either of us write this off as impulsive. I wanted to kiss him, and I meant it. He sat completely still for three heartbeats, and then he was kissing me back, both arms wrapped around my back, pressing me against his chest as if he wanted to absorb me into himself. The gravity had me in its clutches again, and this time I could feel all of him; from his now rapidly beating heart to the song that moved his very atoms in biological dance. Without thinking, I hummed in my chest, making my own frequency a counterpoint to his unique music and feeling the sudden shift in the song as our frequencies fell into harmony with each other.

A shock went through Ronan's big body, and he growled, deepening the kiss until we were locked around one another, his hands tangled in my hair and my arms tight around his neck. Pleasure coiled warm in my chest as the taste and feel of him filled my senses, waking something hot and primitive inside me. Sensing the shift in my body, Ronan pulled back, panting, eyes heavy-lidded.

I felt as if some vital connection had been severed, though my blood was still thrumming. He held me away from himself by my upper arms with shaking hands.

"Allie," he said, then swallowed and closed his eyes, taking a few deep breaths before opening them again, "Allison—"

"You don't have to say anything," I interrupted, "I'm sorry. It's just...I feel like there's something here, Ronan. I don't know how to describe it. It sounds so infantile to say I have a 'crush' on you because," I clenched my hands in the front of his t-shirt as embarrassed heat flooded my cheeks, followed quickly by the sinking fear of rejection that made my mouth feel like it was full of paste.

"Allie," he started to say, but I reached up and covered his mouth with my hand, certain that he was about to let me down gently.

"Whatever I feel," I said, not brave enough to meet his eyes but knowing that I had to speak, "it's more than just simple attraction."

He covered my hand with his own and pulled it slowly away from his mouth, and then lifted my chin, so I had no choice but to look him full in the face. With his other hand, he reached up and slid his fingers into the hair at the nape of my neck and pulled me slowly toward him, his eyes locked on mine. When he kissed me, it was slow and deliberate, and with both eyes open, his lips just as ravishing in their tenderness as they had been in heat, leaving me dizzy when he finally released me.

"Allison, there's something I need to tell you," he said, "I'll still help you, just like I promised to, but if you don't want me...if you don't want me to after this, I can find another Venatore to keep you safe. I'll understand."

My stomach dropped as if I just hit the downward side of a rollercoaster. I slid off his lap and sat next to him on the bed, clasping my hands together. For his sake and for mine, I tried to stay calm so that I didn't jump to conclusions and stamp on whatever had been growing between us, so I just said, "Okay. Tell me."

"I was married once." I held my breath and nodded for him to continue. "Her name was Gráinne. I met her the night of her betrothal feast. She was beautiful, with hair like sunlight and cheeks as round and pink as apples. Her father, the king, had promised her in marriage to the leader of my clan, the greatest warrior of Ireland. Though he was still hale and handsome, he was as old as her father. She was just sixteen and full of fire. She couldn't stomach marrying someone more than twice her age.

She asked me to run away with her to save her from the marriage but my ceannaire—my leader—I loved him well, and I couldn't bear to betray him that way. So, at dinner, she poisoned the mead with a sleeping draft, leaving all but me snoring into their cups. She asked me again, promising to curse me should I refuse and I was drunk enough to believe her. I should have said no."

All this time he'd been looking down at his hands, which were resting on his thighs. They curled into fists, and he looked up with self-loathing drawing the corners of his mouth down. "I should have risked the curse and kept my vows, honored Fionn, my ceannaire. I didn't. I wasn't sure what power Gráinne had but, like a coward, I was more concerned about my life than my honor.

I ran away with her, and we hid in the countryside, moving from place to place, often spending days in pathetic little camps made of twisted branches or in holes in the hillside. Gráinne wanted to be properly married, but I couldn't bring myself to be with her that way. She was meant to marry—well, she wasn't meant to marry me, and my ceannaire hunted us all over the country. At that time, I still had some hope that she would relent and reconcile herself to him. But Gráinne was passionate and willful, so different than I, and so very alive. Emotion would pass across her face like storm clouds one minute, and then she'd be sweet and pliant and as gentle as spring rain the next. One night, after we had been running for almost two years, she came to me, and I gave in. I thought there was no hope for reconciliation after that."

He rolled his left shoulder, almost as if the bullet wound still pained him, and exhaled forcefully through his nose. I could see his jaw muscle clenching and unclenching as he worked over the next part of his story. My hands were clasped so hard in my lap that my knuckles were white from the strain.

"I went to my foster father, finally. I was tired of dragging Gráinne from one hovel to the next, always looking over my shoulder for a spear at my back. Angus is a powerful man, a Walker—I mentioned him to you, remember? He negotiated a truce. We were able to settle down. I built us a home. I thought life would finally move on in peace."

A sense of foreboding warned me that this tale was about to take a turn for the worse. When he didn't speak for a long time, I asked softly, "But it didn't?"

He laughed bitterly and shook his head. "No. No, it didn't. My former clan invited me on a hunt. I had been hoping for a chance to explain, to regain the fellowship lost between us, so I said I would go. We left one morning with spears and bows to hunt boar. Half of us waited, spread out along the foot of a hill and the other half went out to flush the animals toward us.

For a while, it felt just as it had used to; we joked and laughed, and I started to think maybe things could be repaired and I could be forgiven. But the boar that came out of the trees toward me wasn't just fleeing from the noise of hunters hitting their spears against their shields; it was mad. Its mouth was foaming, and its eyes were red and rolling. I can still remember the feeling of its body crashing into my spear. The beast was so huge that the force of it knocked me over and the spear broke off, half-shaft, in its chest. It gored me across the belly before it died."

I swallowed hard and reached out to lay my hand on his leg, less to comfort him than to remind myself that he was alive.

"He left me to die," he said, simply. "He could have healed me, Allie. My ceannaire had the power to heal. Instead, he left me to die by the stream in repayment of my betrayal. The only reason I am alive today is that my foster father Walked me to the monastery in another verse."

I leaned back against the wall and blew a long breath out through pursed lips. Damn. I briefly wondered if there was anyone in this place who didn't have a tragic drama or a horror story in their history. So far, it wasn't looking good.

I couldn't imagine what it must have been like for him, being hunted by a man he'd loved for a sin he was compelled to commit; for the love of a woman. A stab of jealousy interrupted that thought.

I couldn't help but ask, "What happened to your wife?"

He pressed his full lips together between his teeth, then said in a very controlled voice, "She died. A long time ago. Angus said it was grief."

"I'm so sorry, Ronan." His eyes softened a bit but remained wary and tight near the corners.

"I was a traitor, Allison. I betrayed a most sacred vow, stole another man's intended wife, and she died for it. I'm not...a good man, the *right* man for you."

That did it. I leaned forward and stared straight into his eyes. "What choice did you have, Ronan?"

"I could have said no. I should have."

"And what would have happened to you then? What would her curse have done to you?"

"It involved a grisly death," he admitted grudgingly, but then rallied and added, "but death would have been better than betraying my oaths, and a worthy sacrifice to save her life. I acted against everything that I thought made me who I was."

The self-loathing in his voice was enough to make me flinch.

"Would it have been better?" I demanded, unable to bear allowing him to continue. "How many people have you saved since you've been Venatore, Ronan? How many potential disasters have you averted? You may have been happier with a valiant death at the hands of a young girl, but would the Ereverse have been a better place?" He had nothing to say to that and tried to look away, but I put my hands on his face and forced him to look at me.

"If you had died from that curse, I would be dead right now. Tell me I'm wrong."

He shook his head silently once.

"You made a mistake, Ronan. Granted, it was a damn big one, but you know what that means? You're human. Congratulations and welcome to the club. We're all imperfect, here. But I happen to think that you're pretty okay."

Ronan brought his own hands up and covered mine, pressing them to his face for an instant, and then bringing them down onto the blanket between us. "I'm afraid I'm going to hurt you, Allie," he said quietly, "and I don't know what this is between us, but I've never felt anything like it. I think I can feel you sometimes, and when I'm away from you," he floundered for a second, his eyes roving the room as if searching for a word before he gave up and said simply, "there's a hole where you should be, even though we've only known each other a short time. I've tried to ignore it, and after what happened to your family I tried to run away from it because I feared—still fear—that somehow I would hurt you or make things worse. But I couldn't turn it off. I can't. Now I have this feeling that, whatever this is, I'm going to bollocks it up because I don't deserve this kind of connection, not after what I've done."

You beautiful idiot.

"You will," I assured him, "and I probably will, too. We aren't perfect. People hurt each other sometimes, even when they don't mean to. But,"

I said, leaning forward to plant a single kiss on his forehead over the silky brown hair that curled there, "I'm willing to try and make whatever this is work. If there is one thing my life has taught me," I hesitated for a second, swallowing back grief, "it's that none of us are promised tomorrow. If we wait until we're perfect to believe we deserve love, it will never happen. I don't expect you to be perfect, but I know how to forgive. I'm nowhere near perfection, but if you think you can forgive me when I mess up, maybe we can make this work..."

He sat completely still, eyeing me with a heart-wrenching mixture of fear and hope in his eyes that was all the more affecting because I'd never seen him fully vulnerable. I had begun to think that he was lowering his mask around me but, until this moment, I had not seen him entirely as he was, with no defenses.

His hand was warm and solid against my cheek, the callus on his thumb slightly rough as he rubbed it over my lips.

"I can do that," he said quietly. "I can do that."

CHAPTER TWENTY-SIX

E verett wasn't a large city, but kind of a sprawling extension of the greater Seattle Metropolitan area that was far enough away to maintain the feeling of a smaller town but close enough to have big-city ambitions.

"I wonder why they're staying up here," I asked Ronan as I climbed out of the cab half a mile from the apartment building Ben was leasing.

"Dunno," he said as his eyes scanned the tree-lined streets. We'd walked from Avalon that morning and ended up just outside of Everett. I was pleased to note that my body seemed to be handling the trip better each time, and this time around I only felt queasy, weak-kneed, and very thirsty. This was the first time we had Walked back to True Earth in an area not close to my apartment, which was something I had noticed and remarked on. I had asked him why we always seemed to Walk *to* the same places while we could walk *from* almost anywhere.

"It's always the clearing on the hill when we walk to Avalon," I had said to him, "and always just outside my apartment building when we walk to True Earth, except for this time. Can't we just show up wherever we want? Why go to all the trouble of calling a cab and everything instead of just popping up outside the apartment building?"

"There are a few reasons for that," he'd explained, "one is that it's safer for us to get close to Ben's apartment by traditional means. The last thing we want to do is pop into existence in front of someone on the lookout for Walkers."

I had nodded at that, feeling foolish. If I was going to survive, I'd have to pay closer attention to details like that.

"Another reason," he continued, "is that it's always easier to walk to places you're familiar with because you've already established harmony with that frequency. I'd already traced Ben here while you were training. But if you've never been somewhere...imagine trying to Walk yourself to Paris, or Hong Kong."

"I wouldn't know where to start," I had admitted.

"If you had to do it, what would you try?"

"I suppose I'd try to make a mental picture of the city."

"Describe it. Try Paris."

We had been walking down a sidewalk in a neighborhood on the outskirts of Everett, so I stopped for a moment and leaned against a chain-link fence to give myself time to consider. "I'd think of cobblestone streets, small trees surrounded by those little metal fences, stone buildings, cafés along the street with metal chairs and tables set out...that kind of thing."

"How many places in the world do you imagine that mental vision might fit? I mean, how close might the real Paris be to your mental images of it?"

I had shrugged, "I've never been, but I'd guess it's pretty close."

"Well, you're right that there are places in Paris that do fit that description but also places in Spain and Germany. Not only that," he'd said, sounding like a school teacher who was thoroughly enjoying bursting his student's bubble of ignorance, "but the place you described would be busy, wouldn't it? People eating or drinking coffee, walking to and from work, pushing baby carriages and the like."

I had nodded.

"Well then," he continued, "if you were successful, you'd show up on a busy street right out of the clear blue sky and scare the ever-loving shite out of quite a few regular people."

"I hadn't thought of that," I'd admitted, blanching. "I know. That's why new Walkers need Venatore. Not only can we teach you how to use your ability, but we keep you safe while you do it. More than a few myths and legends got their start with Walkers who were making all their own mistakes. Still do."

"I thought your job was to find new Walkers before that could happen?"

"The Eververse is a big place, Allie. Unimaginably big. We do what we can."

"So, we always Walk to the same places because they're familiar?"

"Partly," he had said with a little back and forth tipping motion of the hand, "but also because it's safer. What if you tried to Walk somewhere that used to be an empty street and ended up in a building, or a dump, or—"

"A battlefield?" I'd interrupted with a cheeky grin.

He smiled. "Not only that, certain places tend to pull more."

"The places of power."

"Indeed. The meadow on the hill is one of those. If you try to Walk too close to the Castle City, the place of power will pull you."

"Why?"

"I'm told it has something to do with lines of magnetic force or something like that. It affects your frequency when you come close to it."

"What if you don't have a choice? What if you have to Walk somewhere you've never been?" "There's a chance that the nearest place of power will pull you since you won't have any reference for how to adjust your frequency, but it's best to be sure you have no other choice because there's no knowing what you're in for. I'd hate to show up in a river on the high side of a waterfall."

"That's a distinctly unpleasant thought."

"Unless you've got a death wish."

"So," I said, ticking off the list on my fingers, "when Walking: stick with places you already know if you can, avoid places where too many people will be, be aware of places of power, and be prepared to show up in dangerous situations if you're going anywhere unknown."

He smiled and chucked me under the chin. "Smart lass. If you must Walk somewhere you've never been, your best bet is to go with someone who has already Walked there."

"Do you have to be touching to go with them?"

"It helps," he'd said, "they'll kind of pull you along. But it's not necessary if you already know where you're going."

"Then why do you hold me when we walk to Avalon and back? I know the way."

He had smiled a slow, wicked smile that made my stomach flip and said, "Because I like the feel of you in my arms."

I shivered, remembering the conversation, and handed our driver a handful of cash through the window. I was so used to reserved, serious Ronan that these sudden bouts of playfulness or flirtation were throwing me off balance.

"Let's go over this one more time," Ronan said as he watched the yellow car drive away. He was wearing nondescript clothing and a beanie that made his bangs curl over the knitted edges near his eyebrows.

"How do you manage to look like a hipster now when most of the time you look more like a vigilante biker?"

His mouth twisted into a crooked grin. "I've a lot of practice blending in. Wait till I take you to some of the other verses. Some of the clothing choices are, ah...interesting. In fact," he eyed me up and down for a second, eyes sparkling with mischief, "I know exactly where I'm taking you once this business is over."

Goosebumps ran up my arms. Since we had admitted to each other whatever it was we had admitted, Ronan had been more open and carefree than I'd seen him. He smiled more, which I was trying to convince myself was not turning me slowly into a middle school girl with a crush.

Get it together, Chapter. "You said we were going to get this over with," I reminded him sternly.

He became businesslike right away. "And so we are. Getting in unnoticed should be simple enough. If you sense anything wrong, or if anyone does or tries anything, I want to you to Walk to Avalon. Okay? Walk right away."

"Fair enough. Though I am feeling pretty froggy," I flexed my muscles for him.

"Just be careful where you leap, little toad. I don't want to see you get hurt. Then again, I still have a black eye, so maybe I shouldn't worry so much."

I cringed at the faint purple bruise seeping beneath the skin of his lid but felt a smile start to tug at the corner of my mouth.

"That'll teach you not to mess with me."

"I've learned my lesson," he promised solemnly.

I snorted, and we started walking.

Paying attention to my surroundings was hard with my mind somewhere else. Now that I knew I was only minutes away from seeing my brother, he was all that I could think about. I was so distracted that I barely noticed when Ronan touched my hand and crossed the street so that he could circle the outside of the building to avoid being seen in my company.

Of course, there was a good chance that no one who was looking for me would connect the girl in the long, flowery skirt, oversized sweater, and slouchy pink hat with Allison Chapter, serial jeans wearer, and despiser of skirts. Ben would certainly be shocked when he saw me. He was going to be shocked no matter what I looked like, though, and fresh guilt settled on my shoulders as I rounded the corner to walk to the entrance of the apartment buildings.

He would have woken up in a hospital—I knew what that was like—only to find out that his mother and his girlfriend had been murdered, and that his sister was missing. All the while, I was safely in Avalon learning how to fight, at least knowing what had happened and knowing that Ben was safe.

I should never have promised Ronan I'd stay away, I thought fiercely, I should have gone back myself to let him know what happened, but I was too much of a coward. Again. Stopping my eyes from filling up with tears as I thought about what he had been through took me a good 10 seconds of looking at the sky and taking long, slow, deep breaths.

The stairs up to the second floor had old carpeting that had been worn threadbare in the center by the passing of thousands of feet. I focused on my surroundings and tried to push from my mind everything that wouldn't help me get through what I was about to do without breaking down into a sobbing, hysterical mess.

230. There was the number.

Muted sounds filtered through the door—*are they playing video games in there?*—as I raised my fist to knock. I wasn't surprised to see my hand shaking.

Knock on the door, I told myself. *Quit thinking so much. Just do it.*

What are you, a Nike commercial?

Shut up.

"Oh man," I whispered, "I'm talking to myself."

I swallowed my anxiety and knocked on the door.

"Allie?" I threw myself into Ben's arms as soon as the door was opened wide enough to let me pass. He caught me with a surprised half muttered, "Wha—" as I slammed into him bodily.

"I'm so glad you're safe," I said into his chest.

He smelled like Doritos and stale cologne.

"What the hell is going on, Al?" It wasn't a question. Ben's roommates made a hasty departure when they saw the nature of what was about to happen. Alvin, Ben's oldest friend in the quartet, gave me a once over, tugged at my crocheted pink slouch beanie, and said, "You look good, Allie," winking at me before walking through the open door and into the hallway.

I tried to gather my thoughts into some form of coherency. After I had tackled Ben, he'd hugged me so hard that my ribs cracked, but I hadn't minded. I felt his heartbeat beneath my cheek and tears of gratitude welled up and spilled, unchecked, down my face. After a moment, he'd stepped back and fixed me with a look that reminded me so much of our dad that I felt more tears sting the backs of my eyelids.

"Allie," Ben warned.

Probably best just to drop the bomb. "Trisha poisoned you and Mom, Ben. You passed out, and she pulled out a handgun. Mom tried to attack her because she—she threatened to cut you with a steak knife if Ronan and I didn't drink the poisoned drinks she gave us."

Ben's hazel eyes turned green, a sure sign of danger.

"Trisha?" he asked, incredulous, "little, ditzy, one-hundred-ten-pound Trisha? Are we talking about the same girl, here? She couldn't hurt a fly, even if she tried. The fly would probably out-think her, anyway."

"It doesn't take a lot of strength to poison someone, Ben, or to pull a trigger."

"That makes no sense. Why would she do something like that?"

"Because she was a psycho?"

Ben growled, "Allison, tell me the truth and tell me now."

"This is going to be hard to believe," I started. He snorted, but I ignored him and said firmly, "but I'm going to tell you the truth, Ben; at least, as much of it as I can."

His jaw muscle clenched, and he nodded once.

I swallowed, trying to work some moisture up in my suddenly dry mouth. "I've been...recruited. It's a secret organization, and I can't tell you much about it because it's kind of dangerous. I think Trisha was an enemy of the organization, and she started dating you to get close to me."

Ben's expression didn't change so much as a fraction of an inch. I started to sweat. I couldn't tell if he was just thinking hard, or if I'd shocked him into silence. The moment dragged on until I thought I might scream just to get him to move or speak.

Finally, he said, "Maybe we should go to the hospital, Al. I know the last couple weeks have been hard, it's understandable—"

"How much do you know about Trisha, Ben?" I interrupted savagely. The last thing I would stand for now was my brother trying to have me committed. One stay in the psychiatric ward was more than enough for me. "Who were her parents? Where does she come from? Did you ever meet any of her friends? Do you know anything about her other than her bra size?"

He opened his mouth, but I kept talking, "I do not have post-traumatic stress disorder, and I'm in my right mind. I saw what happened, and so did Ronan. How do you think I was able to get out of there?"

"How the hell should I know? I can't remember anything, Allie! The last thing I remember is telling Trisha about your birds, and then waking up in a hospital with the cops telling me that you and mom were missing, mom was...is suspected dead, and my girlfriend is nowhere to be found. What am I supposed to believe? I spent the last few weeks thinking that you and mom were both dead!"

He was breathing hard, knuckles white and his eyes bright green with fury. The vein in his forehead was bulging, and corresponding guilt ripped up my insides. "I wanted to see you, Ben, but it wasn't safe. I didn't have any way to protect myself, and I might have put you in more danger if I'd come. Ronan thought—"

"Yeah, there's something right there," Ben interrupted, pointing at me and starting to pace as he built up steam, "all this shit happened when Ronan showed up. How is he connected to all this? What has he done to you, Allie?"

He stopped pacing in front of me and grabbed my elbows in earnest hands, fury softened by brotherly protectiveness. "I can keep you safe, Al. If he's done anything to you, I can get you out of here. Let's go right now; we can go to the police station and file—"

"Dammit!" I exploded, jerking my arms out of his grasp and pushing his chest with both hands. "Ronan is not abusing me, Ben! Why can't you believe what I tell you? Have I ever lied to you before? I've told you a million things I'm ashamed of, why would I lie to you now?" I took a few, steadying breaths and said, much more calmly, "I know it's hard to believe, but it's the truth, Benjamin."

Ben started pacing again, turning away from me to stare out the window. "I thought you were dead, Allie. Now you show up and expect me to believe that some 'secret agency'," he said, making air quotes with his fingers, "which you won't name, recruited a random college student with no prior history, no connections, no experience or athletic talent, to do what?" he turned toward me, "counterterrorism?"

The last was said with such scathing derision that I had to clench my fists to stop myself from slapping him out of his diatribe. Suddenly, an arm was around my neck, and I reacted with instant fury and no thought at all. I grabbed the wrist of the arm in both hands and used my feet to thrust myself back into the body. Ducking under the arm I held, I rotated my hip and twisted, turning my back and hip into a lever that threw my attacker over my shoulder to land in a heap on the carpet.

With a solid grip on the wrist, I twisted his arm into a joint lock that Danet had used on me multiple times and pushed my knee hard into the neck of the man on the floor. I'd realized it was Ronan once his unique scent registered on my senses, but the motion of the throw had already begun. The Ambrosia nectar had done its job well, making my muscles remember the moves Danet taught me as if I'd practiced them for years, rather than weeks.

I let go of his wrist and stood, demanding, "Why the crap would you do that, Ronan?"

Ronan rolled to his feet and rotated his shoulder with a half regretful, half-amused grin on his face. "I'm sorry, lass. But your brother needed to see you in action. Since I know you won't try to knock any sense into him, I figured if he saw your skill at hand-to-hand against me, it might get through his hard head. Reason obviously can't."

I looked from Ronan's face to Ben, who had gone still with one arm raised as if he'd intended to interfere, but he had been across the room, and his back had been turned when Ronan had walked in. He'd turned just in time to see the full attack from start to finish and, judging by his open mouth, clearly didn't know what to think.

"Your sister isn't lying, Chapter. Recruited isn't the best word, though. More like she was accepted. She's currently in training, but we have reason to believe that she already has enemies outside the organization." Ben dropped his arm and took a few steps backward to lean against the wall. His eyes had a stunned vacancy to them that reminded me of the look I'd seen on his face after he and Holly had broken things off so long ago.

The woman in front of him, who had just hip-tossed and joint-locked a man twice her weight, was not connecting in his mind with his smart-mouthed, bookish sister. Sympathy tightened my lips into an unhappy grimace. He probably had fifty-million conflicting thoughts and impressions running through his mind. I stepped close and did my best to wrap my arms around him. He was stiff but didn't push me away.

"I know this is a lot to take in, Ben. You can blame me if it makes you feel better. I had no idea that Trisha was anything other than your girlfriend, and I don't know why she would have wanted to hurt any of us, especially m—" my voice broke, but I pushed through, "especially Mom. But I swear to you, I'm going to find out. The thing is, I can't do very much if you don't help me."

"What do you need from me?" Ben's voice was hoarse, half-strangled, and his shoulders slumped.

I forced the pity aside. We didn't have time for it now, and if—by some slim chance—Mom was alive out there somewhere then the longer we waited...I decided not to think about it.

"I need to know everything you know about Trisha," I said, trying to keep my voice even and assured, "where she worked, where she lived, her family, her friends, everything. The more we know, the better chance we have to find out who she really is and who she was working for."

"Holly came to see me in North Carolina. Did I tell you that?"

"No." That surprised me. The last time Ben had talked about Holly it had sounded as if they both would rather eat nails than see the other.

"I didn't even know she was coming. She must have checked the tour schedule on the website or something. One night, after a show, she was just there. She said that she was wrong, and she wanted to get back together." He shook his head as if surprised himself by the turn of events. Then he grunted and gritted his teeth, breathing in slowly through his nose. Clearly, the memory cost him a lot.

"I know I shouldn't have looked at her phone, but when she fell asleep on the couch...I couldn't help myself." He passed his hands over his eyes, looking much too old for a man in his mid-twenties. "She was still seeing Tyrone. He sent her a bunch of texts asking how her trip to Philadelphia was going and telling her all his plans for when she got back to Seattle. I believed her, and she lied to me. I didn't even confront her, I just left her sleeping and caught the next flight home. The guys were pretty pissed at me."

"I bet."

Ben told me everything he could remember about his relationship with Trisha. He had met her right after leaving Holly and checking into their hotel in Seattle. She had been notified by their agent that the band was in town, and the rest was history. She was the opposite of Holly in every way; short and curvy where Holly was tall and willowy, blonde to Holly's almost black hair, bubbly and simple while Holly was more reserved and articulate. Plus, she was blatantly impressed by him, and it was a balm to his bruised ego. "I guess...well; I suppose I kept her around because she didn't require very much of me. She didn't challenge me. I didn't have to do much to keep her happy. Hell, I didn't even have to think much. It was easy. So, I didn't bother asking any questions because, to be honest, I didn't care."

That made sense. Holly had never let Ben get away with anything, and they had been deeply involved in each other's families. I still missed Holly, but I couldn't forgive her cheating on Ben if that's what she'd done. So, Trisha had been an opportunity, and he'd taken it.

"In all that time you didn't learn anything about her that we can use?"

He shook his head, staring down at the floor.

Ronan uncrossed his ankles and stood up from where he'd been leaning against the arm of the couch. "Well then, looks like the next place to check will be her job. Where did you say she worked, mate?"

"Ah, the venue is called Rue 9. It's in downtown Seattle."

Ronan was looking at Ben with his arms crossed over his chest, but there was sympathy in his gaze. It struck me that Ronan knew, too, what it was to love the wrong woman. I bit my lips.

"That's our next stop, then. I'll give you two a minute to say goodbye," he said.

Ben pushed himself away from the wall and said, "I'm coming with you." I started to protest, but he pinned me to the spot with a furious gaze. "I don't know what happened to mom or if she's even still alive. I'm not going to take the chance of losing you, too."

I was powerless against those words, against the look in his eyes, and Ronan could see it.

He considered for a second and then sighed and told Ben, "I can't promise to protect you. If you go, it's on your own steam."

"I can take care of myself."

"He's not kidding, Ben. I've already been attacked three times since I found out—since I was accepted," I corrected, "once by someone who was working as a police officer. I have no idea what we might be walking into."

His shoulders straightened and his jaw, square and stubborn like Dad's, clenched in a way I knew all too well. "All the more reason for me to be there. Knowing some Jiu-jitsu doesn't make you James Bond, Allie."

"Jane Bond," I corrected.

An unwilling smile curved the corner of his mouth, but it was clear that he'd made up his mind. The little sister half of me, the part that always felt safer when her big brother was there to protect her, was relieved. But the part of me that had been uncovered, who knew there was a lot more to the world than I'd ever realized, felt a wrenching fear for this man that I loved and wouldn't be able to protect.

"Okay," I said to cover my unease, "let's do this."

CHAPTER TWENTY-SEVEN

To say that the car ride was uncomfortable would be the kind of gross understatement that only British comedians can pull off. Ben sat in the back seat like a vulture, looming out from between the front two seats with disapproval rolling off him in waves. My hand was practically tingling with the desire to touch Ronan, but Ben's narrowed eyes and audible nostril-breathing stopped me.

He peppered Ronan with all kinds of questions that Ronan dodged easily and with good humor, but his incredulity made it clear that he didn't believe my story. He was accompanying us for reasons of his own.

"Take a right at the light," Ben instructed from the back. We'd gotten into Seattle with little actual drama, but the tension in the car was straining my nerves to their breaking point.

"You'll never find parking on the street down here," Ben said, pointing, "there's a parking garage on the corner, though, just take this right."

As soon as we pulled into the dark garage, anxiety uncurled in my stomach. An image of Rayne, limp on the pavement in the shadow of a parking garage, flashed through my mind, and goosebumps ran up my arms.

"Steady on, Allie," Ronan said in a low voice as Ben climbed out of the back seat.

I forced a half-smile.

When I walked around the back of the car, Ronan calmly took my hand in his and looked at Ben.

"Lead the way." His voice was low and even, and he completely ignored the storm clouds in Ben's eyes.

Just touching Ronan made me breathe easier, and his relaxed confidence made it hard to worry about Ben's opinion of his little sister being physically intimate with a man he distrusted. In the end, he didn't say anything, just turned and headed toward the exit. I bit my lip.

"Remember, mate, we're trying to fly under the radar here, so I'll be in the room if you need me but finding out about Trisha's past will be up to you. Allison is still technically a missing person, and if we want to keep her safe, we need to keep it that way."

"I'm not going to do anything that would put my sister in danger," Ben replied, managing to sound offended and accusatory all in the same breath.

"Not saying you would," Ronan assured him, "but it's easy to make mistakes when you aren't experienced questioning people. Just do your best to keep the questions related to Trisha. Anything you can find out will help us, but if you can get anyone to tell you how to contact her family or friends, that will give us the most to work with."

Ben stopped and turned to face us, his face calm but set. "What exactly are you hoping to find out? I'm going to go along with the pretense that you're part of some kind of organization or agency or whatever, no matter how stupid that sounds, but I want to know what you're going to do with the information you find."

"The more you know, the more danger it puts you in if someone finds out that you know we're alive."

Ben thrust his chin out and turned his hard eyes on me. "I need to know what I'm doing. You can't just give me vague explanations and hope I'll get what you need. I'm not stupid. I can be of more use if I'm not flying blind. And I'm sure as hell not going to give you information if I don't know what you plan to do with it."

Ronan's hand flexed in mine as he measured my brother. I could tell that he was weighing the need to track Trisha's history against Ben's safety. He was also taking Ben's measure, and I could tell by the expression on my brother's face that he knew it.

"I'm going to use whatever we can find out about Trisha and trace it backward until I find out who she was really working for. If I must go through her family and friends and tear her life apart piece by piece, I'm going to find out who's been trying to kill your sister and I'm going to return the favor."

The two regarded each other for a long moment, Ben with tense shoulders and a set jaw, Ronan with calm confidence. Finally, Ben nodded and led us to the entrance of Rue 9. The brick building was older, complete with crown molding above the entrance and leaded glass in the door. I watched Ben enter with trepidation. It was still an hour or so before the club could expect any business, and I couldn't help but feel how indiscreet we were, standing outside.

Ronan must have been thinking the same thing because he turned toward me with mischief in his eyes and used his wide chest to push me toward the wall of the building, pressing my back against the brick. A delicious shiver ran down my arms as he nuzzled at my neck.

"Now we look like nothing more than two proper lovers in the city," he murmured in my ear as the stubble on his cheek rasped against mine, warm breath stirring the sensitive hairs on my neck. I clung to his shoulders, enjoying the sensation even more because I knew it could only last a moment before we were forced to follow Ben into the building.

"When we get inside, keep your eyes and ears open but stay out of sight," he warned me for the hundredth time, "and if things go badly—"

"Walk to Avalon," I cut him off, "I know. But I can help, Ronan. I know that I'm not fully trained, but if anything does go wrong, I can't not help you and my brother. I'm tired of running away. I won't leave if you need me." Ronan leaned back to look at my face, eyes searching as if to find and test my resolve.

"I don't suppose it would make a difference if I ordered you, as a senior Venatore?" he asked hopefully.

"Not a chance. Besides, I'm not sworn in yet, so you can't order me around."

"That's a technicality," he shrugged, then stepped back and tilted his head toward the door. "Après vous, mademoiselle."

"And he speaks French," I muttered under my breath as I walked toward the entrance, "there's no hope for mortal men."

The sound of his soft chuckle followed me through the door.

Faded hunter green stucco was chipped away from the walls inside Rue 9 to show the brickwork beneath. With high ceilings, antique chandeliers, and low candles placed on each of the tables that crowded the small stage, the entire effect was turn-of-the-century intimacy. I could easily picture Ben singing here.

Apparently, the acoustics were more modern, because I could hear Ben's voice clearly from the other side of the room near a booth close to the stage.

"...heard anything from her family," he was saying.

I edged along the wall toward him, trying to move casually while studying the old movie posters on the walls. Audrey stared down at me, regal in her black dress and tiara, making me wish I could eat breakfast at Tiffany's someday.

"Dunno man," the DJ said, "only hired her a week or so before you guys got here. Dwight ran off with some Russian girl right in the middle of a set, dude. I'm telling you, it was crazy. Tim didn't have any time to interview people, but she was there, and we had like, six bands lined up, so we needed somebody. That's all I know. Sorry to hear about your girl, dude. That's loco."

"Thanks. Do you think there's a chance I could talk to Tim? Maybe he could tell me something." The DJ said something too low for me to hear and vaulted up onto the stage to push his way behind the curtain. I moved on to the next poster, this one of Katharine Hepburn and Humphrey Bogart. A little bell rang from the front of the club signaling that Ronan had entered. He'd keep the front of the club covered, so I focused all my attention on the stage. I was too far from the stage to see much of Tim when he walked out from behind the curtain, but the lights shone off his bald scalp when he bent to shake Ben's hand. He also had a voice deep enough that I could only make out a few words here and there.

"Can't give you...police investigation..."

Ben raised his shoulders and lifted his hands to the sides, a gesture of helpless frustration, and Tim said something that ended in 'office.'

No, no, I thought, *don't go into his office.*

Luckily, Ben gestured to the table and said, "Thanks, I'll just wait out here if you don't mind."

I let out a long, slow breath and moved into the shadow between booths where a chandelier had gone out. Ben sat, seemingly unconcerned, and pulled out his phone. That was a good, normal thing to do. Tim walked back into the club with an envelope in his hand and Ben stood as he approached. His stance was wary, almost hesitant, as Tim started talking. His voice was too deep to hear, so I edged closer, trying to be inconspicuous.

"Didn't ask for this," he was explaining to Ben, "so I think it's okay to give it to you. Maybe you can give it to her family; I don't know. They've never called or stopped in to find out anything since she disappeared, and she never gave us a number."

Another bell rang from the front of the building.

"That's strange," Ben admitted, opening the envelope and looking inside.

"Yeah," Tim agreed, "you'd think the family would be interested, you know? But maybe she was on the outs with them, I can't say. She didn't talk much about her life outside the job. Anyway, it's yours if you want it. Hopefully, you get the chance to give it back to her someday."

Ben said that he hoped so, too, and shook Tim's hand before the shorter man turned to walk back through the curtain. The envelope was bulky, with a bulge on one side that didn't look like paper, and might not have been anything promising, to judge from Ben's chagrinned expression.

Sitting in the car felt almost anticlimactic. Everything had gone smoothly, even though we hadn't gotten the information we'd needed. Ben was safe, and Ronan was safe, though not very happy.

"Unless you want to break into the man's office, this is the best I could do," Ben said defensively.

"I know. Alright, let me see it."

Ben pulled the envelope out of his pocket and handed it to Ronan. He turned the white paper over, and a bulky silver bracelet landed on his palm.

"See, just a bracelet, like I said."

Ronan didn't respond. He stared at the bracelet like he'd never seen one before, his expression locked in place. Ben looked at me for some answer, but I could only shrug and watch Ronan's face for any sign of what was unique about the bracelet. After a minute passed, and Ronan still didn't speak, I put my hand gingerly on his forearm. He flinched and jerked his gaze up to mine.

"What's wrong?" I asked.

"I'm not sure, but..." his eyes dropped back to the bracelet as his voice trailed off, studying the ropes of silver that were twisted into an incomplete circular band that ended in a boar's head on either side so that the boars were facing each other across a small open space. The muscle of his forearm was corded with tension beneath my fingers, and I was surprised to realize that Ronan was breathing as if he'd just finished a race. Looking up into his face, skin drawn tight across his cheekbones and mouth pressed flat, eyes burning, it was clear to me that he knew something about the bracelet, and whatever it was, it was profoundly disturbing him.

"I need more answers," he growled, "and I've got a fair idea where to find them."

CHAPTER TWENTY-EIGHT

"**A**bsolutely not, Allie."

If there was any time I needed to keep a tight rein on my temper, it was now. Ronan had agreed to hear my idea before leaving to pursue our latest clue, and was now towering over me, scowling, with his jaw set and his hands curled into fists.

Ben stood behind him with his arms folded across his chest looking equally belligerent.

I could tell that blowing up on these two would only unite them against me so, as calmly and with as much certainty as I could muster, I said, "Ronan, you can't stop me."

He took one sharp step toward me and growled, "You know I can."

"Rayne and Mateo are as close to me as family. They are family. If someone could get to Ben, then someone could get to Ray and Mat, too. I need to make sure they're safe."

"If someone could get to Ben, then what makes you think they're not there right now, watching and waiting for you?" he demanded. "Do you think that's a chance I'm willing to take?"

"It doesn't matter if you're willing or not, Ronan. I am."

Ronan made a strangled noise and veins began to bulge in his neck. Ben stepped up and put both hands on my shoulders, bending to look me in the eye. I clenched my fists, steeling myself against the guilt he was planning to lay on me.

"Dad is dead, and mom might be, for all we know. You're the only family I have left, Allie. Ronan is right; this isn't safe. We could at least call Rayne. That doesn't put you in any danger, and you can still make sure she's all right." He had a fair point. It wouldn't give me the satisfaction of wrapping my arms around her and seeing that she was safe with my own eyes, but it was something.

"All right," I conceded, "we can call first, and if everything is okay, then we'll leave it at that. I'll try to warn her and see if I can get her to stay with her parents for a while." Ben straightened and nodded, satisfied, but Ronan only continued to glower at me. When Ben dug his cell phone out of his coat pocket to hand it to me, Ronan snatched it out of my hand before I could press the first number.

"Nope," he said curtly, shoving the phone back at Ben, "a payphone will do. And you'd be wise to get rid of that phone and buy a pre-paid one. Chances are that whomever Trisha was working for has your line bugged."

Ben flinched and looked down at his innocuous little phone in surprise. "I hadn't thought of that," he admitted as he powered off the phone and pocketed it. Luckily a payphone was only half a block down the street from Rue 9. Since the prevalence of cell phones had made payphones practically obsolete, the phone booth had definitely seen better days. The numbers were jammed and the line from the scummy receiver to the phone box had moss growing from the rings. I rubbed the handle vigorously against the material of my skirt to clean the grime off and listened to the phone ring from an inch away just so that I didn't have to press it to my ear.

"Hello?" I closed my eyes in relief, and my shoulders drooped. She was all right. "Ray, it's me."

"Allie!?"

"Look, I can't stay on—"

"Allie, are you okay? Where are you? Oh my God I heard, I mean, the cops said that you were missing, and they dug through all your stuff and your mom—"

"Rayne, I'm all right, I promise, just listen for a second, okay? There's someone who wants to hurt me, but I don't know why. I can't come home, but I had to call you, I needed to let you know. I don't think you should stay at the apartment for now, at least until I can find out what's going on."

"Wait, what do you mean?" Rayne's voice was low and tremulous, and I could practically feel her unease through the phone line.

"Can you go stay with your parents? I don't think it's safe for Mat to come over, either."

"Allie, you're scaring me. Are you sure you're okay? Is Ronan with you?"

"Ronan?"

"Yeah, is he okay?"

I hesitated. "Yeah, Ronan's fine."

"Where are you, Allie? I can come get you. We could go down to the police department."

"I can't," I started to say, but stopped and thought a moment as an idea began to take root. "I know I'm asking a lot, but do you think you could pack a few of my clothes into my bag and bring it down to Pioneer Square? I could meet you there."

"Done," she promised quickly.

Ronan was not thrilled with the idea, but since it had stopped me from insisting on going to my apartment, he accepted my spur-of-the-moment plan grudgingly. The only part that made me nervous was Ben. He had no training and no idea what he was getting into. I knew we'd have to walk back to Avalon soon, and that meant leaving Ben behind with no guarantee of his safety, but maybe if we could pull this off, then we wouldn't have to leave him ignorant.

Pioneer Square in downtown Seattle was surrounded by old buildings, leafy trees, pedestrian traffic of the hipster variety, and iron lampstands that I always found rather romantic. For most of the year, the trees kept everything shaded, but when I stepped into Occidental Park, the paving stones were slippery with mostly rotted leaves, littered with wet trash, and hosting the occasional panhandler braving the misty rain. There wasn't much foot traffic, so the sound of my heels striking the concrete was uncomfortably loud.

Despite wearing a baggy sweater, a chill ran down my spine and made the hair on my arms stand at attention. I ignored a random whistle and reached up to make sure my hair was tucked neatly into my slouchy pink hat. Red still showed through the holes in the crochet pattern, but with the color of the material such an eye-stinging pink, the red was hardly noticeable unless you were close enough.

We had gotten there about 15 minutes earlier than the time I gave Rayne to meet me so that I could find a safe vantage point.

"You'll need to keep your back to a wall but have an exit nearby," Ronan had told me, "though two exits would be better. Make sure you're able to see all avenues of approach, yeah?"

I sighed. Occidental Park is almost nothing but avenues of approach. I settled on a red brick building covered in climbing ivy and parked myself just inside the doorway of a little art gallery whose hand-painted sign was sitting stolidly in the rain, welcoming the umbrella shunning locals who figured a purchase would be worth wet shoes.

I had three ways out at least, though it was hard to keep my eyes on every possible avenue of approach. A man came around the corner, and I tensed, watching him trudge through puddles along the side of my building, wearing cut-off shorts and flip-flops.

Only in Seattle.

He walked by, muttering under his breath, and I relaxed, feeling a sudden urge to laugh at myself. Who did I think I was? The whole affair abruptly felt like a farce. Here I was, in disguise no less, lurking outside a building and planning routes of escape while waiting for my roommate to bring me a getaway bag.

"This is ridiculous," I said to myself, "you're not Jason Bourne, and the whole world isn't out to get you."

Despite the levity, I couldn't force my nerves to calm down. Up until this point, my MO had been to flee danger...with tragic results. I was determined to protect the people I loved, determined not to fail, so I scanned every face, watched every stranger for any sign that they might be other than what they seemed. What that kind of person would look like, I had no idea, but I stared anyway.

Rayne walked into the park from the opposite end, and her blonde braids were like a candle in the mist, drawing my eye immediately. The urge to fly at her and wrap my arms around her was so strong that I had to fold my arms around myself and hold on tight. When she spotted me, she jogged over, breathless, and threw her arms around me instead.

"Oh God, Allie," she cried, "I thought you were dead."

I held on and did my best to check my own tears.

"I know. I know, Ray. I'm so, so, so sorry. I couldn't come back right away; it wasn't safe."

She let me go, and looked around, crestfallen. "Where's Ronan? I thought he'd be with you?"

"I don't know where he's at right now," I said truthfully, "why?"

She shrugged. "I just figured he'd be with you. I mean," she corrected, her voice growing nonchalant, "all this stuff started happening after you met him. I don't think he's safe, and I think you should come with me to the police station."

I snatched the brown leather backpack from her hand and hugged it to my chest. "Thanks, Ray. But this isn't Ronan's fault, I promise. He got caught up in all of this because of me. Listen," I pulled her closer and took another step back into the doorway of the gallery, and asked in a low voice, "you remember when my Dad died?"

"Yeah, of course."

"I don't think it was an accident."

"What?"

"I don't think the accident was an accident. Someone is trying to kill me, Rayne, and I think it started with the accident that killed my father. I don't think it's safe for you to stay at the apartment until I know what's going on."

"Why would someone want to kill you? Al, just go to the police! Listen," she begged, grabbing my arm, "I've read about this kind of stuff, and the police can protect you and get you help. Sometimes people who've experienced trauma can hallucinate, it's only natural. I know that it feels like it's really happening but—"

I groaned and put my face in my hands, pressing my palms hard against my cheeks. "I. Am. Not. Hallucinating." I pronounced each word separately with as much vehemence as I felt. I was getting tired of trying to convince everyone that I wasn't nuts, myself included. Right now, I just needed to get Rayne safely out of here and make sure she was suspicious enough to keep herself safe.

"I'm going to go somewhere safe for a while, but I'm okay, I promise. Will you warn Mateo for me?"

"Allie," she started to protest, but her eyes were filling up with worried tears, and I cut her off before I could start crying, too. "Will you? Promise me. If anything happened to you or Mat because of me…I don't think I could handle it."

Naked emotions chased each other across her face; doubt, fear, love, anxiety. She bit her lip and gave an infinitesimal nod. I half suspected that she'd still call the cops, thinking she could keep me safe that way. I didn't blame her. I'd have done the same thing.

Dropping the bag at my feet, I hugged my best friend for all I was worth. My partner in crime, my sanity, my anchor and my wings and now, hopefully, my ticket to finding out who was trying to kill me.

"Love you, Rayne-bow."

I felt her swallow before she whispered, "love you, too, Allie-gator."

Then she turned and walked away from me without looking back, wiping at her eyes, shoulders shaking beneath the chunky brown cardigan. Once she was safely out of Occidental Park, I grabbed the bag off the ground, slung the strap over one shoulder, took a steadying breath, and walked out of the square, crossing Washington street and heading into the ally between a vintage pottery shop and a studio with boarded windows.

Alleys in Seattle have a distinct smell. While every alley smells like trash, rotten food, and cigarette butts, Seattle alleys also smell strongly of mold. It makes sense, being so wet in Seattle, that you'd also find moss growing between the red bricks of the closely set buildings. I tried not to breathe the miasma too deeply, but kept my head down and hurried through the darkening passage, ignoring my growing sense of danger. I expected someone to jump out on the other side of the alley when I got to the end, but no one did.

Turning left toward the waterfront, I doubled back, walking beneath the viaduct. The homeless camps beneath the overpass tugged at my heartstrings, just like they always did, and I pinched my lips together with my teeth. I had nothing to offer them right now, and no time to give it if I did. Still, the camp was full of people, so I scanned the area to see if I could find an opening.

Shoddy scaffolding from some old construction project loomed up beside one of the cement supports like an enormous game of pick-up sticks. It was abandoned, so I hurried toward it. Half rotten plywood wobbled beneath my sandals and I stumbled to the side, turning to look over my shoulder at the offending piece of wood and noticing, for the first time, the shadow of a man following me. He was lean, long-limbed, and moving purposefully. I picked up my skirt and hurried around the opposite side of the viaduct arch support.

Control your breath, and you control your body, Danet's instruction repeated in my mind.

With some effort, I slowed my breathing and set my bag down even as adrenaline spiked in my blood. I turned and stepped toward the street, but there was no one there. Panicking, I spun to look in the opposite direction, and there he was, no more than four feet away. I tried to step to the side but tripped over my own feet, yipping in surprise. He was on me before I could regain my balance, right hand fisted in the front of my sweater and the other jabbing toward my face. I jerked my head instinctively to the left so that his fist grazed my right cheekbone and ear, and tried to counter with a heel strike upward to his nose, but he dropped his head, and my blow landed ineffectually on his forehead.

Using my body position against me, my attacker parried in an upward sweeping motion with his arm and then completed the circle, bringing his arm down to his side, which trapped my upraised forearm between his arm and chest. Then he twisted his torso so that I spun to the side leaving my back against his stomach. Only instinct made me able to turn my head to the side and duck my chin just as his left arm came around my shoulders. I tried to drop beneath his reach before he could sink the choke, but he bent with me and jerked my forehead back with one arm so the other could snake beneath my chin.

The hold tightened, and everything went black.

CHAPTER TWENTY-NINE

"Ronan?"

I rolled over, arms flailing, as the world swam back into focus. Pushing myself to my feet was impossible because my legs spasmed and sent me right back to the pavement. Instead, I twisted until I was on my backside and could see my attacker. Ronan was there, and so was Ben, though Ben was rushing toward me and Ronan was grappling with the man who'd ambushed me.

"Al, are you okay?" Ben gasped between breaths.

"What happened?" I asked muzzily. I could remember dodging the jab, my right cheek and ear burned, and my poor attempt at a heel strike, but nothing after that. Ben wrapped his arms around my chest and lifted me easily to my feet, then turned me to look at him, examining my face with an expression I'd never seen before. His eyes were flat and dangerous, and his big body was still.

"He choked you," he told me, his voice emotionless. When he'd finished examining me, he turned to watch as Ronan clinically picked his way through my attacker's defenses and delivered a stunning blow that left the man crumpled on the ground, snoring. The entire ordeal had taken no more than 10 seconds.

Ben and Ronan lifted the man off the ground as I grabbed my bag, and the three of us hurried through the dusk around the corner of South Main and into the loading dock behind a parked catering van that screened us from the road. The stranger was dumped unceremoniously on the ground while Ben jogged down the street to where our car was parked. Ronan rolled his shoulders and flexed his hand, looking daggers at the unconscious man.

"Are you all right, Allie?" He had very tight control over his voice, but it was the kind of control a man has over a wild horse, and I could tell that eventually, the rope would break. My own nerves weren't far from the snapping point.

"I'm okay."

"Are you hurt?"

"Just a little sore."

He looked up from the man on the ground and caught me touching my cheek. Taking a step toward me, he brought his hand up to replace mine and, with gentle pressure, turned my face to the side to look at the mark left by the passage of knuckles. The corners of his eyes tightened.

"I can't believe I agreed to this," he growled, "how did I let you convince me to use you as bait?"

"It worked, didn't it?"

He didn't argue with my defense but shook his head and ran his thumb over my bottom lip. The callouses on his fingertips were rough against the sensitive skin, and I shivered, smelling the subtle hint of leather from his jacket and the stronger bite of fear and sweat.

"When I saw you fall," he hesitated and closed his eyes for a moment, brow creasing with distress, "my heart stopped in my chest. The only thing that stopped me from outright killing the bastard was hearing you say my name."

I pressed his hand against my cheek and then kissed the center of his palm. "I'm okay, and we've got our best chance at finding out who's behind all this, so it was worth it. I knew you and Ben were close behind, so I knew I was safe."

He pulled me into his arms and pressed me against himself, burying his face in my hair, which had spilled from beneath my hat during the fight. "You don't know how quickly things could have happened, Allison. Had he a knife, a gun, or were you not fast enough..." his big body shuddered, and he leaned back to cup my chin in his hand, "I know you to be capable, despite only having a small piece of your training. I know you to be quick and smart, but chance can take down even the best trained of us. It could have happened so quickly."

I opened my mouth, but two things happened simultaneously to distract us. Ben pulled up alongside the parked van, and our prisoner groaned. Ronan kissed me quickly on the lips, leaving them tingling, and bent to see to our captive.

The plan had been simple; if our suspicions were right and someone was watching my apartment, then it was a good bet they'd be following my roommate for any chance she might lead them to me. If we could get our hands on whoever was hunting me, then we may be able to backtrack information directly to the source. Neither Ben nor Ronan had been easy to convince, Ben in particular because he wasn't as pragmatic as Ronan and still didn't whole-heartedly believe that I was a member of a secret organization. He didn't give in gracefully, either. If his silence were any indication, it would take him a while to forgive me for making him watch me put myself in danger.

By the time we got out of Seattle, rush hour was over, and it didn't take us long to find a secluded spot off I-5, screened by evergreen trees and a thick undergrowth of ferns and half-grown cottonwood trees. It was a good thing we didn't have far to go because the unconscious man was dangerously close to waking up. He'd come to less than a minute after we initially moved him, but Ronan had been prepared for that and used a simple blood choke to keep him under. Just now, he lay on his back on the gravel of the pullout, his head rolling around on his neck as he blinked owlishly at his surroundings

"Cá bhfuil mé?" he moaned, trying to roll up to a sitting position but finding the prospect difficult while his hands were bound.

"Why are you trying to kill me?" I demanded.

The man squinted up at me from his seated position, blinking and trying to shake shaggy locks of dirty blonde hair out of his eyes. Once he realized our relative situation; he tied on the ground in the dark and me, flanked by two huge men standing menacingly over him, his eyes became distant, and I felt the vibration of Walking begin. Before I even processed what was happening enough to react, Ronan had stepped around me and slapped the man coolly across the face. The thrumming stopped, and the air around him quieted as he looked up at Ronan in shock.

"Venatore?" he asked scornfully.

Ronan knelt, bringing his face within inches of the other man's, and said conversationally, "That's right, friend. And you'll be answering the lady's question, or you'll answer to me." Then he reached up and deliberately wiped at the stream of blood and saliva dripping from the corner of my attacker's mouth, and continued in a low, dangerous voice that held the same kind of warning as the hiss of a rattlesnake's tail, "and my questions won't be asked so gently."

I felt the humming vibration again, this time quite clearly. Ronan must have felt it, too, because he dealt the man an openhanded blow that rocked his head back and stilled the air.

"Mac soith," the man swore as a thin stream of blood slid out of one nostril. I had no idea what language he was speaking, but I knew a curse when I heard one. His forehead was creased, but he spat to the side and glared at me with more than uncommon dislike.

"I was ordered to," he growled through clenched teeth. I felt a rush of adrenaline spike right up the back of my neck.

"By whom?"

"Gabh suas ort féin."

I looked at Ronan to see if he'd understood the language, and saw a slow flush rising up his neck.

Ronan answered the silent question on my face with coldness. "This ignorant wretch thinks he's got nothing more to say."

"Well, I've got a few questions, and I don't mind beating the answers out of him," Ben offered while audibly cracking his knuckles in anticipation.

I gave him a reproachful glance over my shoulder, but he ignored me, keeping his malevolent gaze fixed on the man. Ronan began to dig in his coat pocket and a second later, held the silver bracelet flat on his palm beneath our prisoner's nose. The man pulled his eyes away from me and fastened them on the bracelet with undisguised shock and recognition. All the blood drained from his face and the air around us leaped to life with desperate tremors that beat against me in panicked staccato.

Despite Ronan's effort to stop him from Walking, the man began to pass, growing indistinct around the edges while his face contorted with inhuman effort and terrible pain. I remembered that feeling far too distinctly, like my very atoms were ripping themselves asunder. I shuddered, wrapping my arms around my chest to keep my body from flying apart.

"What the hell!" Ben exclaimed, stepping back and trying to pull me along with him. Screaming tore at the already tortured air as the panicked man fought to leave, his voice ragged with effort and half-formed words I couldn't recognize. Ronan grabbed the front of the captive's shirt, but the man was pulsing violently now and his legs convulsed as he lurched backward, the motion tearing the dark cloth of his shirt and revealing his tattooed chest an instant before Ronan leaped away, and our prisoner disappeared into thin air.

A shockwave blasted through me, and I stumbled into Ben clutching my chest and dragging in gulps of air that smelled sharp, like ozone. Ronan stood and shook his arms out, clenching his hands and stamping hard on the ground as if his limbs had gone numb.

"What the hell," Ben repeated breathlessly, peering into the darkness and jerking his head around as his eyes scanned shadows beneath the trees. "What the hell..."

"Are you okay?" I gasped while taking an unsteady step in Ronan's direction.

"Enough," he answered ruefully, "you?"

I gave an uncertain nod. "Everything is still attached, but my muscles don't feel very happy about it."

He smiled apologetically and then glanced at Ben, who'd gone wild around the eyes and was looking at both of us as if we were rabid animals who might decide at any point to make a meal of him.

"Did you see that?" he demanded.

"Ben," I began soothingly, but he reeled backward and held both hands out, palm up.

"Don't touch me."

"It's just me, Ben. Ben, look at me. It's okay—"

"This is not okay, Allison! Did you see that guy? He's gone. Oh my God, what just happened?"

He was starting to hyperventilate. "He was right there. I saw him. Oh God, oh God, oh God..."

His hands were shaking.

"Ben," I warned him, "you need to sit down and breathe."

"You knew," he accused me, panting, "you knew about this Allie! What," he panted, "how?"

His knees went wobbly, and he promptly passed out, crumpling toward the ground like a puppet whose strings had been cut.

I jumped forward and managed to get my arms around his torso, but my brother was big and barrel-chested, and my legs weren't yet able to withstand his weight. Ronan eased him off me to lay him on the ground and then pulled up the hem of his shirt began slapping him on the bare stomach. Ben's head lolled to one side, then snapped up, and his eyes flew open. His body jerked for a second, reminding me of a clubbed fish whose body hasn't caught on to the fact that its head has been smashed.

"Ben?" I hesitantly touched his arm, "you okay?"

He didn't answer me but rubbed his hand over his face and fought his way to a sitting position. "I just…" he hesitated, looked at me and then looked away, shuddering, "can I have a minute?"

Ronan clapped him on the shoulder and said sympathetically, "It'll take longer than a minute, mate, but take as long as you need."

"How much can we tell him? He wasn't supposed to see that."

We'd stepped away into the darkness near the fir trees that concealed our car from the road, close enough to see Ben but not so close that he'd feel threatened. I remembered the need to be alone shortly after seeing Ronan disappear for the first time, so I didn't grudge him that, though empathy for him was a cold stone in the pit of my stomach.

"No, he wasn't. I tried to stop that wanker from Walking, but I didn't think he'd nearly kill himself just to get out of here."

I bit my lips. "Do you think he made it to wherever he was trying to go?"

Ronan shrugged and rubbed the back of his neck, looking as tired as I felt. It had been an amazingly long day. He swore in a language I couldn't recognize and shook his head. "I can't say. He was within an inch of being a pile of slime in the dirt. If he did make it, he isn't in very good shape."

"What language was he speaking?"

Ronan's expression closed, like an old lady drawing the curtains when she's been caught spying on the neighbors.

"Irish," he said shortly.

"What did he say?"

"Nothing important. He asked where he was. He swore. That's it."

"Is he from here, then?"

Ronan shrugged.

"What do you think it was about the bracelet that made him freak out like that? It seemed like he recognized it."

His eyes darted away from me, and he shifted his weight. "I've got a few suspicions," he hedged.

"And those are?"

"It's still early to say. I don't want to jump to conclusions. As soon as your brother is somewhere safe, we'll walk to Avalon and talk to someone who might be able to give us some answers."

I glanced over at Ben, who was still sitting on the ground with his head in his hands.

"What can we tell him?"

"What will he believe?" Ronan countered.

"I don't know. I know that we're not supposed to tell normal people what we are, but he's already seen it happen. How do we explain it away?"

"I don't know that we can."

I sighed, exasperated. "Aren't there any standard operating procedures for things like this? People have to have seen Walkers vanish before."

"Indeed, they have. It doesn't often happen to Venatore, but when it does happen it's usually a stranger who sees it, and the event gets passed off as an accident, or a vision, or too much to drink, not sleeping well, fairy rings, kidnapping, that kind of thing. People don't want to believe things like Walkers exist. This... is a bit more personal."

"I guess there's not much danger then, is there? If Ben said anything to anyone, they'd just think he was crazy. I mean, it takes an awful lot to convince just one person that this is even possible, let alone convincing enough people to pose any real danger to Walkers."

"That's true," he conceded, "but you never know what just one person is capable of. It's safer to avoid the issue altogether."

"There's no avoiding this," Ben said, "and you're not going to convince me that I didn't see what I just saw. I want to know what the hell is going on."

Ronan and I both spun, surprised that Ben had managed to walk within feet of where we were standing without either of us having heard him approach.

"It's not that we want to lie to you, Ben," I insisted, "but there are rules—"

"I don't give a shit about your rules, Allie," he cut me off with a slicing gesture of his hand, "and I'm not interested in you trying to keep me safe by keeping me stupid. I want to know what happened to that man and I want to know now."

CHAPTER THIRTY

Early morning crept across the meadow, banishing the darkness by small degrees and chasing every shadow back down into the cracks and hollows beneath the leafless trees. Eyes closed, I breathed in the sweet, chill air of the most peaceful place I knew and savored the clean fragrance of frozen grass and impending snow.

I squeezed my eyes shut and willed Ronan not to speak for just a little while longer so I could hang on to the peace and pull it inside myself. After leaving Ben, I needed the sanctuary. Ben hadn't believed my carefully crafted lies. He thought the man had disappeared through some trick or weapon, or that we'd hypnotized him to see things. When we'd finally left, though still skeptical, Ben had promised to keep looking for details about Trisha. The hug he'd given me was genuine but uncertain and unless I was mistaken, afraid. I sighed heavily and opened my eyes.

Ronan spread his arms, and I walked into them without hesitation. His arms were a barrier between me and the world.

"I was intrigued by you, you know," he said to the top of my head. I leaned back and looked up at him, raising my brows, wondering where that thought had come from.

"It's true," he insisted, "I'd never seen someone take the news so calmly the first time. Most often, we must bind people just to keep them still long enough to convince them." "Calmly? Me? I just about crapped my pants."

"You saw how Ben responded to the fake news. You reacted to the truth far better than most people do. I didn't have to carry you into the house kicking and screaming, or bind your hands, or knock you out, or get you drunk or anything."

I snorted and pinched him, and he jumped, chuckling, grabbing my wrists in one hand and then kissing my palms. I laid my head against his chest. "Can we just stay here?"

He wrapped his arms around me and laid his cheek on the top of my head. "For a bit."

Not moving or talking, just holding each other, we listened as the birds woke up and watched dawn make its way across the sky to fill the valley of Avalon with pale pink light.

"Are you going to explain what happened back there?" I asked, finally breaking the silence that blanketed us. He sighed, stirring the hair at my crown with his breath.

"Not everything, no," he admitted, and let go of me with a regretful twist of his mouth, "but as much as I can for now."

He fished in his jacket pocket and lifted out the silver bracelet, handing it to me. The early morning light picked out the delicate details carved into the boar's heads that completed each side of the twisted silver rope, with the snouts pointing at each other but not touching.

"This is called a torc," he told me, tracing the c shaped metal with one fingertip, "and it's not a bracelet. This one is an armband, though most were made to be worn around the neck."

"Is that what this is? I think one of my textbooks had a brief mention of them, but it didn't look like this one. It seems awfully small for an armband," I noted, picking up the torc and turning it over so that the sunlight shimmered off the twisted bands.

"Trisha had small arms."

"Okay, so it's an armband and not a bracelet. What does it mean? Why did you freak out when you saw it?"

Ronan rubbed the back of his neck with one big hand, rocking on his heels and making a sound low in his throat. We were moving into murky waters for him. "A torc is a piece of jewelry worn by a person of high rank. They were fairly common in the ancient world, but I haven't seen one since I left home."

"So, you think this one is Irish?"

Without looking at me, he nodded.

"You think you know the owner, don't you?" I guessed, assuming that to be the only reason he would have reacted so strongly to seeing a piece of jewelry that used to be commonplace.

Ronan tilted his head to the side and gave a slight shrug, but his lips were closed tight. I tried to remember everything I could about what Ronan had told me of his past; how he'd been betrayed and left his verse, nearly dead, but had never been back.

"Wait...you said these were common in ancient times. These were part of everyday life in your verse?"

Another nod.

"Then your verse isn't as advanced as we are on True Earth?"

"I haven't been back since I left," he hedged, looking away from me, "so I can't say."

My arm went limp, and my hand hung at my side, barely clutching the piece of jewelry as I realized what he was implying.

"How..." sudden dryness in my throat stopped my question, and I had to swallow a few times and try again, "how old are you, Ronan?"

He winced and shoved his hands into his pockets.

"Ronan?"

"I don't really know. Time runs differently in my verse and I've spent a lot of time in different time streams. I haven't kept track."

"Ronan!" I shouted, squeezing the torc so hard in one hand that my nails dug into the skin of my palm.

"Maybe...twenty-five or so...centuries. True Earth moves around the sun a bit faster than earth in my verse does."

My legs went wobbly, and I sank into the wet grass, completely oblivious to the ice melting and seeping through my skirt. Ronan was thousands...thousands of years old. *Thousands of years old.* From my position in the grass, Ronan towered over me with his jaw clenched and his arms folded across his chest, dark brows drawn low over his eyes. His cheeks were unblemished beneath the day's growth of beard. The lines around his eyes were all but invisible, and not a single grey hair lightened the dark curls.

"You look like...I mean...you couldn't possibly be more than thirty!"

I knew I must have sounded ridiculous. He'd just told me he was—my mind shuddered away from the number. The vast expanse of time stretched out hungrily before me. Ronan unfolded his arms and kicked savagely at an unoffending clump of weeds, sending small brown stalks flying in every direction.

"Well, I am," he said bitterly, and kicked again, and again, turning toward me with a flushed face and demanding breathlessly, "Does it matter?"

Unable to bear the sight of his face drawn into taut lines of desperation, I squeezed my eyes shut and bit my lower lip, willing myself to get a grip on my emotions.

"Allie." Softer, more insistent, his voice was pleading, and the urge to look up at him was almost irresistible. By the smell of leather and the sharp tang of sweat, I knew he was close. The warmth of his hands settled on my upper arms and, when I opened my eyes, he was kneeling in the grass before me, the newly risen sun striking amber sparks off his dark hair and lighting up the pale blue-grey shards in the center of his irises like cracks in the ice of a spring pond.

Slowly, he reached up and cupped my face between his hands, making my skin tingle with familiar humming vibrations.

"Does it matter?" he repeated, his voice low and earnest.

"Yes!" I blurted, "no...I don't know."

Looking away from his eyes was impossible. I remembered the time he had saved a little girl's doll from getting trampled on the road to Avalon, and his secret smile when she clutched the toy to her chest. I remembered the smell of his jacket wrapped around me in the cold van, his concern for Rayne and Mateo in the alley, the way he'd held me against his chest when I grieved for my mother. He leaned toward me, his face only inches from mine and his smell rising around me, mixed with the bite of crushed grass. The leather jacket was cool from the morning air and buttery beneath my fingertips.

"Allie," he whispered, pressing his forehead against mine, "does it really matter? What's important is what's beneath our skin. Does it matter how old our bodies are?"

Which one of us initiated the kiss, I couldn't tell, but his lips were warm, soft and tenderly insistent as he held my face delicately between his palms. All the blood seeped into my cheeks then spread outward in a tingling rush that made my limbs weak. He felt me softening beneath his kiss and groaned, wrapping his arms tightly around me, pushing his advantage by nipping at my lips until I gasped then twisting his head and deepening the kiss until I lost all sense of myself in a vortex of heat. Ronan wrenched his lips from mine and, tilting my chin up with the thumb of one hand while his other was fisted in the hair at the base of my head, and forced me to look into his eyes.

"Does it matter?"

There was no room left in my head for the shock of his age or the disparity that number created between us. My initial surprise and fear had melted beneath the naked longing in his eyes, and forced from me the honesty beneath my self-doubt; the truth beneath the fear that someone like Ronan, dangerous, skilled, beautiful, kind, pragmatic, intelligent, loyal, ages beyond me in experience, could possibly love someone like me.

No, his age didn't matter to me; not if he was a hundred times older would it matter. My soul knew him with the bone-deep recognition of a bell for the hammer that struck it. His was the counterpoint to the melody my very atoms sang. I shook my head, never taking my eyes off his.

"No," I admitted, "no, it doesn't matter."

Ronan's expression cleared as he searched my face, eyes lingering on my swollen lips, then he nodded brusquely and pulled me to my feet.

Despite its beauty in the morning sun—glowing like a delicate piece of rose quartz—Avalon didn't stun me with awe as it always had in the past. My mind was too full of everything that had happened in the last twenty-four hours, and too tired to make sense of any of it. Dazed with fatigue and lulled into a kind of numbness by the chilly walk down the hill through the barren trees, I followed Ronan incuriously through the empty streets of the capital toward the castle building. It wasn't until we reached the gates of the castle wall that I began to realize that something was wrong.

Had Ronan not tensed as the rhythm of his gait shifted from purposeful stride to cautious prowling, I probably would have missed the silence that hung over the city, the shuttered windows, empty streets, and six additional guards at the wall, all heavily armored with weapons much more modern than the swords and spears they usually carried. Six black rifles of some kind, rounded and ergonomic rather than angular and intimidating, were lowered at us while making small, high-pitched humming sounds. One of the guards barked something in a language I didn't recognize, and Ronan responded with both arms outstretched non-threateningly.

"We don't speak Avalonian."

I suspected that was for my benefit, as I doubted Ronan didn't speak the language of his home base.

"State your business and show your credentials," the guard snapped.

"Ronan, Senior Venatore and Allison Chapter, apprentice."

With exquisite slowness, Ronan pulled the sleeve of his jacket back to expose his wrist and shifted the bracelets he wore to reveal a tattoo beneath. I tried to move as deliberately as Ronan had when exposing my bracelet and turned my hand, so the sunlight shimmered off the silver wolf etched into the metal. When the guards lowered their weapons and motioned us through, I grabbed Ronan's hand and stayed as close to him as possible.

A sense of dread had begun to settle on me, making my hands cold and my neck and shoulder muscles tense with apprehension. Inside, the castle was starkly different from the city outside its walls. The halls were crowded with people hurrying in every direction, talking in groups, carrying trays of food, whispering, shouting, gesturing wildly, and looking about suspiciously; almost all of them were armed. Despite all the people, I heard no laughing and saw not a single smile. The hum of conversation was excited but uneasy.

Two women spoke in hushed voices to a pale, green-skinned man with limbs so long and thin that he reminded me uncomfortably of a stick bug. I was so distracted by him that I was hit broadside by a woman walking out of a hallway as we passed. I stumbled sideways into Ronan, but we both caught ourselves before falling, and I found myself in a defensive crouch before realizing that there wasn't any danger.

"Megayn," Ronan said with relief, squeezing my hand reassuringly, then made a sweeping gesture at the crowd with his free hand, "what is all this?"

Megayn had skin the color of nutmeg and distinctly feline features, including wide, slanted amber eyes and a delicate nose that seemed too small for a human face. Her dark brown hair was shoulder length and impossibly shiny.

"Ronan! Pruwsh mealahshar au roashm vurla?" Her voice was low and throaty and the language she spoke rolled off her tongue like the purring of a big cat.

"Will you speak English, True Earth? Speaking Vurshemne will take too long."

She switched languages almost without taking a breath. "When did you get back? Don't think on it," Megayn cut herself off with a frantic wave of short-fingered hands and glanced nervously over her shoulder before grabbing his sleeve and yanking him toward the closest door to the inner courtyard and ordering, "come."

Almost as soon as the heavy wooden door closed behind us, she blurted, "Fighting became in the Bastion. There are so many of people here that no one asked of the new ones—the intruders," she clarified.

Words were tumbling out of her mouth like white water over rocks and, while her pronunciation was good, her grammar was alien. She didn't pause where she should have, and her word choice and inflections were strange, which made it hard to keep up with the constant flow of her thoughts.

She continued, "There were three. Molfus caught them into the armory breaking, so he started fighting them. They say Molfus struggled with the fighting until more of Venatore came, and the fighting into the open moved. Molfus killed one, but the other two walked away before they could be stopped. The Pendragon ordered martial law until more can be known. Who's this?"

I blinked and felt the need to catch my own breath after that speech.

"Megayn, this is Allison. She's an apprentice."

Her non-existent eyebrows lifted, and she held out her hand. "Hi."

I took it without thinking and realized that her skin was covered in fine hair. "Um, hi," I offered hesitantly. One corner of her mouth pulled up in a crooked, half-friendly smile that intrigued me.

"The one Molfus killed," Ronan interrupted, "is his body still here?"

Megayn freed me from her amber gaze to nod vigorously at Ronan, sending her hair flying around her head. "He is. In the conservatory, his body is under guard." Ronan thanked her, and we turned to head to the conservatory. I glanced back over my shoulder to watch Megayn prowl around the corner with lithe grace and wondered what could have happened to cause a reality where humans evolved to such a state. I asked Ronan.

"She's not human," he answered absently.

I opened my mouth, but no words came out. In the midst of the chaos that was my life, I wondered whether I would ever get used to having bombs like that dropped on me, and seriously doubted it.

During my stay in Avalon, I'd never gone to the conservatory. All my time was devoted to training, so I was more familiar with the Bastion than any other part of the castle grounds. Near the rear of the castle proper, the conservatory extended out of the main building like a peninsula of leaded glass and high arches, filled with the moist warmth of growing things. I started to sweat as soon as we walked inside.

To circulate some air, I plucked at the front of my sweater and pulled the fabric in and out, but the slight breeze the motion created was still warm and moist, which didn't do much to help. The ceiling was so high that I had to lean my head back to peer at the canopy where the few cultivated trees spread broad, leafy limbs in vegetative ecstasy.

"Why in here?" I whispered to Ronan, "the heat and moisture can't be good for a decaying body."

He turned and walked down a narrow path between thin-leafed plants that flowered with pale pink buds. "There are wards on this place, so things don't decay here."

"Don't plants need decaying things in their soil, though?"

"Not these plants, I guess."

"Why?" Ronan stopped and turned an exasperated expression on me.

"Can't it wait? We've got more important questions to ask than what strange plants The Pendragon keeps in his conservatory."

"Geeze, crabby pants. You could have just said 'I don't know.'"

His mouth quirked into a crooked but unwilling grin. "I don't know. There. Can we go now?"

"I thought you'd never ask," I said breezily, and walked past him down the lane. His snort of amused exasperation made me smile. The grin died as I rounded the corner to be confronted with the bloodied body of the man Molfus had killed.

Guards, holding the same sleek weapons as those at the castle gates, stood to either side of the table where the corpse had been laid. We stopped until Ronan had given our credentials, with tattooed proof, and then approached the table. Molfus had been thorough in his business. The right side of the man's skull had been staved in. I tried to clear my throat and then almost choked on my own spit when I noticed the man's chest. He'd been stripped to be examined and cleaned, and the tattoo on his chest was an exact match for the one I'd seen only a split second before our captive disappeared from the clearing outside Seattle. The blue-black ink was slightly faded in places, but the twisted knotwork was clean and complex, curving back in and through itself until the design formed a circle on his left pectoral muscle, surrounding the stylized head of a boar.

I reached into Ronan's pocket and pulled out the torc, comparing the boar's head on the dead man's chest to the carved boar's heads at either end of the armband. Stylistically, they were strikingly similar.

"How long has he been dead?" Ronan's demeanor was coolly professional, but I sensed violent energy beneath his composure.

"Less than 10 hours," one of the guards replied. Without another word, Ronan turned and strode from the conservatory.

I had to jog to keep up with him as his long legs drove him down corridor after corridor, the tension of his big body palpable in the air around him. I wanted to say something, to ask about the tattoo and the torc I still held, but the barely controlled emotion radiating from Ronan made me hesitate. We stopped at last just outside the armory.

"Molfus!"

I jumped at the crack of authority in Ronan's voice. The heavy door swung open, and the Master at Arms stood there, bare-chested with brass-studded leather pauldrons across his shoulders and upper arms. His dark eyes held lightning beneath the thundercloud of his brows, which were drawn low in suspicion.

"Ronan," he greeted us, face relaxing a bit.

"The men who tried to break into the armory," Ronan asked brusquely, "how did they fight?"

"Brutally," Molfus responded in kind, "straightforward with spears and short swords."

"Technique?"

"Single. I was detecting no secondary martial technique, though they were being skilled enough in their own."

"Did they bear targets?"

Molfus' eyes widened in surprise. "Yes. Wood with carvings on the front and brass bosses in the center. They were being sturdy though, well crafted. Even my hammer was not splintering the wood. How are you knowing that?"

Ronan took a deep breath and expelled it forcefully through his nose, rolling his left shoulder uncomfortably. "The corpse of the man you killed, he had a tattoo on his chest, an Irish design. I suspected that they might have been using Irish weapons, too."

The big man grunted and rubbed at the black forest growing along his jaw with both hands, his formidable arms bunching with the motion. Molfus had successfully fought off three men, and here he stood looking like he was ready for a hundred more. The glare he gave Ronan would have frozen most men where they stood.

"I can tell you are suspecting something more, my friend. Do not be keeping it from me long, eh? No one was being hurt this time, but—"

"This time?" I interjected, "you think they'll come back?"

Molfus shrugged his burly shoulders. "They were trying to stealing weapons from my armory. They were not succeeding. I am not knowing what they were after, so will they be coming back? Safer is better than regretful."

I looked up at Ronan, who was scowling, then back at Molfus whose expression had turned thoughtful.

"I would never put anyone in danger, Molfus," Ronan assured him, though his voice was tight, "you know that."

Molfus hesitated for a split second and then sighed as his heavy shoulders relaxed. "Yes, my friend, I am knowing." Then he turned to me and narrowed his eyes. "I'm glad you are bringing this one to me, however. Allison, am I having something for you."

Ronan interrupted my surprise with a gentle touch on the shoulder. "I need to talk to Cecily," he murmured, "you'll be safe with Molfus until I send for you."

I had only enough time to nod bemusedly before he stalked off down the hallway.

"Coming with me, kishma," Molfus rumbled in a voice like boulders crashing down a hill, "Danet and I have been working on something."

CHAPTER THIRTY-ONE

T he Bastion had a distinctly martial air that reeked of violence, leather, oil, and the bite of sharpened metal. Molfus looked at home amongst the impedimenta of war with his broad, hairy chest flanked by armor, but I felt particularly unsuited to be there.

"Danet is telling me you are not having a killer instinct," he announced without warning. I stared at him, mouth open, feeling like a kitten caught in a bear trap.

"Um..." He studied my face intently, and I got the impression that he saw much more than his burly appearance suggested he was capable of. Embarrassed heat blossomed in my cheeks.

"Venatore must being able to kill," he annunciated each word, "there will be being times when to be upholding our laws will mean to killing. When the time is coming to be choosing between killing or dying, can you choosing to kill?"

The uncomfortable sensation of being a fish in a barrel made any answer I could have given him feel like a lie. My decision to train as a Venatore had nothing to do with a desire to uphold the law, or to protect strangers. I had rage burning in my chest, kindled against whoever was responsible for my parents' death, for attacking my family. I felt completely capable of mayhem where that person was concerned, but I hadn't thought beyond that vengeance, beyond the time when I'd be free of that threat. My experience in Seattle proved how little I was capable of against a trained attacker, and even in that circumstance, I hadn't wished for his death; I had wished to protect Rayne and Mateo, to keep myself safe, to end the threat.

But what if that man had attacked Rayne? Visions of my best friend lying in the alley assailed me, her limp body and tangled blonde hair wet from the puddle on the pavement. The man who attacked me had followed her from our apartment, and when I thought of how vulnerable she'd been, my blood went cold. I locked eyes with Molfus and nodded once. He leaned forward to narrow his eyes at me like a hungry bear, but he must have seen something that satisfied him because he straightened and grunted.

"Very well. I am having something for you." From the table behind him, Molfus lifted what I took at first sight to be leather gloves, and held them out to me. My mouth popped open in wonder when I realized that they were; hardened leather vambraces that would enclose my arms from the elbow to the first joint of my fingers, protecting my forearms, wrists, and the back of my hands. The leather wrapped around my knuckles and through my fingers, with brass studs punched into the ridges so that I had a kind of medieval brass knuckles.

The handguard had surprisingly soft padding inside that would protect my fist from getting beaten up by the boiled leather, which was much harder than I expected. Plate metal, thin and dull silver in color, was attached to the back of the forearms with more brass studs, and swooping designs that resembled vines were etched into the plate. The workmanship was stunning, elegant, and dangerously functional. Anyone who got punched with those wouldn't easily walk away.

"Is that a fox?" I asked as he strapped the vambraces on my arms, fastening them over the sleeve he'd pulled on to protect my skin.

"Ah, yes," he sounded pleased, and flicked a finger at the figure carved into the metal near my wrist, "little was I knowing that the name I was choosing for your hair would be being so fitting, eh? A fox will be being cunning at first, hiding or fleeing, but is being fierce when cornered."

When he'd finished, the leather armor fit the contours of my hands and wrists like it had been molded from my limbs. "It's so thin," I remarked.

"The elves are being clever craftsmen," he agreed. My eyes widened to the point of bulging and Molfus barked out a laugh at the strangling noises I made.

"Elves."

"Yes, Elves."

"You mean...elves?"

"Ventu saving me, yes girl, Elves."

"Like, tiny guys who make shoes for poor cobblers or like, Tolkien elves?"

It was Molfus' turn to be surprised. "Tolkien? Were you knowing him?"

"Ah, no."

He looked crestfallen. "Ahh, I would giving much to know him. He is being famous among Walkers, you know."

I was saved from replying to this by another knock at the door, which turned out to be one of the castle servants in the blue and silver livery of Avalon.

"Sir Ronan asks that you meet him in his chambers, lady."

I could only nod as my mind was still spinning. I stared down at my forearms with renewed awe. "I...thank you, Molfus," I murmured, looking up from my wondrous gift and into the big man's face.

He grunted and shrugged off my gratitude. "I am liking you, little fox, but I am doing this thing as much for Ronan as for you."

"For Ronan?"

"I am liking Ronan," he explained, "He is being a good man, a good Venatore. I have been knowing him a long time, and I am never seeing him looking at someone as he is looking at you. He is never apprenticing new Venatore or staying so long in Avalon. To be being in the light," he continued, "I am never seeing Ronan smile. This is telling me that you are being worth protecting, for his sake as well as for your own."

A million responses sprang to my tongue, but instead, I asked, "He doesn't stay in Avalon?"

Molfus shook his head and leaned back against a wooden table. "Not that one. Ronan is being gone more than any Venatore who is living in Avalon. He is only working and training."

I bit my lip at the thought of Ronan rarely sleeping in the same place, constantly on the move, running from home ever since his fateful decision to flee with Grainne.

"So," the big man stood and clapped massive hands together sharply, "before you are going back to meet your mentor, letting me show you how to be using this new weapon."

Fatigue was beginning to settle back on my mind and in my body. The novelty of the elf-made armor had been enough to stave off impending weariness, but now that I was trudging through the nearly empty corridors behind the servant who insisted he walk me to Ronan's room, listening to the hollow sound of my shoes echo off the stone walls, it was back in full force, dragging my limbs toward the ground and churning my thoughts into pudding.

"Oh God, pudding," I breathed as my stomach gave a sharp twist of hunger, "what I wouldn't do for a snack pack."

"My lady?" The young page's eyes were confused as he glanced over his shoulder at me.

"I didn't realize I said that out loud," I muttered.

The boy gave me a concerned nod before turning the corner and stopping at the oak door, bowing, and hurrying away. When the door swung open, I caught my breath. Ronan stood bared to the waist with a towel around his neck and a plate full of fruit in one hand. Neither my brain nor my body was prepared to handle that sight. A slow flush climbed up my neck as I looked from Ronan's freshly washed torso, carved with corded muscle, to the plate of succulent fruit he held. My stomach growled audibly.

"Come on," he said with a faint note of amusement and stepped forward to urge me in with his free hand. I stumbled over the threshold, only barely stopping myself from falling flat on my face. Ronan grabbed my upper arm and steered me toward the bed before turning to lock the door and saying a few words in a language I couldn't understand. He set the tray next to me on the bed and peered at me critically.

"You're knackered." I tipped to the side and buried my head in his pillow, which smelled enticingly of sandalwood.

"I don't know what that word means," I muttered, "but you're probably right."

Ronan pulled me up and held a peach beneath my nose. I nearly took his finger off when I bit into it and moaned with pleasure as the flavor burst in my mouth and juices ran down my chin.

"How could a tired, bruised woman eating a piece of fruit like a hungry goat possibly be sexy?"

I nearly spit out my peach and then choked trying to swallow it.

"You tell me," I laughed, doing my best to finish the fruit in one bite. He took the chair across from me as I shoveled fruit into my mouth with abandon.

"Did you talk to Cecily?" I asked around a mouthful of another fruit that tasted something like an apple but had the texture of a grape.

"I did."

"And what did she say?"

"That I should check my rooms. It appears that a few unique weapons were stolen: two from the Captain of the Guard and another from the practice ring when everyone was paying attention to the attack."

I looked up from my feast and went to wipe my mouth on the back of my sleeve before I remembered that I was still wearing my vambraces. "You think the attack on the armory was just a diversion so that others could steal those weapons?"

"Maybe," he conceded, "or it could have been a multi-pronged attack so that they were sure to walk away with something one way or another. It could even have been a local taking advantage of the distraction, but I doubt it."

"Is this kind of thing common?"

"No. It's never happened before. There's too much concentrated power in Avalon. That's why the city is locked down. There are squads searching the houses."

"Aside from attacking the Venatore, if those men stole weapons and walked with them then that's against the law, isn't it?"

"For non-Venatore, yes. Even for Venatore, there are rules regarding what kind of weapons can be taken and used in other verses. Magical weapons are prohibited to everyone, and the weapons they stole have properties that cannot be found outside of Avalon."

I looked down at my own newly acquired armor and turned my arm so that the light caught the carving, making the fox stand out in relief.

"Elf make?" Ronan asked, examining the leather with a professional eye.

"That's what Molfus said. Am I allowed to walk with these?"

He nodded, sending wet locks of slightly curling hair bouncing on his forehead. "You are. What the elves do isn't exactly magic. Magic has to do with forces and energies being controlled by the will of a person, sometimes with spells or potions or other means. But what the elves do is part of what they are, like a skill or ability. It's hard to explain, but it's not the kind of thing that could retard the growth of a society or conquer a continent."

"Good," I said with a yawn, "I didn't want to leave these behind."

"What you need to do," Ronan informed me, taking the mostly empty plate from my lap and setting it down on the table before climbing over me and making himself comfortable on the bed next to me, "is get some sleep."

I bit my lips and looked down at him as heat suffused my face. Ronan was already ridiculously handsome, with rugged features, a sensual mouth, and a jawline that seemed to be made for nuzzling. But lying there, his dark head on the pillow and a gentle smile on his lips while the early afternoon sunlight made his skin glow, he was almost painfully beautiful.

"Sleep," he coaxed.

"I need a bath," I disagreed, scowling down at my dirty, sweat-stained shirt, "I didn't have time."

Ronan reached up and pulled me down next to him, tucking me into the hollow of his arm with my head pillowed on his chest. "I like your smell," he whispered into my hair, "besides, you're so tired you'd probably drown in the tub. Sleep now, wash later."

I was wrecked, he was warm, and the rhythm of his heartbeat beneath my ear was as soothing as waves crashing on the beach.

"Why did she want you to check your room," I mumbled sleepily as my mind drifted between thoughts, "do you have some magic weapons or something?"

Ronan's long fingers slid up through my hair and gently began massaging my scalp. I was asleep before I could start purring.

CHAPTER THIRTY-TWO

W armth, like the sun on the first day of summer, cocooned me, making my skin prickle deliciously and the hairs rise on my forearms. Heat bathed my back from my shoulder blades to the back of my knees, and I stretched languorously, enjoying the warmth and the peaceful, sleepy lassitude that made my limbs heavy but my skin exquisitely sensitive. Air stirred near my ear and sent goosebumps down my neck and back as a warm weight settled across my ribs just beneath my breasts, which tightened in a swift rush of anticipation.

My eyes flew open. Darkness had settled on Ronan's room, but pale, silvery moonlight was pouring through the window behind us, stealing all the color and outlining the inside of the chamber with surprising clarity. I was lying on my side, and the heat behind me was Ronan's body, curled against my back with his nose pressed just behind my ear and one arm flung across my ribcage, his hand curled underneath me, tucked between my ribs and the blanket, millimeters below my breast. Something between panic and anticipation fluttered to life inside my belly. I resisted the urge to take a deep, rib-expanding breath and settled for shallow pants that wouldn't disturb his arm.

Ronan grunted softly in his sleep, and his arm tightened, pulling me securely against his chest as he burrowed his face in my hair. The basso rumble of his voice in my ear made another cold wave of shivers run all the way down the backs of my legs.

I can't handle this, I thought as his breath warmed the skin of my neck and his hand flexed, thumb spreading from his fingers so that it rested on my breastbone with his palm flat against my ribs and his long fingers curled beneath my breast. I bit my lips to stifle the impulse to squirm against his body.

He's sleeping. He has no idea what he's doing. It's only reflex, just relax.
Easier said than done.
Thank you, Captain Obvious.
That is not reflex!

A knee had inserted itself between mine, and his lean hips flexed against my backside. Warm tremors shot through my belly and settled heavily between my thighs. His hand slid up the outside of my sweater over the curve of my breast and squeezed lightly, sending electricity zinging along every nerve ending until it was almost painful.

"Mmm," he hummed against my hair.

Need began to build low in my belly, something I'd experienced during my admittedly limited teenaged make-out sessions, but those had been mere shadows of this compelling hunger. A second hand slid beneath my body to grip my hipbone and squeezed, pulling my hips back against him as the other hand tightened and warm lips settled against my neck.

I gasped and arched involuntarily. Ronan went completely still. I barely breathed. His hands slid slowly away from my sensitive parts and halted on more unassuming areas. I fought the urge to writhe, to encourage his hands to move.

"I'm sorry," he breathed against my ear.

My heart plummeted. "Um...I didn't mind it."

There was a ghost of a chuckle behind me in the darkness. "Didn't mind it, eh? That's not exactly a stellar recommendation."

"Well," I floundered, "I, ah, actually kind of enjoyed it."

He wrapped both arms tight around my rib cage and laughed into my hair. "Someday I'll have to get a stronger review than 'kind of enjoyed it.'" Then he continued, more seriously, "but I didn't intend to ravish you in your sleep."

Ronan pushed up onto one side, holding himself up on his elbow and rolling me toward him so that I looked up at him from my back. His eyes were heavy-lidded from sleep, his finely carved lips curved into a sensual smile that made my heart stutter.

"I've never had a woman in my bed here, and I've dreamt about doing that to you so many times...I suppose my subconscious decided to take advantage of the situation."

His sheepish expression was absurdly endearing. My mouth felt dry. It was one thing to kiss Ronan and let passion lead where it may in the heat of the moment, but it was another to admit it aloud, from the flat of my back, when we weren't touching each other. I knew what I wanted to say, but nervous tension stopped the words in my mouth so that I could only respond by shaking my head.

His eyes tightened. "I didn't mean to take advantage, Allie. I am sorry."

"No," I said blurted, upset that he'd misinterpreted my response, "there's nothing to apologize for, I—well, it's just that I—"

"You've never done this before, I know. I can tell. But there's no hurry, and I won't try to pressure you, I swear."

I cut him off by putting my hand over his mouth. "No, Ronan, I just," I paused for courage and then forced the words out, "I didn't want you to stop."

I felt him catch his breath as his eyes narrowed at me. Gently, his right hand settled against my jaw, thumb running along my bottom lip as he studied my face. "I meant it, Allison. There's no rush. As much as I want you, you're still young, and there's time."

I could tell that he felt my lips tighten into a scowl beneath his thumb because he hurriedly went on, "These last couple of months have been hard for you. You've been attacked, lost loved ones, been thrust into a reality you never imagined for yourself. It's natural that you'd feel close to the person who's been with you through all the trauma. I don't want to take advantage of that. I don't want you to regret being with me when you've adjusted to this life, once all this is over. You can make that decision when there isn't so much at stake."

Pushing his hand away from my face I sat up and turned toward him, then caught my breath again at how beautiful he was in the moonlight, like a statue carved from alabaster. Even the pale line of the scar on his belly glowed silver.

"This isn't some kind of," I floundered, searching for a word, "some kind of bond of adversity. I'm not attached to you because you're my mentor, Obi-Wan. I *know* you."

He shook his head. "You've only known me for a couple of months, Allie."

Frustrated, I pulled his hand off the bed and pressed it over my heart, closing my eyes. The skin of his wrist under my fingers was fine-grained and very warm, with coarse hairs on the back. After a moment, I could begin to feel the pulse of blood in his veins, and concentrated hard on the rhythm, letting my body relax until my own heartbeat mirrored his. I felt the sharp intake of his breath and my awareness followed as oxygen rushed past his lips and into his lungs, filling his blood with life that pulsed out from his core.

More faintly than the brush of butterfly wings or the brief, gentle kiss of newly falling snowflakes, I could sense the infinitesimal movement of the electrical field around him as it pulsed with the unique frequency that cried to me, over and over again.

"*I know you*," I repeated with certainty.

His eyes were black in the moonlight, framed with dark lashes and wide with a mixture of shock and recognition. I remembered vividly the first time he'd left me, in the park in front of my apartment building, when I'd looked up at him and had the sense that, somehow, I knew this man on a level deeper than understanding. I could see the knowledge of it in his eyes.

"This isn't the kind of thing that's going to fade with time, Ronan."

His shaking hand lifted from my breast and traced the lines of my face as if I were made of glass.

"I've known for some time," he said slowly, "that you were special to me. Your bravery, your strength," his fingertips traced the curve of my brow and down around my cheekbone, "I don't know how, but my soul knows you. I've been fighting it for a while. It feels..."

"Dangerous?" I suggested.

"Yeah. Dangerous."

I turned my face toward his right hand and held it against my cheek, pressing a kiss into the center of his palm, and closed my eyes. "I am tired," I admitted, "and scared, worried for my brother, and still struggling to find my place in all of this." Then I opened my eyes, locked them on his, and said with as much conviction as I could manage, "but I also want you. Very much."

He took both of my hands in his own, imprisoning them so I couldn't use them to force the issue, and drew in a steadying breath before saying softly, but firmly, "This isn't the right time, Allison. This is something I know a bit about. No, dammit, listen to me," he said fiercely, cutting me off before I could argue, "do you know how much I would give to lose myself in your arms? To forget everything and spend myself in your body over and over again, to pull cries from your lips and make you scream my name till it's written on your soul? And I would do it, Allison," he threatened, "I'd use you till neither of us had the power to think or feel anything else."

I cleared my throat and offered, "That doesn't sound too bad."

He laughed unwillingly as he squeezed my hands, but his voice was tortured. "Grief and danger make poor advisers. They want you to feel alive at any cost, even if that cost means the kind of regret that tears at your soul. I'll not have you live with regret, Allie. I know what it is, and your pain isn't a price I'm willing to pay."

"What makes you so certain that making love to you would hurt me?"
"

I don't have the best track record," he admitted, "but even without that, this is the wrong time to make this kind of decision. If you had more experience, maybe...but no. To give yourself to someone changes you on the inside in ways I can't fully explain. When I have you," he said, letting go of my hands and holding my face gently, "I will have all of you, Allison Chapter, with no room for regretting decisions made in the grip of danger. I want you to choose me when you know the consequences."

My throat went dry as I thought of Grainne and the weight her death had left on his shoulders.

"I can't imagine I'd ever regret choosing you, Ronan."

"That's where the danger comes from, love."

I sensed defeat as he retreated behind the walls that protected his heart, but a sudden idea took hold, and I said, "I do want to try something, though, if you're willing."

He eyed me suspiciously for a second, then nodded once. Carefully, deliberately, I leaned forward to kiss him. The first touch of our lips was hesitant; he was restrained, and I was hungry. Within seconds, though, his hands were on me, and the kiss had deepened until we were locked around each other. As soon as I felt his restraint weaken, I reached for that nebulous sense that allowed me to feel Ronan on a level I couldn't understand, and I pushed.

He groaned under my mouth, deep in his chest, in what sounded like a mixture of pleasure and pain. The noise spurred me to push harder until we were both frantic. His hunger rolled into me with physical force, and I shoved it back at him, mixed with my own desire. Whatever boundaries made us two separate beings began to blur, the same way my own body blurred as it came into harmony with a different verse only, this time, I was forcing us into harmony with each other.

With a wrenching sensation that sent the world spinning, I realized that I could feel the fine-grained texture of my own skin through Ronan's fingertips, taste the salt of my own mouth with his tongue, feel the cool silk of my unbound hair as it slid across the backs of his hands and forearms. The resiliency of my flesh beneath his palms as they slid down the curve of my waist to my hips felt as real to me as the sensations of my own fingers, which were tangled in the hair at the nape of his neck as I pressed myself against him. We *were* each other, and there was no way to know who was moving or touching or tasting. The sense of being joined was so acutely sensual that my body spasmed with it.

We pulled apart at the same time, gasping and staring wildly at each other. I ran the pad of my thumb across the tips of my fingers, felt the hardening of callouses from my training, and pressed my other hand to my head to steady myself. "I didn't really...expect that...to happen," I gasped, "but you did say...I could try it."

"I feel like I've been hit by a truck."

His hand was on his chest with his heartbeat thundering in the hollow of his throat. "What did you just do to us?"

"I don't really know."

Ronan reached out and took my hand and stared at it, turning it over as if there might be some clue to what I'd just done in the lines on my palm. "I thought I was going to die," he said with a mixture of awe and amusement, "and I wouldn't have even cared."

"You won't let me...be with you right now," I tried to explain, "but I needed you to have something of me. I mean, I didn't actually know what I was doing, but that was the only way I could think of to give it."

He shook his head in a mixture of wonder and resignation. "Remind me to clarify things the next time you try to give me gifts."

My stomach sank. "Are you mad?"

"No," he said ruefully, "I'm not mad. I don't know what that was, but I can't say I didn't enjoy it."

There was a wry twist to his lips that was incredibly sexy. "But," he said, flopping back onto the bed, "I think I need to sleep for a good week to recover from whatever it was."

The experience left me exhausted as well, and I didn't resist when Ronan pulled me toward himself and tucked me into the crook of his arm. "Let's get this mess with interdimensional assassins sorted before we tackle any of the physical stuff, though, shall we? Maybe you can try that trick again when things are settled, and I'll do my best to distract you in a few other ways."

I fell asleep with a smile on my face.

Late morning sunlight was blazing in through the window, bright red behind my eyelids when I woke up to the sound of Ronan's slow, steady breathing. Sheets were tangled around my feet, and I twisted to pull them free but stiffened as every muscle tightened in protest. Memories of the night before filled my mind like water through a floodgate. Whatever I'd done to us had taxed me physically to an almost frightening degree.

With sore muscles and a fuzzy mind, I pushed myself up and yawned. Ronan's face was serene in the hazy light, and I shifted to my side—wincing at the discomfort—so I could watch him sleep, feeling unspeakably tender. Never having slept in the same bed with a man, the novelty of the experience made me want to catalog every detail. His lips were parted ever so slightly, arms folded across his chest, and the direction of the light picked out the lump in the bridge of his nose from a break sometime long ago. The thick hair that usually obscured his forehead was slightly askew. I was reminded suddenly of Cupid and Psyche; Cupid lying in their marriage bed and Psyche, standing over her lover with a candle, enraptured by her husband's beauty.

"I must be Psyche," I murmured, reaching up to brush away the curls that always fell over his forehead, a gentle smile on my face.

Ronan jerked at my touch, and his hand shot up to close around my wrist. "What're you doing?" he demanded sleepily, throwing my arm away from him and shaking the hair back into place before scooting backward into a sitting position and rubbing his eyes. Shocked, I said nothing and dropped my own eyes to my wrist, and then raised them back to Ronan, who looked disoriented as he blinked owlishly.

"I'm sorry if I startled you," I offered, biting my lips. He made a dry noise in his throat and then closed his eyes tight before raising his brows to open them, and looked back at me.

"What?"

"You were sleeping; I'm sorry I startled you awake, I didn't mean to."

"No harm, love," he assured me, yawning. He appeared not even to realize he'd grabbed my wrist, and it occurred to me that there might be unforeseen complications in sleeping next to someone who was used to waking up in dangerous places. He winced as well and shook out his arm muscles, confused by the soreness.

Before he could ask me any questions I couldn't answer about my impulsive metaphysical attack on our senses the night before, I said, "You shouldn't let your birthmark embarrass you, you know."

Both of his hands dropped, and I leaned away from the intensity of his gaze when he asked, "What birthmark?"

"The one on your forehead. You don't have to hide it with your hair. I've got this whopper on my shoulder," I turned to look at the dark brown mark on the back of my shoulder that bore a mild resemblance to South America, but when I turned back to Ronan, my wry smile died. Face completely stiff and impassive, he looked just like he had the night I'd first met him. Unease coiled in my chest. He worked hard at a swallow, and the muscle in his jaw clenched, but he didn't speak. I shivered and tried to look anywhere but at him, not trusting myself not to burst into tears at the sudden coldness in his face, the distance in his eyes.

"I should never have let you stay the night."

I bit my lips together and swallowed before asking in a whisper, "Is this because of what I did last night?"

He flung the blankets off his legs and surged out of bed, stalking across the room toward the washbasin but stopped and grasped the corners of his dresser so hard that the wood squealed. The muscles of his arms and upper back flexed and tightened as if he could break the wood with his bare hands. When he groaned and bowed his head, the sound was so broken that a knife twisted in my guts.

"You should go get washed up," he said tonelessly, "I need...I need you to leave."

There was no point in trying to reply; I wouldn't have known what to say even if I could've forced words past the lump in my throat. Sliding silently off the bed, I glanced one last time at his wracked form, and fled.

CHAPTER THIRTY-THREE

The hallways between Ronan's room and the communal baths were vacant as I hurried through on silent feet, and when I stepped into the pungent air of the cellar, the baths themselves were blessedly empty.

Brass pipes brought water from the hot springs in the mountain behind the castle and the large stone tubs separated by wooden dividers steamed with mineral-rich water that filled the air with moisture that stuck to my skin.

I peeled off the oversized sweater and skirt, splashed into the hot water, and held my breath to sink beneath the surface. While the warm water couldn't ease the ache of my confusion and hurt at Ronan's sudden coldness, for a little while, at least, I was surrounded by warmth...even though I knew the cold floor still waited for my naked feet.

When I broke the surface, my mind was somewhat more composed, if not less pensive. As I scrubbed away several days' worth of sweat and dirt, I realized that my own body felt strangely alien. Whatever I had done last night hadn't just made my muscles sore and achy, it seemed to have altered me on an elemental level, as if my own body had betrayed me; one more thing that was far more complicated than I ever dreamed.

Clean skin and hair did me some minor good. At least my body odor was under control. I pushed the worst of my mental turmoil to the back of my mind—something I seemed to be getting good at—and set about preparing myself for whatever Ronan had planned. It was impossible not to suspect that my assault on his defenses last night had something to do with what happened this morning. He'd been hesitant to take my virginity after all, and, though I disagreed with him, at least I understood his reasons. So what had made me think that a different kind of joining, even one I didn't understand, would be less catastrophic for him?

His behavior completely confused and hurt me but, with a calmer mind, I knew that he wasn't giving up on finding my attacker. The man had killed for me, protected me, and comforted me while barely knowing me. That knowledge kept the tears at bay, but only barely.

When I walked into my room it was clean, with a wrinkle free bed and clothing tucked into the single chest of drawers. Silently thanking whichever of the castle's industrious servants had tidied my room, I pulled out a dark, buttery pair of leggings that would give me ease of movement, and a closely fitted black cotton shirt. Mid-calve leather boots with soft soles completed the ensemble, along with the vambraces Molfus had given me, which I'd carried back from the baths. My arms were still back above my head, twisting my hair into a braid when I spun at a sharp knock to see Ronan halt just inside the doorway. He was similarly attired, in almost all black utilitarian clothes that closely fitted his powerful frame. My fingers hesitated a moment, then flew through the rest of the braid as I fought to keep my features relaxed. Ronan's face was carefully neutral as he turned back to me after closing the door.

"I've got a hunch," he said without preamble, "that whoever has been behind the attacks comes from my verse."

I opened my mouth, then closed it as angry heat suffused my cheeks. "That's nice. How about you tell me why you closed off on me this morning."

His jaw tightened. I pursed my lips and raised my brows expectantly. Ronan ducked his head and ran his hand through the hair at the nape of his neck, suddenly looking half ashamed.

"Come here to me," he said.

When he opened his arms the instinct to walk into them was so great that I started to step forward before I consciously decided what to do. Instead, I shook my head. The air would be cleared here and now.

His arms dropped, and his lips tightened. "The last time I was with a woman it was Grainne. I mean, I have been with other women, but it's not the same, not the way—aw hell, I'm—" he made a frustrated noise and linked his fingers behind his neck, dropping his head and looking at his feet long enough to gather himself and say, "What you did last night, it was so intimate. Hell, that's not even a strong enough word for what it was. But it made me—I dreamed about her last night."

Sympathy washed through me, unasked and unwelcome. I walled it off and folded my arms over my chest.

His voice was raw as he continued, "Because of her, I have painful memories about my birthmark. So, I woke up thinking of her, and when you mentioned my birthmark—" his voice died, and he growled in the back of his throat, "you didn't deserve that, and I'm sorry. I was feeling raw, but I didn't have any right to talk to you that way."

"You hurt my feelings."

He groaned and took two quick steps toward me, folding his arms around me, kissing my forehead and cheeks and eyelids.

"I'm sorry," he breathed, "I'm sorry, Allison. I don't ever want to hurt you, and I'm so damn scared that's exactly what I'll do. God, I've already done it."

His pain and regret felt as present and clear to me as my own emotions ever had, and it surprised me so much that I stiffened in his arms and pulled back to stare at him. He was looking back at me, a mirror of my surprise on his face.

"Did you..." I hesitated, unsure how to phrase what I had just felt so that it would make any sense, "did you feel that?"

Ronan closed his mouth, swallowed, and nodded.

"What was it?" I asked, "I didn't do anything that time."

He shrugged, looking as baffled as I felt, and said, "I don't know. I've never even heard of anything like that."

"Was it my fault?"

"I don't know that, either."

As the silence began to stretch, I wanted him to pull me back into his arms and tell me that whatever had happened it would be okay but, instead, he held me slightly away from himself by my upper arms. For a moment, his eyes were filled with longing, and he leaned forward to kiss my forehead, his fingers tightening around my arms as his lips pressed against my brow once, tenderly. Then he let go of me and stepped back until we were out of arms reach. His eyes had become opaque, his face blank.

"Let's go find out who's been trying to kill you."

A knife was strapped to my thigh, another tucked inconspicuously into my boot, and two were sitting crosswise at my lower back, sheathed and held in place by a wide leather belt that sat low on my hips. Ronan strode next to me as we left the Bastion in the mid-afternoon sunlight, crunching through areas of frost that still clung to the grass in the shadow of the stone buildings. I had been right in my certainty that, despite the debacle that morning, Ronan was committed to finding my father's killer. Unfortunately, I was now less certain about the state of our relationship.

He had retreated behind the mask again, and while he was still more relaxed than he had been when we first met, I felt as if he was withdrawing from me as slowly and surely as the tide from the shore. With no idea what to do, I fell back on pretending that nothing was wrong.

"What's the plan?" I asked, and then added, "why do I feel like I'm in a heist movie when I ask you that?"

"A what?"

"A heist movie."

He made a confused noise in response, and I rolled my eyes.

"You've seen Star Wars, but you've never seen a heist movie?"

"I was in True Earth when Return of the Jedi was released. The movie poster looked intriguing."

I pursed my lips and raised my eyebrows at him while he held a tall blackberry vine out of the way for me. "Leia in the bikini?"

He shrugged, then asked, "So what exactly is a heist movie?"

"Never mind, tell me what your plan is."

He sighed. "I recognized that boar on the torc when I saw it," he told me, "it's the sigil of a family in my own verse, a very particular sigil. I've never seen it's like. But I wasn't sure if it was a coincidence or not until our prisoner nearly killed himself trying to get away from us. That tattoo on his chest linked everything, especially since he spoke in Irish Gaelic."

"That brings up something I want to know," I interrupted, "why was a simple slap enough to stop him from Walking in the first place?"

"You remember when I told you that being in pain makes Walking harder, more dangerous?"

The memory of my own experience bubbled to the surface and ice slid down my spine. "Yes."

"Well, it's possible to interrupt someone's ability to Walk by breaking their concentration. Doing anything that stops their train of thought effectively will make it difficult or nearly impossible to Walk. It takes a very disciplined or a very powerful Walker to ignore the pain enough to Walk without harming themselves."

I thought of Ronan Walking me to my own verse with a gunshot wound and shivered at the chance he'd taken. Right on the heels of that emotion came a burst of resentment that he would be withdrawing from me now, after all we had been through since then. "Okay, that makes sense. Pray continue, Obi-Wan. Tell me about the boar."

He scowled at my tone and said, "When we saw the dead body with the same tattoo, and Molfus told me about the weapons the attackers were using, weapons common to my Ireland, that was confirmation. Whoever is still behind this sigil, they're the one trying to kill you."

"But, I've never been to your verse, " I protested, "why would someone from your verse be after me?"

"That's what we need to find out."

I jumped over a moss-covered log and scrambled up the steep hillside to keep up with Ronan's long strides. While the sun was out, the air was chill with the breath of winter, and the tip of my nose had started to go numb.

"Are you sure we should be doing this alone? We don't know what we're walking into."

"More people aren't always an advantage. Too many people would make us more conspicuous, and the only people I would trust to come with us...well, they wouldn't exactly blend in."

"Megayn?" I asked on intuition.

"She's one of them."

"Yeah, I suppose she'd be fairly obvious anywhere but here. She's Venatore though, right?"

"She is." "How can she do her job, then? She can't walk to all the verses, can she? Or are there more worlds with...cat people?"

"Neither can we, but that's not a requirement. She's still helpful in her own verse, and there are plenty she can walk to without being noticed."

"Why do you trust her?"

He glanced back over his shoulder at me and replied, "I trained her."

That surprised me. I'd always thought of Ronan as a bit of a lone wolf, but imagining him training Megayn the way Danet had begun to train me, cast him in a different light. Molfus had told me that Ronan was in Avalon less than most Venatore, but of course, he must have trained at least a few new Walkers during his long years of service.

"You said your foster father was a powerful Walker, right?" I asked, "What was his name? Adolf?"

"Angus. And no, he won't help. He was in Endre, last I knew, with no intentions of leaving. He does things for his own purposes. I wouldn't trust him with your life."

"What about Cecily or Abasi or Molfus?"

"Cecily has more important things to do, Molfus has duties here, and Abasi wouldn't exactly go unnoticed in Ireland in my verse."

"What does Cecily do that's so important?"

"That," he said as we gained the top of the hill, "is something I can't tell you unless you become full Venatore and not just a trainee."

I frowned at him and pushed a stray lock of hair out of my eyes. "I can't become Venatore just to satisfy my curiosity, Ronan. I hate unanswered questions."

His tone was wry as he said, "I've noticed."

"And you still haven't told me what we are going to do, exactly."

Ronan grabbed the end of my braid as it lay over my breast and tugged on it, widening his eyes at me. "Maybe I would if you'd stop asking—so—many—questions," he pulled on the braid with each word and then tossed it over my shoulder. I touched my mouth with my thumb and forefinger pinched together and ran my fingers over my lips with a mumbled zipping noise while looking at him expectantly. His eyes were far away as he began pulling his own knives out of various sheaths and double-checking the edges.

"I haven't been back to Eiru since Fionn let me die, so I don't know what they're wearing now or how the culture has changed, which means we've got to be careful about getting involved with the locals until we find out. If things aren't too different, or if we blend in enough, then we can start asking questions. Well," he amended, "I can start asking questions."

"I can't ask questions?"

"Do you speak Irish?"

"Erm, no."

"Then you can be quiet."

I scowled at him, and he smirked then spun and, with a long over-hand throw that looked almost lazy, released his knife at the dead tree across the clearing from us. The tip sunk into the wood with a heavy thunk.

"Your turn. You drank the nectar?"

I nodded and looked dubiously at my knife. "I don't know if that's going to help me. It's not like throwing a baseball, and I only started to learn how to do this with Danet a couple of days before you came back."

"You don't need to be an expert before we leave. I just want you to get some experience throwing with your vambraces on. It will feel different than it did during your training."

While my efforts weren't laughable, my success wasn't anything to brag about either. The blade struck home more often than not, but the distance wasn't great, and the angle of the knife wasn't always ideal. I'd be more likely to anger someone than hurt them.

"Don't be hard on yourself. Knife throwing isn't something you can pick up in a single afternoon. You've got enough of the basics to operate, though you need to make sure you've got space between yourself and your target. A person can close the distance quickly, and a knife in your hand is more effective than one you throw away."

"We aren't planning on any knife throwing during this trip, are we?"

Ronan worked his own knife out of the tree trunk and tested the tip with his thumb. "Nope. But I'd rather have the knife and not need it than need it and not have it."

The hilt of my knife was still warm from my palm when I pulled it from the tree, and I considered the blade, trying to imagine myself using the steel on another human being. "What if I can't use it?"

If Ronan was curious about the plaintive note in my voice, it didn't show on his face when he looked up from sheathing his own knife. "If the time ever comes when you must use that knife, you won't have time to think about the moral dilemma of whether it's right or wrong to take a life. Your own life will be in danger, and you'll either do everything within your power to protect yourself, or you'll probably be dead."

"Well," I gulped, "that was direct."

"A knife is a direct weapon, Allison. What it does is ugly. There's no use trying to soften that."

My blade slid home with the whisper of steel against leather, and I imagined what it would be like to push the knife up under someone's ribs, as Danet had taught me. I couldn't stop myself from shuddering.

"Don't worry," Ronan placed his hand over mine where it still clutched the hilt, "anyone who forces you to use that will deserve what they get. All 5 inches of it."

"Using my fists is one thing," I told him, trying to ignore the surge of hope I felt as his skin touched mine, "but stabbing someone is something else. Logically, I know that I might have to use a weapon to save myself, but the thought of cutting into someone..." I shrugged and flexed my hands.

"You come from a sanitary culture, Allison. Where you grew up, people can afford to practice non-violence. Where you're going," his eyes hardened as he reminded me, "where you *insisted* on going, non-violence may not be an option. There are places where the strong can take from the weak or kill the weak, without repercussion, unless another strong person stands in their way."

He took my wrist in his hand and turned my arm over to the place where the silver of my bracelet showed through the straps of my vambraces and tapped it with one fingernail, making a muted metallic sound that vibrated against my skin. "There's someone out there who thinks they can hurt you and the people you love because they're stronger than you are. Men who thought they could hurt Rayne and Mateo because they were willing to be violent, and they knew your friends couldn't defend themselves."

"So, I make myself stronger," I finished.

"You can do that, or rely on someone else who is strong enough. But someone must be willing to stand in the gap, and if that person is you and your fists aren't enough..." He left the implication hanging there.

I wanted to believe there could be a world where people respected one another, where people didn't take advantage or hurt others simply because they could, or because it was convenient. And maybe someday there would be. But that wasn't the reality I lived in. Safe places existed because some people were willing to be violent, willing to take life, to stand in the gap between the innocent and the aggressor. Could I be that person?

"Come along, little philosopher," he urged, "no more time for thinking. The longer we wait, the colder the trail will grow. It's been two days since the attack on the Bastion. We know from the tattoos that the person who has been trying to kill you, and the attack on the Bastion are related. We know, based on the evidence, where the attacks originated from. Let's go find out how we can put an end to this."

CHAPTER THIRTY-FOUR

E vening sun had forced its way through broken clouds, backlighting the gently sloping carpet of grass in a golden haze that haloed the entire countryside. I blinked hard and waited for the blazing imprint of the sun to fade from behind my eyelids, but my first impression of the land wasn't ever likely to fade; rich, verdant green under an achingly blue, broken sky.

Luckily for us, the sun was minutes from descending beyond the tree-lined horizon, and we'd soon be protected by darkness. But, for the moment, I was awed by the countryside that rolled away from the hill we stood on. Stone fences divided the land into parcels, pierced here and there by rocks and boulders that stood solitary sentinel over grazing animals. Thin coils of chimney smoke rose in the distance between the trees only to fade into the evening sun. I turned toward Ronan to exclaim at the beauty of the place, and the words died in my chest.

He was bathed in golden light, his bold features cut cleanly by the slanting rays. Stark longing and sorrow mixed with regret had drawn the skin around his eyes tight and flattened the line of his mouth. Whatever barrier he had erected between us, it wasn't strong enough to stop me from reacting to Ronan's pain. His hand was cold when I slipped my own into it.

"I meant never to see this place again," he admitted in a voice raw with emotion. I squeezed his hand.

A double circle of mounded earth ringed the hill we stood on, which was swiftly falling into shadow. It struck me that the ground falling away on all sides of us meant that we were sky-lined against the setting sun and, if anyone were looking, our silhouettes would be easily visible from the entire countryside. It wasn't the best place to show up suddenly, but I knew we hadn't had much choice in that; this was a place of power, and the inexorable pull of it captured us as we Walked. Ronan didn't resist as I pulled him down to recline against the side of the innermost circle, hiding us from outside eyes.

"I'm sorry," he murmured, "I had convinced myself that coming here wouldn't affect me but, suddenly I feel like a stag chased by hounds. I'm either going to give in or run until my heart bursts."

I scooted against the side of his body and watched the last rays of the sun set fire to the clouds, hoping to give the comfort of closeness since I had no advice to give. He hadn't been exaggerating. His heart was only beginning to slow.

"I'm the one who should be sorry," I countered after a moment, "after all, you wouldn't be here if it weren't for me."

"Maybe not, but I don't regret it, Allie. I missed this place to my very soul. Besides," he said with a shrug, beginning to sound more like himself, "the attack on the Bastion would have led me here, eventually. So, no need to feel guilty."

All traces of melancholy were gone from his face, which was schooled once again into a business-like mask. Was the ability to control emotion something he had gained with the passage of so much time or was it the self-protective result of suffering? If suffering, then I hoped it was a skill I could learn, and soon. I suspected that I could only push my emotions aside for so long before they would start trying to claw their way out of my ribcage. Sarcasm, my usual defense, now seemed insufficient armor.

Ronan lifted his arm and wrapped it around my shoulders to pull me against his side while we waited for the cover of darkness. He was always warmer than I and his scent, that mix of leather and sandalwood spiced with whiskey, was absurdly comforting to me in the face of what we were about to attempt, despite the fact that his embrace felt less like intimacy and more like utility; body heat was body heat, after all.

"This shouldn't be that dangerous," he told me as if reading my mind or, more likely, the sudden tension in my muscles, "since we're only gathering information."

"Right. And we can always walk back to Avalon if things start to get hairy."

"Get hairy? That's an interesting euphemism."

"Better than a boring euphemism."

"Fair enough, but I don't see why hair would be a choice descriptor for trouble."

"You've never tried to shave your armpits," I pointed out.

He snorted in amusement and glanced at the sky. "Looks like the last of the light is as good as gone. Let's have a look around."

While it appeared to be a smooth carpet in the sunset light, the hillside was nowhere near as easy to navigate in the dark as I'd imagined. Grass grew in hillocks that seemed to reach up to snag the toes of my boots, and I rolled my ankle more than once in the valleys between mounds. Ronan seemed as sure-footed as a cat as he strode down the hillside.

We reached a hard-packed dirt track that skirted the base of the hill and followed it west toward the area where I'd seen chimney smoke rising. Darkness was complete beneath the trees, and I had to rely on

Ronan's sense of direction and confident strides to keep from tripping over imagined obstacles. Luckily, the path was well worn, and the going was easy, at least until Ronan came to a sudden halt and I ran into his back.

"Oww," I moaned, fingering my nose where it had struck Ronan's shoulder blade. The number of times we ran into one another was beginning to get ridiculous. He reached behind, grabbed my arm, and pulled me off the path to crouch in the undergrowth. Seconds later the muted, rhythmic thump of horse hooves broke the silence.

The rider was a darker shadow against the night, though I could hear the creak of saddle leather and the clink of tack as the horse plodded down the path. We waited several minutes after the sounds had disappeared before making our way back to the road.

"No industrial revolution here, I guess," I noted.

Ronan made an uncertain noise in the back of his throat. "Maybe not, but it's hard to say. Even in True Earth, there are places in the countryside where horses are still regularly used."

"I didn't see any signs of modern cities from the top of the hill. And no light pollution."

"Fair point, but I'd still wait to count my ducks."

"Chickens."

He turned toward me. "What?"

"Count chickens," I corrected, "you don't count chickens before they're hatched, not ducks."

"Who says so?"

"I don't know, everyone."

"They both hatch from eggs, yeah?"

"Yes."

"And people eat them both, right?"

"Yeah."

He started walking again, brushing off my correction. "Then I like ducks better. They don't attack you with their spurs or wake you up early. Chickens are crabby wee bastards."

I shook my head and followed him into the darkness.

We made our way to a path beneath the trees at the bottom of the hill, feeling out each step on the hard-packed earth as crickets started their nightly symphony. Wood smoke in the air forced Ronan to slow our pace as the scent of humanity grew stronger. Pale light was visible around the bend in the path where the trees thinned. We followed the road until it opened into a clearing where a circular house with a peaked roof, much like a witch's hat, stood with whitewashed walls glowing in the pale moonlight.

I had assumed that the smoke rising was from a chimney, but I was right only by association. There was a large white dome that reminded me of a beehive rising out of the ground near, but not touching, the house, while smoke rose from something like a chimney that came out of the ground directly opposite the beehive on the other side of the house. The style of the home reminded me of movies I'd seen set during medieval times but, even in the weak moonlight, it was clear that the construction was much more advanced, almost as if the circular shape was the stylistic choice of some avant-garde architect rather than a building of necessity.

As we neared the home, creeping carefully across the yard at the back between a smallish kitchen garden and a wattle chicken coop, radiant heat from the beehive oven warmed the side of my body from more than two feet away. Ronan motioned for me to wait and crept as silently as any night creature around the side of the house.

We'd discussed the kinds of things we could look for to give us clues about the advancement of society, like the kinds of tools people would be using. Of course, we'd need to see more than just one or two homes to justify our observations, but what we found tonight could set us up for another trip where we could move amongst the people to find out more about the boar's head sigil without drawing too much attention to ourselves. If this was truly where my attacker originated, I certainly didn't want to go flaunting myself openly. I was still considering how much we could learn before Walking back to Avalon when a sharp pain stabbed the side of my neck, and I slapped at the sting with a surprised squeak of alarm. There was a disconcerting, wet crunch beneath my hand and disgust made an involuntary shudder run down the back of my arms as I wiped the body of whatever bug had bitten me on my thigh.

A male voice rose suddenly in the night, shouting a challenge in a language I couldn't understand, and I spun to put the beehive heater between myself and the home, crouching down and holding my breath as the challenge was repeated. Pale yellow light spilled from the doorway of the home and showed a large, wavering shadow against the ground. Where was Ronan?

A woman's voice raised in question. There was a break in her voice, which sounded raw and tired.

The man responded in a calming tone, and his voice was nearer to me. I bit my lips and shifted to the balls of my feet in case I needed to move quickly, pulling in a slow, quiet breath and tensing my muscles. There was a short conversation between the man and woman, who I assumed to be husband and wife, in the same rolling, musical accent that sounded like it was spoken with the whole mouth and throat. He sounded conciliatory, she worried, and both tired. I gritted my teeth, hoping they'd go back inside, but they seemed content to stand just outside their threshold. The more I listened to them speak, the more I felt as if I should understand what they were saying, even just by the lyrical cadence of the speech, but the words were too foreign, and the pain on the side of my neck was distracting.

Finally, the duo re-entered their home, and I sighed in relief, easing toward the chicken coop when a hand clamped down over my mouth, hard. My elbow shot back instinctively but was caught and held tight.

"Be still, you little troublemaker; it's just me."

I resisted the urge to growl at Ronan and peeled his hand away from my mouth to turn and give him the evilest eye I could manage. He was less than impressed and urged me back toward the tree line.

"What was that all about?" he asked, exasperated, "I figured you'd know better than to go hollering while we're trying to sneak around."

"Something bit me on the neck, something big. I couldn't help it!"

His hand followed mine up to my neck, and he swore softly when he felt the lump left by my nighttime visitor.

"You're all right?"

"Fine. So?" Ronan looked back over his shoulder at the house in the clearing and then crouched and motioned for me to do the same.

"You know that horse that passed us on the road?"

"Yes," I whispered.

"It sounds like that was their daughter. When you made that noise, they thought she'd come back. I get the feeling that something's very wrong, here."

"What do you mean?"

"Well," he began, but stopped and rubbed his hand along his jaw, making a sandpaper noise against his palm while he thought. "It sounds like their daughter is in some kind of danger from a powerful person. The woman was asking if she'd come home, and her husband said, 'of course she didn't. You know what will happen to her if she's found here.' The wife said that maybe they wouldn't know, wouldn't find her, but the husband seemed sure that someone would come to find their daughter and take her away."

"Maybe she committed a crime," I suggested.

"I don't know, maybe. But I'd like to know who this 'they' is."

"Probably the police, or whatever they have here."

"You may be right." Then he shook his head and gestured with his chin toward the road where it curved away from the clearing and back into the woods. "Let's see what else we can find."

The forest began to thin until the land opened into wide patches with homes here and there or in small groups, much the same as the thatch-roofed house we'd first seen. Nearly every home was similar, with beehive ovens and several smaller outbuildings and, here and there, herds of grazing cattle or sheep. What tools we did find were well made, though there seemed to be a shortage of metal and not a single piece of recognizable technology. One large home, which was rectangular rather than circular and sported several wings, even had a large barn where we found a huge wooden plow.

"It's like they've not gone beyond the 17 or 1800's," I whispered to Ronan, fingering a block of peat from atop a pile of fuel as tall as I was.

"The man we saw at the first house was wearing a pair of short trousers and stockings, similar to what I saw in Europe in the 1700's," he mused.

"Should we wait for daylight to see more?"

He thought only a second before shaking his head. "No, it's not worth the risk. I've got a pretty good idea. There are quite a few verses where the industrial revolution hasn't happened yet, and many of them are a lot like this," he gestured around us as we walked back through the brush toward the path, "so you were likely right."

Light was just beginning steal back into the sky, which was now deep indigo shifting into purple-grey.

"How far have we walked?" I asked, surprised to see the stars beginning to fade. Ronan looked behind us toward the sleeping village and then toward the sky, getting his bearings. "We must be close to the River Boyne," he speculated.

"Is that far?"

"Maybe six or seven kilometers."

"Dang, that's not a bad distance in the dark."

"Not for what we needed to do," he agreed.

"What happens now?"

Ronan's eyes strayed to my lips, which began to tingle, and then his jaw clenched, and he shifted his gaze toward the horizon. I wanted to grit my teeth.

"We go home," he said, "and get some sleep and then come back, but this time in costume and prepared to snoop around in people's lives a bit. We'll have to be prepared to stay more than a couple of days, but..." He hesitated and his mouth twisted, "I still get the feeling that something is wrong here. I don't want to be caught unprepared when we come back."

As if he'd uttered a prophecy, the sound of galloping hoofbeats rolled like distant thunder from the direction we'd just come. Leaping a low stone wall that fronted the road, we crouched behind the rock as the sound grew louder. There was a sudden, terrified shout followed so closely by an animal scream of pain that the two noises sounded like one prolonged cry, save that both were cut off abruptly by a crash and thud that shook the ground near us.

I had twisted my head just as I'd heard the first cry, so I was in time to see a horse and rider go down, hitting the ground with bone-crunching force and a tangle of limbs. Ronan and I glanced at each other once and then vaulted the wall to run toward the accident. The rider was a girl, no more than 17, who lay with arms flung wide, half stunned with the pain of impact, skirts thrown haphazardly about her waist. I slid to a stop on my knees near her head and looked down into her pale face as she struggled for breath.

"Shhh, it's okay, you've got the wind knocked out of you. Calm down," I said in the most soothing voice I could manage, "just try to relax, the breath will come."

Her lips were pulled together as she dragged at the air like a landed fish, eyes wide with fright and confusion.

Ahhh, I thought, giving myself a mental forehead slap, *she can't understand you, idiot.*

The girl tried to sit up but winced and fell back, finally pulling in a bit of breath and whimpering as she curled on her side toward me. I looked down and realized that her wrist was lying at the wrong angle, bent slightly toward the inside of her arm. I winced as well and rubbed her back.

"Shhh, it's okay," I murmured, trying to sound soothing even if she couldn't understand my words, and looked up as Ronan approached.

"The poor beast was run half to death and full of arrows, broke its leg in the fall," he gritted, rubbing his hands briskly against his pants. I glanced over at the horse, then at Ronan.

"Did you..." I swallowed and gestured with my chin toward the horse.

He nodded, and I grimaced. "She's got a broken wrist. She hit the ground pretty hard. I didn't want to check her yet since she can't understand what I'm saying, and I don't want to scare her by feeling all over her body."

I shifted so Ronan could kneel close to the girl, and he said something in a low, fluid voice. Her wide eyes fixed on him, and she nodded, stammering out a response as tears started to run from the corners of her eyes. Ronan lifted her easily, though she whimpered and held her arm against her chest. He asked something else, gesturing back toward the village with a jerk of his head and I saw her body stiffen as she responded in a voice dripping with panic.

He leaned the girl gently against the stone wall and asked her something. She looked up at me, then back to Ronan and nodded shakily, murmuring something I couldn't' understand.

"She says you can check her for other injuries, but asks that you hurry. Someone is chasing her, and she's frightened."

"I can tell," I said, running my hands along her limbs to check for other breaks, "what is she running from? Who the hell would shoot up her horse like that?"

Ronan didn't answer since he was already talking to her in the rolling language of this land. In an effort to concentrate, I pushed their voices to the back of my mind and tried to remember everything my mom had taught me about first aid. There was enough light in the sky now that I could clearly see her pupils, both moving evenly and contracting to the same size as she spoke. Her neck muscles felt tense but supple with youth, and the bones of her neck were thankfully straight and smooth beneath the skin. I closed my eyes to recreate the spinal column in my mind, feeling the edges of each bone to make sure there were no fragmented pieces. I opened my eyes abruptly and jerked my hands away from her with a gasp.

"Allie?" Ronan asked, looking from my shaking hands to my face.

"She's," I squeaked and cleared my throat then took a slow breath to steady myself, clasping my hands in my lap to still them. In as normal a tone as I could manage, I said, "she's a Walker, Ronan."

His head snapped toward me. "What? How do you know that?"

"I don't know," I admitted, looking down at my hands and shuddering as I remembered feeling down beneath her skin and bones as the subtle vibration ran up my fingertips.

"I felt it," I whispered, "I can feel what she is."

For a moment he looked as if he didn't want to believe me, but then his face cleared and he nodded briskly before firing off another series of questions at the girl, which she could only answer in whimpers as her breathing became more ragged. Color started to drain from her face, and I leaped forward to catch her as she fainted.

"She's in shock," I said, and shifted her so that her head was pillowed on the grass. "Raise her feet."

Ronan lifted her feet and placed them on a rock. "We've got to get her out of here, Allison."

I looked up and shook my head, "No, not yet. Shock could kill her."

"She says the King's men are chasing her, and they can't be far behind."

"Maybe we should let them take her, she needs help, and I can't give it to her."

"No, we can't do that. They're trying to kidnap her, she says. I knew something was wrong here. She's running."

"What would the King's men want with her?"

Ronan's jaw clenched as he looked down at the girl, sympathy and disgust in his eyes. "If she's a Walker like you said, then I suspect he's breeding himself an army."

"What!?"

"She said he takes all the gifted girls. Magic is more common in this verse than in many others, or at least it was when I...before I left. From what I could get out of her, the King takes all the people who have any magic into his service, whether they want to or not."

I scowled, sliding my fingers underneath the girl's jaw to settle on her carotid artery, feeling her pulse push back against the pressure of my fingers in a reassuringly steady rhythm.

"How could they do that?" I asked quietly. Ronan didn't answer me, but he didn't have to. I knew full well what lengths evil people would go to, and suspected how powerful a man could be if he managed to control people with the kind of gift, or curse, this girl was born with.

"Okay, let's get her out of here," I agreed.

We had just started to lift her when the sound of thunder shook the ground beneath our feet. Ronan swore viciously and looked from the girl's face to the tree line, nearly a hundred yards up the road.

"Get out of here," he barked at me, stepping to the side and taking the girl from me with a powerful twist of his body. "Walk back to Avalon. I'll distract them and follow with the girl as soon as I can."

The first horse came around the bend in the road near the village behind us, and we both took off toward the trees at a dead run.

"Go," he huffed at me as he tried to concentrate on running while holding the girl.

"Not a chance, Obi-Wan," I gasped, hearing shouts as the ground rolled beneath us with thundering hoofbeats. The sound of buzzing passed within an inch of my ear as I hit the tree line and a red-shafted arrow buried itself in the bark of the tree near me. I spun, shocked, to see the first rider bearing down on us while Ronan was still twenty feet from even the minimal safety of the trees. I'd outstripped him, running with no burden, and the rider was already nocking another arrow. Without stopping to think, I pulled a knife from the sheath at my thigh, drew my arm back, and threw. The distance was too great for accuracy, but the knife came close enough that the rider flinched, drawing off his shot as Ronan passed safely into the trees with his burden.

Seconds later the horseman drew up, his mount sitting fully on its haunches to kill their forward momentum, and leaped from the horse. There was no way Ronan could outrun the man and, if he wasn't interrupted quickly, he'd have another arrow on the string.

"Get her out of here!" I yelled at Ronan while pulling both knives from the small of my back. I closed the distance in a rush to stop him from having the opportunity to draw another weapon and started a series of slashes and thrusts that Danet had drilled into me. The man dodged my first cut, took a long slash across his arm meant for the body, and then kicked me solidly in the stomach. I saw the shift in his bodyweight an instant before he kicked me and tightened my stomach muscles to deflect the full power of the blow, but it still sent me stumbling backward. He rushed in, and I swung a slashing cut toward his face, but I was off-balance, and he batted the knife from my hand with a backhanded swing that made my arm go numb to the elbow.

I caught him as he bulldozed me and both of us hit the ground with a jarring crash, all the air crushed out of me by the combined weight of his body and the force of our fall. Though dazed, I wrapped my arms and legs around him to keep him from getting enough leverage to rain blows down on me as I fought for air with my face pressed hard against his neck. Though he couldn't get a full swing, the strike to my side made me grunt in pain, and I tightened my legs, trying to squeeze the air out of him. We couldn't stay locked that way for long, so I took a gamble, letting go with my freehand long enough to pull the knife from my boot and twist my body for a blow. The tip struck but skittered off a rib.

The man arched off me with a cry of pain, hands going involuntarily to his back. The knife sunk up to the hilt in his side with the second thrust and he cried out, bucking backward so forcefully that the knife jerked out of my hand and disappeared into the leaf mold. I scrambled to my feet in time to see another fifteen men on horses leaping to the ground just beyond the trees. I turned and ran after Ronan, who hadn't made it as far away as I'd hoped. My fight had lasted only a handful of seconds, not nearly enough for Ronan to disappear in the growing light.

"You," I panted as I caught him, "have to...get her...out. Walk her...too many of...them."

Ronan shifted the girl in his arms and growled, then stopped and turned to me. Men were coming at us through the bushes not fifty feet away, with swords drawn and shields held over their torsos. It was too late. Even if Ronan tried to Walk with the girl right now, they'd be on us before he could bring a second, inexperienced person into harmony with Avalon.

"Walk out of here with her," he ordered me, "and I'll hold them until you're gone."

"No! I can't leave you here," I gestured sharply at the girl, "and I don't know how to do it."

He grabbed the front of my shirt and kissed me hard, then pulled one of his knives out and sunk it into the right eye of the man closest to us with a throw so fast it was a blur. I fell on the girl, covering her with my body as Ronan rushed the next two men, moving like a dancer between sword thrusts, catching one man by the wrist and twisting his body with a sudden hard snap that sent the man's sword tumbling to the ground while he aimed a front kick at the shield of the other, who stumbled sideways into the man that had been trying to flank him, giving Ronan a precious second to snatch the sword off the ground and go to work.

I tore my eyes away from him and wrapped my arms around the girl, focusing on her and trying to bring my body into harmony with Avalon, but she flinched awake and cried out, pulling at her arm and whimpering. I could feel myself starting to slip, but the girl's body remained tense, frightened, and in pain. Ronan had said it would be both hard and dangerous to try and Walk when your mind was distracted.

"You have to calm down," I told her urgently, "I can get you out of here, but you've got to relax." She only cried and cradled her arm, repeating something I couldn't understand over and over. Frustrated I looked up to see that Ronan had killed five men and now stood holding two swords as the rest of the men on horseback dismounted, five swordsmen and three archers with bows drawn. Ronan held both blades low, his stance relaxed but ready. The archers fired, and Ronan's arm pivoted in its socket, slicing two arrows clean out of the air as the third went whizzing by over my head. I tried to cover the girl with my own body as a battle broke out again. There was another twang of releasing arrows, and then a voice shouted, "Stad!"

I looked up to see a large man, almost as tall as Ronan, with a beard and light brown hair, striding behind the line of archers. He had a gold torque around his neck and a face set in lines of pure astonishment. The men, who were clearly under his command, stopped the attack and backed up a few steps from Ronan's blades, one of them limping.

"Diarmuid?" the man asked in disbelief.

Ronan stiffened.

"Diarmuid Ua Duibhne?" the man repeated.

"Niall? How are you..." Ronan's voice died away, not seeming to realize he hadn't replied in his native tongue.

"English?" The man asked, incredulous, but went on to demand, "How is it ye'r still breathing, Diarmuid? It is you, but I watched ye die. And where have ye been, these many years?"

Ronan didn't answer the question, but adjusted his grip on the swords and asked in a low, flat voice, "What is the meaning of this, Niall?"

"Ye'r stealing the property of the King, boyo."

"She's a person, Niall, not property."

"She's a Faery. She's not human."

"Since when do the Fianna persecute the Fae?"

"The Fianna?" the man laughed derisively, "nay, Diarmuid, the Fianna died when you did. The King takes all the Fae into his service."

"Allison, take the girl and get out of here." Ronan's voice was low and calm but urgent.

"I'm trying," I whispered, "but she's fighting me. She's in too much pain, and I don't know how."

The frantic need to flee made my whole body shake with urgency, but I couldn't Walk at the expense of leaving Ronan or abandoning this girl, who was holding onto my shirt with her good hand in white-knuckled desperation while she buried her face in my neck.

"Concentrate, Allison. You can do this."

The man Ronan had called Niall gave a low whistle, and his eyes widened as they fixed on me. "She's Fae too, is she not?" He studied me for a moment, and his brow lowered as his eyes flicked back to Ronan. Realization stole slowly across Niall's features, and he breathed, "Ye all are," then gave a sharp command in Gaelic.

Bowstrings were drawn tight, and Ronan shouted, "Allie, go!" before leaping forward in a vicious attack that left one man dead before I could turn my head.

"Come on," I begged the girl, closing my eyes again and focusing will all my strength on Avalon, dragging my scattered mind and frantic atoms into harmony with all the force of my will. It wasn't until I started to hum in my chest that her body relaxed a bit. She must have realized what I was trying to do because I felt it when her own frequency began to alter as she tried to match the tone I was creating. We were starting to fade when she cried out, and fiery pain shattered my concentration, slamming me back into the present moment with a force that made me shudder.

An arrow had pierced my right biceps, entering just above my vambrace and passing cleanly through the muscle, out the other side, and right into the neck of the girl. She was making a gurgling noise while blood seeped from her wound to run hot down my arm. "No!" I screamed and tried to reach my other hand up enough to put pressure on the bleeding, but I was half laying on the ground, and my right arm simply wouldn't hold my body weight long enough for me to pull my other arm free of her body, which was quickly going limp and heavy.

"No, no, no, no," I cried, completely helpless to do anything to save the girl beneath me, pinned to her dying body by the red-shafted arrow.

A foot came into my vision on my left side, clad in a brown leather boot caked with mud. The man bent over me, and I shied away reflectively, only to be pulled up short by the burning pain in my arm. His hands clasped the arrow, one wrapping around the shaft close to my arm and the other holding the fletching. When the arrow snapped, white-hot pain blazed up my arm. The man above me wrapped his left arm around my torso, took a firm grip on my right elbow with the other, and forced my arm down the broken shaft. I screamed, and the world went white for a blindingly painful instant.

"Allison!" Ronan roared, his voice seemed to come from a long way off. I blinked hard, and the world came slowly into focus. Ronan was fighting 3 men, moving with deceptive ease as he twisted away from one thrust, spun, and blocked an overhand blow only to slide the attacker's blade down the length of his own and follow up with a kick to the knee that sent the third man stumbling to the ground. A hand fisted in my hair, and I was jerked to my feet and pulled hard against the body of the man who'd released me from the arrow.

"Stad!" he shouted again and forced my head to the side so that the pressure on my neck made me gasp. The sounds of fighting had stopped, and Ronan stood still amidst the three remaining men, chest heaving. Niall shook me and snapped another command at Ronan, whose jaw clenched and unclenched several times. His eyes were flat and deadly as he looked at Niall, and I saw for the first time that he had been injured; blood was dripping from the fingers of his left hand.

He growled something at Niall, something that sounded like a threat or a warning, but Niall answered by forcing my head farther to the side, and I couldn't' stop the sharp hiss of breath through my teeth at the stab of pain.

"No!" Ronan barked. He raised both swords threateningly, but his eyes looked almost panicked as they searched my face.

"Allison," he whispered, eyes pleading. "Go."

I knew that he'd never Walk without me, not even to save himself, and if I couldn't make a way out, he'd stay until one or both of us were dead. *He can walk once you're gone,* I told myself.

I closed my eyes and thought of Avalon. Niall must have recognized what I was doing because he tightened his grip on my hair and twisted, but the shift in my frequency didn't waver. I'd rather him break my neck than be the reason Ronan died.

Save him, I thought desperately, *save him, save him.*

Peace washed over me as I shut the pain out. I could save Ronan. *Save him.* I opened my eyes to focus on Ronan's face. *Save him, save him.*

His eyes had lost their frantic pleading, and his face seemed to relax into relief as he recognized the signs of my departure. I was going, and not even Niall pulling out clumps of my hair, screaming in my ear, or punching me viciously in the kidney, could stop me. Ronan could Walk as soon as I was gone, and I could save him.

I felt completely calm when I Walked, locking eyes with Ronan as my body fell out of harmony with his verse. My last sight as the world disappeared was of Ronan's eyes rolling back in his head when one of the king's men used the hilt of his sword to knock him unconscious

CHAPTER THIRTY-FIVE

When I opened my eyes in Avalon, I was so frantic that I ran all the way from the glade at the top of the cliff to the city gates without stopping, breath sawing in and out in ragged gasps as tears mixed with sweat to pour down the sides of my cheeks. I had left to save him, and my leaving may have damned him.

If Ronan was unconscious, then he was incapable of Walking, and that left his captors free to take additional steps to secure him when he awoke...if he did. The panic was so strong that my first instinct had been to turn around and Walk back to him, but I was no match for that many men, especially not wounded. My arm, cradled against my chest, was still oozing blood that dripped down my fingertips and spattered the ground as I ran. There was no way for me to help Ronan against trained men when I could barely flex my arm.

When I reached the gate my knees went weak, and my head started to spin from blood loss as I collapsed into a panting, sobbing heap. Pushing myself to my feet with my good arm, I took a wobbling step toward the gate only to notice that the portcullis had been dropped and there were no guards on the ramparts. I realized then that there had been no people walking the lane toward the city, either, which was unusual for the farmers of the surrounding countryside came to the capital to sell their produce. Deep unease condensed at the base of my spine.

"Hello!" I shouted up at the parapets, "someone help, please!"

There was no answer, and no one appeared between the embrasures to challenge me. I stumbled down the length of the city wall, shouting, hoping that a face would appear between the crenellations, but there was only silence. The capital of Avalon was walled entirely, and there was no way for me to climb the edifice, not even if my arm were whole. The stones had been fitted so smoothly together that not even a hand-hold could be found in the mortar between them.

"Somebody help me!"

I screamed myself hoarse, pounded on the portcullis with my good hand, and finally sank down with my back against the wood to cry out my frustration. Something was clearly wrong in the city for the gates to be closed and unmanned, very terribly wrong, but all I could think about was Ronan, alone and helpless. Were he conscious, I knew that he would find a way to escape. I knew it. But the girl had said that the King kept all the 'fae,' which I assumed meant those able to Walk between realms as the Irish gods were supposed to have done. That meant that he had some way to keep them under his power.

To make matters worse, I had no idea how time passed between Avalon and Eiru. So far, I'd only stayed a month or so at a time in Avalon, and the same amount of time seemed to have passed on True Earth, but was that true for every verse? What if I was able to find help, only to make it back to Eiru and discover that Ronan was long dead?

For a while I simply cried, helpless to stop the flow of pain and agonized frustration that tore up through my chest and leaked down my cheeks. Ronan needed help, and the only people I knew who could help were inside those walls, while I was trapped outside of them.

"Wait a minute," I muttered as a thought rose from the tangled welter of emotion. I was a Walker. Why couldn't I just Walk myself into my own room in the Bastion or, better yet, into Ronan's room? His room was in the Castle proper, and I was more likely to find help faster if I walked there. Plus, Ronan had weapons in his trunk, and I'd lost all my knives in the fight with the soldiers.

I did my best to tie an improvised dressing around my right biceps with the damaged length of the sleeve, tearing the arrow hole until the material separated. Taking a moment to catch my breath, I steadied myself as the fiery pain subsided into a throbbing sting. I'd already Walked under duress, and I thought I could do it again, but clearing my mind proved much harder than it had when Ronan was in immediate danger in front of me. Visions of what might be happening to him swam before my closed eyes, making it almost impossible to focus on redirecting my frequency. I hadn't realized how much harder it would be to Walk to another place within one verse than it was to Walk to an entirely new verse: the fluctuations in frequency and harmony were much subtler and required smaller, more exact changes.

I pictured Ronan's room, his furniture, the smell of leather and sandalwood, the fur on his floor, and the oaken trunk at the foot of his bed, and felt myself begin to vibrate the same way your chest feels when you hum, only deeper and extending through my entire body. I altered the pitch slightly, accounting for being indoors rather than being outside, and my substance slipped from the concrete reality of feet standing on the solid earth, to the unseen realm of atoms, electrons, and protons in a continuous cosmic dance of energy transfer. I felt Ronan's room, felt the solid wood of his chair and the flannel quilt on his bed, but I couldn't get there. The feeling was akin to swimming against a riptide that constantly dragged at your straining muscles, towing you farther from the safety of the shore despite exhausting yourself fighting it. And it was exhausting.

I opened my eyes in the clearing at the top of the cliff, looking down to where Avalon stood silent, miles away, and screamed at the sky. My arm throbbed with the ache of the wound and the pressure of the dressing, my chest hurt from the pointless run down the hillside and the weight of the fear that threatened to pull me under.

"Pull yourself together," I ordered myself aloud, pushing escaped strands of hair away from my face, where they'd stuck in my mouth and the wet tracks of my tears. The place of power had pulled me to itself, just as Ronan had warned me it would. It would take a significant amount of power and practice to avoid those places when trying to Walk close to them, and I had neither the power nor the training to do it, not to mention a clear enough mind to manage the intricacy; so, Walking myself into Avalon Castle was out.

With no idea what was going on in the city, I couldn't chance waiting for someone to open the portcullis. It could be a matter of hours or days, and who knew what I would find inside. The problem was that the only people I knew with the ability to help Ronan would be inside that castle. Was there any chance...

"Angus!" I burst out, catching the memory as it flitted past. A surge of hope, followed immediately by a stab of terror, raced through my veins. Ronan's advice about Walking came back to haunt me, and I shuddered at the thought of Walking right into a fight, a pit, the ocean, or some other dangerous situation, but gritted my teeth and decided to give it a go, anyway. I'd been too weak to save my father, not fast enough to save my mother, my relationship with my brother was strained, and Rayne would probably never trust me again. I was the only person who knew where Ronan was, and I'd be damned if fear would stop me from doing everything in my power to get him out of there.

Pulling together everything Ronan had told me about Walking and pushing the dangers aside, I focused on what he'd told me about the verse in which—I hoped—Angus might be found. Every specific piece of information I could remember that described that world and its people tied itself together in my head as I tried to build a picture of the place without relying on a mental image, which was an amazingly difficult psychological exercise. Like a child letting go of the edge of the pool to flounder clumsily toward the outstretched arms of its parent, I let go of Avalon and pushed myself toward the deep water knowing I might drown.

Stomach cramping with nausea, mouth dry, and blinking sand-papery eyes against the blazing sun, I stumbled and fell to my side onto pale, cool bricks and tipped over into darkness.

A blunt impact on my shoulder shocked me awake, and I started up then stilled with a groan as the pain in my arm shot fire up to my armpit. A hundred sore muscles and stiff joints cramped in protest. The push was repeated, only a nudge against my shoulder this time, and I scrubbed at my face, careful not to move my injured arm. I was no longer on the cool bricks, but sitting on the wooden bed of a cart while a woman crouched in front of me with a look of wary speculation in her wide, tilted eyes. I tried to clear my throat, but it was so dry that I only managed a raspy wheeze.

She cocked her head, sending red-brown curls tumbling over her shoulder, then spoke to me in a language of hard consonants and repeating sounds. I shook my head and shrugged my shoulders, wincing at the pain that caused in my right arm. The woman clucked at me and pointed at the arm as a line formed between her brows. After thinking a moment, I mimed, in small scale, shooting a bow and arrow and made a '*pshew*' noise, and then looked meaningfully at my wound.

She rocked back onto her heels, eyes gone wide. Trying to work up some moisture for speech, I shifted my tongue around inside my mouth before croaking, "Angus?" in a voice that sounded like it belonged to a 75-year-old career smoker.

The woman looked just as confused as I felt, and rattled off another series of unintelligible words while she leaned forward and untied my improvised bandage. The ragged hole was crusted with blood. I looked away as my stomach lurched. It had been far easier to ignore the wound when I was overcome with frantic urgency. With a sympathetic grunt, she retied the bandage and then made sitting motions. I was too tired to argue. She climbed onto the wagon seat, handling the reins with casual competence, and made a clicking noise while flicking the leather against the rumps of the animals drawing the cart. They reminded me of water buffalo, but their tails were more akin to horses, and they had a ruff of shaggy black fur around their necks.

I closed my eyes and swayed with the motion of the animals as the wagon bumped along, trying to orient myself and nail down a plan of action. But the motion was making my nausea worse, so I gave up and opened my eyes to stare out at the city.

The entire place was built of smooth, pale stone that reflected the sun and diminished all shadows, wrapping the city in a subtle halo. The lack of contrast in the light gave the place a strange two-dimensional appearance, where the streets and buildings were watercolor washes, and the golden-brown faces of the people stood out stark against their pastel clothing.

After some time, we passed into a courtyard before a broad two-story building with rounded cupolas and curving doorways. The trees that lined the outside of the walls were palm-like, with shorter, pear-shaped trunks and pale bark. The woman climbed down and tied off her animals only to disappear into one of the arched doors. I closed my eyes against the radiant heat that reflected from every surface and leaned gratefully against the sideboard. My stomach had finally calmed, and I could move my eyeballs without feeling like they were peeling off against the sandpaper inside my eyelids.

Shouting came from the doorway and the woman who'd found me hurried out of the building accompanied by a short man who also wore the loose-fitting robe, though his was pastel blue tied with a black sash at the waist. Two more men in identical robes walked out to flank him. His skin was honey brown and creased like well-worn leather around hooded eyes that twinkled merrily. The woman stopped just in front of me and clicked at me with her tongue, waving her finger and gesturing at my arm. I got the distinct impression that she was scolding me. She spoke to the older man for a moment, who reached into a leather bag that hung from the sash at his waist and passed her a handful of pale green glass beads. She counted them and nodded to him, then looked at me sternly and pointed from my chest to the pale robed little man before shooing me away from her wagon.

He gestured for me to walk forward with both of his hands as he nodded encouragingly, like a bobblehead, I thought bemusedly.

"I'm looking for Angus," I said slowly, making a vague circular gesture toward my face.

He smiled and nodded and cheerfully motioned me to follow him toward the building. Relief made my knees weak. As soon as we got close to the doorway, the other men closed ranks behind us and followed as the priest—for that was how he struck me—led the way, continually turning back and nodding at me with a reassuring smile. We walked down long, shaded hallways that opened on one side to center courtyards filled with trees and fountains, open to the sky but shaded by the high walls of the building around it. The priest stopped walking at the end of a long corridor and opened an ornately carved wooden door to motion me inside.

"Is this where Angus is?" I asked and repeated, "Angus?" for clarity's sake.

He nodded and gestured toward the room. I passed his smiling face and walked through the door into a dark, cool room with a cot along one wall and filmy curtains over a small window; a window with a decorative metal grate on it that was uncomfortably reminiscent of bars. There was no man in the room. I turned to walk out but froze at the sound of a lock snicking into place.

It took me a long, drawn-out moment to remember that I wasn't really trapped but, during those few, panicked heartbeats, I was back in the psychiatric ward, alone and scared. When the little priest gave the cart woman those glass beads, I hadn't stopped to think that the transaction might have been payment, and that I may have inadvertently entered a slave trade.

I had hoped that my intent when Walking, centering on Ronan's erstwhile foster father, would guide me to an area within a reasonable distance of him but I had no way to know whether that was even possible.

A creaking sound alerted me to the woman standing in the doorway, wearing the same pastel blue gown that the others had worn, but her black sash was wider and more intricately tied. She was as tall and thin as a crane with a long, bony neck and stooped shoulders. Peeking out from the edges of her robes was a young boy of ten or eleven with a wooden case held tightly against his thin chest. His skin was the same golden brown, but his curly hair was pure white, which made him look as if his head were surrounded by clouds.

She walked into the room with slow, elderly grace and a no-nonsense manner. It wasn't long before she had me seated on the cot and her deft fingers were probing, cleaning, and dressing my arrow wound with swift efficiency and a mixture of ground herbs and minerals that I couldn't identify. Her little assistant procured supplies from her wooden box without saying a word, but couldn't keep his eyes from roving over my skin and hair in fascination.

Whatever the healer had used to treat my injury worked quickly, because the pain receded from a dull roar to an inconvenient throb. I touched the clean, white bandage with the fingertips of my left hand and then smiled up at her.

"Thank you."

Apparently, that was universal enough for she smiled gently, making the skin of her cheeks furrow into layers of wrinkles, before saying something to the boy. He began packing the healer's tools into the box with careful precision.

"I'm looking for a man named Angus," I told her, carefully annunciating each word, "An-gus."

She tilted her head at me, making her resemblance to a bird even more pronounced, and said something that sounded like 'mother whirl' in a voice as thin and fragile as herself before patting my forearm and walking toward the door with her young assistant in tow. I tried to follow, but she turned toward me with a swiftness that belied her age and shook her finger at me in a motion that clearly said 'stay.'

"Wait," I said, knowing that she couldn't understand me but hoping my urgency would translate, "I need to find Angus. My friend is in trouble, and I can't help him without Angus. I don't know how long I can look for him."

She gave me a gentle, sad-eyed smile. I was torn between pushing my way out the door to try searching on my own and waiting to see what happened next. On impulse, I stepped toward her and reached out to take her hand. She didn't try to stop me, and I closed my eyes, concentrating hard, trying to feel my way below her skin and bones to the woman beneath.

She pulled her hand out of mine and regarded me with an intense expression of wary wonder, rubbing absently at the hand where our skin had touched.

"Mother whirled?" she said again, shaking her head in a motion that looked more like shock than denial, before pulling the boy out the door behind her. I stood back and let her go. While I couldn't make sense of what I felt or how I'd been able to tell, much the same way I'd known the Irish girl to be a Walker, I knew this healer didn't mean me harm. Until that point, the pain in my arm was enough to distract me from the fact that I hadn't slept in more than 24 hours, but now that the pain was abated—though every muscle ache and bruise was evident—the lingering discomfort wasn't enough to slow the wave of fatigue as it washed over me.

I took a few stumbling steps backward so that the cot was behind me when my knees gave out. With one breath, I was thinking of how long I could afford to search for Angus before Walking back to Avalon, and in the next, I'd slipped over the edge of wakefulness and into the welcoming darkness.

CHAPTER THIRTY-SIX

S liding off the bed and hitting the floor on a fresh wound isn't the best way to wake up.

Searing pain shot up my arm and into my shoulder so that I cried out and rolled to my unwounded side, clutching my arm against my chest with gritted teeth until the pain dwindled to a throbbing ache. Golden evening sunlight poured through my tiny window and lit up the small room like the inside of an amber jewel. I swore under my breath, rolled into a sitting position, and tried to make a guess at the hour. Five o'clock, maybe? That left Ronan in unfriendly hands for far too long. Of course, he could have come to and walked back to Avalon by now but, from what the girl had said, I could only infer that the king of that place had some way to force magic users into his service.

I had to assume that meant the man had some way to control or stop Walkers from using their gifts. Better to charge to the rescue than assume he was safe in Avalon and waste the extra time checking.

As if I'd summoned it, the door to my room swung open on creaking hinges. It must have been the turning of the lock that woke me up, I realized as I pushed myself to my feet. The little priest walked in, a gentle smile on his face as he nodded at me.

"Mother whirled," he told me confidently.

I opened my mouth to ask what on earth everyone meant by "mother whirled" when a man stepped into the room behind the little priest, dwarfing him into almost childish proportions. My mouth shut with an audible clicking of teeth as I stared up at the man. He was as tall as Ronan, though clearly older, with a significant amount of iron-grey peppered through the light brown hair tied into a tail at the nape of his neck. High, broad cheekbones, an aquiline nose, and eyes the pale green of a frog pond made the man quite striking, if not exactly handsome.

Despite appearing to be in his mid-sixties, he was incredibly hale beneath the loose blue robe, with wide shoulders and capable hands. His apparent fitness wasn't what had surprised me, though. His skin was as fair as my own.

"Mother whirled?" slipped out of my mouth. I could have bitten my own tongue off. Of all the questions I could have asked, that was the first thing to pop out? Clearly, my parents had raised a genius. To my surprise, the man threw his head back and laughed in a smooth tenor voice that was as warm and clear as honey. Once his amusement had passed, he looked down at the little priest and said something in the man's own language. The little priest still smiled and nodded, which seemed to be his perpetual state, and then left the room. I noticed that he did not lock the door behind himself.

Light green eyes considered me for a moment, and then he asked with an apparent Irish accent, "Do ye speak English, then?"

"How did you know that?"

He shrugged and gestured toward my head. "You've red hair and skin as fair as a bucket of milk. More redheads in Western Europe than anywhere else and English seemed the most likely guess. Besides, you said 'mother whirled' like an American. I'd have tried Gaelic, next." He pointed at my vambraces. "And, those are elf make, unless I miss my guess. Walkers from Avalon generally speak English, even if it isn't their first language."

"What is mother whirled?"

A merry light twinkled in his eyes, and one corner of his mouth turned down in a half-crooked smile.

"They murder the language, don't they?" he asked fondly, glancing toward the closed door, "it's partly my fault. What they're trying to say is 'another world.' It's how they distinguish me."

I looked down at the pale skin of my right arm, exposed by the section of the sleeve I'd torn away to use as an improvised dressing, and mused, "So they must have guessed. I suppose there aren't many light-skinned people here."

"Nay, there are none, at least not in this part of the world, and none anywhere with dress such as you're wearing."

"Is that why they brought me here, because they knew you were from another world, too?"

"It's yer arm, lass. The monks have a standin' reward for anyone who delivers someone in need of help."

"Wow. That's rather altruistic."

His brow rose at my skepticism. "It's naught but common sense. Most people will have sought out the skill of the monks at some time. Their gratitude means the monks lead comfortable lives, and they see that good deed is returned to the people."

I could only nod, suitably chastised.

"How'd ye get here? To Endre, I mean."

"I Walked."

"Endre isn't a common destination for Walkers. Too quiet and altruistic," he said, flinging my words back at me, "that's why I'm here. I prefer to be left alone."

I ignored that less than subtle hint, released a slow breath and said, calmly, "I came from Avalon. I was looking for you, Angus."

He started back, brows lowering, and regarded me with an entirely new intensity that was almost intimidating. "How do you know me?"

His voice had that same note of command that Ronan used so casually.

"Ronan told me about you. I wasn't sure whether you were here or not, but it was my best guess, based on what I knew of his past."

"Ronan?"

I nodded.

"How does this Ronan know me?"

"I...but I thought..." I stuttered, frowning hard and running through my actions in my head with as much speed as I could manage. I'd walked here with my mind focused on Angus, on Ronan's foster father. Was it possible that there was an entirely different Angus here than the one I was looking for?

"I mean, he said you were his foster father, I don't understand how I could have the wrong place. I was so focused."

Angus took two steps toward me and stopped with his face mere inches from mine and said quietly, "Who said this to you, that I was their foster father, who said it?"

"Ronan did, I told you."

"I know of no one by that name."

"But," I started to argue, but he cut me off with a curt gesture and asked, "what did he tell you of me?"

"That you were his foster father, that you brought him here when a boar gored him, that you were a powerful Walker..."

His face cleared a bit, but the suspicion was still apparent in his eyes. "Ronan, you say?"

I nodded.

"Can ye describe this Ronan?"

"Dark brown, slightly curly hair," I began, "blue eyes, around six-foot-four, broad shoulders, has a penchant for leather jackets with hoods...oh and he has a birthmark on his forehead."

Angus let out an explosive breath through pursed lips and leaned back, closing his eyes for a second as the tension in his body relaxed.

"Be damned, Diarmuid, what d'ye mean by it?" he muttered to himself.

"Wait a second!" I interrupted, rising excitement making the words come flying out, "that's what the captain of the guard said to him! He said it to him more than once after they attacked us, um..." I snapped my fingers in time with my rushing thoughts as I sifted quickly through the memories, "ah! Diarmuid Ua Duibhne! What does it mean?"

Angus stiffened again and turned toward me with a lowering brow. "What do ye mean, attacked ye? Who? When? Where is Diarmuid?"

"I don't know what that means," I burst out, frustrated.

"It's his name," he snapped impatiently, "Dermot O'Dyna, in English. Now tell me what happened to him, and be quick."

I recounted the events of the previous morning, including our suspicions about what the King was doing to those gifted with magic.

"I don't know what they'll do with him," I confessed as fear weakened my voice, "but the leader of the King's men seemed to know him and guessed that we were Walkers. If what that man said is true, then they have him, and I don't know what they'll do with him. I have to find Ronan, or—" I swallowed and tamped down the stab of betrayal, "or Dermot. And I can't do it myself."

Angus sat on my cot and was utterly still, but it wasn't the stillness of shock or fear, it was the way a coil is still when it's been pressed all the way down by a heavy weight, thrumming with restrained energy.

"And so, you came to me," he muttered.

"I tried to get to Avalon, but something is wrong there. The gates were closed, and the walls were empty. I couldn't Walk inside because the stones pulled me." Angus nodded, eyes still on the floor as he thought.

"Wouldn't have mattered, anyway. If he wasn't on a mission for the Venatore, they'd not have sent anyone after him."

"Wha—" I sputtered, "why not?"

Angus surged to his feet and stalked to the other side of the room. "It's not an army, girl," he snapped, "and it operates in secrecy. Venatore can't go interferin' in the normal events of other verses. They don't topple regimes or stop wars, or save men."

"But, you're not Venatore, are you? You can help me get him out of there."

There was a long, frustrating silence as Angus stood with his arms folded across his chest and an introspective scowl on his face. I wanted to pound on the walls in agitation, to shout at him to hurry now that I knew who he was, but I got the sense that those kinds of things would not move this man. He would make his own choices in his own time and for his own reasons; but it wasn't easy to keep my mouth shut, and I couldn't stop myself from whispering, "You can help me get him out of there."

His green eyes snapped up to mine, and he said, "That I can." Then, before I could react, his hand shot out and locked around my wrist, turning it over to expose the silver of my bracelet beneath the buckles of my vambraces, and he nodded to himself as if he'd been expecting to find the metal beneath.

"I can help you, but are ye sure you sure that I should?"

I jerked my hand out of his grasp, surprised and angry. "What do you mean? Of course I'm sure! Anything could be happening to him, and I'm the only one who knows where he is!"

Angus snorted in disgust and dropped my arm. "Have ye even thought this through, lass? Ye say he was taken by guards, did you not? Where d'ye think he's being held? You think the two of us will have an easy job of it? Just walk in and demand the boy, if you please?"

I hesitated and looked at him helplessly.

"So, if it's you and me only," he continued mercilessly, "then we need something to even the odds. But it's unlawful to Walk with the kind of weapons we would need. Worst case scenario, from what you've told me, you and I both die. The best we can hope for is to get him out alive, and after that, I can't promise you what will happen. Both of us may be brought up on charges before the Concilium," he pointed at me and said, quietly emphatic, "especially you, as you're in training to uphold the laws we would need to break." I took a moment to rein in my churning emotions. Everything he'd said was true. We'd gone to Eiru in the hopes of saving my life, and the result could easily be that I lost it anyway.

"I can't leave him there."

"A student may say as much for their teacher," he admitted. His tone was placating, but his gaze was penetrating when he added, "But there's something more than duty in your eyes."

I felt my face flush, but I didn't respond, only kept my eyes locked on his in stony silence.

"Ye said he's a birthmark on his forehead?"

I nodded.

"And ye've seen it?"

"That would be a logical assumption," I said as impatience and frustration warred with my good manners.

In a soft, gently regretful voice, he said, "Then what ye feel for Dermot may be merely a lie; feelings created by magic."

My stomach did a roller coaster drop at his words, and my own voice came out as an incredulous, breathy whisper. "What?"

"It isn't a birthmark, the ball-seirc. It's a curse, lass." Angus must have seen my incomprehension because he blew a hard breath through his nose and explained, "It's a love spot. Dermot was cursed with it when he was but a lad by a hag, bitter at his refusal of her. He does his best to hide the cursed thing, for any woman who sees it falls in love with him."

He said the last in the same gentle voice a parent might use to tell their child that the family dog has been hit by a car. "Ye were right in one thing: I'll go after him. But I'd not have you risk your life for a love that is merely a spell, and no real love at all."

My mind went blank, and I shambled backward until I could let the cot catch me when my knees gave out.

"Gráinne?" I asked weakly.

"Aye. Though it wasn't his fault, the lad never forgave himself." There was regret in his voice, both for me and for Ronan-Dermot's, dead wife; the woman who'd defied her father, shunned her betrothed, and lived on the run, in huts and caves, for a man who'd trapped her in a cage of her own love. That he'd never intended to earn her love made no difference to her. I closed my eyes, and two hot tears burned their way down my cheeks.

Angus was silent for a moment as my emotion spilled onto my clasped hands. Could I believe that everything I felt for Ronan was manufactured by some spell? Had Gráinne felt the same way, that her love was untainted by the curse?

"I'll need to know where ye were when they took him."

"He said we were near the Boyne." My voice sounded lifeless, even to my own ears. I wanted to chastise myself for questioning the truth of my own emotions, but Ronan had told me about Gráinne himself, and his haunted eyes seemed as clear to me as if he was in the room with us.

"More'n a few places are near the Boyne. Where'd you walk from?"

"A hill with some kind of earthen circles at the top."

"Tara?" he asked intently.

I shrugged, "He didn't say. It had pull, though. We couldn't have walked anywhere else nearby."

"And ye were in the woods, ye say, when the attack happened?"

I nodded as Ronan's face flashed before my closed eyes, the last three months playing in rewind across the screen of my mind to end with his eyes quietly pleading with me to get myself to safety while his own life was in jeopardy. My jaw clenched as resolve solidified in my chest, and I opened my eyes to growl, "I can show you when we get there."

"Have ye trained to use a sword?"

"Not well enough," I admitted as Angus knelt at the foot of a simple wardrobe and pulled a leather-wrapped bundle from beneath a stack of robes. His rooms were spartan, but the sword he unwrapped was anything but plain. Even the scabbard had beautifully tooled, intricate carvings down the length.

"I gave this to Derm—ah—Ronan, once. He bade me keep it, but I've a feeling it's time for the blade to go to work." He laid the sword on the blanket atop his cot and then began to pull clothing from the wardrobe, woolen garments that were clearly not native to the area. With a casual shrug, the robe dropped off his frame, and my cheeks went up in flames before I turned away from his broad, flatly muscled back and lean hips. He might be nearing old age, but he was still clearly fit.

"Have ye trained in anything useful, then?"

"Unarmed combat and a bit of knives," I admitted to his back.

"Some's better'n naught, I suppose, though skill at archery would've been a greater help."

I peeked over my shoulder to see that he'd fastened his britches and breathed a quiet sigh of relief.

"I can also...well," I hesitated and tried to think of a way to frame what I'd only recently realized I could do. "I can tell whether someone is a Walker if I can touch them. I can tell other things, too, though I've only tried it a couple of times."

Angus turned toward me after pulling a dark brown linen shirt over his head, eyes keen. "Can ye, indeed?"

I cleared my throat, and shrugged one shoulder, feeling self-conscious beneath his scrutiny. He held out his hand and said, "Do it."

"I, well, I've never tried to do it on command."

He only pushed his hand closer to me. I took a deep breath and reached out. His palm was calloused, warm. I closed my eyes and felt the crisp hairs on the back of his hand and the subtle, unique vibration that indicated his ability to shift his frequency and...I caught my breath as a different sensation became apparent to this new sense I'd developed. It wasn't just the elusive frequency that Walkers emanated, which I could sense almost like placing your hand on the top of an old record machine while the music played, but a discordant hum wrapped around and within Angus's frequency.

As the sensation washed through me, I felt beneath the skin, the bone, the electrical impulses that moved his muscles, to the very seat of his will, an indomitable force that glowed with kinetic energy. It was at that point I realized that I had stopped breathing. Angus caught me as I stumbled forward, gasping as oxygen surged again through my veins, making me lightheaded.

"You're," I gasped, one hand to my throat, "what are you?"

He tilted his head at me, eyes narrowed. "Tuath de," he said, quietly.

"It was—it was magic that I felt, wasn't it?"

He nodded.

"When Ronan said you were powerful, he didn't mean just your ability to Walk."

Angus smirked, then turned away as if dismissing me and began pulling on his boots. "This skill of yours," he said over his shoulder, "will it help us find Dermot?"

"Um...yeah, I think so. I can sort of, feel him if that makes any sense."

"Well then, at least we'll know where we're headed."

He reached down into the bottom of the wardrobe again and tossed me a belt with two silver-handled daggers, one sheathed on the backside of each hip.

"Hold this while I fasten my buttons," he said and passed me the sword in its scabbard. I took it without thinking and almost dropped it just as quickly. It thrummed with the same energy I'd felt from Angus. I gaped at the sword that reverberated against my palms like a struck guitar string, and then looked up at Angus, who was watching me with narrowed eyes. He nodded, as if a question had been answered, and went back to strapping on various implements of violence.

"Is this," I hesitated, not sure exactly what to ask. "A magic sword?"

"That it is." There was a certain amount of irony in his voice, and I suspected he was completely aware of how ridiculous that phrase sounded. I held it out once Angus stood, eager to get rid of the feel of it, but he declined.

"You'll have to walk it," he said seriously, "I'll be taking this." He held up a long-handled dagger with a tooled sheath and strapped it to his thigh, motioning for me to do the same with the sword.

"This is one of those laws we are going to break?"

Angus didn't bother to answer since it wasn't a question but more of a sick-stomach acknowledgment of what I was about to commit myself to. I kept my mouth shut for the rest of the time it took Angus to procure supplies.

It was full dark when we were finally prepared to Walk, and impatient anxiety coiled inside me like a snake waiting to strike, making my muscles tense and my stomach sick.

"Ye've agreed to do exactly as I say," Angus reminded me as we stood in the open courtyard inside the Monastery.

I nodded.

"And you'll be taking the sword, of your own free will?"

I nodded.

"D'ye need a hand, or can ye walk unaided?"

"I'm fine."

"Alright then, let's be off."

I focused on Eiru and began to shift, knowingly and willfully committing my first crime.

CHAPTER THIRTY-SEVEN

"Y ou've got to be kidding me."

With the back of my wrist pressed firmly against my nose, I stared at the black mouth of the tunnel. The air was so thick with the reek of human waste that my stomach backed up into my throat.

"Not what ye had in mind, eh?" the wry amusement in Angus' voice made me want to slap him.

We'd arrived at the same place Ronan and I had walked to, an ancient site Angus said was the original seat of the kings of Ireland. Though we'd arrived after dark, Angus hadn't had much trouble orienting us toward the nearest town and setting off at a pace that covered the ground quickly despite the uneven footing. We'd been lucky enough to stumble across a beggar who had been more than happy to point us in the direction of the King's castle for half the loaf of bread that was tucked in a leather satchel Angus wore over his woolen cape. The old man had snatched the bread with the quick dexterity of a hungry rodent and began gnawing at it with teeth that were as sharp and yellow as any rats.

Between mouthfuls, he'd looked up at me and asked Angus something in a mildly interested tone. Angus responded blandly, the beggar cackled to himself and raised the crust in a salute as we stalked away into the darkness.

"What did he ask you?"

Angus had chuckled at the suspicion in my voice. "Your lack of Irish could get us in trouble."

"Well, I can't help that."

Angus reached up and placed both hands on either side of my head. A sensation, uncomfortably like what soil must feel when earthworms burrow through it, made my scalp crawl and goosebumps ripple down my arms. When he dropped his hands, the world started to spin, and I'd had to hold onto his arm to keep myself from falling over.

"It'll pass," he'd assured me.

When I demanded to know what he'd done, he simply shrugged one shoulder and asked, "Can you not tell?"

I realized then that he'd responded in English to a question I had asked in Irish Gaelic or, at least, the version of Irish Gaelic spoken in this verse.

I had no idea if or how it was different from the Irish spoken on True Earth. He'd given me no time to ask how it was possible to teach someone a language they didn't know in mere seconds because he'd turned his back and disappeared into the darkness before I could formulate the question.

We had headed south and east all through that night, encountering no one, and took shelter the following morning in a copse of newly budding trees. I had pulled the surprisingly warm woolen cape Angus provided around my body and fallen asleep as soon as my head hit the ground. We had awakened just before nightfall, staying in our hide as the last rays of light died out. When my stomach had growled audibly, he'd tossed me the last piece of our bread, and I'd choked it down with a bit of water from the flask at my hip.

"How did you teach me Irish?" I'd asked as soon as I forced the dry bread down.

He had shrugged but kept his eyes on the road through the trees as he said, "A few shifts in your grey matter. Don't worry," he'd grinned as my face went stiff, "it's much easier to put something in than take something out. Your secrets are safe."

I'd snorted. I hadn't the mental resiliency for the kind of sarcasm I'd wanted to fling at Angus for brushing me off, not with Ronan weighing so heavily on my mind, so I had kept my mouth shut for the rest of the evening.

We'd followed the road at a safe distance once night descended to conceal our movement, and the salty tang of seawater on the air was apparent long before we saw the city spread out along the harbor. Angus kept us far from the walls, skirting the outside of the sprawling city until we reached the coast. The walls of the city were reminiscent of the walls of Avalon, made of light stone that glowed in the moonlight with crenellations along the along the top, even on the rocky coastline.

We had headed toward the largest building—which was distinctly castle-like—that reared above the rest of the city on the highest point of a peninsula. Once I was sure the crashing of the surf would cover the sound of my voice, I'd asked Angus the question that had been weighing on my mind since I'd first seen the steady glow of the city lights behind high walls.

"How are we supposed to get into the city?"

We had been scrambling over wave-washed boulders when I asked him and now, standing and staring into the black void of the sewage tunnel that was leaking a constant stream of refuse into the seawater fifty feet below while Angus grinned at me, I wished I hadn't asked.

He reached into a pocket of his woolen cloak and pulled out a small glass ball hanging from a thin chain connected to it at 3 sides, like a potted plant. Holding the ball firmly between both hands, he twisted the top and bottom of the ball in opposite directions. Fine, colorless powder in the top half of the ball had dropped into the liquid in the bottom half as the barrier between them broke, and the ball immediately began to glow with a faint but steady blue light that reminded me of my father snapping a chem-light in one hand and shaking it until our tent glowed.

Light from the sphere reached just far enough to illuminate the top and bottom of the sewage tunnel. Angus lifted the strange lamp by a ring in the chain and took a deep breath. "

That'll do it."

"Can't we just steal some clothes and walk in by the front gate or something?" I groaned.

"Ye want to commit a crime against the innocent people, here? Or do ye happen to know where to find clothes to fit you and me both, or what time the gate closes, or what the routine of the city is so that you don't make any mistake obvious to eyes trained to see magic users?"

I ground my teeth.

The sewage tunnel was everything I hoped it wouldn't be; dark, moist, thick with stench and far, far longer than I could have imagined. What little bread and water I'd eaten since waking that morning joined the river of sludge heading out to the sea as my stomach muscles burned in protest. Angus hadn't heaved once. I wiped my mouth and stared mutinously at his back as we began to climb, imagining hooking my foot around his ankle, shoving his back and watching his arms windmill as he fell forward to get a whiff of whatever the residents of the city had eaten that day...up close and personal.

I was smiling at that mental image until another wave of smell hit me and I had to stop to retch again. We slowed down as the tunnel widened into a room-sized opening that split in 4 directions with a ladder that reached from the floor in the middle of the room up into the darkness above.

Angus lifted the light to illuminate the ladder and jerked his chin at the top, gesturing for me to climb.

"You have the light," I objected and immediately regretted opening my mouth.

Angus pointed at the ladder and tilted his head while raising one brow, as if to say, "What, are you scared?"

I blew a disgusted breath out through my nose and began to climb. The air that drifted down toward me through the grate was blessedly fresh, and once I reached the top, I pressed my nose as close to the grate as possible. Angus didn't seem to care much for being kept waiting if the pinch on my calf was anything to judge by, so I curled my fingers around the grate and pushed.

In movies, people always make it look so easy to push manhole covers out of the way, so I wasn't expecting the grate to weigh as much as a small pony. The noise that resulted from my effort to lift the grate could have woken the entire town if the room we climbed up into hadn't been closed behind a bolted door.

"Is this a service room?" I asked. My voice echoed off of the high ceiling. Angus lifted the light and peered at the various tools secured to racks along the walls; shovels, rakes, large drills with hand cranks and other devices I couldn't name.

"So it would appear," he gestured toward the wooden door, "shall we?"

I took a step forward only to stop as my foot squelched loudly inside my boot, the sound followed by a noxious whiff of sewage.

"Aren't we going to sound pretty conspicuous?"

Angus looked down at my legs, wet to mid-shin, and muttered, "Our smell won't go unnoticed, either."

He handed me the glowing light and knelt near my feet. Frowning in concentration, he placed both hands on either side of my legs without touching the wet material and murmured to himself. My feet and calves began to grow warm as a cloud of steam rose from my lower legs toward my face. I gasped at the sight and then recoiled, sure that I was about to get a nasty mouthful of sewer smell, but the moist air that touched my cheeks was surprisingly odor free. Within another few seconds, my pant legs were dry, and my socks only mildly damp inside my pleasantly warm boots.

Angus let out a forceful breath and leaned back, rolling his shoulders as if he'd lifted a heavy weight.

"What the hell did you just do?" I asked, wiggling my toes in my dry boots.

"I broke the chemical bonds of the molecules that caused the smell. Breaking chemical bonds produces energy, which I used to dry your clothes."

He grunted as he pushed himself to his feet.

"How did you do it?"

"Not an explanation we've time for. C'mon."

As we crept through the shadows, I ran over the bones of the plan Angus had laid out before we'd Walked to this verse. The city was still and quiet in the night, lit with the same steady blue light as the glass ball Angus now kept concealed inside his shirt. Seen from the higher vantage point of the capital structure, the city stretched out for miles along the coastline.

Despite what we suspected was the lack of an industrial revolution, the city before us was surprisingly modern and angular, created on a grid of wide roads dotted with buildings of several stories and even what appeared to be city parks. We edged around the side of a building on silent feet. Before us, a courtyard opened wide with manicured gardens decorated here and there with abstract knot-work statues and a fountain with frozen water crusting its surface.

I tried to ignore the unease that uncurled in my belly as I halted behind Angus, watching from the tentative safety of the shadows as a guard made a pass along the walkway that led to the porch of the Castle building. Seconds later another guard appeared, walking in the opposite direction. Both men carried spears across their bodies and swords strapped to their hips.

"How are we supposed to get inside the castle?" I breathed as a second round of guards crossed in front of the building thirty or so seconds later.

"We could knock on the front door," he suggested.

It was too dark for him to see my scowl.

A small building adjoined the castle at the rear, connected by a narrow hallway. Moving between patrols and keeping to the shadows, we managed to follow two guards back to the building and watched from cover as they passed inside.

"That'll be the guard room," Angus whispered.

He motioned for me to follow, and we pressed ourselves against the wall around the corner from the door until Angus had the watch rotation timed. His words were no more than a breath, nearly drowned out by the low chatter of the guards keeping warm inside, and the breaking waves in the distance.

"Seems to be about ten minutes between rotations. We'll have to work fast."

I nodded and burst into the room as soon as the departing patrol was out of earshot. Two of the guards fell beneath Angus' hammer-like fists, which left the third man just enough time to draw a short sword from his side. The close quarters of the guardhouse didn't leave him much room to maneuver, so he closed with a thrust toward Angus' unprotected ribs.

I slid in from the side and raised my forearm in time to deflect the thrust with the armored side of my vambrace, sliding the blade along the metal with a steely rasp. The guard was no slouch and lifted a booted foot to kick me. Danet had trained me well though, and I reacted to that opening instantly, grabbing his extended leg with my right arm, driving my shoulder into his stomach and bearing him to the ground with the force of all my weight. We landed with a grunt of expelled air, and a meaty 'thunk' as the back of his head struck the stone floor.

I watched, with numb detachment, as the man's eyes rolled back in his head, rubbing my injured arm as the adrenaline started to ebb and the fiery pain of my wound came burning back to life.

"Well done. Now, this is the tricky part," Angus said, and I had to blink a few times to focus on his face, "getting into the city at night, under cover of darkness, didn't take much skill—"

"Only wading through a river of crap," I interrupted sourly.

He glared at me and continued, "But moving through a castle without being seen, even at night, is going to require all my concentration. We've maybe five minutes before our guards don't make their rounds and the alarm goes up, and five more after that before things get exciting. That's assuming we don't stumble upon any magical tripwires. Think ye can find Der—ah, Ronan, before that?"

"I don't have the slightest idea," I began, and then stopped as understanding broke. "Right, gotcha. My whatever-it-is power," I sighed and clenched my fists. "I suppose we'll find out." I reached for the handle of the door leading to the castle proper, but Angus grabbed my wrist.

"I'm going to be hiding us," he warned me, "by bending the light so that anyone who looks in our direction will see what's behind us. It's not easy, and it's not perfect. It'll hide a stationary person so they're near invisible, but two moving people..." he shook his head, "we'll be a bit of a blur. So, move slowly and as quietly as you can manage, yeah?"

I reached down to unbuckle the sword, pushing it at him. "Take this, then. I can't move in this thing."

He took it with one hand while his other tightened on my arm. "I'll be concentrating. If there's any fighting to be done, it'll be up to you unless you absolutely need me, so it'll be best to end things quickly and as silently as you can."

I nodded stiffly and turned the knob.

Ronan is somewhere in this building, I told myself.

It took concerted, conscious effort to open my ability as I stepped outside the dark pantry to prowl through the empty kitchen with Angus at my back. Up until that point, I'd only tried to use my newly discovered gift when I was standing still, touching someone. Even my sense of Ronan had always been clearest while I was touching him. While I did seem to be able to tell when he was near, I'd only done it unconsciously and only while we were in the same room. Trying to get a feeling for where he was in a huge space while skulking through a castle I had just broken into—on a timeline no less—was rather more difficult than simply knowing that he was in the room with me.

Thanks to Angus' unique gift we moved through the first floor without incident, aside from the time I smacked my forehead on the mental embrasure that held a large glass sphere like the one Angus had used, only 4 times larger. While his magic, or whatever it was, bent the light around us so that passersby wouldn't notice us, is also threw off my depth perception and skewed my own vision so that things tilted slightly to the side depending on which way I was leaning. Angus choked back a laugh as I rubbed my forehead.

"Ah, the spell can cause a wee problem with yer perception." I clenched my jaw and glared in his general direction through eyes squinted in pain.

"Thanks ever so much."

It took me a few more turns before I could adjust to the change in perspective and, by that time, I was certain that Ronan wasn't on the bottom floor of the building. We were halfway up the darkened staircase when pale blue light lit the curved wall above us. I froze as the sound of laughter echoed off the stone, and flattened myself against the wall.

Five men stumbled down the stairs surrounded by the reek of beer, sweat, and a cloud of raucous laughter. I didn't dare to breathe.

"His face turned purple," one of the men chortled as he bounced off one wall and into his neighbor, who caught and steadied him with an expression of long-suffering amusement.

"Looked like his head would catch fire."

"I would do the same had my prized hound died on the floor at my feet."

They were a mere three steps above us, and the sour smell of alcohol mixed with body odor was nearly too strong for my composure. I drew the knife from my belt as silently as possible and held it low, ready to move quickly if one of the drunks stumbled into me. The stumbling man turned to his companions and said, with a note of steel in his voice, "That's what the pompous fool gets for refusing to sire pups on my bitch. 'Not fit to raise a pig,' indeed!"

"He was right, O'Connor," laughed another, "I'd not lend ye my horse even had ye a broken leg! I never saw a man so hard on beasts as you are."

"I'd not be seen on one of your nags anyway, you bleedin' heart. We'll see how proud that self-righteous prick is now. He'll never win another bait with his other sorry hounds."

The man behind O'Connor pushed at his shoulder and warned, "You had better keep an eye on your blind side. He'll find a way to repay you for poisoning that hound."

O'Connor shrugged and stumbled down two more steps until he was even with me, laughing menacingly. "Aye, he will. Then I'll have cause to kill him and seize his property...including that pretty new wife of his."

The other men jeered, and I clenched my fists in fury. As O'Connor turned back to make his unsteady way down the stairs, I stuck out my foot. With a cry of surprised alarm, the man lost his footing, wind-milled his arms, and went tumbling down the stairs beneath the shocked eyes of his friends. I didn't get to see O'Connor land at the bottom of the stairs, but I did get to hear the half-strangled laugh of one of the men with him when he blurted, "Ye've broken yer leg, ye sodden fool. Damn me if fate doesn't intervene quickly."

There was a pained groan, and another voice said, in a no-non-sense manner, "Don't let him puke on my boots, fergodsake! Hoist em up; we'll have to carry his wine-soaked arse to the healer."

I didn't move until there was only silence from the floor below.

"That was a bloody stupid thing to do," Angus snarled from behind me.

"He deserved it."

"And maybe he did. Had you given us away, though, who would have saved my foster son?"

I hissed, "That jerk deserved a lot more than he got. Besides, they were all drunk anyway; they probably can't see half of what's in front of them."

"Be that as it may, if you don't keep your mind on our task this place will be crawling with guards before we can find out if the lad is even in the castle!" Then his voice lowered menacingly, and he said, "Now move."

I tightened my grip on the knife and peeked out into the hall. It was empty. The wide passage stretched to the right and left of the stairwell with doors and other hallways opening toward the inside of the building. I turned to the right and made my way down the corridor, hesitating, and then hurried past each passage, certain that a door was going to open or a person was going to walk out as soon as I stepped in front of it.

One did.

A door opened less than ten feet in front of me, and a woman stumbled into the hall with a torn dress hanging from stiff shoulders. She clutched the material to her chest with one hand and wiped savagely at her mouth with the back of the other, eyes blazing. When the door slammed at her back, she flinched visibly, and her shoulders slumped as she turned to walk away from me down the hall, turning left down a long passage that appeared to lead toward the inside of the building. When I saw the silver sheen of tears on her cheeks as she disappeared around the corner, my mouth tightened.

That's four, I thought angrily, ticking off offenses against this place and, by extension, it's King, as I passed in silence behind the crying woman, pausing just long enough to concentrate my seeking efforts on the hallway. There was no sense of his familiar presence, that elusive tremor of molecules against my skin that said *he's been here.*

While we had only actively been searching for a matter of minutes, it felt like hours, and the knowledge of the unconscious guards in the building below, just waiting to be stumbled upon by the returning shift, increased the urgency tying my stomach in knots. If I couldn't find Ronan soon, our job would get a whole lot more difficult, and considerably more dangerous.

Come on, Allie, I thought, sharpening my focus on Ronan's unique signature and struggling to shut out everything else, *you can do this. Do or do not; there is no try.*

The hallway slipped away from my conscious mind as I prowled, but I didn't stop seeing it, it simply became unimportant, like the background in a photograph; all that mattered was the frequency of the air around me and whether it held hints of having been touched by Ronan's signature. It was like knowing what song is playing in someone else's car even when your own radio is on.

"Yes!" I exclaimed, and turned toward Angus in mid-stride, "he's here! Maybe one floor up—" The impact sent me stumbling to the side with a surprised gasp. I tripped over my own feet and instinctively clutched whatever struck me as I hit the stone wall shoulder first, only to be flattened by the man who'd bowled straight into me while crossing the open passage to my left.

"What," the man croaked while he tried to push away from me, his eyes jerking wildly from side to side, frantic to see whatever was holding him. I was still behind the blur of bent light Angus had provided for us, which must have made the man think he was being molested by a ghost. He managed to crush the toes of my left foot in his struggle, and air hissed through my teeth at the shooting pain. I planted both hands against his chest and shoved hard. He stumbled backward and pulled a long dagger from his belt, panting and holding the weapon low as his eyes rolled wildly.

"Wha...what..."

I had to deal with him quickly, since distant yells were now echoing up the hallway, signaling that we were out of time. A swift kick to the wrist sent his knife clattering to the ground, but I hadn't counted on his panicked response. He bellowed in fright, like a spooked cow, and charged me, swinging wildly. The blow took me by surprise, and my cheek exploded with pain as his weight slammed me against the wall and we both fell to the hall floor. He was whimpering in fright, battering at me with fists, knees, and feet. While only a few of the blows landed with any force or accuracy, it was painful and distracting enough that it took a moment for me to get my bearings.

I planted the sole my left foot on the ground, arched my hips and pushed with all the strength in my lower body to lever us over and topple the man. He fell to the side with a high-pitched grunt and then screamed with the ear-piercing power of a 6-year-old girl. Wincing at the sound, I pushed myself to my knees, waited for an opening in the flailing limbs, and swung.

The strike was clean, but his head had shifted just enough to the side that the punch that should have knocked him out cold only stunned him.

"Crap," I muttered, coming to my feet. It was going to take more force than a simple punch, and I realized as I looked down at him that this wasn't a man at all. He could have been no more than sixteen. He was tall with the gangly length of youth, but his cheeks were rounded, and the hair on his chin was still soft. I bit my lips, pulled back my foot and kicked. Blood ran from the boy's nose, and the side of his face was already purpling. I stared down, feeling sick, as his blood began to pool on the stones beneath his cheek and fought a sudden, startling memory of my mother's blood as it spread on her white blouse like a blooming flower.

The boy had freckles on the bridge of his nose.

"Go!"

I blinked and turned toward Angus but couldn't see any more than a hazing of the air where he stood.

"Move yer arse, girl," he snarled, and pushed me forward as the sound of boots and shouts echoed up the hallway.

I ran.

CHAPTER THIRTY-EIGHT

D oors, glowing metal sconces, and surprised faces blurred by as we ran down the hallway. I skidded to turn up another flight of stairs, my sense of Ronan growing stronger with every step. I was so distracted by his closeness that I barely had time to move out of the way of a small detachment of guards who were rushing down the stairs toward us. Wind from their passage pulled at loose strands of my hair as I pressed myself flat against the wall.

"Well, things are getting exciting," Angus murmured as they disappeared.

I ignored him and took the rest of the stairs three at a time, nearly tripping over my feet as I reached the top. The hallway opened into a kind of foyer with carpeting in the center and a modest chandelier hanging from the ceiling. Additional hallways opened from each side of the room. I pulled to a stop in the middle, stretching out my senses.

Please be here, please, please, please.

My head snapped up, and I bared my teeth. Of course, Ronan was in the very back. I took a few running steps and then slowed again when I realized that the faint footsteps I heard were coming from every direction.

"Sounds like a full mobilization," Angus breathed against my ear. His voice sounded strained.

"We're close," I returned, craning my neck around the corner of a passage that opened off the main hallway before skipping lightly to the other side.

"Hurry then."

I felt, more than heard, Angus pull the sword from its sheath beneath his cape. My knives leaped into my hands in response to the tension of impending violence in the air as we strode onward. Rising noise came from the end of the hall, but the sound wasn't what I expected. With as many guards as we'd passed, it seemed logical that the alert had gone out, so I'd anticipated hearing sounds that were a bit more martial in nature. What I heard instead was music and, if I wasn't mistaken, drunken laughter mixed with the snarling of hounds.

The door to the room beyond was wide, arched, and opened into a banqueting hall that seemed to stretch all the way to the back wall of the building. Ceilings higher than any on the first two floors opened the room up to grand proportions, but there was no elegance to the rectangular construction. Everything had sharp corners.

People dressed in jewel-toned brocades were gathered around the outside of the room, either standing in groups or lounging on low couches. There were several serving girls, clad in the same red as the guards but with much more skin on display, moving listlessly through the crowd with pitchers and trays. At the center of the room, about two feet deep, were two pits with wooden walls and dirt floors. One pit held two mongrels, snarling and tearing at each other as red-faced men cheered, and the other showcased a large hound, as tall as a pony, casually ripping out the insides out of a young fawn whose slender legs jerked grotesquely beneath its teeth.

My eyes caught all this as I scanned the room from behind Angus' veil of bent light, but the place was too crowded to see Ronan easily amongst the throng. I closed my eyes and focused. The room hummed with life, half a hundred unique frequencies mixing and forming a minor harmony that gave the room a spirit and vibration of its own. It was like noting the contribution of each instrument in a symphony; the sound existed separately from, but because of, the people inside.

Every single person was contributing to the aura of the place in a mixture of drunkenness, ambition, lust, fear, and hopelessness that was so overwhelming it made me nauseous. The sensation was so strong that I almost missed the one discordant note at the back. I recognized the signature of Ronan's aura, but his frequency was dampened like he was under water. My eyes flew to the place my senses told me Ronan would be, and I had only to wait a few seconds until the group of people standing between us parted to mingle with other partygoers.

Ronan lounged on a low bench, leaning on the bosom of a dark-haired woman dressed—or undressed—in red. His eyes were heavy-lidded, glazed and completely empty of anything resembling coherent thought. His bare chest expanded with slow, deep breaths, and the brass collar around his neck glowed dully against his skin. The dark-haired woman was cupping his head against her chest, whispering in his ear, and occasionally tipping a cup against his slack lips. Some of the liquid ran out the corner of his mouth, his lips too lethargic to tighten around the rim.

Random guests would stop in front of the tableau to peer at him, to test the muscles of his arms and nod in approbation to each other at what a fine specimen he was. He was on display like a pet monkey.

My chest went tight with rage, and I growled, "He's in the back on the right."

Angus grunted in response and said in a low voice, "I can't hold this crafting and fight, too. I'll have to drop it as soon as someone notices. Keep moving. Whoever gets to Dermot first walks his arse out of here, and the other will follow as soon as he's gone. I told you where we're going, where to take him?"

"Yes."

"Alright then" and he added in a dry, slightly amused tone, "try not to get killed."

We stepped into the room. I hadn't walked more than twenty feet before I heard the first person ask, "Did you see that?'"

"See what?"

"That, that...I don't know what it is, right there!"

Becoming suddenly visible in the middle of a room full of people who weren't previously aware of your presence is a fantastic way to make a splash at a party. A few piercing screams, yells of surprise, and quite a lot of backward stumbling will make it quite clear that something is wrong. Of course, it's understandable; people who had been glancing into an empty space one second were now, inexplicably, staring at a wild-eyed redhead holding a pair of knives as if she knew how to use them.

No one immediately attacked me, which had been my initial fear, so I started walking toward the back of the room as guests scampered out of my way. The moment someone grabbed my arm, demanding, "Who are you?" all hell broke loose.

I ducked and spun, pulling the sharp edge of my knife hard against the underside of the arm that clutched me, severing muscles and tendons just above the elbow. Someone screamed, and the room catapulted into a frenzy of motion. I lost sight of Angus while shifting between moving bodies and pushing past fleeing guests. One woman stumbled into me, having tripped on an abundance of skirt, and we wobbled drunkenly to the side, instinctively clutching each other's arms for support. The blade of a sword went slicing through the space my head had occupied mere seconds before, so I dropped to my knees and rolled to the right just in time to avoid a booted foot.

I raised my knife to deflect a hasty swing from the man who'd tried to take my head off seconds before. The blade slid off the knife and down the armored side of my vambrace just as I caught sight of a fist blurring toward my face. Fortunately, there wasn't much power behind the blow, but my top lip split none the less, and my teeth cut into the tender flesh inside. Blood filled my mouth.

I tried to step back but collided with another fleeing partygoer who thrust me forward just in time to get inside the next swing of the attacker's sword. With all the strength I could manage, I tried to drive the point of my knife up beneath his breastbone, but instead felt the shock of impact all the way up to my shoulder as the tip of the knife caught on something hard, slipped to the side, and sank a good three inches in the man's abdomen. He screamed.

I released the knife, pushed away, and leaned against the wall just in time to catch my balance as a flash of incandescent blue light blinded the entire room. Seconds went by as my eyes readjusted to the dim atmosphere. Once I could see, I discovered that the back of the room was now mostly empty, leaving me a nearly clear path toward Ronan.

Surging forward, I leaped over a drunken form on the floor, dodged a surprised swing from another partygoer and then landed with a teeth-clacking crash on the floor as something large and hard hit me in the back of the head. I rolled onto my stomach, vision swimming. The floor beneath my cheek shifted like the deck of a ship in a storm. From my prone position, I could see Angus off to my left on the other side of the room, glowing with a faint blue nimbus and swinging his sword in wide arcs. The few guards in the room correctly pinned him as the larger threat, as he was fighting off four men. He was smiling.

When I put my hands on the floor to push myself to my feet, I realized that I was no longer holding my knife. Someone had thrown an empty bowl at my head—the evidence was still twirling in a lazy circle a foot from where I had fallen—and I'd dropped my weapon on impact. I spun, scanning the floor as warmth began to tickle a path down my scalp, and saw that more guards were pushing their way through the bottlenecked entrance, shoving people violently out the way. The nearest guard was too close for me to outrun.

"Shit."

This time, I struck first. The man had a sword on his hip, and I knew I couldn't give him the chance to draw it. He dodged the jab I threw with my left but wasn't fast enough to avoid my right cross. The vambraces increased the power of my blow, making up a bit for the weakness of my wounded arm, and my leather and brass-clad knuckles crunched against the man's left cheek with bone breaking force that left him dazed on his knees. I reached down and jerked his sword from the sheath on his hip, stepped back, slipped on the stupid bowl that had busted my head, and landed unceremoniously on my butt; which was lucky, because an arrow went buzzing inches above my head.

I heard a high-pitched crack as it ricocheted off the wall in the corner and thought, detachedly, that would have sunk right into my belly. Two more men were bearing down on me, and I scrambled to my feet to meet them, sparing a second to glance over my shoulder at Ronan, who was still slumped at the back of the room some 20 feet away, abandoned by his busty companion.

Both guards had their swords drawn, so I took a firm grip on the hilt and held the tip of my own sword low. The blade felt natural, despite my lack of training, like an extension of my arms, and I found myself parrying blow after blow; not with any skill or finesse, but I'd managed not to die in the first few seconds, which was long enough for Angus to dispatch the last two men he'd been fighting and cross the room toward me.

The sword made the air around it ring like a gong still humming after being struck, and I could feel the throb of its magic press against my skin without even having to look. Apparently, my opponents couldn't feel the magic blade because it struck the first man's hand off at the wrist before he realized Angus was there. The wound turned black within seconds. Instead of clutching his arm and screaming, the man simply stiffened and fell backward without another sound.

"Get Diarmuid," Angus snapped at me as two more guards made it through the thinning press at the door to close in on us. I turned and took two running steps before sliding to a stop as my heart dropped to my feet. Standing next to Ronan was an older man, not tall but broad across the chest and shoulders, with a black handgun in his meaty fist, the muzzle resting almost delicately against Ronan's temple.

He said, in a casual tone, "It's been a while since last we met, Angus Og. If you want to keep yer foster son's brains inside his skull, ye'll drop yer weapon."

Chapter Thirty-Nine

H is voice was surprisingly soft for such a burly man, but the room fell as silent as if he'd shouted the words. I didn't dare to look over my shoulder and away from Ronan.

"It hasn't been long enough, Goll. Ye're getting fat." Angus' voice was as bright and cheery as if we had just met an old friend for coffee.

"Drop the sword, Angus."

"I'll tell ye what: you free the lad and I'll let ye live. Moralltach hasn't tasted blood for a long while, and she's not yet slaked."

The man's eyes, so pale they were almost white, dropped to the sword in Angus's hands. I realized with a shock that his left eye was white, the iris covered by a milky film. A flicker of emotion crossed his face, hunger I guessed, but was replaced instantly by the same bland expression he'd used while threatening to blow Ronan's brains out.

"I don't think I'll do that, no. My breeding stock has been dwindling, and I've rarely had so nice a stud as Diarmuid Ua Duibhne. It's glad I am that he still lives. I regretted setting that boar on him, bonny fighter that he was, but something had to be done. Fionn could no longer be trusted, and leadership of the Fianna should have been mine. Diarmuid was a sacrifice indeed, but now that he's here, my daughters will give me fine, strong grandsons off him; so long as you don't force me to kill him...again."

Behind me, Angus warned in a low voice, "Ye've my vengeance on ye already, Goll McMorna. Hurt the lad, and I'll see ye rot in hell."

"Ye're not in a position to be giving me orders, are ye? Drop yer weapon, Angus, and don't bother tryin' to Walk from this place. The second you go, I'll put a bullet through the lad's head."

"Kill the lad and ye'll never be free of me, that I can promise."

Goll tilted his head slightly to the side, his eyes unblinking and flat as a snake's, and clicked the hammer into place. That got a low growl from Angus, followed by a curse and the clatter of steel against the stone floor. The hollow sound of more booted feet striking the stones filled the room. I risked a second to peek over my shoulder at Angus, who was surrounded by guards and grinding his teeth, both arms held behind his back and his eyes spitting fire.

Two more guards came up and grabbed me roughly by the upper arms. I cried out as pain knifed up into my shoulder from the arrow wound. Goll turned toward me, clearly taking note of me for the first time, and his eyelids lids peeled back in recognition as his face drained of color.

"You've brought her to me," he said bemusedly, and jerked his chin at the guards who hauled me forward until I was close enough to see the ragged scar of the wound that had damaged his right eye; a puckered line of pale skin that ran crossways from the inside corner of his brow near the bridge of his thick-set nose, and down through the eyeball itself, disappearing into his silvery beard. Whiskey fumes rolled off the man in waves. Gripping my chin with one paw-like hand, his pale eye roamed over my face with the poorly veiled contempt of a jeweler examining a flawed stone.

"Aye," he spat, pushing me away with a disdainful twist of his lips, "Fionn always left his mark on his get. I can see him in yer face, even if you've not got his bones."

I knew that I shouldn't say it. The room was so thick with the promise of violence that the atmosphere alone almost choked me, but I couldn't stop myself. Issues with authority notwithstanding, I had to let this man know that I wasn't afraid of him before I ruined everything and peed my pants in terror.

"So, you can see out of that eye," I exclaimed in mock surprise.

Angus groaned, I imagined him dropping his face into his hands, but Goll bared his teeth at me.

"Interesting that you should mention my eye since it was your grandfather who took it from me...before I removed his head from his body."

Though I had no idea what he was talking about, the venom in his voice was quelling, and I bit my lip to stop myself from saying something even stupider.

"Oh, aye," he continued, mistaking my silence for understanding, "your grandfather died by my hand, your father's death was my doing twice over," his upper lip curled back to reveal yellow-stained teeth, "and now your fate is in my hands."

My mouth dropped open. "My father?"

Amusement at my surprise mingled with a kind of gleeful contempt to form on his rough features the expression that must be on the face of every little boy who ever fried ants with a magnifying glass. The look only lingered for a moment before he mastered himself.

"I didn't know he was still alive, you see. So, when my son..." his eyelids flinched, and he paused as the muscle in his jaw tensed, "when my son found your father was unexpectedly alive and well, we engineered a little accident for him. The fire was a lucky circumstance, and quite a fitting funeral for the slayer of Aillen, all things considered. Speaking of my son, perhaps you would be so good as to tell me where he is?"

This last I heard only in part because my mind was suddenly full of flames. I was lying on the ground, swamped with pain that left me balanced on the knife edge of consciousness, face stinging with the heat of the fire that was devouring my father's crushed 67 Mustang, burning his body so thoroughly that my mother had nothing left to bury.

"Where is my son?"

I looked up from my feet where my eyes had unconsciously drifted in the grip of memory. Fat tears rolled down my cheeks, but I ignored them. The fire that had been banked in my chest was sparking to life. Goll stared back at me, his one good eye grey as storm clouds. The realization hit me like a blow to the stomach, and the face of his son floated behind my eyelids, grey-eyed and intent as he demanded to know why I still lived, furiously implacable as his hands settled over my neck.

"Officer O'Goll," I whispered, shaken.

"Where is my son?"

The fire leaped furiously to life and cast its light back onto the past three months. My teeth ground together, and every muscle in my body tightened in fury.

"He's saying hello to my father," I hissed through clenched teeth, feeling terribly satisfied as Goll's face went pale and wooden. I continued mercilessly, "I'd imagine his body is rotting in an unmarked grave somewhere in another verse."

Aside from the blood draining from his face, the man made no other movement or acknowledgment. The gun was still steady on Ronan's temple, and Goll's expression was pond-water still, which made his conversational tone more disconcerting.

"That's three lives your family owes me, daughter of Fionn. You will replace them for me before I kill you. I'll breed out the last of your cursed line, and make them mine."

Ronan groaned and rolled onto his back, his breath catching as his arms twitched toward his chest, eyelids beginning to flutter.

"Mona!" the bald man barked, all traces of civility gone from his voice, "bring our guest more wine."

A brown-haired girl who had been huddling in the corner stumbled forward, picked up the cup from where it lay on the floor at the foot of the couch and filled it with a thick, dark liquid from the pitcher on the table near him.

"Wait," I pleaded as she tipped the cup against his lips, but the liquid slipped over the side and dribbled from the corner of his mouth to run down his cheek. Ronan ceased struggling, and his breathing deepened. I pulled against my pinned arms in hopeless rage, but the guards held me tight. Even if I were to free myself, it would have done no good because the gun in Goll's hand held me as immobile as if it were pressed against my own head.

"Don't worry, daughter of Fionn. Diarmuid doesn't suffer. The wine is sweet. It takes your mind away and leaves your body behind. He'll give me many grandsons even though his mind is lost. My daughters know their work."

"You sick son of a bitch," I said with as much disgust as I could manage, "you're breeding people like animals!"

The skin tightened across the older man's cheekbones, and his eyes narrowed dangerously.

Unable to stop myself, I said, "It must really sting that drugging a woman is the only way to tempt one into your bed."

He gestured to one of the guards, who took the gun and leveled it at Ronan's head in his master's place. With a curt nod from their king, the guards pulled me up the short stairs until Goll and I stood toe to toe. From so close, every detail of the man was shockingly apparent, from the sharp reek of his body odor to the broken blood vessels on his cheekbones and the golden torc that wound around his neck, ending in stylized boar's heads.

"You'll be grateful for the wine, daughter of Fionn," he purred, bathing my face in alcoholic stench, "you won't know when I come to you, and you won't fight me, but I'll plant my seed in your belly, and your father's grandchildren will be mine. I'll take my sons back from you, and then send you to hell with the rest of your cursed line. Mona!"

The girl squeaked and hurried to pour more liquid into the cup, spilling some over her shaking hands in the process.

"Goll," Angus warned from behind me, his voice rough with emotion, but Goll never took his eyes from my face. Mona hurried to my side and held the cup out, eyes downcast and shoulders slumped. I was shaking, too, but with fury.

Goll took the cup from her and held it up before me, victory burning in his eye, and said, "Drink up."

I bit my lips between my teeth and pulled my head as far back as possible. Goll's hand shot out to clamp my nose shut as one of the guards twisted my hair around his fist and wrenched my head back. The lip of the cup pressed hard against my closed mouth, waiting for the lack of oxygen to force me to betray myself as my lungs started to burn. Stars burst behind my eyelids, and I knew that self-preservation would override my willpower in mere seconds. I gasped, gaining half a lungful of air before my mouth was filled with a thick, sickly sweet liquid that tasted vaguely of dates, and made the roof of my mouth numb.

I had a sudden vision of myself laying limp, pliant, and vacant-eyed on a bed while Goll straddled my body. Bile rose, burning the back of my throat, to choke me. Wild with fear and defiance, able to do nothing else, I spat the liquid into his smug face and kicked out with my right leg to plant the man's balls firmly in his abdomen.

Goll grunted, curling protectively around his crotch while purple-brown syrup dripped down his cheeks. I wasn't fast enough to get away from my guards, who pinned me in place by my arms. Struggling was useless, so I turned my head toward Angus. I knew he had gifts far beyond simply his skill as a swordsman, but he was looking at me with shocked, almost panicked eyes that didn't belong in the face of the competent man who'd led me through the dangers of last two days.

"Angus," I whispered, but he clenched his jaw and closed his eyes to shut me out.

"Give me that bottle," Goll snapped as he righted himself, pulling at the front of his trousers.

The servant girl scurried forward. He snatched the bottle from her, straightened with a grunt of discomfort, and punched me in the solar plexus with a short, sharp strike that made the edges of my vision go black. All the strength went out of my legs, and I crumpled to the floor, dragging at the air as if an elephant was sitting on my chest. I was so focused on trying to breathe that I had no resistance to offer when Goll casually pushed me flat and straddled my hips. Two guards dragged my arms away from my stomach and pinned them to the floor just as I pulled my first breath in with a sobbing gasp.

"They all fight, at first," Goll said softly, leaning over me and sliding a lock of hair off the side of my face with the tip of one finger, "but once you've whelped your first brat, you'll settle. After all, no mother wants to see harm come to her child, does she?"

He patted my cheek with the side of the bottle and smiled in away that made my already sick stomach knot in disgust. "Open your mouth."

I bit my lips together and turned my face to the side just in time to see Angus disappear out of the hands of the guards. He was gone, and so was the sword. I was alone. Luckily, the guard who had the gun trained on Ronan was watching me instead. Goll shifted until he was all but sitting on my chest, then gripped my face in one hand and squeezed until pain and pressure forced my jaws apart. Again, my mouth filled with the sickly-sweet liquid but he clamped a hand over my mouth before I could spit it out, using the other hand to pinch my nose shut.

I kicked and squirmed and tried to twist my head, but I knew I was only fighting inevitability. My oxygen starved body would rebel, and I'd be forced to swallow. Squeezing my eyes shut, I held the poison in my mouth. I had no doubt that if I choked to death, Goll would simply sit on top of my body with his hand pressed against my mouth and watch.

The poison slid down my throat like molasses, clinging and choking so that I coughed and gagged trying to breathe. Gol stood over me and reached down to grab a fistful of my shirt, hauling me to unsteady feet with a malicious glint in his eye.

"Welcome to the family, daughter of Fionn."

I curled my lip in a snarl; at least, I tried to curl my lip, to bare my teeth, to growl at him and spit profanities in his face, but my body wasn't responding to my commands anymore. Goll reached out and took my face in one hand, turning it from side to side with a smile. "There, you see? Nice and pliant. She'll give us no more trouble."

Oh, yes I will, I thought, but an assiduous lassitude had stolen over me, weighing down my limbs as my mind seemed to detach itself from my body and float somewhere off to the side. Everything took on a kind of hazy glow that made me think what I was seeing wasn't quite real. Had I fallen asleep? Goll gave me one, last, dismissive glance before he turned on the guards who'd been holding Angus. They both cowered back from him and shook their heads, waving hands and gesturing at the thin air between them.

I watched indifferently as Goll pulled the sword from one of the guards trembling hands and buried it, hilt deep, in his partner's belly. At some point, we left the room, and I realized that we were moving down a long, darkened hall behind another detachment of guards, who were supporting Ronan between them. His head lolled to the side, and the toes of his boots scraped against the stone floor as two of the guards carried him under the arms. I was struck by the beauty of him, even in repose, and my eyes cataloged every detail I could see in the dim light. An exquisite kind of sadness washed over my thoughts, and I had the vague notion that if I was capable of this kind of melancholy while my mind was so detached, then my feelings for Ronan weren't rooted in my body at all.

The guards turned to haul Ronan into one room and deposited me on the bed in another. I sunk into the bed and lost myself, floating somewhere above my body, catching thoughts and impressions as they drifted by, but they were too slippery to hold on to, and I'd lose them after a second or two. I did think briefly about walking out of Eriu, but my body wasn't taking orders from me anymore, and I didn't know how to begin. Time had no meaning since there was nothing to measure it by.

My mother's voice echoed in my head sometimes, but it would always fade away into white noise that became the crackling hiss of fire; fire was devouring my dad's car, burning in my chest, burning at the bottom of a deep well, where I'd sink down and down into the darkness.

Sometime later, I came to myself and realized that I was being bathed. My body was naked on the bed, and two girls were rubbing rough, wet cloths over my skin, rinsing them out in a bucket of water near my bed.

I began to feel cold.

The sensation pulled me back toward my body like an anchor. My toes were cold, my fingers, my breasts, and the tip of my nose as well. My skin was raw and tingling where it had been scrubbed. I tried to cover myself with my arms but could only get them to twitch spastically. A groan of effort escaped my lips, and one of the girls dropped her rag and lifted a cup to my lips.

No, I thought, desperate to hold onto my body, but the thick liquid slid, slug-like, down my throat to pull me under with it.

The next time I came to myself, Gol MacMorna was standing next to my bed.

"Not the red, no," he said, "she'll wear the green. I want my sons to bid high for the use of her womb."

A girl in a red dress passed by with a green garment draped over one bent arm, her head hung low. Everyone seemed to move through a filmy haze that glowed around the edges, leaving afterimages just behind them when they shifted. I watched as Goll lifted my arm to examine the silver bracelet around my wrist with a furrowed brow.

"Aileen," he snapped. A girl stepped up behind him, her sandy brown hair falling over her lowered face. "When ye come back to dose her, see if you can get this off," he shook my arm by the wrist, and I watched my fingers dangle limply, "I want no ties to Avalon if I can help it."

The girl nodded stiffly, and I noticed she wore a white cloth or collar around her neck. Goll dropped my arm and looked toward my feet.

"Have you checked her maidenhead?"

"Not yet my lord," a trembling voice replied.

"How can I drive up her price at the banquet tonight if I know not the state of her maidenhead? Quiet," he raised his hand dismissively, "I'll check her myself. In fact, leave the dress and go prepare the others for auction."

The sandy-haired girl seemed to hesitate, pausing by the door as the others passed quietly through. Her eyes looked tortured and vaguely familiar. Had I seen her somewhere? In the hall where I'd fought for Ronan? The other girls pulled on her arm with frightened expressions that shifted to terror when Goll stiffened. She allowed herself to be dragged from the room, and I lost sight of them as the door closed.

The haze around him had dimmed somewhat, and some of my objectivity seemed tenuous as the rope that anchored me to my body tightened.

"I'm going to sell you to my sons, daughter of Fionn, and be revenged against the man who took all I held dear," he said, but he didn't seem to be talking to me at all, "I'll strengthen my line with Cumhaill's blood. Let us see how well you'll fill my coffers, too."

I could feel my body shift and jerk beneath his hands before he wiped his fingers on the blanket. "My nobles will pay well for a fallow field. You'll be of value only so long as you bear my line fey sons," he said, leaning down to look in my eyes as he pinched my cheeks between his fingers, "fail in this, and I'll have no use for you."

A wave of dizziness rolled over me, and I let the blackness draw me under.

CHAPTER FORTY

Ronan touched me, kissed me, laughed with me under the bright canopy of fall leaves as shafts of sunlight danced across his features, turning everything into a shifting, golden haze.

Rayne sat on the end of my bed and patted my leg.

"They killed Mat," she told me calmly, "but he'll be all right, so don't worry."

Then she grabbed my hand and fell over backward, pulling me with her. We plunged into cold water and my head sunk beneath the surface as slimy tendrils dragged at my flailing legs.

My mom brushed the hair from my face, and I felt her lips warm on my forehead.

"I'm here, baby girl. You just be brave."

Momma.

I felt tears slide down my cheeks. Her hand on my face felt so real, so warm that I opened my eyes and found myself looking into the eyes of the sandy-haired girl with the white fabric tied around her neck. Her lips were pale, pinched together between her teeth, and her eyes had the hunted look of a hare chased by foxes.

I felt the pang of recognition again.

She looked back over her shoulder toward the door and then at me, and held up a stoneware bottle that reeked of the sickly-sweet blackness. I heard myself whimper, a pathetic sound that vibrated in the back of my throat, but I couldn't so much as raise a hand to stop her from pressing the bottle against my lips. She raised one finger to her mouth as she locked eyes with me, and then poured the liquid against my closed lips, letting a few drops run down the line of my mouth to slide slowly down my cheek. It tickled, and I felt it.

With another frightened glance over her shoulder, she poured a generous portion of the bottle into the chamber pot and replaced the cover quietly. When she looked up at me again with round, frightened eyes, I recognized her at once. The girl from the forest.

You died, I tried to say, but all that came out was a breathy grunt.

She shook her head and then winced, pressing her fingertips against the bandage and sucking a painful breath in through clenched teeth. Once more, the girl pressed her finger to her lips with imploring eyes. I tried to nod but couldn't force my head to move, so I simply blinked once, slowly. That earned me a tremulous smile before she turned and hurried from the room.

My body came very slowly back to life. The haze began to fade from the world around me, but dizziness and nausea crept in to replace it, followed sluggishly by emotion as my critical thinking crunched into gear. The girl was alive, how? She'd been choking on her own blood when Niall broke the arrow shaft off and pulled my arm free. I'd been certain she had died, even felt her frequency fade away, but there she was. Perhaps there was someone in the king's service with a healing gift?

The thought of Goll made me recoil.

As sensation anchored me firmly to my body and the feeling of detachment faded, everything I'd experienced since swallowing the drugged wine began to take on the surreal quality of a vivid dream. Had the girl even been real? I was sure she'd died, but I could feel the dried line of liquid against my cheek and could even force my fingers to move as the effect of the drug started to wear away. How long would it take to wear off completely? I still didn't have enough control to Walk out of Eriu. I tried, and then remembered watching Angus fade away, his face twisted in anguish. Heat suffused my cheeks. He'd left us.

The logical part of my brain said that there wasn't anything I could have done.

Welcome back, I thought acerbically. *I could have done without that reminder, thank you.*

That bastard left me here to be—I couldn't continue the thought; my entire being shied away from it even as I caught the hazy memory of Goll sliding his hand between my legs. With every bit of will I possessed, I forced myself to focus on immediate concerns, like how the hell I was going to get myself and Ronan out of this mess.

The door to my room swung open, and three guards walked in, followed by a homely girl in a plain brown dress carrying a basket. My mind began to work furiously. As far as these people knew, I was still being drugged by doses of the wine. I wasn't in control of my body enough to walk out of Eriu, and unless I wanted to give away my only advantage by fighting, it was best if they thought I was still completely under the influence of the drug.

The guards took hold of my arms and lifted me into a sitting position. My head fell limply to the side and I saw that I was wearing a sheer green dress that did nothing to hide my body. Hands gathered up the heavy curtain of my hair, and I felt a comb or brush being pulled none-to-gently through the tangles. Soon my hair was twisted and braided into some semblance of order, and the guards lifted me.

We passed through hallways, only encountering a few servants as I tried to keep my body limp and unresponsive while paying as much attention to my surroundings as possible. Sifting through my hazy memories was getting more difficult as my mind sharpened and control of my body slowly returned. I didn't remember the layout of the castle enough to know where we were going, but I was carried down several flights of stairs and into a room much grander than the one in which I'd found Ronan.

Tapestries lined the walls, though I could only see the bottom of the rich embroideries as my head hung on my limp neck. We passed ornately carved tables, highly polished leather shoes and dresses dyed in rich colors, all the while the air was full of the scent of roasted meat and herbs. The room buzzed with whispers while the guards dragged me to the front and deposited me in a chair, the last in a line of four. I joined two other women, both young girls in red, one with skin the color of red clay and—my heart hesitated and then pounded hard—Ronan, all of us seated limply in our padded wooden chairs. I had to force myself not to lift my head and look around, to gain my bearings and assess how I could get myself to Ronan and get out. I focused inward for a moment, trying to see whether I could affect my body enough to change my frequency, but the response was weak.

"Nobles of the King's court," a voice boomed from my right, silencing the whispers, "the quarterly bidding will begin after we feast. If you've been selected to bid, please be sure to view the stock before the auction begins."

There was a clapping of hands, and the voices in the room rose in excited chatter. A line was beginning to form to my right, near the girl farthest from me, and I could distinguish the voices.

"Nice wide hips," a man was saying conversationally, "small in the chest, though, and a bit too short for my liking. I want my sons tall and brawny."

"She's a pretty one, isn't she? Look at that hair, Meryl," said a woman's voice, "as yellow as a fall leaf. Connor is sure to bid for that one; you know how yellow hair turns his head. Not that I mind," she added in a whisper, "at least he'll leave me be for a few months."

"She's too soft, feel her? Breasts like empty sacks of flour. What did you say her gift was?"

"Oh my, he's a big one. I'll bet he's big all over. It's been quite some time since we've had a male to bid on. Lift his clout, would you? Ahhh. To have his sons...how much do we have to bid with, my lord?"

Finally, someone stepped into my field of view. A coal gray jacket fastened with buttons as black as jet filled my vision as a hand reached up to lift my head while I tried to keep my eyes as vacant as possible. "Damn me if she's not one of the Sihde. Look at her eyes."

Keeping my eyes unfocused, I couldn't clearly see the face of the man who was examining me, but it took everything in my power not to bite his finger when he drew the tip of it across my lips.

"She's got freckles," the next man said derisively, but the man who was holding my face answered, "but they're like little flecks of gold."

He pinched my cheeks together, forcing my lips apart, and noted, "nice teeth," and then dropped my face.

His hand cupped my breast over the sheer fabric before he said breathlessly, "Sons from this wench. She's as tall and firm as a young tree." My skin seemed to shrink away in disgust, and I couldn't disguise a shiver of revulsion.

"Look how she rises to my touch, even with the potion still in her blood."

The second man shoved in and forced the grey-suited man away from the rows of chairs. "Most like she's just cold," he sneered and pinched my nipple so that it tightened in a rush and retreated against my skin.

Remaining still and quiet was the single hardest thing I'd ever done. I began to repeat a constant litany of *please, please, please, please,* to my body, willing myself to be rid of the drug so that I could get myself the hell out of there.

My fury was stoked to even greater fire when I heard a woman say, "I don't care if my children foster at the castle or no, I'd empty my coffers just to have this one in my bed. Did you touch him? I've never seen so fine a stud." Then she added, in a conspiratorial whisper, "I could even cast aside the first few babes to keep him a while longer. Iona knows herbs that will do it."

Fire began to burn in my belly as I imagined Ronan, limp and helpless in his chair while woman after woman examined him like an animal, touching his body with lascivious fingers. At least I was awake, I could scream inside my own head, but Ronan and the other women didn't have even that small luxury.

The line seemed to last forever, man after man pulling at my hair, pushing my knees aside to peer between my legs, sinking their fingers into my hips and examining my face with hungry eyes. Even the women stopped to look me over, some remarking with venomous jealousy, others with pity, all of them remarking that a child of mine born with my gift would be a boon for their families.

One man, the last in the line, held my face carefully with both hands and looked hard into my eyes.

"Are you the one?" he asked, but he was talking to himself. "If I don't have a fae child soon..." his voice died away, and his eyes dropped to examine my body, "wide enough hips, that should do, and taller than the others. I need a son," he whispered, biting his bottom lip. "I can't let Goll cast my family out. Little Brigid is still at the breast, oh god, she'd never survive it." He lifted my chin to peer at my features again and said, "I'd be kind to you."

Don't you dare, I thought to myself furiously, summoning every bit of disgust and fury I could, stoking the flames in my chest until they were hot enough to burn away any trace of traitorous pity.

They had taken their seats to gorge themselves, and I fought to spare my energy for Walking, but my mind was boiling. I pushed, turning my mind inward with all the force of my will, to attempt the healing Molfus hinted was possible. Maybe I could speed up my metabolism and hurry the drug out of my system. I tried to feel my way down through the chambers of my heart, following my blood through its long path toward my brain. Where would I need to go to speed my metabolism?

"Goll Mac Morna!" The basso roar filled the room, crashing toward us with the sound of ringing steel and the grunts of fighting.

My head snapped up as another man called, "The strength of our arms!"

I'd been so focused on my own body that I'd completely missed the sound of men fighting their way into the room. Men filled the back of the hall, guards in red locked in battle with men wearing greens and browns and carrying outdated weapons. One man, a head taller than the rest, stood alone with fury riding his features like a thunderhead on a mountaintop. His hair was white as snow.

Guards from Goll's table rushed the back of the room and one swung at the white-haired man, who parried the blow lazily, kicked the guard in the stomach and brought the edge of his shield down on the crown of the guard's head. He moved with the confident grace of an actor in a Chinese action flick, every move perfectly choreographed and executed with the precision of a dancer. Angus strode behind him in mismatched armor carrying his greatsword.

"Fionn!" Goll's voice rose above the din of panicked diners like a bull elk in challenge. The white-haired man turned at the sound, and his gaze settled on the front of the room. I couldn't take my eyes off the man as he advanced through the fight and the fleeing guests, parrying blows and negligently knocking men aside with his own weapon. The men in green and brown closed ranks behind him, twenty at least, fencing him off from the back of the room where the fighting was progressing in earnest.

"Goll Mac Morna," he said, his voice quiet but ringing with authority, "I'll have a word with you."

The tables emptied in a rush of stumbling bodies as people huddled against the walls or tried to bolt between the fighting men. Goll stood rigid, voice and body tightly controlled, and said "So, the prophecies are true. You live, after all."

"Despite your best efforts, I do. What have you done, Goll?"

His blank façade cracked and broke. "I've made Eriu mine," he spat, "I've made her people mine."

The white-haired man shook his head sadly. "Enslaved them, you mean."

"I protect them!"

"You kill them."

"You dare speak to me of killing?" Goll demanded, his face flushed with blood and his pale eyes glowing beneath his brows. Both huge fists clenched at his sides as he shouted, "You who were sworn to protect them? What blood stains your hands, Fionn Mac Cumhaill? The blood of children and of old women!"

White brows rose in surprise, and Fionn said, "Is that why you've been hounding me? She didn't die by my hand, Goll Mc Morna and well you know it. She was yours to protect."

Goll's face went the color of spoiled milk and then darkened in seconds to purple, pulsing with his hammering heartbeat. "Her death was your fault! Yours! And so was Fer Tai's! Mac Airt gave you the Fianna and naught but death followed!"

Goll drew the pistol from his side, his face split into a rictus grin, and pulled back the hammer.

"Is this how it ends, Goll? Will you hide behind a coward's weapon? Come, mo dheartháir, and face me as a man of Eriu."

Goll's face stilled. His blind eye twitched, and I caught my breath. I'd forgotten to pretend to be drugged; I was too wrapped up in the action. The king's face underwent a surprising transformation as he set the pistol down carefully on the wooden tabletop. His former outrage had been replaced by the hungry competence of a starved predator. Fionn brought the tip of his sword up into a low guard and nodded as Goll drew his own sword with a violent 'whoosh' of air.

"Here is your chance for vengeance, then, Goll," the white-haired man said with satisfaction, "come and take it."

"Daddy!" I screamed.

CHAPTER FORTY-ONE

All three men turned toward me in slack-mouthed surprise. My mind fought against what my heart knew to be true. I'd seen him lying on the roof of his car, bloodied and breathless, and yet there he stood, with hair white rather than red, but just as virile and alive as my fondest memories.

"Allie girl," my father said, relieved.

"Go, Allison!" Angus shouted.

Goll took advantage of the distraction my scream created and leaped the table to bring his sword down in an arcing blow. I screamed, and my father twisted his arm to slide the stroke aside. Angus rushed toward me, leaping fallen bodies and calling, "Go!" just as the line of green-clad fighters began to break, spilling crimson guardsmen into the room like blood through an open wound.

I pushed myself to my feet and wobbled, holding onto the chair for balance and staggering toward Ronan, who was pushing himself out of his chair dazedly.

"Allie," he croaked, falling to his knees and retching. My heart broke as I pushed myself past the chair next to mine, and stumbled to his side.

"Diarmuid," Angus breathed as he knelt next to us, grabbing Ronan's chin and examining his face, then gripping my shoulder and pushing me toward him, "Get the two of you out of here, Allison. He'll never make it on his own."

My eyes strayed toward the two men only half a room away from us, fighting with the skill of thousands of years, and I said weakly, "My father."

"I'll stay with him," Angus promised, standing with his sword held protectively over us, "go now!"

I took one last, longing glance at my father as he blocked a stroke with his shield, stepping inside Goll's guard and thrusting toward his middle only to have Gol slide to the side as the two twisted in unison, like a pair of dancers. Ronan groaned, shifting under me and I jerked my eyes away, pressed my cheek against his chest, and began to hum.

Tremors ran from my neck to my feet and back again as my body fought against the lingering effects of the drug, coming under my direction reluctantly. It was like trying to button a jacket with numb fingers. I knew what to do, but my body fumbled with my responses, and the sounds of fighting drew near.

"Allison get out of here!" Angus growled, and the sound of metal clashing rang in my ears. I squeezed my arms around Ronan but they were weak—so weak—and I couldn't protect him. I struggled to bring him within my electromagnetic field, to bend both his body and my own to my will, but I couldn't make us match up.

"GO!"

Ronan, come on, I pleaded silently, beginning to feel the pain of separation as my will forced our bodies to do something they weren't capable of. Ronan groaned and twisted, his face contorted in pain, and I knew that he felt as if his body was about to fly apart into a million tiny pieces while the room around us filled with screams.

I grabbed his face and kissed him.

Ronan's chest rose and fell steadily—reassuringly—beneath my cheek, and I hesitated to open my eyes. We were somewhere cool, quiet, and together. That was all that I could process. Shortly, I was distracted by tickling on the inside of my arm, like the tiny feet of a bug crawling from my biceps down toward my wrist. With a sigh, I opened my eyes. Blood was dripping down my arm from the bandage, an almost brown line down my pale skin in the dim light. Had our traveling torn open the half-healed arrow wound?

We were lying on the ground in a cave-like room, two ants trapped under a bowl. The arched ceiling was as smooth as an egg, rounded from the wide circle of the floor up to the curved roof, the walls pale and featureless. At the center of the room was what looked like a broken pillar, wide as a man is tall and two or three times as high. Smooth-sided, but not as perfect as the walls, the top looked to have been broken off at some time in the past.

Ronan began to stir, groaning and rolling to his side, and I climbed unsteadily to my feet. Four arched doors opened from the circle room in each of the cardinal directions, like surprised mouths, black in the pale walls. There was no light source, as far as I could see, and no way to know for sure that I had walked us to the right place.

A steady, throbbing pain was beginning to intrude on my thoughts, pulsing from the pit of my stomach where nausea boiled like a cauldron on fire, complimented by the rising fire in my shoulder. The violence of our travel had dislocated my left shoulder again and sweat began to bead on my forehead.

"Hello?" I called weakly. Ronan began to retch. I shambled toward the closest door and shouted down the corridor, "Hello?"

My voice didn't echo back. I knelt on the ground near Ronan, rubbing his back with my right hand absentmindedly as he was noisily sick, trying to think back over what Angus and I had discussed and pinpoint where I was supposed to take us, but my mind peeled off and started floating somewhere else to escape the pain. When Ronan finally stopped heaving, I pulled him away from the dark stain of his sickness with the last of my strength, pillowed his head on my lap, lay back on the cold floor, and closed my eyes.

I woke up suddenly and completely. The room around me snapped into instant focus in the absence of my usual morning fog, and my first impression of the room was, sterile. Everything was flat, ergonomic, and in various shades of pale. Where was Ronan? I sat up and kicked my legs off the bed, prepared to wince at a cold floor when my feet touched the ground, but the surface was surprisingly warm and smooth. My clothes were nowhere to be seen.

I jerked the blanket off the bed, wrapped it around myself, and went in search of a human being. Before I could reach for the door, which had no handle and was only indicated by a narrow seam that broke the even surface of the wall, a thin blue light glowed along the door seam, and it slid open to reveal a tall, slim man with widely spaced eyes and aquiline features.

"Allison, may I help you?" He reminded me strongly of Cecily, airline pilot voice and all.

"Yeah, um, where's Ronan? Where are we and can I have some clothes, please?"

He gestured graciously toward the bed and said, "You are in the Valetudinorium Venatores. Please sit, and I will answer as many questions as I can. First, do you mind if I ask you about your health?"

I pulled the blanket more tightly around myself, trudged back toward the bed, and plopped down on it frowning but relieved that I had walked us exactly where I'd meant to despite the struggle.

"I suppose."

He walked gracefully into the room and stood in front of a waist-high table, pressing the fingers of both hands against the surface. Blue light glowed beneath the tabletop and sectioned itself off into something resembling a keyboard but with no visible letters or numbers.

"How do you feel?" he asked.

"Fine."

"No pain in your arms?" I started to say, 'a bit' but then looked down at my biceps to see nothing but a smooth oval of slightly raised skin, pale pink around the edges. "Ah...no. No pain. What?"

I prodded the freshly healed scars with my fingertips. "Nothing," I said in wonder, glancing at my left shoulder as it moved smoothly in its socket.

"That is well. Is there any residual pain in your stomach?"

"How the hell—I mean—what did you do to me?"

His fingers flew over the glowing tabletop, but he paused to look at me quizzically. "We healed your injuries, naturally."

"Naturally."

"Is that not why you came to the Valetudinorium?"

"Yeah, but I didn't think—" I reached up to search for the knot on my scalp where the bowl had cut me, "I didn't think you could just make them disappear!"

"We do not heal the injuries, in a technical sense. We simply encourage the body to heal itself."

There didn't seem to be anything simple about healing a wound that quickly. I stifled my natural curiosity and repeated, "Where is Ronan?"

The man dragged the fingers of both hands across the surface of the table from top to bottom, and the blue light disappeared. "Your companion is quartered in his own room, across the hall. They are still removing the poison from his stomach."

I felt sick. "Poison?"

"Such mind-altering substances in large doses are poisonous. He had much more of the drug than you did."

"But he...will he be okay?"

"Naturally."

"Can I see him?"

He shook his head. "Not until he is cleared. Now, do you feel any discomfort or mental turmoil from your assault?"

"My what?" He turned his impassive face toward me and said, "When we treated you we found bruising on your breasts and slight tearing in your reproductive tract. There was no trace of semen, and since you had strong doses of the sedative in your system, we assumed it was assault. Was it consensual?"

"No, it wasn't...I didn't—I mean—" my voice died away as my mind went blank.

"Ah," the man said, "as we suspected. You will be glad to know that we found no sign of infection or serious damage, and with no traces of semen, we did not have to cleanse your womb to prevent unwanted fertilization."

"Unwanted..." I looked down at the blanket, imagining my body beneath it, and resisting the sudden urge to press my hand against my stomach, and breathed out the only syllable I could utter. "Um."

"Ah, yes, clothing. I will see that you are supplied with something suitable."

He walked over to the wall and ran his fingers down a section, causing it to glow with blue light, and pressed a few squares. Next to the keyboard, a drawer-shaped piece of the wall slid out silently. He reached down into it, pulled out a bundle of cloth and walked it over to me.

"I hope this will be sufficient. I will have food sent to you." He nodded to me and left.

I sat on the bed covered by a loose-fitting grey robe for a full five minutes before I tried to escape. The place was too much a hospital room for my comfort. I put the fingers of both hands against the door, imitating the way the nurse had brought the light-keyboard to life, and the door lit up before popping an inch toward me and sliding silently to the side. The hallway was much the same as the room had been, sterile and pale, broken only by unmarked doorways and a faint glow that seemed to have no source. I stepped out and then backed up in almost the same motion. Just to the right of my room were two guards wearing seamless white uniforms that reminded me vaguely of Stormtroopers without the stupid helmets; the weapons they were holding were infinitely more intimidating than plastic laser blasters.

Both men turned to look at me with expressions that convinced me that exploring might not have been the best idea. Before I could pull my head back into my room, four people turned the corner into the hallway behind the guards. One was Cecily, as calm and unperturbed as ever, followed by two more guards in white, and the other was Angus, who limped toward me with blood on his face and shirt.

"Angus!" I stepped out into the hall, and the guards immediately turned and raised their weapons.

"Let her pass," Cecily ordered.

"Are you okay?" I huffed after skidding to a stop in front of them, "Did my—"

He held out a hand and silenced me, eyes stern, and said, "I'll do. How's Diar—ah, shite—how is Ronan?"

"I haven't seen him; I was hoping you had."

"I've not seen him, I only just arrived." He turned to Cecily and asked, "Might I have a word with the girl?"

She studied me for a moment, folded her arms, and nodded. "Feel free, but make sure your wounds are seen to before you come to the Hall."

He agreed and motioned me back toward my room.

"What happened?" I asked as soon as the door slid closed. Angus sank against the wall with a long, weary sigh.

"We were overwhelmed before Fionn could finish the fight, and forced to flee before suffering more loss of life. He left Goll in a state of rage, I can tell you. I saw Fionn Walk before I came here. I don't know where he went."

"My dad's name is Patrick."

Angus stood, rolled his shoulders with a wince, and said calmly, "No. His true name is Fionn Mac Cumhaill. Just as Ronan's true name is Diarmuid."

I ignored the stab of betrayal I felt at the knowledge that the two men I had trusted and loved most in my life had lied to me about who they really were, and accused Angus, instead. "You left us."

He took my limp wrist, guiding me over to the bed and nodding at it. For lack of anything better to do, I sat.

"I think it's time you learned a few things," he said, sighing. "No one else knew that Fionn was a Walker. He was a gifted fighter, a strong leader. He had other gifts, too, in the way of some of the people of Eriu. He was greatly respected, even loved, until the falling out with young Diarmuid."

"Gráinne?"

"Gráinne, indeed. The Fianna—the band of fighters led by your father—they knew Diarmuid wasn't to blame for the girl's actions. He wasn't responsible for the ball sierc, that damned witch was the one who cursed him with the love spot, yet Fionn hunted them. He felt betrayed by Diarmuid, a man he loved and trusted above any other."

I saw the entire story play out in my mind again, this time from my father's point of view. I could imagine his sense of deep betrayal, of his injured pride as his young bride-to-be ran off with his trusted captain. Vengeance would only grow during the desperate hunt for the man and woman who had spurned him, choking out the love he'd once held for them and leaving only wrath.

"Ronan said that—" I swallowed, trying to reconcile his description of Fionn Mac Cumhaill with my memories of my father, "that Fionn let him die after he was gored by that boar."

Angus sat heavily on the armless chair near my bed, groaned, and nodded. "That he did. You see, Fionn had—has—the gift of healing. He could have healed Diarmuid but," he shrugged, "his vengeance was stronger than his mercy. Diarmuid was on the edge of death when I took him to Endre."

"I can't see my father doing that," I objected, "my dad was a good man, he'd never let anyone die if he could help them."

Angus sighed, looking far older than the day we'd first met, and said quietly, "Time changes many things, Allison."

"What happened to my father after you saved Ronan, why did everyone think he was dead?"

"Remember that no one knew your father was a Walker. His grandson, Oscar, loved Diarmuid much, and he shamed your father when he let Diarmuid die. The Fianna imprisoned him in a cave as punishment. Guilt is a powerful thing, lass. As far as anyone knew, Fionn Mac Cumhaill starved to death in that cave."

I pictured my father in the dark, alone and wracked with guilt. Thanks to the last few days, I also knew about the body's unreasoning will to live and guessed, "he Walked to True Earth?"

"He must have done."

We sat in silence for a long time as I played the timeline out in my mind. My father Walking to True Earth, living lifetime after lifetime, finally meeting my mom. How many wives were in his past, how many children? The recurring feeling that my own reality couldn't be trusted, and that nothing was what it seemed, came washing back over me like I was riding a riptide, being pulled farther out to sea with no way back to land, except the land had never really been there in the first place.

If everything Angus said was true, I was the daughter of the man who'd scarred Ronan, hunted him, and ultimately chased him from the home he loved for more years than was comprehensible. How could Ronan possibly look at my face and not see my father?

"But you left us." I accused Angus, ready to say anything to keep my own thoughts at bay.

"I left you to find him."

"You knew he was my father?"

"I knew he was alive; I didn't know he was in Eriu and I didn't know he was your father until Goll said so. I couldn't have saved you both on my own before I was cut down."

"How did you know where he was?"

"You remember the beggar we traded with for information?"

I nodded.

"He asked me if we were from the 'Fair One's' army. That's what your father's name means, more or less. I thought nothing of it at the time, but when Goll said you were his daughter, the connection made sense. I gather he's been building a resistance force among the people, so I took the chance that it was Fionn, and it was."

"Why would he have asked you if we were part of the army, I thought we were dressed to blend in?"

"The regular folk don't walk around armed."

I laid my head in my hands. "Okay. But none of this explains why Goll Mac Morna has been trying to kill me." I said the words, but it was incredible to me how little they mattered. I'd spent so much time thinking, training, hunting to find the man I believed was responsible for my father's death, for attempts to murder me, and for the death of my mother, that this single detail should mean more to me than anything else and yet...

"I won't pretend to know the whole story, but maybe a bit of history will help."

Angus told me that leadership of the Fianna, a band of the fiercest fighters in Ireland, had been taken from Goll by the King, Cormac mac Airt, and given to my father for having defeated a fearsome enemy of the crown.

"Which means Goll blamed my father for losing his position."

Angus rubbed his face with a weary hand, made an affirmative noise and added, "But I've a feeling it goes deeper than that."

"He said that my father had blood on his hands?" I was afraid to ask whose blood it was and more afraid that Angus would tell me. The shoreline of reality was growing more indistinct as the pull of the current grew stronger.

"Goll lost his mother and his son. I think his mother may have been the only person in the world he did love, and he blames your father for the fight that took her life, and for the battle his boy died in. And that's not all there is. There has been a prophecy in Eriu since your father left."

I bit my lips, closed my eyes, and stopped fighting the current.

"Which was?" I asked numbly.

"In many verses, they say the same thing of your father that they say of Arthur. He'll return to Ireland in a time of great need."

"So, my father—who is not dead—is an ancient, magic warrior who took control of a band of warriors from the original leader, which was Goll. Then Ronan betrayed my father, so he left Ronan to die, then ran away from his guilt. Somehow, Goll found out my dad is still alive, so he tries to kill him because he thinks Fionn will come back to Eriu and save everyone?"

"That seems right enough."

"Did he try to have me killed because I'm my father's daughter, or because I could find out who was behind it all?"

"I don't know, lass."

Overwhelmed and tired, I decided to change the subject.

"Can you tell me why there are guards in the hallway?"

Angus cleared his throat, and I opened my eyes to study the uncomfortable expression on his battered face, his sandy brows drawn up in the middle and crusted with dried blood.

"You remember I warned you about walking with magical weapons? You knew the rules."

I did.

"We're to be brought up on charges before the Concilium. Once Avalon is secured, anyway." Though I'd known that being caught walking with weapons had been a possibility, the knowledge still froze my insides.

"What do you mean, secured?"

"Avalon was attacked."

Chapter Forty-Two

I could run.

I could Walk away from this verse and disappear somewhere; my father had done it, after all. It appeared that running was in my blood.

Run, and go where?

Anywhere. Away from here.

You'd never see Ray or Mat again. It would never be safe to go home.

I thought I could live with that, as much as it hurt. Harder to accept never saying goodbye to Ben, never seeing his eyes wrinkle up when he smiled, never teasing him again.

You'll never know what's going on with your dad.

That thought made me wince. Angus had left me after breaking the news, limping badly and on the verge of collapse. He'd put a hand on my shoulder, given me a solemn nod, and disappeared down the hallway. I was too anxious to lay on the bed but too dejected to pace. I found myself alone once more, hugging my knees in the corner of a sterile room and having a conversation with myself.

You'll never get to say goodbye to Ronan.

"But he's alive," I said aloud, ignoring the stab in my chest, "at least he's safe and alive. I brought him back."

Sure, he's alive, but what are the chances of you ever being happy with him once he finds out what happened to you?

This thought made every muscle in my body tighten as if flinching away from some unseen hand. The irony of having experienced the thing I had been careful to avoid since puberty only made the experience more painfully surreal. I could still see hands touching me callously, examining me for suitability as breeding stock.

When my father died or, when I thought he died, the paramedics had found me fifty feet away from the car. At some point, I'd crawled away from the wreckage, and away from my father, to safety. The psychiatrists told my mom I had survivor's guilt, but I didn't. I had coward's guilt. I knew that I'd crawled away while half-conscious, and must have been acting on instinct. But surely, I thought, what a person does when they're not thinking is the most accurate indication of their character, and my character was selfish and cowardly. I'd left my father to burn and managed to save myself.

I'd run away from every boy who'd ever been interested in me. I'd gone to college for years with no real goal in mind. I'd made no plans for my future. I'd run away from the shooting in the diner. I'd failed to help Rayne and Mateo in the alley. I'd run from my mom's house after Trisha had attacked my family. I remembered Ronan telling me what the consequences might be for a Venatore who broke the Second Law, and I could only imagine what the Concilium would sentence me to for breaking the First. I was terribly, sickeningly afraid that I would run this time, too.

But at least you'll be alive.

Alive.

What good was being alive if there was no one to love? What good was being alive if the only thing that kept me company was my guilt? If I ran, I'd be sitting on an island in the middle of the ocean. Yes, I would be alive, but I would be alone and wishing I had the courage to jump into the water. If I drowned, at least I'd drown having used every ounce of will to fight.

My hands went unwillingly to my stomach. I had been avoiding unwanted attention since I was thirteen years old. While I tended to get along easily with men, I was in the habit of rebuffing their advances. I was more comfortable being in control, being the initiator, because being pursued felt exactly like being pursued; someone bigger and stronger chasing me down did not make me feel desired, but hunted.

With Ronan, I had been the initiator. I felt in control, even if things were equal between us, and he made me feel safe. I looked down at my body and felt again the hands touching me impersonally, without my permission, as if I were no more than a hound at a dog show.

There was no sound as the door opened, but I knew instantly that there was someone in the room. Taking a deep breath for courage, I opened my eyes and looked up from my knees expecting to see the two guards and their sleek guns, but instead saw Cecily standing in the doorway once again. She wasn't wearing scrubs this time, but a black shirt that billowed out from her slender frame and leather pants that fit her long legs like a second skin.

"You're not here to break me out of the hospital this time, are you?"

She didn't smile. Of course, she didn't. "No, I am not. I am here to take you back to Avalon to await your trial."

"What will happen to me?"

"I do not know, Allison. You have broken the First Law, the very reason the Concilium was founded."

I stood up, straightened my plain grey robe, and clapped my hands brusquely in front of myself. "All right then. Let's get this shit over with."

She blinked at me.

"I'm not fond of hospital rooms," I explained, feeling as if I should be embarrassed by my joviality but unable to squash the sudden lightness I felt as resolve settled on me like armor. I might have broken the law, but I'd saved Ronan's life. I had accomplished that much. I might have been abused, but so had many other women. I wasn't going to hide or cry over what couldn't be undone. For this one time, I was not going to run away.

I followed Cecily out of the room without a backward glance but hesitated just outside my door as a chink in my armor made itself painfully known. The door to Ronan's room slid open as silently as mine had, and a tall, willowy woman stepped out. For the space of a few heartbeats, the door remained open and I saw Ronan lying on his bed, face pale but peaceful and relaxed, not with the slackness of a drug but with honest sleep. His lips were parted, arms crossed over his chest. I almost walked into the room.

The desire to touch him, to reassure myself that he would be fine, was almost a physical need, but I hesitated long enough for the door to slide quietly closed. Would I ever see him again? If I did, would he even want to see me, knowing—as he must soon know—who my father was, and knowing what I must now tell him about what happened to me in Eriu?

Cecily led me down the hall, feet falling soundlessly on the floor. My surroundings passed in a kind of dim, pale blur while I considered how grace seemed to be a natural part of Cecily's people, while warmth was not. My nurse had delivered the news as if he was reading the statistics of a baseball game. This place was the center of advanced healing for the Venatore, at least that was what Angus told me when we made plans to bring Ronan here before walking to Eriu, but the people didn't seem to exhibit any kind of emotional concern for their patients. Did they practice medicine, or their version of it, simply from the pragmatic standpoint of functionality?

We turned a corner and were suddenly in the bowl-shaped room with the stone pillar in the center.

"Why here?" I asked, focusing on the room I had brought Ronan to when we'd first arrived.

"Surely you noticed that this is a place of power?"

"I wasn't very coherent when I got here," I admitted, "are all places of power marked with stones?"

"No, but many are. Are you prepared?"

I swallowed and tried to tamp down the sudden urge to turn around and sprint down the hallway.

"You cannot run from this, Allison," she said, correctly interpreting the tensing of my muscles.

"I could."

She eyed me for a second and then shook her head. "No, you could not. I would find you, wherever you ran."

"What? How?"

Cecily's blonde brows shifted—the first expression aside from perfect calm I'd ever seen on her face—and she seemed to consider something for a moment before her face cleared. "You see that this place is possessed of advanced technology?"

I didn't need to respond to that, and we both knew it, but I slid my hand along the side of my head, where the thrown bowl had cut me, and my fingers encountered only smooth skin.

"Suffice it to say that we have technology that can allow certain of my people to sense the atomic signature of Walkers."

"But how can they tell the individual signatures apart?"

She'd already turned away from me to walk toward the center of the room. A man appeared out of thin air before her, his face red as a lobster. Blisters popped out on his skin as I watched, horror-struck. The air was filled with the acrid stench of burning hair—most of it had been burned off his head—and Cecily caught him easily as his legs gave out. She laid him gently on the ground, turned his head to the side, checked the pulse in his wrist, and then stood, looking at me expectantly.

"Are you ready?"

"But," I sputtered, staring down at the man, "aren't we going to help him?"

"What can you and I do for him?"

I opened my mouth, but no sound came out.

"Healers will be along shortly to tend to his wounds. Prepare yourself, please, and follow me," her eyes hardened, and she added in a voice as sharp as shattered glass, "and do not attempt to escape, Allison. You have created enough trouble for yourself and, if you run, it would be within the rights of the Venatore to kill you on sight."

I cleared my throat to ease the sudden tightening and started to think of Avalon.

Soldiers patrolled the streets of the capital city in groups of four with rifles instead of swords. Farmers, artisans, and other people once more crowded the roads, but there was a subdued, hushed quality to the way they moved through the city, as if loud noises were somehow dangerous.

The blanket of oppression lay so heavily on the city that I felt myself stepping carefully. In many places, the brightly colored buntings that had hung from the sky bridges were singed, burned, or torn, hanging limply to flutter against the walls like broken butterfly wings.

When we reached the central marketplace, my legs went stiff, and I jerked to a stop. Wooden coffins were laid out in row after row on the grey cobblestone, some of them heartbreakingly small, with little dolls or stuffed animals placed on top. I hadn't realized that I was walking toward the coffins until I bent, reached out to pick up a tattered doll that lay on the ground, and saw that my hands were shaking.

The doll had brown yarn for hair, tied into two braids, and a blue dress. Dried brown stains marred one side of the doll's linen skin. Something heavy sat hard on my chest, and all the air in my lungs squeezed out in a moan. I kissed the doll on the forehead and placed it neatly in the center of the coffin at the end, smallest in the row.

Cecily brought us past each guard station with relative ease, and we entered the main castle building. I noticed the chipped stone in the walls, splintered bullet holes in some of the wooden doors, and groups of soldiers on patrol with suspicious expressions.

"How many did we lose?"

Cecily didn't turn toward me as she answered, "Fifty Venatore and civilians."

I followed her through the rest of the castle without asking any more questions. At least, not until we were standing just outside the cell I was going to call home for an unknown period. The room was circular, the metal walls fifteen feet or so in diameter, with a bed in the center, a little table with a lamp, and a discreet toilet against one wall. There were no windows. I dug my fingernails into my palms.

"Meals will be brought to you three times a day as well as books if you are so inclined."

And that was it. The door closed with sickening finality.

I sat on my bed in my cell, thinking about a little brown-haired girl and her doll, and cried for her...and for myself.

CHAPTER FORTY-THREE

"Y ou done, yet?"
    I sat up, wet-cheeked, and blinked at the door, but there was no one there. Most of the first evening I'd spent in self-pity until finally exhausted, I'd drifted into an uneasy sleep. I had just decided that the voice had been the last figment of a dream when it said, quite clearly, "because if you're going to cry some more, I'll wait."

I stood up and backed against the wall, waiting for some mysterious figure to appear when the voice said, "What'd ya do?"

"What is this, magic? Where are you?"

A low chuckle. "In my own metal cell, crazy. Look at the vent."

That was when I saw the grated vent in the wall about a foot across and six or so inches high.

"Who are you?" I asked into the opening.

"Name's Rich," the voice came back with a hollow echo, "welcome to the tinfoil box. What'd ya do to get in here?"

"The what?"

"The box. You know, the iron. Messes us up when we try to Walk, like a tinfoil hat."

I laid my hand flat against the cool metal wall of my circular cell. "Oh. I didn't know they could do that."

"Shoot, they can do just about anything. I mean, just think about all the stuff they can get their hands on."

Looking down at my wrists and seeing the bare skin there made me feel strangely naked without my vambraces. The silver cuff had been removed during my stay at the Valetudinorium. I'd seen futuristic weapons, as well as a magic sword that seemed to kill someone even when the wound wasn't deadly on its own. Hell, I'd learned an entire language within seconds, and I'd only been to a very few of all the possible verses.

"Yeah," I admitted, rubbing the bare skin, "I guess they can."

"So, what'd you do to get put in the box?"

"I, um...I walked with a magic weapon."

A whistle. "Whew, that's a doozie. First Law, ya know."

I slid down the wall to sit on the floor near the vent, grateful to have someone to talk to, even a disembodied voice. "Yeah, I know. What about you, why are you here?"

"Aw, I told my wife about all this, and they found out."

"That's it?"

"Yeah, I didn't want to lie to her anymore, ya know? We got kids and all."

I did a mental rewind to remember all the rules Ronan had told me about. Artifacts, technology, or weapons from one verse may not be walked to another verse; this is the First Law of the Founding, he'd said. You shall not endanger your fellow Walkers' existence by revealing your gifts to normal men; this is the Second Law of the Founding. Your actions shall not deprive another Walker of freedom, property, health or life; this is the Third Law of the Founding.

My stomach did a little flip-flop as I remembered telling Ben about what I was. Of course, he'd already seen it with his own eyes, but I wasn't sure how that would play against me if anyone knew about it. Had this man's wife had the capacity to endanger Walkers in some way? Did Ben?

"So, you try to get rich or something? I heard some Walkers make good money selling fancy guns."

"Rich?" I almost laughed, "No. I was just trying to stay alive."

"Instead you ended up in here, eh? Yeah, those Venatore are some hard-nosed sons of bitches. Not like they don't break the rules all the damn time, but does anybody ever do anything to them? Hell, no."

He made a disgusted noise that sounded like a bad starter on a car. I looked down at the place the silver bracelet used to occupy on my wrist.

"The Venatore aren't all bad."

"No? I suppose you think the Concilium is as clean as a virgin's sheets, too, ha! They're as crooked as any politician."

I mulled that over, twisting my now bare wrist and remembering the way light used to play on the engraved wolf's head.

"Did you try to run?" I asked.

"Oh, hell no, why would I do that? I don't got a death wish. You?"

"No."

"Well," he sighed, "you got that goin for ya, at least. Don't want to get caught by one of them cyborgs."

I turned to look at the grate like it could give me answers, and asked, "What do you mean, cyborgs?"

"Damn girl, don't you know nothin'? There's always one on the pick-up teams; I bet you met one yourself. Those sons-a-guns are colder than a witch's tits."

"Ah," I said, picturing Cecily, "yeah, I have. I guess they are kind of like robots, aren't they?"

"They ain't like robots; they are robots! They got crap inside 'em, you know, gadgets, and circuits, and stuff."

"Are you serious?"

"Yeah, the Concilium has some kinda deal with 'em. They let the Venatore use the cyborgs, and the Concilium gives 'em...something. Nobody knows what. It's some kinda big secret."

"How do you know that?" I demanded. The vent was silent for a while.

"I don't like to say."

I snorted, recognizing the sound of a conspiracy theory when I heard one. "Where are you from? What verse, I mean?"

"Earth, of course."

"True Earth?"

"What kind of other Earth is there?"

The next day I had my first chance for a bath and a change of clothes. It was a relief to be out of my cell, more to get a moment of peace without Rich chattering through the vent about how the Walker black market, apparently called 'the Exchange'—in some language that he couldn't wiggle his tongue around enough to pronounce—paid off members of the Venatore for protection, and how Elvis had been a Walker and become president of the United States in some other verse.

I paced my room, scratched designs into the stone walls with the handle of my soup spoon, and fine-tuned my self-defense by practicing the movements Danet drilled into me. Often, I wondered why Ronan hadn't come to see me, but no one would tell me anything. Had the poisoning been worse than they'd suspected? My nurse seemed certain that he'd recover, and my last sight of him had been in a healthy sleep, but I couldn't stop myself from thinking that he had learned who my father was. Angus would have told him, I was sure of it. Would he be able to face me again, knowing that? I wanted to believe he would have come to me if he could, but doubt gnawed away at my insides like a rat chewing through a wall.

Our relationship had been strained when we left Avalon. Maybe he was done with me. By the end of the fourth day, my curiosity was a raging monster that managed to overpower even my self-pity and wrestle it into submission. I was ready to plead guilty to starting world war three on Mars if someone would just tell me something.

I was talking to Rich through our shared vent, complaining loudly and with particular zest, when a knock on my cell door made cold dread condense into ice in my stomach.

"Miss Chapter," the voice said, "I am here to take you to trial."

"Abasi?" The door swung open, and there he stood, round belly sitting merrily in front of his sturdy frame. His mild, dark eyes changed from commiseration to panic as soon as he saw my face.

"Oh, don't cry, my dear! Please, do not. Things may not be as bad as they seem."

"I'm not crying," I insisted. It was a close thing, though. My eyes filled up as soon as I recognized his voice and the tears were hovering dangerously close to the edge. I hadn't seen anyone I recognized since Cecily left me in my cell, and something about Abasi had always felt comfortingly safe to me. The urge to throw myself at him and cry on his sturdy shoulder was nearly irresistible.

"Why you?"

Abasi shrugged. "I heard what was to happen and I thought you would like to see a friendly face before your trial."

He reached out and patted my shoulder consolingly when he saw my lips begin to tremble.

"Don't go borrowing trouble, my dear. Wait and see what happens, and then cry if you need to. Who knows what the future may bring, eh?" He was flanked by two guards in the silver and blue livery of the Pendragon who escorted us through the castle building and down a flight of stairs that wound at least three stories below the bottom floor. With every step downward, my muscles clenched in increasing anxiety until, reaching the bottom floor, I wasn't sure I could force my legs to move forward anymore.

The room was laid out like an amphitheater, with tiers of seats staggered down toward a lower center floor. Directly in front of the stairs we walked down, and at the opposite side of the room, was a dais, raised above the floor level, shaped in a semi-circle and sporting nine chairs arranged so that the center chair was flanked evenly on either side. One chair sat empty on the right, slightly apart from the others.

We walked toward the center of the room where a short wooden platform stood in isolation, a single chair at its center. With a hesitant glance, I peeked at the chairs rising around me and sighed in relief to see that only a bare few were occupied, and those in a single group just to the right of the dais. I thought those must have been what passed for my jury. At least I wouldn't be on public display.

Abasi led me to the chair, gave me an encouraging smile that didn't quite pass as honest, and sat in the lowest row of seats to my right. Guards flanked my platform. Torches lined the stone walls, casting fitful, shifting light and providing a low murmur that made the darkness in the pit and the silence of the watchers all the more disconcerting. Had they gone out of their way to make this room as intimidating as possible? Biting my lips, I slid into the wooden chair, which squeaked beneath my weight like a mouse beneath a cat's paw.

Courage, I told myself and squared my shoulders to face my judges.

"Allison Chapter," intoned the Pendragon, who sat in the center of the crescent of chairs, "you have been called before the Concilium on the charge of smuggling a magical weapon, violating the First Law of the Founding. There will be a trial to determine guilt or innocence as well as sentencing that will be ratified or rejected by a group of your peers. Do you understand these charges?"

"Yes."

Arthur turned to his right and asked an old woman, "Can we confirm the charges?"

"According to our eyewitness," she began in a voice like brittle paper, "the girl walked from one of the lesser verses with a blessed weapon—a sword I believe—and brought it to Eriu."

"I assume we have the witness?"

"He should be here."

"We cannot have a trial with no witness."

"You have a witness," said a voice from the back of the room. My spine stiffened as if someone had hit me with 50,000 volts. Angus walked into the center of the room, his stride long and confident, and stopped in front of my platform without so much as a glance in my direction.

"Shall we truly hear testimony from this deserter?" The dark-skinned man who spoke in stilted English was sitting to Arthurs's left, glaring at Angus.

"It was his choice to leave the council, Oronowe. That doesn't make him a liar," Arthur said and gestured toward Angus, "your testimony, please."

I didn't hear a word Angus said because blood was pounding in my ears, throbbing in thunderous pulses that shook my brain inside my skull and rattled all the arguments I'd spent the last couple of days building up to defend myself.

He betrayed me.

I hadn't stopped to wonder why Angus wasn't in the courtroom, despite the fact that he'd told me we were both being brought up on charges. Ronan's words about his foster father rushed back to my mind with stinging irony, words I'd been too consumed with desperation to remember when I had asked him to help me.

'He does things for his own purposes. I wouldn't trust him with your life.'

Cheeks burning, I stood up and said furiously, "I would like to speak."

Arthur pursed his lips but glanced at the other members of the Concilium, who shrugged or nodded vaguely. I told them everything. Everything I knew or suspected, and everything I'd done to try and help Ronan.

"And did this man coerce you to carry the sword, or deceive you in any way?"

The speaker was taller than average, lean, and sharp-featured. I started to say yes, that he'd told me I would have to carry the sword because he would be walking a magical dagger, when the memory of our conversation stopped me. Angus had never said the dagger was magical, only implied it. Besides that, I'd known the penalty for my actions and made the decision anyway. I gritted my teeth.

"No, he did not."

"And you Walked with the sword in full knowledge that doing so is a violation of the First Law?"

I straightened my shoulders and said calmly, "I did."

The members of the Concilium looked back and forth between themselves, and I turned to whisper in Angus's direction, "I'd like to kick you in your perfect teeth, you manipulative, lying weasel."

He didn't move.

"She is in training," someone mentioned.

"This was not a sanctioned mission, however," Oronowe pointed out, "and our policy is one of non-interference where the legless are concerned."

Murmured discussion began that was inaudible to me, but I noticed one member of the Concilium not speaking at all. He sat at the end of the row on the left, his single eye locked onto me like a heat-seeking missile while he tugged at the end of a long, grey beard. Unlike Goll, whose eye was damaged but still whole, this man's eye socket was empty beneath the wrinkled lid. I had the uncomfortable feeling that he was looking right through me.

"She did try to gain approval—"

"Knew the laws—"

"Presents a danger to entire verses—"

"Does it not strike anyone as strange," said the one-eyed man in a deep, resonant voice that immediately silenced the others, "that this happened just as Avalon faced its first armed attack, and that those attackers spoke Irish Gaelic?"

They all had troubled expressions on their faces as the man continued, "and that the weapons stolen in the attack all had magical properties?"

"I don't see how that relates to this case," the old woman pointed out.

"You said that his man, Goll Mac Morna, had a modern firearm, modern by True Earth standards?" the one-eyed man asked me.

"Yes, sir.".

"And we know that Eriu has not yet experienced anything like an industrial revolution, correct?" He looked at Angus when he said this, and Angus nodded.

"You are also under the impression that this Mac Morna is pressing Walkers into his service."

I bit down hard on my back teeth and grated out, "He's breeding them."

Thinking about my what my future would have been in Goll Mac Morna's hands still made bile rise in the back of my throat.

The old man nodded, as if he'd expected that, and looked toward the center of the half-circle where Arthur sat meditatively with his chin in his hand. "Does it not appear that this Goll Mac Morna is accruing magical weapons for himself, then, by creating slaves of our people?"

"So it would seem," Arthur allowed.

"Perhaps the girl was simply trapped, then, as we were trapped here in the city. Can she truly be blamed for trying to save her own life and that of her mentor, a Venatore of great renown?"

"Her life was in no immediate danger," pointed out the old woman as the elaborate bun on top of her head wobbled.

"But her life has been in continuous danger from the time she first exercised her abilities."

"She knew the Law. There is no honor in defending your own life by breaking the law that upholds the safety of all."

"But I wasn't trying to defend myself," I said, "I was trying to save Ronan!"

The woman gave me a sour look but continued speaking as if I'd never corrected her. "What if the sword had fallen into the hands of this man? What ability does the sword possess?" she asked Angus.

"Any blow landed with Moralltach is a killing blow," he answered, "even a scratch."

Her feathery brows rose. "Formidable."

"This is a dangerous prospect, my lord," said a lean, pale-skinned man.

"Indeed, it is." Arthur sat for a moment with the fingers of his hands steepled in front of him, his eyes solemn and distant.

"Allison," he finally said, sitting up straight and folding his hands in his lap, "you have purposefully and knowingly violated our First Law, the very law that brought the Concilium and our society into existence. The Law protects not only the safety of Walkers but also protects normal humans within reach of the Venatore from being subject to those with the power of alien weaponry. The penalty in such cases is death."

All the breath rushed out of my lungs. The word "death" hung in the air with the gut-wrenching finality of a shut coffin lid.

"Your unique circumstances will be considered," he allowed, with a slight bow of the head, "but given the power of the weapon and the magnitude of damage it might have caused in the hands of a man such as Goll Mac Morna, whose actions, we suspect, have already caused great loss of life..." he let the implication hang and turned to look to the left and right, letting the weight of his eyes fall on each member of the council. "All these things must be considered when you make judgment. Council members, what do you recommend."

They answered one at a time in ringing, formal tones.

"Probation."

"Death."

"Imprisonment."

"Death."

"Death."

I stopped hearing the words, stopped noticing who was speaking and sat in the center of the room, alone and buffeted by the roaring in my ears.

"Miss Chapter?" I saw his mouth move but heard no sound at first. "Have you understood me?"

"No," I croaked.

Arthur pressed his lips together for a moment, then repeated, "Based on the recommendations of my fellow council members, I will now make a judgment to be ratified or contested by a group of your peers. Do you understand?"

I nodded.

"Allison Chapter," he intoned, "as punishment for breaking the First Law of the Founding, I recommend—"

"This woman is an Augur." The voice split the air, silencing Arthur in mid-speech and I spun, breathless, to see Ronan striding out of the shadow of the stairwell in the back of the room. Confused chatter broke out in the jury and wide, surprised eyes were turned in my direction.

"You have proof of this, Venatore?" Oronowe demanded, standing halfway out of his chair.

"I do. But all you need do is let her touch you, your Grace, if you doubt me." Ronan stopped just to Angus's side, his chin held high, jaw clenched, and drops of sweat leaving lines down the sides of his face.

"Very well," Oronowe said after conferring with other members of the Concilium. He stood up to extend his hand toward me.

When I took it, I felt the thrum of energy that distinguished Walkers from normal humans, but the sense was woven with something else, something ephemeral that I couldn't quite distinguish. I closed my eyes and focused, pushing myself beneath his skin, feeling myself slip away from the solid stone under my feet and sink into his body. Almost a minute later I gasped and staggered to the side. His gift had been deeper and much harder to find than Angus's had been.

"Plants," I panted, gulping air, and trying to hold myself upright, "something about growing things, I think."

There was more murmuring, and Oronowe turned a speculative eye on me, rubbing his palms together as I caught my breath. The other members stood and gathered into a tight knot, gesturing, nodding, or shaking their heads and occasionally looking over their shoulders at me. Neither Ronan nor Angus so much as glanced in my direction and seemed to be doggedly ignoring one another despite being only feet apart.

What is an Augur? I wanted to ask, but instead walked slowly back to my chair, careful not to look at either man and stood clasping my hands and willing myself not to shake or fidget as the conference wore on. Finally, each member of the Concilium took their former place, standing in front of their chairs as Arthur cleared his throat.

"In light of recent events," he said, "the members of the Concilium have decided to grant partial clemency on the grounds that you agree to be fully inducted into the Venatore, swear fealty to the Concilium, and agree to a term of service not less than 5 years. Should you choose not to accept these terms, the penalty is death, to be carried out immediately. Do you accept?"

My mouth dropped open, but nothing came out.

"Miss Chapter?"

"Ah," I cleared my throat, mind racing through the possibilities but no other option for escape presented itself, so I swallowed hard and said, "Yes."

"Does the council agree to ratify this decision?"

After a few seconds of murmuring with his peers, a man stood up, leaned over the rail, and said, "We do."

"This concludes the meeting of the Concilium. Please take Miss Chapter to the Ritual Hall." Arthur nodded to Ronan, who dipped his chin respectfully and then spun on his heel and stalked out of the room without looking back.

CHAPTER FORTY-FOUR

"I, Allison Erin Chapter, do solemnly swear to enforce the Laws of Founding, to obey the orders of the Concilium and to protect the life and liberty of Walkers in the Eververse."

The words echoed inside my head as I sat at the dining room table, staring at the stain that had sunk into the pale grain of the wood while itching absentmindedly at the tender skin around the newly inked tattoo on my wrist. Ben had driven to the hardware store to buy more dust cloths, leaving me to finish packing, but neither of us could bear to get rid of mom's things. I'd been given a short leave from my training, which would begin in earnest soon, to handle family matters.

When I showed up at Ben's apartment he hadn't said a word, simply stepped forward and hugged me. Important documents had been boxed up, our old rooms packed up and the furniture donated, but neither of us had the heart to move or touch anything that belonged to Mom. The Kitchenaid mixer still sat on the countertop, waiting for her deft fingers to flick the switch on a batch of Belgian waffles.

I'd wandered around the house after Ben left, touching random things like the glass elephant that had always stood sentinel on the bookshelf and the spider plant mom had lovingly nursed back from death a thousand times, but the stain on the dining room table kept drawing me back. I laid my hand on the stain, my head on the cool wood, and closed my eyes.

"Allie girl?" My breath only caught for a second before I responded, but it was the longest second of my life.

"Hi, daddy."

"Won't you let me see your face?"

I squeezed my eyes shut hard, drew in a shaking breath, and sat up. He was standing in the dining room doorway wearing everyday jeans, a blue hooded sweater, and a baseball cap. His face was as cleanly carved as I remembered, with more wrinkles and deeper lines bracketing his mouth, but his green eyes hadn't changed.

"You've grown so much," he said.

"They killed momma."

His mouth compressed into a tight, white line and his eyes closed for a moment. When they opened, they were haunted.

"What happened to you, daddy?"

He rubbed his hands on his jeans. "You remember when our rubber boat sank?"

As if I could forget.

"That wasn't the first time something like that happened to me. Twice before that, I had almost fatal accidents that were just too convenient. That was the first time it could have killed you and Ben, too, though. I searched for a couple of years, but I couldn't find out who was doing it, so I thought it would be safer for you all if I left."

"The car accident?"

He nodded.

"How could you let me think you were dead? That I could have saved you..." my voice broke.

"Allie girl," he knelt on the ground near my chair, "it was better for you to think I was dead than that I left you, and safer for you, and your mom, and Ben. If they thought I was alive, they'd try to draw me out by hurting one of you. I couldn't let that happen."

"We could have died that day. I thought you did!"

"I know, and I'm sorry. When I woke up the car was on fire, and I realized that would probably be my only chance to get away cleanly. When the assassins showed up, I was in no condition to fight, so they needed to think I was dead. The sound of the ambulance scared them off before they could do anything to you," his voice broke, and he took a second to steady himself before continuing, "and that's when I learned they were Walkers. I healed myself enough to pull you away from the car so I could heal the worst of your injuries, and then I waited in the bushes for the paramedics to take you. I had to leave after that because I knew they'd come back."

I shook my head in disbelief.

"I had to, Allie. They would have kept trying to kill me if I didn't and I—" he swallowed, the adams-apple bobbing in his throat, "I couldn't forgive myself if something happened to you because of me."

My hand slapped flat on the table in the center of the stain. "Something did happen! If you had been here, you could have healed her, right? Now Momma is dead." He flinched, and I demanded, "Where have you been?"

"Tracking. It took me a long time to find out who had been trying to kill me. Once I knew, I started organizing a rebellion. Goll has destroyed Eriu, and the people are ready to fight."

"You underestimated him."

"I did. I didn't know about the weapons he'd been gathering."

"You left me." My father looked like he'd been punched in the gut. I didn't care.

"I know," he whispered and swallowed, repeating in a stronger voice, "I know. It was the hardest thing I've ever done, Al, and I've lived a long life. But I missed you and Ben and your mom every day. I started to forget what you looked like after a while. You lose the details of people's faces when you haven't seen them in a long time, did you know that? I didn't even have any pictures of you or Ben, but..." his voice died away, and he pulled off his hat to jerk his fingers through his white hair. "Sometimes I would come back to find you," he reached out to touch my cheek with one finger "just so I could watch you think about something when you didn't know I was watching. You grew up so much. I knew I couldn't talk to you or hug you but... I missed you."

I threw myself at him, and he caught me in the same strong arms that had rocked me to sleep as a baby. I was a daughter again, even if only for a moment.

The sound of Ben's jeep pulling up outside slammed us both into the present. I leaned back, and he slapped the ball cap back on his head before grabbing my upper arms. "Allie listen, there are things I need to tell you. I didn't know you were a Walker. None of my other children ever have been. I would have told you everything if I had known, but—damn—there's no time," he looked over his shoulder as the car door slammed, "there's something more going on here. I'm not entirely sure what, but keep your eyes open, okay? Don't trust anyone. Protect yourself. I'll find you again, I promise."

He disappeared just as Ben opened the front door.

We had a small memorial service for my mom in a secluded cove on Whidbey Island that had always been her favorite getaway. Ben, Rayne, and I stood on the rocky coast, battered by early Spring rain, and threw bottles stuffed with messages into the surf. We didn't get to watch the bottles float languidly away as if the tide were bearing the messages to her; they were swallowed as soon as they hit the turbulent waves. Since her body had never been found and I wouldn't be able to attend her service, still being a person of interest, this was the only memorial we could have.

"I miss her," I said, shivering, and looked at Ben.

"I know. Me too." He wrapped Rayne and me into a group hug and promptly knocked our heads together.

"I'll go warm up the car," he yelled over his shoulder as he ran away up the slope, successfully dodging the handfuls of wet sand we lobbed at him. Rayne took my hand as we walked back toward the road, her mouth thoughtfully pursed.

"What about school?" she asked.

"I don't know. Until we get all of this figured out..." I shrugged and kicked at a clump of weeds.

"Are you sure you can't go to the cops? I just feel like, I don't know, somebody has to be able to do something."

Someone was going to do something.

"I don't have any proof, yet," I reminded her, "and it was a cop who tried to kill me first. Besides, until I've got some way to prove I wasn't involved, it just doesn't seem like a risk worth taking."

"Where will you go?"

"I'm not sure, yet. Somewhere safe. Anyway, it's safer for you if you don't know. I couldn't live with myself if something happened to you, too."

She squeezed my hand, and I squeezed back.

The ride to Rayne's parent's house was filled with lighthearted banter, and I forced myself to participate even though I felt despair dragging at me with every mile of wet pavement. Knowing what I had to do didn't make doing it any easier. I thought of Rayne's easy smiles, her compassion, her stupid fuzzy socks.

"Don't forget," I said as we stood on the sidewalk in front of her parent's home.

"I won't," she assured me as she pulled the can of mace from her oversized purse and wiggled it.

"I'm taking precautions, see?" Then her eyes filled up with tears, and she smiled bravely at me.

"Tell Mat for me, will you?" I asked around the lump in my throat, "I hate not being able to see him but…"

"I will. I miss you, Allie-gator."

I wrapped my arms around her shoulders and pressed her wet cheek against mine, squeezing hard and fighting back my own tears. "I miss you, too, Rayne-bow. I don't know how long I'll be gone but…but I'll see you soon, okay?"

I almost choked on the lie, but I couldn't say goodbye to my best friend. The lie would protect her, and so it was worth it, no matter how much it hurt me to say it.

"You okay?" Ben asked when I pulled the car door shut.

"No. But it's done. She won't look for me if she thinks I'm coming back. You'll check in on her, right?"

"I will. But Al," he said, turning toward me to fix me with a gimlet eye, "you're my only family. You'd better come back."

I tried to smile at him, but it was too hard. Instead, I hugged him, let the tears flow, and lied again. "I will."

I was holding the last family photo we'd ever taken hard against my chest when I left True Earth. Rayne had brought it for me from our apartment, and it was the only thing I was taking with me into my next life. While I had every intention of going home again as soon as I thought it would be safe, I had no idea how long that would be—or whether I'd live long enough to do it—so the family photo seemed more precious to me than ever.

Walking alone toward Avalon from the meadow reminded me uncomfortably of my desperate run after Ronan had been captured. I pulled my mind away from that day and watched the countryside pass, grateful that I'd dressed warmly. There was no snow to soften the hard edges of the frozen landscape, just wilted grasses and trees naked to the biting wind, everything painted in shades of grey. Even the hardy Rhododendron bushes were hunkered down against the cold. Avalon was still under guard, but the people were resilient.

New buntings had been draped from the sky bridges, and garlands of pine boughs hung bravely above shop windows. One woman exited a shop just as I was passing. She wore black, from the scarf about her head to the skirt rustling above her boots. A small boy, maybe six or seven years old, hurried behind her with his arms full of paper-wrapped packages. His head swiveled on his little neck, eyes darting all over the square and his thin shoulders were up around his ears, expecting danger at any moment.

His mother noticed and paused, taking the packages and setting them on the ground. She looked intently into his eyes and put her fingers under his chin, lifting it to a proud tilt, and then stood and squared her own shoulders. The boy's mouth firmed; he puffed out his chest and took the packages, this time leading his mother down the street.

By the time I reached my room in the Bastion, I had two hours until I was supposed to report, and no way to fill the time. Despite having stayed in the room for weeks, it still felt more like a hotel than a home. With a trembling hand, I set the frame down gently on the chest of drawers and wrapped my arms around myself, taking in the scene of familial happiness. My father stood in front of the lake with his red hair afire in the sunlight—I wondered if he had dyed it all those years—a fat, large-mouthed bass dangling from his fingers, a satisfied smile on his lips as blood and slime dripped down his forearm. Ben and I stood in front of him with our own catches held out toward the camera. Ben was eyeing me suspiciously because my bass was twice the size of his. I had a gap-toothed grin because mom had secretly given me her catch, and she stood behind Ben with her hands on his shoulders, a conspiratorial smirk on her face. I'd been ten years old.

Everything I'd believed about my life then, everything I'd known about the world, had been turned upside down, and I might never have the chance to reconcile it. My face in the photo was innocent and mischievous. I had been safe and loved. I grieved for the girl who was me, for everything her life should have been, for everything that would be taken from her.

A tentative knock made me flinch.

When I pulled the door open, Ronan stood on the threshold with wary eyes and clenched fists.

"Can I come in?" I nodded and stepped to the side.

He walked into the center of the room and stood completely still. I tried to warm my suddenly cold fingers by rubbing them together in front of me. He cleared his throat, rubbed a hand over his mouth, and shook his head. "I, ah...I understand if you don't want to see me, it's just—I've got something for you." He dug into the pocket of his jeans and pulled out his fist. "I was afraid I would hurt you," he said, swallowing and looking down at his palm, "I thought—I knew—that I was the wrong man for you.

When they told me that you were being charged, I ran all over creation trying to find something that would free you from the charges; God help me, I trapped you instead." His eyes plead to me to understand. "It was the only thing I could think of."

"How can you apologize for saving my life?" I asked, incredulous.

His jaw clenched, and his eyes tightened. "I trapped you, Allie. I knew they'd want you if they knew you were an Augur. Enforcing the law isn't as important to them as securing someone with a gift like yours. Once I realized what you were doing, when you read that girl, I meant to get you out, but I didn't get the chance."

"Wait," I held up a hand, "what do you mean, get me out?"

"I was going to end your official training. Venatore only serve as volunteers and only for as long as they're willing. But people like you...you're too rare and too valuable, especially now. I wanted it to be your choice." He looked down at his hand again, tightening his grip until his knuckles went white, "I wanted all of it to be your choice."

"If you hadn't told them, I might have been killed."

"You could have been paroled," he countered, "Arthur isn't unfair, but it wasn't a chance I could take. I made that choice for you, and I'm sorry, but I didn't have a way to ask you. They wouldn't let me near the cells."

"Who told you I was being charged?"

His face hardened. "Angus."

My own features underwent a similar shift, accompanied by an angry flush. "I don't understand why he did that! He helped me save you, why would he set me up?"

"Angus can't be trusted. He's motives of his own, and you can never be sure what they are."

"It would have been nice to know that beforehand."

"I didn't know you'd go looking for him."

"I couldn't think of anyone else who could help me get you out of there!" I threw my hands up in the air, feeling an echo of the frantic need I'd experienced that day mixed with frustration. "Avalon was closed from the inside, and I couldn't get past the gate."

"Maybe you should have left me," his voice was low, and he wouldn't make eye contact with me.

"Would you have left me?"

"Never."

I bit my lips and took a deep breath through my nose.

"I'm the reason you were there in the first place. I couldn't leave you, Ronan, especially not after that what that girl said about the king. I had no idea what might happen to you, and I knew it was my fault." He nodded, eyes still fixed on the ground, fidgeting with whatever he held in his hand. "

Do you know what did happen?" His voice was plaintive, and my mouth opened, closed, and opened again.

"You don't remember?"

He looked up at me and winced. "I woke for a second, with a splitting headache, choking on some kind of fluid. Everything went into a haze after that. There were, ah," he flushed but went on doggedly, "women. It's like remembering something when you're drunk; it's all fuzzy. I don't know what was real and what wasn't."

I steeled myself and told him, "Goll was going to 'breed' you."

His eyes snapped, the cords in his neck standing out visibly.

"What do you mean?"

"He's been building an army of gifted people by breeding Walkers and other magic users. He said you'd give him grandsons, and he said—" I had to take another deep breath and hold it for a second just to muster the strength to force the words out, "he said I was going to give him sons. Before he killed me, anyway."

The last was said with a shrug to indicate less emotion than I felt, but a shiver still went down my arms when I remembered the icy hatred in the man's eye. Ronan's body went as taught as a drawn bowstring.

"He threatened to...to rape and kill you."

"He knew who my father was."

I held my breath as Ronan's eyes narrowed and the muscles in his arms flexed. It wasn't the way I would have wanted to confront this problem, but there it was, and I couldn't un-say it.

"How? Goll isn't Walker; he had no magic as far as I know. Our race is long-lived, but not that long. How was he still alive?"

I shrugged, even though I knew it was a rhetorical question. "My father found me at my mom's house. Or, I guess, he already knew where she lived. He said there was more going on than we suspected." I hesitated, then added softly, "My father is the reason we were able to get you out." Ronan's eyes were far away, and I wondered what he saw that made the corners of his lips turn down.

"I understand," I started, and then cleared my throat, looking over Ronan's shoulder at the portrait sitting on my dresser, "I know it must have been hard to hear he was still alive, and that I am his daughter."

Ronan took two steps toward me and reached out to take my hand in a tentative grasp. His skin was warm, compared to my own, and the calluses on his palm felt shockingly familiar, and yet my first reaction was to pull my hand away and rub the feeling of him off on the leg of my pants. Hurt flashed across his features but he mastered it quickly, looking down at his hands for a moment before saying softly, "I've known, Allie."

"What?"

"After Trisha...well, when I went back to investigate I covered your mom's house top to bottom to find anything that might help me figure out what was going on. I found photographs of your dad. It's been a very long time since I've seen him but," he shrugged one shoulder, "I'd never forget his face. When I came back to Avalon, I decided that I'd find someone else to protect you, given my—history—with your family, but I couldn't give you up. I couldn't trust someone else to keep you safe. I tried."

The pain in his voice affected me like nothing else could have, and I ignored the fluttering of discomfort in my belly to take his hand in my own. After a moment, the nerves wore away and the warmth of his hand began to steal into my own.

"When you kissed me," his voice trailed off, and his hand tightened on mine. I looked up at his face, watching his long-lashed eyes blinking rapidly. "I wanted it to be your choice. But then you saw the ball seirc," he squeezed my hand once more and let go. "I thought for a little while that I could make this work, that maybe someone really could love me...you were so determined, so honest with me...but I can't trap you with a curse. If you loved me, I'd fight the world to keep you, but," he pushed the heel of his hand hard against his forehead and grimaced as old pain dug sharpened claws into him, "I can't let my curse hurt you, too, and I know that it already has. I can't ever make amends for it." Ronan grabbed my hand again, tilted his own hand and slid a bracelet onto my palm. He closed my fingers over the warm beads, squeezed once, hard enough to press the beads almost painfully into my skin, and then walked past me toward the door.

When I opened my shaking hand the pale blue glass beads that lay against my palm caught the light and seemed to glow with icy fire.

I heard, as if in a dream, Ronan's voice in the car on Thanksgiving Day. "Love for you has made me clean."

The door clicked quietly closed.

CHAPTER FORTY-FIVE

"I already loved you!"

I was breathless when I caught him, just before the corridor turned toward the main entrance of the Bastion. Ronan's eyes were shuttered but I grabbed his forearm, and I could feel the hope he was desperately battling as it arced through him like a current of electricity.

"I already loved you," I repeated between breaths, "before I saw your stupid birthmark."

"You can't know that Allie," he said, "you might have seen the ball seirc at any time, no matter how hard I tried to keep it hidden. I let you get too close to me too many times."

"I can know it," I insisted, tightening my grip, "I never saw it until that morning. I think," I hesitated and then pushed on, "I think I started loving you when you gave that little girl back her doll."

The memory of it registered on his face before disappearing behind the mask.

"But we can never be sure. I won't tie you down with a lie, Allie. It's manufactured love, and it's not fair to either of us." He said it calmly, and I could physically feel him shutting his emotion down, hobbling it like an unruly horse.

"It's not a lie," I insisted, forcing him to look me in the eye, "it's not a lie that made me find Angus, not a lie that made me break the first law to save you, not a lie that made me fight my way to you inside Goll's castle; I can prove it to you."

I let go of his arm and lifted his shirt, sliding both hands up over his stomach to rest against his chest. He flinched in surprise but didn't move. Closing my eyes, I focused on my feelings for Ronan and found that I didn't have to close my eyes or even concentrate the way I did when reading someone else. All I had to do was look at him and let everything I felt wash through me.

His heartbeat redoubled under my hands, and his breathing sped up. I watched his pupils dilate, watched his mouth drop open as the truth of my feelings surged into his body with physical force.

"I can feel magic, Ronan," I told him softly, "I can feel the way it wraps itself around and through things, and I'm telling you, there is no magic in this," and I pushed again.

His knees started to shake.

"Stop," he breathed.

I let the flow taper off and relaxed my hands but didn't take them off his chest. "I love you. For your selflessness, and your courage, and your unexpected humor, and for being the kind of man willing to stand between the weak and the strong. Not for your beauty, although," I smirked, "it is kind of a nice bonus."

An unwilling laugh rumbled in his chest, and his hands came up to cover mine. "I don't want to believe you," he admitted, pressing my hands, "I don't want you to get hurt, and people who love me always seem to get hurt. But whatever that was, I can't argue with it. I've never felt anything so true in my life."

"I've already been hurt, Ronan."

"My fault," he said, and squeezed his eyes shut.

You're not running anymore, I reminded myself, and focused on the energy humming between us instead of my memories. "In Goll's castle, they were going to—um—auction us off."

His entire body went rigid.

"They touched me and the other women, and you, too. Everywhere." I swallowed and fed the fire in my chest all the fury my body had saved up over the last few months, "But it was not your fault, and it wasn't mine," I growled, "It was the fault of those vile, disgusting, sick people that Goll has bred. He's created them, Ronan, and he uses their own children as chains to tie them all to himself. I'm putting the blame exactly where it lies, and I refuse to let you shoulder any of it, you hear me?"

"How," he choked on the word and then swallowed, his big body thrumming with tension, "how can you still want me? How can you forgive me when I cannot forgive myself? Were it not for me—" I covered his lips with my fingers, unable to let him finish. Had I not been there, holding him immobile with my touch, he'd have been gone already, hunting.

"If it weren't for you," I said, "I'd already be dead. If it weren't for you, I wouldn't know what I am, or what I'm capable of, or how deeply I can love. No," I pulled him close and savored the warmth of him, all hesitation gone, "I'm done running, Ronan. I've been letting things happen to me for too long. You are the first thing in my entire life that I chose for myself, and I'm not letting guilt or anything else take you away from me. Not even you. You're mine."

Whatever restraint he had been using to keep his emotions in check broke like a damn before a flood that washed over my hands and filled me with his hope and joy, but also his pain and fear and regret. Ronan let go of my hands and cupped my face gently, dragging a thumb over my lips and tracing the lines of my face with eyes wet with tenderness. Unlike the pawing hands of the men in Goll's court, Ronan's hands were there by my desire, and his need to protect me was as clear in his touch as it was in the aura that pulsed around him.

When his lips touched mine, as gently as if I were made of glass, the flood of our emotions became a wildfire that burned away the last restraints, the last inhibitions, and charred my insides until nothing was left but sparks rising from the ashes. We stood there for a long time, holding each other.

Love didn't fix everything, I realized. I still had a lot of problems to tackle. My world was turned upside down, and it felt like there were more questions than answers. I hadn't lied to Ronan, there was no magic in the bond that lay between us, but there was something else there that was inexplicable. Love wasn't magic that bent other things to its will; I could have walked away from Ronan, if I had to, just like he'd tried to walk away from me. It would have been like cutting off a limb, but I could have done it.

I chose not to. That choice, I thought, changed things inside of us as significantly as the choices that split the universe and changed the fabric of reality. Because of what we were, maybe the choice to love had even farther-reaching consequences than I could fathom.

Love didn't somehow make everything all better; I wasn't sure even time could do that. Love made everything worthwhile, and that made all the difference.

"You have to learn where to place your focus."

We sat on the ground in the center of the practice field surrounded by sparring Venatore, and I was drenched in sweat. The heaters placed at intervals on the field to keep the snow from sticking—and the Venatore from freezing—weren't helping to cool me off.

"Focus. That's easy to say," I grumbled, wiping the back of my hand against my forehead before more sweat could drip into my eyes.

"Focus! It's not so hard. You do it all the time. Just think, you're looking at me right now, yes?"

I scowled at him. "Yes."

"But you still know what is happening around you, yes?"

"Yes."

"So, it is just knowing what to pay attention to. That is all."

I sighed. Yeah, that is all.

Alika and I had been training since I'd gotten my first set of orders from the Concilium two days before. His wrinkled face was the color and consistency of well-tanned leather, which seemed even darker next to his vividly white eyebrows. He had a habit of lowering them at me so that they seemed to perch on the bridge of his bulbous nose like vultures. I took a few seconds to calm my nerves and tried again. Alika didn't allow me to close my eyes when I read.

"You are vulnerable if you are blind!" he'd say, and slap me with the dried reed he carried around. I couldn't deny that he was right, but it made focusing on differences in the energy that pulsed in the air around me incredibly difficult.

There was somebody in the arena who had skill in manipulating water. Alika wouldn't tell me who. I tried to reach out but kept getting distracted, mostly because he would periodically whack me with his reed. Of course, I was supposed to move out of the way before the reed hit me, which made the entire process more mentally taxing than my physical training with Danet had been.

From what Molfus told me, this kind of training—when it did happen—usually started out with knowing who the subject was so that you learned to recognize the signature of the gift, which made it easier to distinguish in the future. Alika had waved his bony hands in the air and said, "Too many gifts, there is no time for that."

Being the only other Augur in the Venatore, no one was in a position to argue with him. Even though I was pushing out with my mind and my senses, my muscles still tensed with effort and I frequently had to stop to catch my breath. I was still panting when the brassy note of a horn sounded above the din. Molfus stepped onto the practice ground, bare-chested in defiance of the cold.

"Garsh, Chapter, Belquis, be reporting for orders!"

Alika waved his hands in dismissal, and I sighed in relief.

"Kishma!"

I stopped and turned to see Molfus smiling at me, beckoning with his broad hand.

"Hey Molfus."

His grin shifted into a glower as I stopped in front of him.

"Am I in trouble?" I asked.

"Yes."

Unease uncurled in my belly. What now?

"There is not being a 'lost-and-found' in the Eververse, Kishma," he said, reaching behind his back and producing a pair of vambraces, "the next time you are losing these, you will not be being so lucky."

I took the vambraces gratefully, smiling up at him until his grimace broke and he smiled back. I was genuinely fond of the big, gruff man; he had an unexpected soft side.

"Thank you, Molfus. Really."

"Do not be thanking me, just don't be losing any more of them. They are being expensive."

Garsh and Belquis joined me in the circle room in Arthur's tower. The three of us looked warily at each other.

"So," said one of the men, "you're the Auger, eh?"

"That's me. And you are?"

He held out a thick-fingered hand. "Name's Garsh," he said cordially, and I only hesitated a second before he was shaking my hand with a rough enthusiasm, "Rich Garsh."

Relieved that the sudden disgust I'd experienced when Ronan took my hand the other day hadn't come back to haunt me this time, I asked blankly, "Rich?"

"Yup."

A flashback of the metal grate that was my only solace during my imprisonment shocked me into reality and I said, "You told your wife about us all, eh?"

His eyes widened for a second, and then he laughed out loud, slapping his knees. "Hot damn, they got you, too, eh? You never told me you were an Augur!"

"I didn't know I was. You never told me you had any special skills, either."

He shrugged, and his eyes twinkled mischievously, "You're the Augur, why don't you tell me?"

"I'll pass for now, Rich, thanks." I turned toward the other man, who stood silently near the Roundtable with one hand flat on its surface and held out my own.

"You must be Belquis. I'm Allie Chapter."

He looked at my hand as if I'd just wiped my butt with it, and then turned back toward the window.

"I am," he said, not looking at me. "And you're the traitor who broke the First Law."

I stepped back, shocked at the venom in his voice.

The oak door swung open, and Ronan stepped in. He'd shaved, and the purple smudges beneath his eyes had faded considerably. His expression warmed when he saw me.

"Ronan," Belquis said, leaving the table to shake Ronan's hand, "it's good to see you back."

"Thank you. How's your wife?"

"She's well, thanks. She's almost as big as a house," he said, "but don't tell her I said so."

Ronan laughed and clapped the man on the shoulder. "When is she due?"

"Next month, God willing."

Ronan turned toward Rich, who wore a bemused expression on his sun-tanned face, and held out his hand. "I'm—"

"You're Ronan!" Rich interrupted, "I've heard stories about you, man. Damn, it's good to meet you in person. Feels like I'm meeting a movie star or something! I'm Garsh, Rich Garsh."

Ronan disengaged his hand and said in a level tone, "Nice to meet you, Rich."

An awkward silence ensued, where each of us looked at the others with half friendly expressions that said, 'this is awkward, right?'

Except for Belquis. He wouldn't look at me at all.

Finally, Arthur appeared on the stair, and we all breathed a collective sigh of relief, reassured by the authority he wore like an invisible cape.

"Welcome, Venatore," he said. His voice was calm, but his eyes were troubled. He gestured to the table and said, "Please, sit."

The men pulled out chairs, but I just stood there, staring first at the Pendragon and then at the Roundtable.

"For real? I mean...I get to sit at the Roundtable?"

Arthur smiled faintly. "Indeed, you do, Miss Chapter. In fact, if you sit right here, you'll be sitting in the same place Lancelot once occupied."

My mouth dropped open, and I leaped into the seat he indicated, before remembering just exactly what happened between Lancelot and Arthur.

He laughed at my embarrassed flush.

"I'm sorry," I breathed, so mortified that I almost couldn't look at him.

"The pain of that betrayal has long passed, Miss Chapter. Now, shall we discuss why you are here?" Arthur folded his hands on the table and looked at each one of us gravely. "You know that Avalon was attacked just over a week ago."

We all made noises of affirmation.

"The city was breached by a small force armed with automatic firearms and wearing body armor. Fighting raged in the streets and through the castle building as well. This force was well trained, effective, and unexpected. Thus, we lost many lives and, I'm afraid, quite a few weapons with magical qualities."

"Not—"

"No, Miss Chapter," he cut me off with a raised hand, "not that particular weapon."

I sighed in relief.

"However, the weapons that were taken were highly powerful. Of the men we captured, only one lived long enough to be questioned. What we learned from the prisoner, together with the report of what is taking place in Eriu, forced us to assume that the King of Eriu, Goll Mac Morna, is enslaving Walkers and using them to amass weapons of unusual power. It is the position of the Concilium never to interfere in the affairs of mortal men. As far as we know, Goll Mac Morna is a mortal man. His knowledge of Walkers, and his use of their skill, on the other hand, presents a problem, as does his potential possession of so many weapons."

Arthur paused, taking a steadying breath, and continued, "We also have recent reports from other Venatore bases that several verses have experienced a rash of the theft of magical weapons that don't appear to have natural causes."

I sat back in my chair and rubbed my face with my hands.

"We do not know what his goals are, and yet he has already caused great harm to Walkers in this verse, as well as his own. After a vote, the Concilium has decided to intervene. You have been chosen to investigate the cause of all this and report your findings, so a plan of action can

be decided upon. This may result in the first large-scale action of the
Venatore since its inception, and that is a matter we do not take lightly."

"Your Grace," Ronan said, with an apologetic glance at the rest of us,
"forgive me, but, this isn't the team I would choose."

Pride warred with pragmatism at Ronan's words. Pride won, and I
couldn't help but feel stung at his lack of faith in me. "It is not your
choice, Ronan."

"I understand, sir, but their lack of experience could put their lives and
the mission in danger."

"Ronan," Arthur said patiently, "each of these Venatore has been
chosen very carefully to fulfill this mission, hand-picked by myself."

Ronan's mouth flattened, and he nodded once. Arthur clapped his
hands together, businesslike, and said, "Very well, then. Ronan, you
are to take command of this team and lead them to Maa, Jorth, and
Eriu to bring back intelligence. The Domus Venatorum there have been
instructed to assist you. I will need to know what has been taken, by
whom, how Goll is commanding these Walkers, and what he plans to
do with them. You may choose one additional team member as you see
fit, so long as these three are not replaced. Do you have any questions for
me?"

"Not at this time, sir." "Very well. You are dismissed."

When the door closed behind us, Ronan sent Rich and Belquis off to
dinner on the condition they stay in the castle proper so he could send
for them. Rich grinned broadly at me and winked, then followed Belquis
down the long corridor. When they were gone, Ronan turned to me and
asked,

"Did you read them?"

"Rich is a thief," I answered wryly.

"Arthur gave me a thief?"

"He's lucky, I think. Or, something like luck, anyway. Facility, maybe?
I don't really know how to describe it."

"What about Belquis?"

"He wouldn't shake my hand," I admitted.

"You couldn't read him from a distance?"

"Not yet. I've been working with Alika but it's a lot harder without a
physical connection."

Ronan sighed and nodded, his shoulders slumping a bit. "He's a
skilled fighter, and seems to be a good man, but I don't know much
about his personal life at all."

"It sounded like you knew his wife?"

"His second wife. He married an Avalonian. She's often at the castle."

"I see." I turned to look at him, taking in the long, graceful lines of
his body, the breadth of his shoulders, and the tilt of his head. My entire
body tightened with desire even as my mind recoiled. I knew that Ronan
would wait for me, and I had no idea how much my stay in Goll's castle
was going to affect my life but, at that moment, I wanted to be close to
Ronan like I wanted air to breathe.

"I want you," I said, and his eyes narrowed as they fixed on my lips, though the concern was plain in the lines of his face.

"We have time," he reminded me, slowly running his hands down my arms and back up to my shoulders over and over, as if gentling a wild animal...and maybe I was. The conflicting desires—to be in his arms and to keep my body inviolable—held me painfully suspended, unable to take a confident step in any direction.

"Maybe we can just cuddle," I suggested.

He smiled and kissed my forehead. "We can do that."

We lay in his bed, limbs tangled, with the sound of Ronan's heartbeat under my cheek and his hand tracing lazy circles down my back. My shirt was no barrier to his touch, and each of his fingers left a trail of heat behind it. For the first time in ages, I felt safe and, more importantly, like I understood my reality. When I was with Ronan no turn of fate could conquer me, and that was absurdly comforting.

"He didn't give us much time to train before the mission."

Ronan made a sound in his throat, something like a verbal shrug, and said, "The Ambrosia nectar will help with that. Just hope that nothing happens in the meantime. You'll want every bit of training you can get."

"You think it will be dangerous?"

"If what we've experienced so far is any indication, I do."

"Well, at least I know what I'll be doing for the next couple of months," I sighed, then a thought struck me, and I stiffened in surprise.

"What?"

It took a moment for me to relax against Ronan's chest, as I reconciled myself to the realization that had shocked me.

"I just realized that I've been kind of floating along for years. Ever since my dad died, really. I just felt lost, you know? I went to college, but I never had any kind of plan for my life. I mean, what am I going to do with a degree as a history major? And then all of this happened," I shrugged, indicating not just Ronan and I but everything, "and then I felt like a boxer just trying to dodge punches and make it to the next round."

He made a sympathetic noise.

"It seems like my old life or, at least, the life I should have had, has burnt away. The possibility for everything that my life might have been is gone. It hurts."

"I know. I'm sorry, love." He kissed the top of my head.

I pushed myself up and looked at Ronan, examining the striking blue eyes that were soft with compassion, the high planes of his cheekbones, the slight lump where his nose had been broken, and said, "But it also feels...freeing, in a way. There are no expectations left to chain me to anything. Does that make any sense?"

"It does."

I kissed him and laid my head back on his chest. "I'm going to miss Ben and Ray and Mat so much, but at least I have a purpose, now. It feels good to have a purpose."

There was a hesitant pause before he said, "You can't do it, you know."

I stopped breathing for a second, then raised up on my elbows and looked down at him. "Can't do what?"

"Come on, Allie, you know what."

"Accidents happen."

"Not those kinds of accidents."

"Sure they do, they happen all the time."

"Allie," he warned, "you can't kill him."

"Why not? He tried to kill my father, he's responsible for my mother's death, he's been trying to kill me, he threatened to rape me, and let a bunch of sick creeps paw at the both us. We were this-freaking-close," I illustrated the point with my thumb and forefinger, "to becoming breeding stock, Ronan. The girl who saved my life is still stuck there. I had to give up my entire life because of him. I have more right to kill that son-of-a-bitch than anyone. And," I said, remembering, "he said he'd tried to kill once you already!"

Ronan's brow furrowed for a second, his eyes drifting off to the right as he thought, and then his face cleared, and he shook his head, bemused. "That wily old bastard. He's the one that sent the boar at me. He must have harried the poor beast must have gone mad."

I narrowed my eyes and said, "Yep. I'm definitely going to kill him."

"No," Ronan said firmly, wrapping both arms tight around my ribcage and pressing his face into my hair, "you can't, Allie."

"Why not?" I demanded, pulling myself up to glare into his eyes.

"Because we're under orders find out if these thefts in other verses are connected to the attack on Avalon. Because this might go deeper than Goll and what he's doing in Eriu. I know what happens when you betray the trust of your leader. Besides," he told me with a wolfish smile, "when the time comes, I'm going to kill him."

Ronan slept peacefully by my side as I stared up into the darkness. If I found it comforting to sleep next to Ronan, did that mean I would be able to sleep with him? The thought was both tempting and terrifying, and made me regret letting him talk me into waiting. I was lucky enough to have someone to love, someone who wanted to help me heal, but what about the women I'd left behind in Goll's castle? What did they have?

My stomach was flat and hard under my hands. If Angus and my father had taken another day or two to break into the castle, would it have stayed that way? Yes, I'd escaped being raped, but what about the rest of the women who had been sold to the highest bidder? How long before they were forced to bear children they didn't ask for only to be held hostage by the maternal need to keep those children safe? And the girl who had effectively rescued me by not giving me the drug, she was a Walker, how were they keeping her hostage? Her parents, maybe? I decided that I was going back for those women and men whether the Concilium authorized it or not. I couldn't leave them there to be used like animals, sold to the highest bidder, and bred for their bloodlines.

It was almost me.

This should have been the time when Ronan and I could finally be together. As much as I wanted that, I was afraid the pleasure I felt at Ronan's touch would turn to fear unexpectedly, as it had when he'd come to my room to apologize. The hurt in his eyes when I'd rubbed off the feeling of his touch still stung when I thought of it. If we tried to make love, would that trigger all the feelings I was afraid of? Would I ever be able to give myself to the man I loved if my reaction to his touch was disgust?

My fists tightened on the blankets as I remembered having my legs forced apart, the sense of violation so strong my stomach clenched and heaved. I pressed my palms flat against my stomach, as if I could quiet the violence by mere pressure. A large, warm hand settled on mine, but it was comfort, and not disgust or fear, that radiated outward from his touch.

"What if..." I began, but I was unable to finish the question, and my voice died away.

Ronan kissed my cheek and curled his fingers around mine, pulling me into an embrace that shut out the rest of the world.

After taking a deep breath, I continued, "What if this ruins everything for us? What if I can never..." the words choked off and I couldn't bring them back.

He rolled to the side, curling around me as if his body could shelter mine, and pillowing my head on his arm as his other hand tilted my chin so he could look me in the eye.

"I love you for who you are, Allison, not for what you can or cannot do with your body. Whatever happened in the past, we will overcome it. Whatever the future holds, we'll face it together," he promised.

I sighed and closed my eyes. "Together."

The End

The story continues in book 2, The Founding Lie. Turn the page to read the first chapter for free!

T he knife flew in a deceptively lazy arc and buried itself in the target.
Not fast enough, Allie, they're trying to kill you.

I spun, giving myself a mere split-second to aim, then released the second knife with a flick of my wrist.

Keep moving!

I dove into a roll and pulled the last two knives from the sheaths at the small of my back, coming to my knees with a knife in each hand, fighting to control my breathing.

Now!

The blades sailed through the air, point first, and hit with a satisfying thunk. My sheaths were empty, but only one knife had hit the bullseye.

Not good enough, I thought sourly. *If the wooden target had been an enemy, you might be dead.*

I sighed and rubbed my forehead with the back of my left arm to stop sweat from dripping into my eyes. I'd been throwing knives all morning, forcing myself to try weighted throws, blind throws, throws off the wrong foot, and anything else I could think of that might simulate a real combat experience. My muscles burned and my aim got worse as I grew tired. Of course, that was the whole point. If I was forced to throw a knife at someone, it wouldn't be under ideal conditions. If I had to throw a knife, it would likely be a split-second, life-or-death decision.

"That is not being the most practical use of a knife, Kishma," the deep, disapproving voice said from over my shoulder, "a knife is not being a ranged weapon, it is being a weapon for close work."

He jabbed a finger into my back below my floating ribs and I squeaked, spun, and punched the Master at Arms in his beefy shoulder.

The big man grinned down at me, but that didn't stop a cold trickle of unease from running down my spine. Molfus, the Master at Arms of Avalon, was making a point—pun intended. He'd poked me in the exact spot you would use to stab someone in the kidney.

"I know," I said, trying not to think about a blade sliding into my flesh, "but there aren't many ranged weapons I can take to other verses without breaking the Laws of Founding."

"A sling would be being better for range, and small enough to put in the pocket."

"But no use for close work."

"Mmm." The sound rumbled in his barrel chest as he nodded, then pointed at the small piece of armor lying in the grass at my feet. "Are you being tired of my gift so quickly?"

I bent to pick up the vambrace, strapped it to my left forearm, and smiled up at the man I considered a friend. "Of course not. I wanted to practice throwing with different weights on my arms. That's why I left the right one on," I held up my right arm and wiggled it as proof.

"This is not being such a bad idea," he approved, then dropped one meaty paw on the top of my head, "even from such a tiny brain."

"That's rich coming from you," I stepped out from under his touch and backed toward the target while squinting at his overdeveloped shoulders. "I'm surprised all those muscles in your neck haven't squeezed your brains out through your ears."

Molfus threw his shaggy head back and laughed. I smiled, too. I couldn't help it. He was like a huge, friendly bear. Although, I had seen the results of Molfus's handiwork, and there was nothing friendly about it. The last man foolish enough to fight the Master at Arms in earnest combat had his skull staved in. He wasn't merely a big man, but an uncommonly strong one. I didn't know if he carried the same guilt I did over having killed people, but if he did, he never showed it.

"Ronan has been sending a summons for you," he told me.

I plucked one knife from the bulls-eye where the wood at the center was all but chipped away from more successful throws earlier in the day, two from the center ring, and one from about an inch inside the last ring. Each blade slid silently into its sheath.

One out of four. Not good enough, Chapter.

If I was going to use these knives to help keep my team and myself safe, then I was going to have to be more accurate under pressure. A couple of inches could mean the difference between a disabled or distracted enemy, and one still capable of mayhem. I sighed.

"Yeah, our team has to go pick up tech from Alfar before our mission. I stayed on the practice field too long so I'm probably messing with his schedule."

"Ronan could be standing to have his schedules messed with. He is being entirely too serious."

I agreed.

My boyfriend was one of the Senior Venatore and a serious kind of person in general. I'd made a point to tease a smile or laugh out of him as often as possible, but I couldn't blame him for being edgy where this mission was concerned; his team was inexperienced, and we were counting on gathering the information we needed to take down the man who had been trying to kill me for the last year.

"This is an important operation," I said, "he wants to get things right."

Molfus snorted. "Every mission is being important, or Arthur would not be sanctioning it."

I didn't bother to correct him. Molfus might be a high-ranking member of the Guard of Avalon, the center of power for Walkers in the Eververse, but he wasn't Venatore and he wasn't privy to the details of this assignment. All of us would be looking for information about who was stealing magical weapons from different verses, but as far as I knew, only the members of the Concilium itself—the ruling body that ordered the Venatore around—and the individual teams knew exactly what they would be doing in the verses to which they were assigned. Then again, I was about as junior as it was possible to get, so I probably didn't have all the information, either, despite being on one of the reconnaissance teams. So, I ignored his comment, thanked him for giving me the message, and headed toward my room.

The Bastion was a fortress inside the Castle grounds where Venatore trained or lived while in residence on Avalon. I crossed the training field with a watery, early autumn sun on my back, and climbed the stairs into the barracks. Three-quarters of our number were on assignment on different worlds in the Eververse at any given time—finding and training new Walkers, or chasing down anyone suspected of breaking the Laws of Founding and hauling them back to face the justice of the Concilium—so I didn't see anyone else as I snagged a change of clothes from my room and hurried toward the baths.

As the air filled with moist warmth, my skin tightened in apprehension.

Please, let the baths be as empty as the rest of this place, I thought.

When I turned the corner and entered the steam-filled room, I was relieved to find it empty. I slipped behind the screen near a prepared tub, stripped as quickly as my sore muscles allowed, and lowered myself into the hot water, splashing some over the side of the basin in my rush to cover myself. If someone came in now, they'd see no more than my head and the steam rising out of the dark water.

As much as I wanted to stay, to let the heat seep into my sore muscles, I knew Ronan would come looking for me if I didn't meet him soon. I scrubbed the dirt and sweat from my skin, lathered my hair, and sunk beneath the surface of the water for a few blissful moments before scanning the room again and reaching for a towel. Over the last few months, I'd become a pro at quick changes beneath a towel. The cold stone floor didn't exactly invite naked feet to stand for long, anyway, but sometimes the custodians would enter to clean a bath before the bather had finished dressing and, while that wasn't an issue for most Avalonians, I preferred a bit more privacy. After what happened in Eriu last year, the idea of a stranger seeing me naked was enough to make cold sweat bead on my upper lip.

A young woman walked around the screen that gave my tub a negligible amount of privacy and dropped a quick curtsey.

"Are you finished with the tub, ma'am?"

"Yeah," I grabbed my dirty clothes off the back of the chair and held them between my knees as I braided my damp hair, "please, be my guest."

She nodded and drained the tub to wash it as I tied off the braid and hurried out of the room. Back on True Earth, my roommate and I had divided the household chores between us, and who should clean the bathtub was always hotly debated, but that had been when I was just a college student with no more to worry about than midterms. Now, I was Venatore—what amounted to an interdimensional cop—and my main worry was staying alive long enough to lose my virginity.

Okay, so my main goal wasn't losing my virginity, but it was something I'd been looking forward to until I'd been forced to travel to Eriu to save my boyfriend from the man who'd been sending assassins to kill me. We had both ended up drugged and on an auction block as strangers examined us with greedy hands and lecherous sneers, deciding how much to bid for the use of my womb and Ronan's 'stud services.'

"You're safe now," I whispered to myself, and stopped to lean on the cold stone wall for support while I controlled my breathing.

In for four, hold for seven, out for eight, I thought, repeating the breathing practice until the tension relaxed and my heartbeat slowed.

"Venatore Chapter?"

I nearly jumped out of my skin and spun on the young boy who snuck up on me. His brown eyes widened when I scowled at him, and I had to remind myself to calm down. It wasn't the boy's fault I'd worked myself up. With an effort of will, I schooled my face into a more welcoming expression.

"Yes?"

"Venatore Ronan asked to see you in his rooms."

"What's your name?"

"Horace, ma'am."

"How old are you, Horace?"

"I'm seven years old, ma'am."

"Well done, Horace. I'll go right now, but I have another job for you first, is that okay?"

Horace was several sizes too small for the blue uniform worn by those who worked in the castle, and the hem of his pants pooled around his tiny feet. He peered up at me like a turtle in a too-large shell, but his skinny chest puffed up with pride and he gave me a solemn nod.

"I want you to go to the kitchen and find Mirta and tell her I said you could have an apple tart."

He beamed at me as I hurried down the corridor.

"You're late."

"I had to take a bath," I said as I closed the door behind myself. "I was on the practice grounds when I got your message."

Ronan stood next to his dresser holding a leather satchel in one hand, and an apple in the other. Mid-morning sunbeams crept between the curtains, showed the light brown tones in his dark hair, and made the center ring of his irises look like snow on a frozen pond.

"Knives?" he took a bite of the apple.

I watched him for a moment and reminded myself that somehow, this beautiful human being thought I was worth spending time with. My regard lasted a moment too long, and the corner of his mouth curled in a slow, sensual smile, revealing a dimple on one side, as his eyes fixed on my lips.

"Yeah," I said and took a steadying breath, "I was practicing weighted throws."

His eyes took a lazy trip down my body, giving me a taste of my own medicine by letting his gaze linger until heat bloomed in my cheeks, and I was as warm as if I'd swallowed a mouthful of whisky. He finally relented, releasing me from the gravity of his stare, and slung the satchel over his shoulder.

"Good plan. It might make a difference to know how much you'll have to alter your throw if you lose one of your vambraces."

"That was the idea."

"Still, a knife is more useful in your hand."

I sighed. "Yeah, that's what Molfus said."

"Smart man."

"If you didn't think throwing knives was a good idea, why did you teach me how to do it?" I demanded.

"Because I think it's a good idea to know how to use your weapons in every conceivable way."

"Well, being able to throw a knife has come in handy before, and I have more than one knife to spare. Besides, it saved your butt in the forest and I didn't hear you criticizing me, then."

Ronan grinned, held my chin between his thumb and forefinger to stop my grumbling, and gave me a quick kiss. "That's fair enough. I wanted to make sure you'd thought it through, that's all. You know, just in case you were practicing because movies make knife throwing look cool."

I pinched his stomach and he jumped back, laughing. "Okay, okay."

"I've had enough lessons today, Obi-Wan. Can I have Ronan back, please?"

He sighed and shook his head in mock regret. "If you insist, padawan. Shall we go meet the rest of our team and head to Alfar?"

"I suppose we'd better."

I followed Ronan out of his room and toward the courtyard, admiring the breadth of his shoulders and the unconscious grace of his stride as his hips shifted smoothly.

"What are we picking up from Alfar?" I asked, in the hopes of changing the direction of my lascivious thoughts.

"Tech that will help us understand foreign languages."

"That's handy."

"We'll need them. No one else on the team speaks the languages of Jorth, Maa and Eriu, and we're going to need to know what's being said if we're to learn who has been stealing magical weapons."

"It's Goll MacMorna. I know it."

"The Concilium will want solid proof that he's responsible, Allie. They won't approve our request to raid Eriu otherwise."

My chest tightened. Goll MacMorna's grey-eyed face hovered at the back of my mind, sneering at me with the kind of loathing I'd never known existed.

"You won't know when I come to you," he had told me while his guards held me fast by my arms, "and you won't fight me, but I'll plant my seed in your belly, and your father's grandchildren will be mine. I'll take my sons back from you, and then send you to hell with the rest of your cursed line."

I choked back the bile that rose up my throat at the memory, and told Ronan, "Then let's get to Alfar. The sooner we find proof that man is responsible for the theft of magic weapons, the sooner the Concilium will let us kill him."

When Goll was dead, all the people he abused would be free. When the memories didn't have power over me anymore, I would be free, too.

T hank you so much for coming on this adventure! If you enjoyed the book, will you leave a review on Amazon or Goodreads to help other readers know if this is the right book for them?

And if you'd like to read Ronan's side of the story as I write it, I'd love to have you join The Reader's Lounge member area on my website, nicoleyork.com! You can see the writing process from the inside and read new books a chapter at a time as I finish them, even give feedback if you'd like.

Book 2: The Founding Lie

The monsters we face aren't always the ones we expect...
As the newest member of the interdimensional police force, it's Allie Chapter's responsibility to find out who is stealing magical weapons and bring them to justice before war breaks out.

She's certain the thief is Goll MacMorna, the man who still haunts her nightmares, and she intends to prove it...no matter the cost.

Book 3: The Founding War

Coming Soon

The best description of Nicole was written by her kindergarten teacher on a report card: Nicole has a hard time telling the difference between fantasy and reality.

As an author, artist, and photographer, Nicole lives firmly in the realm of fantasy and is committed to telling stories that build bridges back to fairyland and explore human nature in all its subtleties and contradictions.

Made in the USA
Las Vegas, NV
28 September 2022

56153232R00184